LISA JACKSON

DELORES FOSSEN

PROOF OF GUILT

Previously published as *Yesterday's Lies* and
Gunfire on the Ranch

ISBN-13: 978-1-335-00886-2

Proof of Guilt

Copyright © 2019 by Harlequin Books S.A.

First published as Yesterday's Lies
by Harlequin Books in 1986 and
Gunfire on the Ranch by Harlequin Books in 2017.

The publisher acknowledges the copyright holders
of the individual works as follows:

Yesterday's Lies
Copyright © 1986 by Lisa Jackson

Gunfire on the Ranch
Copyright © 2017 by Delores Fossen

Recycling programs
for this product may
not exist in your area.

Printed in U.S.A.

www.Harlequin.com

CONTENTS

Lisa Jackson is a #1 *New York Times* bestselling author of more than eighty-five books, including romantic suspense, thrillers and contemporary and historical romances. She is a recipient of the *RT Book Reviews* Reviewers' Choice Award and has also been honored with their Career Achievement Award for Romantic Suspense. Born in Oregon, she continues to make her home among family, friends and dogs in the Pacific Northwest. Visit her at lisajackson.com.

Books by Lisa Jackson

Illicit
Proof of Innocence
Memories
Suspicions
Disclosure: The McCaffertys
Confessions
Rumors: The McCaffertys
Secrets and Lies
Abandoned
Strangers
Sweet Revenge
Stormy Nights
Montana Fire
Risky Business
Missing
High Stakes

Visit the Author Profile page
at Harlequin.com for more titles.

YESTERDAY'S LIES

Lisa Jackson

Chapter 1

The sweating horse snorted as if in premonition and his dark ears pricked forward before flattening to his head. Tory, who was examining the bay's swollen hoof, felt his weight shift suddenly. "Steady, boy," she whispered. "I know it hurts...."

The sound of boots crunching on the gravel near the paddock forced Tory's eyes away from the tender hoof and toward the noise. Keith was striding purposefully toward her, his lanky rawboned frame tense, the line of his mouth set.

"Trask McFadden is back."

The words seemed to thunder across the windswept high plateau and echo in Tory's ears. Her back stiffened at her brother's statement, and she felt as if her entire world was about to dissolve, but she tried to act as if she was unaffected. Her fingers continued their gentle probing of the bay stallion's foreleg and her eyes searched inside the swollen hoof for any sign of infection.

"Tory, for God's sake," Keith called a little more loudly as he leaned over the top rail of the fence around the enclosed paddock, "did you hear what I said?"

Tory stood, patted the nervous stallion affectionately and took in a steadying breath before opening the gate. It groaned on its ancient hinges. She slipped through the dusty rails and faced her younger brother. His anxious expression said it all.

So Trask was back. After all these years. Just as he said he would be. She suddenly felt cold inside. Shifting her gaze from the nervous bay stallion limping within the enclosed paddock to the worried contours of Keith's young face, Tory frowned and shook her head. The late-afternoon sun caught in her auburn hair, streaking it with fiery highlights of red and gold.

"I guess we should have expected this, sooner or later," she said evenly, though her heart was pounding a sharp double time. Nervously wiping her hands on her jeans, she tried to turn her thoughts back to the injured Quarter Horse, but the craggy slopes of the distant Cascade Mountains caught her attention. Snow-covered peaks jutted brazenly upward against the clear June sky. Tory had always considered the mountains a symbolic barrier between herself and Trask. The Willamette Valley and most of the population of the state of Oregon resided on the western side—the other side—of the Cascade Mountains. The voting public were much more accessible in the cities and towns of the valley. The unconventional Senator McFadden rarely had to cross the mountains when he returned to his native state. Everything he needed was on the other side of the Cascades.

Now he was back. Just as he had promised. Tory's stomach knotted painfully at the thought. *Damn him and his black betraying heart.*

Keith studied his older sister intently. Her shoulders slumped slightly and she brushed a loose strand of hair away from her face and back into the ponytail she always wore while working on the Lazy W. She leaned over the split rail, her fists balled beneath her jutted chin and her jaw tense. Keith witnessed the whitening of the skin over her cheekbones and thought for a moment that she might faint; but when her gray-green eyes turned back to him they seemed calm, hiding any emotions that might be raging within her heart.

Trask. Back. After all these years and all the lies. Tory shook her head as if to deny any feelings she might still harbor for him.

"You act as if you don't care," Keith prodded, though he had noticed the hardening of her elegant features. He leaned backward, his broad shoulders supported by the rails of the fence. His arms were crossed over his chest, his dusty straw Stetson was pushed back on his head and dark sweat-dampened hair protruded unevenly from beneath the brim as he surveyed his temperamental sister.

"I can't let it bother me one way or the other," she said with a dismissive shrug. "Now, about the stallion…" She pointed to the bay. "His near foreleg—I think it's laminitis. He's probably been putting too much weight on the leg because of his injury to the other foreleg." When Keith didn't respond, she clarified. "Governor's foot is swollen with founder, acute laminitis. His temperature's up, he's sweating and blowing and he won't bear any weight on the leg. We're lucky so far, there's no sign of infection—"

Keith made a disgusted sound and held up his palm in frustration with his older sister. *What the hell was the matter with her? Hadn't she heard him? Didn't she care?* "Tory, for Christ's sake, listen to me and forget about the horse for a minute! McFadden always said he'd come back; *for you.*"

Tory winced slightly. Her gray-green eyes narrowed against a slew of painful memories that made goose bumps rise on her bare arms. "That was a long time ago," she whispered, once again facing her brother.

"Before the trial."

Closing her eyes against the agony of the past, Tory leaned heavily against the split cedar rails and forced her thoughts to the present. Though her heart was thudding wildly within her chest, she managed to remain outwardly calm. "I don't think McFadden will bother us," she said.

"I'm not so sure…."

She forced a half smile she didn't feel. "Come on, Keith, buck up. Let's not borrow trouble. We've got enough as it is, don't you think?" Once again she cast a glance at the bay stallion. He was still sweating and blowing. She had examined him carefully and was thankful that there was no evidence of infection in the swollen tissues of his foot.

Keith managed to return his sister's encouraging grin, but it was short-lived. "Yeah, I suppose we don't need any more trouble. Not now," he acknowledged before his ruddy complexion darkened and his gray eyes lost their sparkle. "We've had our share and we know who to thank for it," he said, removing his hat and pushing his sweaty hair off his brow. Dusty streaks lined his forehead. "All the problems began with Mc-Fadden, you know."

Tory couldn't deny the truth in her younger brother's words. "Maybe—"

"No maybe about it, Tory. If it hadn't been for Mc-Fadden, Dad might still be alive." Keith's gray eyes clouded with hatred and he forced his hat onto his head with renewed vengeance.

"You can't be sure of that," Tory replied, wondering why she was defending a man she had sworn to hate.

"Oh, no?" he threw back at her. "Well, I can be sure of one thing! Dad wouldn't have spent the last couple of years of his life rotting in some stinking jail cell if McFadden's testimony hadn't put him there."

Tory's heart twisted with a painful spasm of guilt. "That was my fault," she whispered quietly.

"The hell it was," Keith exploded. "McFadden was the guy who sent Dad up the river on a bum rap."

"You don't have to remind me of that."

"I guess not," he allowed. "The bastard used you, too." Keith adjusted his Stetson and rammed his fists into his pockets. "Whatever you do, Sis," he warned, "don't stick up for him. At least not to me. The bottom line is that Dad is dead."

Tory smiled bitterly at the irony of it all and smoothed a wisp of hair out of her face. She had made the mistake of defending Trask McFadden once. It would never happen again. "I won't."

She lifted her shoulders and let out a tortured breath of air. *How many times had she thought about the day that Trask would return? How many times had she fantasized about him? In one scenario she was throwing*

him off her property, telling him just what kind of a
bastard he was; in another she was making passionate
love with him near the pond.... She cleared her throat
and said, "Just because he's back in town doesn't mean
that Trask is going to stir up any trouble."

Keith wasn't convinced. "Trouble follows him
around."

"Well, it won't follow him here."

"How can you be so sure?"

"Because he's not welcome." Determination was
evident in her eyes and the thrust of her small proud
chin. She avoided Keith's narrowed eyes by watching a
small whirlwind kick up the dust and dry pine needles
in the corral. Governor snorted impatiently and his tail
switched at the ever-present flies.

Keith studied his sister dubiously. Though Tory was
six years his senior, sometimes she seemed like a little
kid to him. Especially when it came to Trask McFadden. "Does *he* know that you don't want him here?"

Tory propped her boot on the bottom rail. "I think I
made it pretty clear the last time I saw him."

"But that was over five years ago."

Tory turned her serious gray-green eyes on her
brother. "Nothing's changed since then."

"Except that he's back and he's making noise about
seeing you again."

Tory's head snapped upward and she leveled her gaze
at her brother. "What kind of noise?"

"The kind that runs through the town gossip mill
like fire."

"I don't believe it. The man's not stupid, Keith. He
knows how I—we feel about him. He's probably back
in town visiting Neva. He has before."

"And all those times he never once mentioned that he'd come for you. Until now. He means business. The only reason he came back here was for you!"

"I don't think—"

"Damn it, Tory," Keith interjected. "For once in your life, just listen to me. I was in town last night, at the Branding Iron."

Tory cast Keith a concerned glance. He scowled and continued, "Neva's spread it around town. She said Trask was back. For you!"

Tory's heart nearly stopped beating. Neva McFadden was Trask's sister-in-law, the widow of his brother, Jason. It had been Jason's mysterious death that had started all the trouble with her father. Tory still ached for the grief that Neva McFadden and her small son had borne, but she knew in her heart that her father had had no part in Jason McFadden's death. Calvin Wilson had been sent to prison an innocent victim of an elaborate conspiracy, all because of Trask McFadden's testimony and the way Tory had let him use her. Silent white-hot rage surged through Tory's blood.

Keith was still trying desperately to convince her of Trask's intentions. "Neva wouldn't lie about something like this, Tory. McFadden will come looking for you."

"Great," she muttered, before slapping the fence. "Look, I want you to tell Rex and any of the other hands that Trask McFadden has no business on this property. If he shows up, we'll throw him off."

"Just like that?"

"Just like that." She snapped her fingers and her carefully disguised anger flickered in her eyes.

Keith rubbed his jaw. "How do you propose to do that? Threaten him with a rifle aimed at his head?"

"If that's what it takes."

Keith raised a skeptical brow. "You're serious?"

Tory laughed nervously. "Of course not. We'll just explain that if he doesn't remove himself, we'll call the sheriff."

"A lot of good that will do. We call the sheriff's office and what do you suppose will happen? Nothing! Paul Barnett's hands are tied. He owes his career—and maybe his whole political future—to McFadden. Who do you think backed Paul in the last election? McFadden." Keith spit out Trask's name as if it were a bitter poison. "Even if he wanted to, how in the hell would Paul throw a United States senator out on his ear?" Keith added with disgust in his voice, "Paul Barnett is in McFadden's back pocket."

"You make it sound as if Trask owns the whole town."

"Near enough; everyone in Sinclair thinks he's a god, y'know. Except for you—and sometimes I'm not so sure about that."

Tory couldn't help but laugh at the bleak scene Keith was painting. "Lighten up," she advised, her white teeth flashing against her tanned skin. "This isn't a bad western movie where the sheriff and the townspeople are all against a poor defenseless woman trying to save her ranch—"

"Sometimes I wonder."

"Give me a break, Keith. If Trask McFadden trespasses—"

"We're all in big trouble. Especially you."

Tory's fingers drummed nervously on the fence. She tried to change the course of the conversation. "Like I said, I think you're borrowing trouble," she muttered.

"What Trask McFadden says and what he does are two different things. He's a politician. Remember?"

Keith's mouth twisted into a bitter grin and his eyes narrowed at the irony. "Yeah, I remember; and I know that the only reason that bastard got elected was because of his testimony against Dad and the others. He put innocent men in jail and ended up with a cushy job in Washington. What a great guy."

Tory's teeth clenched together and a headache began to throb in her temples. "I'm sure that central Oregon will soon bore our prestigious senator," she said, her uncertainty carefully veiled. "He'll get tired of rubbing elbows with the constituents in Sinclair and return to D.C. where he belongs, and that's the last we'll hear of him."

Keith laughed bitterly. "You don't believe that any more than I do. If Trask McFadden's back it's for a reason and one reason only: you, Tory." He slouched against the fence, propped up by one elbow. "So, what are you going to do about it?"

"Nothing."

"Nothing?"

Her gray-green eyes glittered dangerously. "Let's just wait and see. If Trask has the guts to show up, I'll deal with him then."

Keith's lower lip protruded and he squinted against the glare of the lowering sun. "I think you should leave…."

"What!"

"Take a vacation, get out of this place. You deserve one, anyway; you've been working your tail off for the past five years. And, if McFadden comes here and finds out that you're gone for a few weeks, he'll get the idea and shove off."

"That's running, Keith," Tory snapped. "This is my home. I'm not running off like a frightened rabbit, for crying out loud. Not for Trask McFadden, not for any man." Determination underscored her words. Pride, fierce and painful, blazed in her eyes and was evident in the strong set of her jaw.

"He's a powerful man," Keith warned.

"And I'm not afraid of him."

"He hurt you once before."

Tory squared her shoulders. "That was a long time ago." She managed a tight smile and slapped her brother affectionately on his shoulder. "I'm not the same woman I used to be. I've grown up a lot since then."

"I don't know," Keith muttered, remembering his once carefree sister and the grin she used to wear so easily. "History has a way of repeating itself."

Tory shook her head and forced a smile, hoping to disarm her younger brother. She couldn't spend the rest of her life worrying about Trask and what he would or wouldn't do. She had already spent more hours than she would admit thinking about him and the shambles he'd attempted to make of her life. Just because he was back in Sinclair... "Let's forget about McFadden for a while, okay? Tell Rex I want to try ice-cold poultices on our friend here." She nodded in the direction of the bay stallion. "And I don't want him ridden until we determine if he needs a special shoe." She paused and her eyes rested on the sweating bay. "But he should be walked at least twice a day. More if possible."

"As if I have the time—"

Tory cut him off. "Someone around here *must* have the time," she snapped, thinking about the payroll of the ranch and how difficult it was to write the checks each month. The Lazy W was drowning in red ink. It had been since Calvin Wilson had been sent to prison five years before. *By Trask McFadden.* "Have someone, maybe Eldon, if you don't have the time, walk Governor," she said, her full lips pursing.

Keith knew that he was being dismissed. He frowned, cast his sister one final searching look, pushed his hat lower on his head and started ambling off toward the barn on the other side of the dusty paddock. He had delivered his message about Trask McFadden. The rest was up to Tory.

Trask paced in the small living room feeling like a caged animal. His long strides took him to the window where he would pause, study the distant snow-laden mountains through the paned glass and then return to the other side of the room to stop before the stone fireplace where Neva was sitting in a worn rocking chair. The rooms in the house were as neat and tidy as the woman who owned them and just being in the house—Jason's house—made Trask restless. His business in Sinclair wasn't pleasant and he had been putting it off for more than twelve hours. Now it was time to act.

"What good will come of this?" Neva asked, shaking her head with concern. Her small beautiful face was set in a frown and her full lips were pursed together in frustration.

"It's something I've got to do." Trask leaned against the mantel, ran his fingers under the collar of his shirt and pressed his thumb thoughtfully to his lips as he resumed pacing.

"Sit down, will you?" Neva demanded, her voice uncharacteristically sharp. He stopped midstride and she smiled, feeling suddenly foolish. "I'm sorry," she whispered, "I just hate to see you like this, all screwed up inside."

"I've always been this way."

"Hmph." She didn't believe it for a minute and she suspected that Trask didn't either. Trask McFadden was one of the few men she had met in her twenty-five years who knew his own mind and usually acted accordingly. Recently, just the opposite had been true and Neva would have had to have been a blind woman not to see that Trask's discomfiture was because of Tory Wilson. "And you think seeing Tory again will change all that?" She didn't bother to hide her skepticism.

"I don't know."

"But you're willing to gamble and find out?"

He nodded, the lines near the corners of his blue eyes crinkling.

"No matter what the price?"

"What's that supposed to mean?"

Neva stared at the only man she cared for. Trask had helped her, been at her side in those dark lonely nights after Jason's death. He had single-handedly instigated an investigation into the "accident," which had turned out to be the premeditated murder of her husband. Though Trask had been Jason's brother, his concern for Neva had gone beyond the usual bounds and she knew she would never forget his kindness or stop loving him.

Neva owed Trask plenty, but she couldn't seem to get through to him. A shiver of dread raced down her spine. Trask looked tired, she thought with concern, incredibly tired, as if he were on some new crusade. His hair had darkened from the winter in Washington, D.C., and the laugh lines near his mouth and eyes seemed to have grown into grooves of disenchantment. His whole attitude seemed jaded these days, she mused. Maybe that's what happened when an honest man became a senator....

At that moment, Nicholas raced into the room and breathlessly made a beeline for his mother. "Mom?" He slid to a stop, dusty tennis shoes catching on the polished wood floor.

"What, honey?" Neva stopped rocking and rumpled Nicholas's dark hair as he scrambled into her lap.

"Can I go over to Tim's? We're going to build a tree house out in the back by the barn. His mom says it's okay with her...."

Neva lifted her eyes and smiled at the taller boy scurrying after Nick. He was red-haired and gangly, with a gaping hole where his two front teeth should have been. "If you're sure it's all right with Betty."

"Yeah, sure," Tim said. "Mom likes it when Nick comes over. She says it keeps me out of her hair."

"Does she?" Neva laughed and turned her eyes back to Nicholas. At six, he was the spitting image of his father. Wavy brown hair, intense blue eyes glimmering with hope—so much like Jason. "Only a little while, okay? Dinner will be ready in less than an hour."

"Great!" Nicholas jumped off her lap and hurried out of the living room. The two boys left as quickly as they had appeared. Scurrying footsteps echoed down the short entry hall.

"Remember to shut the door," Neva called, but she heard the front door squeak open and bang against the wall.

"I'll get it." Trask, glad for the slightest opportunity to escape the confining room, followed the boys, shut the door and returned. Facing Neva was more difficult than he had imagined and he wondered for the hundredth time if he were doing the right thing. Neva didn't seem to think so.

She turned her brown eyes up to Trask's clouded gaze when he reentered the room. "That," she said, pointing in the direction that Nicholas had exited, "is the price you'll pay."

"Nick?"

"His innocence. Right now, Nicholas doesn't remember what happened five years ago," Neva said with a frown. "But if you go searching out Tory Wilson, all that will change. The gossip will start all over again; questions will be asked. Nick will have to come to terms with the fact that his father was murdered by a group of men whose relatives still live around Sinclair."

"He will someday anyway."

Neva's eyes pleaded with Trask as she rose from the chair. "But not yet, Trask. He's too young. Kids can be cruel…. I just want to give him a few more years of innocence. He's only six…."

"This has nothing to do with Nick."

"*The hell it doesn't!* It has everything to do with him. His father was killed because he knew too much about that Quarter Horse swindle." Neva wrapped her arms around her waist as if warding off a sudden chill, walked to one of the windows and stared outside. She stared at the Hamiltons' place across the street, where Nicholas was busily creating a tree house, blissfully unaware of the brutal circumstances surrounding his father's death. She trembled. "I don't want to go through it all again," Neva whispered, turning away from the window.

Trask shifted from one foot to the other as his conscience twinged. His thick brows drew together into a pensive scowl and he pushed impatient fingers through the coarse strands of his brown hair. "What if I told you that one of Jason's murderers might have escaped justice?"

Neva had been approaching him. She stopped dead in her tracks. "What do you mean?"

"Maybe there were four people involved in the conspiracy—not just three."

"I—I don't understand."

Trask tossed his head back and stared up at the exposed beams of the cedar ceiling. The last thing he wanted to do was hurt Neva. She and the boy had been through too much already, he thought. "What I'm saying is that I have reason to believe that one of the conspirators might never have been named. In fact, it's a good guess that he got away scot-free."

Neva turned narrowed eyes up to her husband's brother. "Who?"

"I don't know."

"This isn't some kind of a morbid joke—"

"Neva," he reproached, and she had only to look into his serious blue eyes to realize that he would never joke about anything as painful and vile as Jason's unnecessary death.

"You thought there were only three men involved. So what happened to change your mind?"

Knowing that he was probably making the biggest blunder of his short career in politics, Trask reached into his back pocket and withdrew the slightly wrinkled photocopy of the anonymous letter he had received in Washington just a week earlier. The letter had been his reason for returning—or so he had tried to convince himself for the past six days.

Neva took the grayish document and read the few sentences before shaking her head and letting her short blond curls fall around her face in neglected disarray. "This is a lie," she said aloud. The letter quivered in her small hand. "All the men connected with Jason's death were tried and convicted. Judge Linn Benton and George Henderson are in the pen serving time and Calvin Wilson is dead."

"So who does that leave?" he demanded.

"No one."

"That's what I thought."

"But now you're not so sure?"

"Not until I talk to Victoria Wilson." *Tory.* Just the thought of seeing her again did dangerous things to his mind. "She's the only person I know who might have the answers. The swindle took place on some property her father owned on Devil's Ridge."

Neva's lower lip trembled and her dark eyes accused him of crimes better left unspoken. Trask had used Victoria Wilson to convict her father; Neva doubted that Tory would be foolish enough to trust him again. "And you think that talking with Tory will clear this up?" She waved the letter in her hand as if to emphasize her words. "This is a prank, Trask. Nothing more. Leave it alone." She fell back into the rocker still clenching the letter and tucked her feet beneath her.

Trask silently damned himself for all the old wounds he was about to reopen. He reached forward, as if to stroke Neva's bent head, but his fingers curled into a fist of frustration. "I wish I could, Neva," he replied as he gently removed the letter from her hand and reached for the suede jacket he'd carelessly thrown over the back of the couch several hours earlier. He hooked one finger under the collar and tossed the jacket over his shoulder. "God, I wish I could."

"You and your damned ideals," she muttered. "Nothing will bring Jason back. But this…vendetta you're on…could hurt my son."

"Even if what I find out is the truth?"

Neva closed her eyes. She raised her hand and waved him off. She knew there was no way to talk sense to him when he had his mind made up. "Do what you have to do, Trask," she said wearily. "You will anyway. Just remember that Nicholas is the one who'll suffer." Her voice was low; a warning. "You and I—we'll survive. We always do. But what about Nick? He's in school now and this is a small town, a very small town. People talk."

Too much, Trask thought, silently agreeing. *People talk too damned much.* With an angry frown, he turned toward the door.

Neva heard his retreating footsteps echoing down the hall, the door slamming shut and finally the sound of an engine sparking to life then rumbling and fading into the distance.

Chapter 2

As dusk settled over the ranch, Tory was alone. And that's the way she wanted it.

She sat on the front porch of the two-story farmhouse that she had called home for most of her twenty-seven years. Rough cedar boards, painted a weathered gray, were highlighted by windows trimmed in a deep wine color. The porch ran the length of the house and had a sloping shake roof supported by hand-hewn posts. The house hadn't changed much since her father was forced to leave. Tory had attempted to keep the house and grounds in good repair...to please him when he was released. Only that wouldn't happen. Calvin Wilson had been dead for nearly two years, after suffering a painful and lonely death in the penitentiary for a crime he didn't commit. All because she had trusted Trask McFadden.

Tory's jaw tightened, her fingers clenched over the arm of the wooden porch swing that had been her father's favorite. Guilt took a stranglehold of her throat. If only she hadn't believed in Trask and his incredible blue eye—eyes Tory would never have suspected of anything less than the truth. He had used her shamelessly and she had been blind to his true motives, in love enough to let him take advantage of her. *Never again,* she swore to herself. *Trusting Trask McFadden was one mistake that she wouldn't make twice!*

With her hands cradling her head, Tory sat on the varnished slats of the porch swing and stared across the open fields toward the mountains. Purple thunderclouds rolled near the shadowy peaks as night fell across the plateau.

Telling herself that she wasn't waiting for Trask, Tory slowly rocked and remembered the last time she had seen him. It had been in the courtroom during her father's trial. The old bitterness filled her mind as she considered how easily Trask had betrayed her...

The trial had already taken over a week and in that time Tory felt as if her entire world were falling apart at the seams. The charges against her father were ludicrous. No one could possibly believe that Calvin Wilson was guilty of fraud, conspiracy or *murder*, for God's sake, and yet there he was, seated with his agitated attorney in the hot courtroom, listening stoically as the evidence against him mounted.

When it had been his turn to sit on the witness stand, he had sat ramrod stiff in the wooden chair, refusing to testify in his behalf.

"Dad, please, save yourself," Tory had begged on

the final day of the trial. She was standing in the court-room, clutching her father's sleeve, unaware of the re-porters scribbling rapidly in their notepads. Unshed tears of frustration and fear pooled in her large eyes.

"I know what I'm doin', Missy," Calvin had assured her, fondly patting her head. "It's all for the best. Trust me…"

Trust me.

The same words that Trask had said only a few days before the trial. And then he had betrayed her com-pletely. Tory paled and watched in disbelief and horror as Trask took the stand.

He was the perfect witness for the prosecution. Tall, good-looking, with a proud lift of his shoulders and piercing blue eyes, he cut an impressive figure on the witness stand, and his reputation as a trustworthy law-yer added to his appeal. His suit was neatly pressed, but his thick gold-streaked hair remained windblown, adding to the intense, but honest, country-boy image he had perfected. The fact that he was the brother of the murdered man only added sympathy from the jury for the prosecution. That he had gained his information by engaging in a love affair with the accused's daugh-ter didn't seem to tarnish his testimony in the least. If anything, it made his side of the story appear more poignantly authentic, and the district attorney played it to the hilt.

"And you were with Miss Wilson on the night of your brother's death," the rotund district attorney sug-gested, leaning familiarly on the polished rail of the witness stand. He stared at Trask over rimless glasses, lifting his bushy brown eyebrows in encouragement to his star witness.

"Yes." Trask's eyes held Tory's. She was sitting behind her father and the defense attorney, unable to believe that the man she loved was slowly, publicly shredding her life apart. Keith, who was sitting next to her, put a steadying arm around her shoulder, but she didn't feel it. She continued to stare at Trask with round tortured eyes.

"And what did Miss Wilson confide to you?" the D.A. asked, his knowing eyes moving from Trask to the jury in confidence.

"That some things had been going on at the Lazy W...things she didn't understand."

"Could you be more specific?"

Tory leaned forward and her hands clutched the railing separating her from her father in a death-grip.

The corner of Trask's jaw worked. "She—"

"You mean Victoria Wilson?"

"Yeah," Trask replied with a frown. "Tory claimed that her father had been in a bad mood for the better part of a week. She... Tory was worried about him. She said that Calvin had been moody and seemed distracted."

"Anything else?"

Trask hesitated only slightly. His blue eyes darkened and delved into hers. "Tory had seen her father leave the ranch late at night, on horseback."

"When?"

"July 7th."

"Of this year—the night your brother died?"

The lines around Trask's mouth tightened and his skin stretched tautly over his cheekbones. "Yes."

"And what worried Miss Wilson?"

"Objection," the defense attorney yelled, raising his

hand and screwing up his face in consternation as he shot up from his chair.

"Sustained." Judge Miller glared imperiously at the district attorney, who visibly regrouped his thoughts and line of questioning.

The district attorney flashed the jury a consoling smile. "What did Miss Wilson say to you that led you to believe that her father was part of the horse swindle?"

Trask settled back in his chair and chewed on his lower lip as he thought. "Tory said that Judge Linn Benton had been visiting the ranch several times in the past few days. The last time Benton was over at the ranch—"

"The Lazy W?"

Trask frowned at the D.A. "Yes. There was a loud argument between Calvin and the judge in Calvin's den. The door was closed, of course, but Tory was in the house and she overheard portions of the discussion."

"Objection," the defense attorney called again. "Your honor, this is only hearsay. Mr. McFadden can't possibly know what Miss Wilson overheard or thought she overheard."

"Sustained," the judge said wearily, wiping the sweat from his receding brow. "Mr. Delany…"

The district attorney took his cue and his lips pursed together thoughtfully as he turned back to Trask and said, "Tell me what you saw that convinced you that Calvin Wilson was involved in the alleged horse switching."

"I'd done some checking on my own," Trask admitted, seeing Tory's horrified expression from the corner of his eye. "I knew that my brother, Jason, was investigating an elaborate horse swapping swindle."

"Jason told you as much?"

"Yes. He worked for an insurance company, Edward's Life. Several registered Quarter Horses had died from accidents in the past couple of years. That in itself wasn't out of the ordinary, only two of the horses were owned by the same ranch. What was suspicious was the fact that the horses had been insured so heavily. The company didn't mind at the time the policy was taken out, but wasn't too thrilled when the horse died and the claim had to be paid.

"Still, like I said, nothing appeared out of the ordinary until a company adjuster, on a whim, talked with a few other rival companies who insured horses as well. When the computer records were cross-checked, the adjuster discovered a much higher than average mortality rate for highly-insured Quarter Horses in the area surrounding Sinclair, Oregon. Jason, as a claims investigator for Edward's Life, was instructed to check it out the next time a claim came in. You know, for fraud. What he discovered was that the dead horse wasn't even a purebred Quarter Horse. The mare was nothing more than a mustang, a range horse, insured to the teeth."

"How was that possible?"

"It wasn't. The horse was switched. The purebred horse was still alive, kept on an obscure piece of land in the foothills of the Cascade Mountains. The way Jason figured it, the purebred horse would either be sold for a tidy sum, or used for breeding purposes. Either way, the owner would make out with at least twice the value of the horse."

"I see," the D.A. said thoughtfully. "And who owned this piece of land?"

Trask paused, the corners of his mouth tightening. "Calvin Wilson."

A muffled whisper of shock ran through the court-room and the D.A., while pretending surprise, smiled a bit. Tory thought she was going to be sick. Her face paled and she had to swallow back the acrid taste of deception rising in her throat.

"How do you know who owned the property?"

"Jason had records from the county tax assessor's office. He told me. I couldn't believe it so I asked his daughter, Victoria Wilson."

Tory had to force herself not to gasp aloud at the vicious insinuations in Trask's lies. She closed her eyes and all the life seemed to drain out of her.

"And what did Miss Wilson say?"

"That she didn't know about the land. When I pressed her she admitted that she was worried about her father and the ranch; she said that the Lazy W had been in serious financial trouble for some time."

The district attorney seemed satisfied and rubbed his fleshy fingers together over his protruding stomach. Tory felt as if she were dying inside. The inquisition continued and Trask recounted the events of the summer. How he had seen Judge Linn Benton with Calvin Wilson on various occasions; how his brother, Jason, had almost concluded his investigation of the swindle; and how Calvin Wilson's name became linked to the other two men by his damning ownership of the property.

"You mean to tell me that your brother, Jason, told you that Calvin Wilson was involved?"

"Jason said he thought there might be a connection because of the land where the horses were kept."

"A connection?" the district attorney repeated, patting his stomach and looking incredulously at the jury. "I'd say that was more than 'a connection.' Wouldn't you?"

"I don't know." Trask shifted uneasily in his chair and his blue eyes narrowed on the D.A. "There is a chance that Calvin Wilson didn't know exactly what was happening on the land as it is several miles from the Lazy W."

"But what about the mare that was switched?" the D.A. prodded. "Wasn't she registered?"

"Yes."

"And the owner?"

"Calvin Wilson."

"So your brother, Jason McFadden, the insurance investigator for Edward's Life, thought that there might be a connection?" the D.A. concluded smugly.

"Jason was still working on it when the accident occurred." Trask's eyes hardened at the injustice of his brother's death. It was just the reaction the district attorney had been counting on.

"The accident which took his life. Right?"

"Yes."

"The accident that was caused by someone deliberately tampering with the gas line of the car," the D.A. persisted.

"Objection!"

"Your honor, it's been proven that the engine of Jason McFadden's car had been rigged with an explosive device that detonated at a certain speed, causing sparks to fly into the gas line and explode in the gas tank. What I'm attempting to prove is how that happened and who was to blame."

The gray-haired judge scowled, settled back in his chair and stared at the defense attorney with eyes filled with the cynicism of too many years on the bench. "Overruled."

The D.A. turned to face Trask.

"Let's go back to the night that Victoria Wilson saw her father leave the ranch. On that night, the night of July 7th, what did you do?"

Trask wiped a tired hand around his neck. "After I left Tory, I waited until Calvin had returned and then I confronted him with what Jason had figured out about the horse swapping scam and what I suspected about his involvement in it."

"But why did you do that? It might have backfired in your face and ruined your brother's reputation as an insurance investigator."

Trask paused for a minute. The courtroom was absolutely silent except for the soft hum of the motor of the paddle fan. "I was afraid."

"Of what?"

Trask's fingers tightened imperceptibly on the polished railing. "I was afraid for Jason's life. I thought he was in over his head."

"Why?"

"Jason had already received an anonymous phone call threatening him, as well as his family." Trask's eyes grew dark with indignation and fury and his jaw thrust forward menacingly. "But he wouldn't go to the police. It was important to him to handle it himself."

"And so you went to see Calvin Wilson, hoping that he might help you save your brother's life."

"Yes." Trask glared at the table behind which Tory's father was sitting.

"And what did Calvin Wilson say when you confronted him?"

Hatred flared in Trask's eyes. "That all the problems were solved."

At that point Neva McFadden, Jason's widow, broke down. Her small shoulders began to shake with the hysterical sobs racking her body and she buried her face in her hands, as if in so doing she could hide from the truth. Calvin Wilson didn't move a muscle, but Tory felt as if she were slowly bleeding to death. Keith's face turned ashen when Neva was helped from the courtroom and his arm over Tory's shoulders tightened.

"So," the D.A. persisted, turning everyone's attention back to the witness stand and Trask, "you thought that because of your close relationship with Calvin Wilson's daughter, that you might be able to reason with the man before anything tragic occurred."

"Yes," Trask whispered, his blue eyes filled with resignation as he looked from the empty chair in which Neva had been sitting, to Calvin Wilson and finally to Tory. "But it didn't work out that way…"

Tory continued to rock in the porch swing. A gentle breeze rustled the leaves of the aspen trees and whispered through the pines…just as it had on the first night she'd met him. All her memories of Trask were so vivid. Passionate images filled with love and hate teased her weary mind. Falling in love with him had been too easy…but then, of course, he had planned it that way, and she had been trapped easily by his deceit. Thank God she was alone tonight, she thought, so that she had time to think things out before she had to face him again.

It had taken a lot of convincing to get Keith to leave the ranch, but in the end he had gone into town with some of the single men who worked on the Lazy W. It was a muggy Saturday night in early summer, and Keith had decided that he would, against his better judgment, spend a few hours drinking beer and playing pool at the Branding Iron. It was his usual custom on Saturday evenings and Tory persuaded him that she wanted to be left alone. Which she did. If what Keith had been saying were true, then she wanted to meet Trask on her own terms, without unwanted ears to hear what promised to be a heated conversation.

The scent of freshly mown hay drifted on the sultry breeze that lifted the loose strands of hair away from her face. The gentle lowing of restless cattle as they roamed the far-off fields reached her ears. She squinted her eyes against the gathering night. Twilight had begun to color the landscape in shadowy hues of lavender. Clumps of sagebrush dappled the ground beneath the towering ponderosa pines. Even the proud Cascades loomed darkly, silently in the distance, a cold barrier to the rest of the world. *Except that the world was intruding into her life all over again.* The rugged mountains hadn't protected her at all. She had been a fool to think that she was safe and that the past was over and done.

The faint rumble of an engine caught Tory's attention. *Trask.*

Tory's heart began to pound in anticipation. She felt the faint stirrings of dread as the sound came nearer. He'd come back. Just as he'd promised and Keith had warned. A thin sheen of sweat broke out on her back and between her breasts. She clenched her teeth in renewed determination and her fingers clenched the arm of the swing in a death grip.

The twin beams of headlights illuminated the stand of aspen near the drive and a dusty blue pickup stopped in front of her house. Tory took in a needed breath of air and trained her eyes on the man unfolding himself from the cab. An unwelcome lump formed in her throat.

Trask was just as she had remembered him. Tall and lean, with long well-muscled thighs, tight buttocks, slim waist and broad chest, he looked just as arrogantly athletic as he always had. His light brown hair caught in the hot breeze and fell over his forehead in casual disarray.

So much for the stuffy United States senator image, Tory thought cynically. His shirt was pressed and clean, but open-throated, and the sleeves were pushed over his forearms. The jeans, which hugged his hips, looked as if they had seen years of use. *Just one of the boys...* Tory knew better. She couldn't trust him this night any more than she had on the day her father was sentenced to prison.

Trask strode over to the porch with a purposeful step and his eyes delved into hers.

What he encountered in Tory's cynical gaze was hostility—as hot and fresh as it had been on the day that Calvin Wilson had been found guilty for his part in Jason's death.

"What're you doing here?" Tory demanded. Her voice was surprisingly calm, probably from going over the scene a thousand times in her mind, she thought.

Trask climbed the two weathered steps to the porch, placed his hands on the railing and balanced his hips against the smooth wood. His booted feet were crossed in front of him. He attempted to look relaxed, but Tory noticed the inner tension tightening the muscles of his neck and shoulders.

"I think you know." His voice was low and familiar. It caused a prickling sensation to spread down the back of her neck. Looking into his vibrant blue eyes made it difficult for her not to think about the past that they had shared so fleetingly.

"Keith said you were spreading it around Sinclair that you wanted to see me."

"That's right."

"Why?"

His eyes slid away from her and he studied the starless sky. The air was heavy with the scent of rain. "I thought it was time to clear up a few things between us."

The memory of the trial burned into her mind. "Impossible."

"Tory—"

"Look, Trask," she said, her voice trembling only slightly, "you're not welcome here." She managed a sarcastic smile and gestured toward the pickup. "And I think you'd better leave before I tell you just what a bastard I think you are."

"It won't be the first time," he drawled, leaning against the post supporting the roof and staring down at her. His eyes slid lazily down her body, noting the elegant curve of her neck, the burnished wisps falling free of the loose knot of auburn hair at the base of her neck, the proud carriage of her body and the fire in her eyes. She was, without a doubt, the most beautiful and intelligent woman he had ever known. Try as he had to forget her, he had failed. Distance and time hadn't abated his desire; if anything, the feelings stirring within burned more torridly than he remembered.

He had the audacity to slant a lazy grin at her and Tory's simmering anger began to ignite. Her voice seemed to catch in her throat. "Leave."

"Not yet."

Righteous indignation flared in her eyes. "Leave, damn you…"

"Not until we get—"

"Now!" Her palm slapped against the varnished wooden arm of the swing and she pushed herself upward. "I don't want you ever to set foot on this ranch again. I thought I made that clear before, but either you have an incredibly short memory, or you just conveniently ignored out last conversation."

"Just for the record; I haven't forgotten anything. And that was no conversation," he speculated. "A war zone maybe, a helluva battle perhaps, but not idle chitchat."

"And neither is this. I don't know why you're here, Trask, and I don't really give a damn."

"You did once," he said softly, his dark eyes softening.

The tone of his voice pierced into her heart and her self-righteous fury threatened to escape. "That was before you used me, senator," she said, her voice a raspy whisper. One slim finger pointed at his chest. "Before you took everything I told you, turned it around and testified against my father!"

"And you still think he was innocent," Trask said, shaking his head in wonder.

"I know he was." Her chin raised a fraction and she impaled him with her flashing gray-green eyes. "How does it feel to look in the mirror every morning and know that you sent the wrong man to prison?" Hot tears touched the back of her eyes. "My father sat alone, slowly dying, the last few years of his life spent behind bars, all because of your lies."

"I never perjured myself, Tory."

Her lips pursed together in her anger. "Of course not. You were a lawyer. You knew just how to answer the questions; how exactly to insinuate to the jury that my father was part of the conspiracy; how to react to make the jury think that he was there the night that Jason found out about the swindle, how he inadvertently took part in your brother's death. Not only did you blacken my father's name, Trask, as far as I'm concerned, you took his life just as certainly as if you had thrust a knife into his heart." She took a step backward and placed her hand on the doorknob. Her fingers curled over the cold metal and her voice was edged in steel. "Now, get off this place and don't ever come back. You may be a senator now, maybe even respected by people who are only privy to your public image, but as far as I'm concerned you're nothing better than a egocentric opportunist who used the publicity surrounding his brother's death to get him elected!"

Trask's eyes flashed in the darkness. He took a step closer to her, but the hatred in her gaze stopped him dead in his tracks. "I only told the truth."

Rage stormed through her veins, thundered in her mind. Five long years of anger and bewilderment poured out of her. "You sensationalized this story, used it as a springboard to get you in the public eye, crushed everyone you had to so that you would get elected." The unshed tears glistened in her eyes. "Well, congratulations, senator. You got what you wanted."

With her final remarks, she opened the door and slipped through it, but Trask's hand came sharply upward and caught the smooth wood as she tried to slam the door in his face. "You've got it all figured out—"

"Easy to do. Now please, get off my land and out of my life. You destroyed it once, isn't that enough?"

Something akin to despair crossed his rugged features, but the emotion was quickly disguised by determination. "No."

"No?" she repeated incredulously. *Oh, God, Trask, don't put me through this again...not again.* "Well, once was enough for me," she murmured.

"I don't think so."

"Then you don't know me very well. I'm not the glutton for punishment I used to be." She pushed harder on the door, intent on physically forcing him out of her life.

"I wouldn't be so sure about that."

"What!"

"Look at you—you're still punishing yourself, blaming yourself for your father's conviction and death."

The audacity of the man! She felt her body begin to shake. "No, Trask. As incredible as you might find all this, I blame *you.* After all, you were the one who testified against my father..."

"And you've been hating yourself ever since."

"*I* can look in the mirror in the morning. *I* can live with myself."

"Can you?" His skepticism echoed in the still night air.

"I don't see any reason for discussing any of this. I've told you that I want you out of my life."

"And I don't believe it."

Once again she tried to slam the door, but his broad shoulder caught the hard wood. "You've got one incredible ego, senator," she said, wishing there was some way to put some distance between her body and his.

"You were waiting for me," he accused, his eyes sliding from her face down her neck, past the open collar of her blouse to linger at the hollow of her throat.

"Of course I was."

"Alone."

She was gripping the edge of the door so tightly that her fingers began to ache. "I didn't want the gossip to start all over again. Keith told me that you were looking for me, so I decided to wait. I prefer to keep my conversations with you private. You know, without a judge, jury or the press looking over my shoulder, ready to use every word against me."

His eyes slid downward, noticing the denim skirt and soft apricot-colored blouse. "So why did you get dressed up?"

"Don't flatter yourself, senator. I usually take a shower after working with the horses all day. The way I dress has nothing to do with you." Her eyes narrowed slightly. "So why don't you just take yourself and that tremendous ego of yours out of here? If you need a wheelbarrow to carry it there's one in the barn."

He shoved his body into the doorway, wedging himself between the door and the jamb. Tory was strong, she put all of her weight against the door, but she was no match for the powerful thrust of his shoulders as he pushed his way into the darkened hallway. "You're going to hear what I have to say whether you like it or not."

"No!"

"You don't have much of a choice."

"Get out, Trask." Her words sounded firm, but inwardly she wavered; the desperation she had noticed earlier flickered in his midnight-blue eyes. As much as she hated him, she still felt a physical attraction to him. *God, she was a fool.*

"In a minute."

She stepped backward and placed her hands on her hips. Her breath was expelled in a sigh of frustration. "Since I can't convince you otherwise, why don't you just say what you think is so all-fired important and then leave."

He eyed her suspiciously and walked into the den.

"Wait a minute—"

"I need your help."

Tory's heart nearly stopped beating. There was a thread of hopelessness in his voice that touched a precarious part of her mind and she had to remind herself that he was the enemy. He always had been. Though Trask seemed sincere she couldn't, wouldn't let herself believe him. "No way."

"I think you might change your mind."

"You've got to be kidding," Tory whispered.

She followed him into the den, her father's den, and swallowed back her anger and surprise. Trask had placed a hand on the lava rock fireplace and his head was lowered between his shoulders. How familiar it seemed to have him back in the warm den her father had used as an office. Knotty pine walls, worn comfortable furniture, watercolors of the Old West, Indian weavings in orange and brown, and now Trask, leaning dejectedly against the fireplace, looking for all the world as if he truly needed her help, made her throat constrict with fond memories. *God, how she had loved this man.* Her fist curled into balls of defeat.

"I'm not kidding, Tory." He glanced up at her and she read the torment in his eyes.

"No way."

"Just listen to me. That's all I ask."

Anger overcame awe. "I can't help you. I won't."

His pleas turned to threats. "You'd better."

"Why? What can you do to me now? Destroy my reputation? Ruin my family. Kill my father? You've already done all that, there's nothing left. You can damned well threaten until you're blue in the face and it won't affect me...or this ranch."

In the darkness his eyes searched her face, possessively reading the sculpted angle of her jaw, the proud lift of her chin, the tempting mystique of her intelligent gray-green eyes. "Nothing's left?" he whispered, his voice lowering. One finger reached upward and traced the soft slope of her neck.

Tory's heart hammered in her chest. "Nothing," she repeated, clenching her teeth and stepping away from his warm touch and treacherous blue eyes.

He grimaced. "This has to do with your father."

She whirled around to face him. "My father is dead." Shaking with rage she pointed an imperious finger at his chest. "Because of you."

His jaw tightened and he paced the length of the room in an obvious effort to control himself. "You'd like to believe that I was responsible for your father's death, wouldn't you?"

All of the anguish of five long years poured out of her. "You were. He could have had the proper medical treatment if he hadn't been in prison—"

"It makes it easier to think that I was the bad guy and that your father was some kind of a saint."

"All I know is that my father would never have been a part of anything like murder, Trask." She was visibly shaking. All the old emotions, love, hate, fear, awe and despair, churned inside her. Tears stung her eyelids and she fought a losing battle with the urge to weep.

"Your father was a desperate man," he said quietly.

"What's that supposed to mean?"

"Desperate men make mistakes, do things they wouldn't normally do." The look on his face was pensive and worried. She noticed neither revenge nor anger in his eyes. *Trask actually believed that her father had been nothing better than a common horse thief.*

"You're grasping at straws. My father was perfectly fine."

Trask crossed the room, leaned an arm on the mantel and rubbed his chin. All the while his dusky blue eyes held hers. "The Lazy W was losing money hand over fist." She was about to protest but he continued. "You know it as well as anyone. When you took over, you were forced to go to the bank for additional capital to keep it running."

"Because of all the bad publicity. People were afraid to buy Quarter Horses from the Lazy W because of the scandal."

"Right. The scandal. A simple scam to make money by claiming that the purebred Quarter Horses had died and offering as proof bodies of horses who resembled the blue bloods but weren't worth nearly as much. No one around here questioned Judge Benton's integrity, especially when his claims were backed up by the local veterinarian, George Henderson. It was a simple plan to dupe and defraud the insurance companies of thousands of dollars and it would never have come off if your father hadn't provided the perfect hiding spot for the purebreds who hadn't really met their maker. It all boiled down to one helluva scandal."

"I can't believe that Dad was involved in that."

"The horses were found on his property, Tory." Trask frowned at her stubborn pride. "You're finding it hard to believe a lot of things these days, aren't you?" he accused, silently damning himself for the torture he was putting her through. "Why didn't your father defend himself when he had the chance, on the witness stand? If he was innocent pleading the fifth amendment made him look more guilty than he was."

A solitary tear slid down her cheek. "I don't want to hear any more of this…"

"But you're going to, lady. You're going to hear every piece of incriminating evidence I have."

"Why, Trask?" she demanded. "Why now? Dad's dead—"

"And so is Jason. My brother was murdered, Tory. Murdered!" He fell into a chair near the desk. "I have reason to believe that one of the persons involved with the horse swindle and Jason's death was never brought to justice."

Her eyes widened in horror. "What do you mean?"

"I think there were more than three conspirators. Four, maybe five…who knows? Half the damned county might have been involved." Trask looked more haggard and defeated than she had ever thought possible. The U.S. senator from Sinclair, Oregon, had lost his luster and become jaded in the past few years. Cynical lines bracketed his mouth and his blue eyes seemed suddenly lifeless.

Tory's breath caught in her throat. "You're not serious."

"Dead serious. And I intend to find out who it was."

"But Judge Benton, he would have taken everyone down with him—no one would have been allowed to go free."

"Unless he struck a deal, or the other person had something over on our friend the judge. Who knows? Maybe this guy is extremely powerful..."

Tory shook her head, as if in so doing she could deny everything Trask was suggesting. "I don't believe any of this," she said, pacing around the room, her thoughts spinning crazily. *Why was Trask dredging all this up again. Why now? Just when life at the Lazy W had gotten back to normal...* "And I don't want to. Nothing you can do or say will change the past." She lifted her hands over her head in a gesture of utter defeat. "For God's sake, Trask, why are you here?"

"You're the only one who can help me unravel this, Tory."

"And I don't want to."

"Maybe this will change your mind." He extracted a piece of paper from his wallet and handed it to her. It was one of the photocopies of the letter he'd received.

Tory read the condemning words and her finely arched brows pulled together in a scowl of concentration. "Who sent you this?" she demanded.

"I don't know."

"It came anonymously?"

"Yes. To my office in Washington."

"It's probably just a prank."

"The postmark was Sinclair, Oregon. If it's a prank, Tory, it's a malicious one. And one of your neighbors is involved."

Tory read the condemning words again:

One of your brother's murderers is still free. He was

part of the Quarter Horse swindle involving Linn Benton, Calvin Wilson and George Henderson.

"But who would want to dig it all up again?"

Trask shook his head and pushed his fingers through his hair. "Someone with a guilty conscience? Someone who overheard a conversation and finally feels that it's time to come clean? A nosy journalist interested in a story? I don't know. But whoever he is, he wants me involved."

Tory sank into the nearest chair. "And you couldn't leave it alone."

"Could you?"

She smiled bitterly and studied the letter in her hand. "I suppose not. Not if there was a chance to prove that my father was innocent."

"Damn it, Tory!" Trask exclaimed. "Calvin had the opportunity to do that on the witness stand. He chose to hide behind the fifth amendment."

Tory swallowed as she remembered her father sitting in the crowded courtroom. His thick white hair was neatly in place, his gray eyes stared straight ahead. Each time the district attorney would fire a question at him, Calvin would stoically respond that he refused to answer the question on the basis that it might incriminate him. Calvin's attorney had been fit to be tied in the stifling courtroom. The other defendants, Linn Benton, a prominent circuit court judge and ringleader of the swindle, and George Henderson, a veterinarian and local rancher whose spread bordered the Lazy W to the north, cooperated with the district attorney. They had plea bargained for shorter sentences. But, for reasons he wouldn't name to his frantic daughter, Calvin Wilson accepted his guilt without a trace of regret.

"Face it, Tory," Trask was saying. "Your father was involved for all the right reasons. He was dying of cancer, the ranch was in trouble financially, and he wouldn't be able to take care of either you or your brother. He got involved with the horse swindle for the money…for you. He just didn't expect that Jason would find out about it and come snooping around." He walked to the other side of the room and stared out the window at the night. "I never wanted to think that your father was involved in the murder, Tory. I'd like to believe that he had no idea that Jason was on to him and the others. But I was there, I confronted the man and he looked through me as if whatever I said was of no significance." Trask walked across the room and grabbed Tory's shoulders. His face was twisted in disbelief. *"No significance! My brother's life, for God's sake, and Calvin stood there like a goddamn wooden Indian!"*

Tory tried to step away. "Not murder, Trask. My father wouldn't have been involved in Jason's death. He…" Her voice broke. "…couldn't."

"You don't know how much I want to believe you."

"But certainly—"

"I don't think your father instigated it," he interjected. "As a matter of fact, it's my guess that Benton planned Jason's 'accident' and had one of his henchmen tamper with the car."

"And Dad had to pay."

"Because he wouldn't defend himself."

She shook her head. "Against your lies." His fingers tightened over the soft fabric of her blouse. Tension charged the hot night air and Tory felt droplets of nervous perspiration break out between her shoulders.

"I only said what I thought was the truth."

The corners of her mouth turned bitterly downward and her eyes grew glacial cold. "The truth that you got from me."

His shoulders stiffened under his cotton shirt, and his eyes drilled into hers. "I never meant to hurt you, Tory, you know that."

For a fleeting moment she was tempted to believe him, but all the pain came rushing back to her in a violent storm of emotion. She felt her body shake with restraint. "I trusted you."

He winced slightly.

"I trusted you and you used me." The paper crumpled in her hand. "Take this letter and leave before I say things that I'll regret later."

"Tory..." He attempted to draw her close, but she pulled back, away from his lying eyes and familiar touch.

"I don't want to hear it, Trask. And I don't want to see you again. Now leave me alone—"

A loud knock resounded in the room and the hinges on the front door groaned as Rex Engels let himself into the house.

"Tory?" the foreman called. His steps slowed in the hallway, as if he was hesitant to intrude.

"In here." Tory was relieved at the intrusion. She stepped away from Trask and walked toward the door. When Rex entered he stopped and stared for a moment at Trask McFadden. His lips thinned as he took off his dusty Stetson and ran his fingers over the silver stubble on his chin. At five foot eight, he was several inches shorter than Trask, but his body was whip-lean from the physical labor he imposed on himself. Rugged and dependable, Rex Engels had been with the Lazy W for as long as Tory could remember.

The foreman was obviously uncomfortable; he shifted from one foot to the other and his eyes darted from Tory to Trask and back again.

"What happened?" Tory asked, knowing immediately that something was wrong and fearing that Keith was in the hospital or worse…

"I got a call from Len Ross about an hour ago," Rex stated, his mouth hardening into a frown. Tory nodded, encouraging him to continue. Ross was a neighboring rancher. "One of Ross's boys was mending fence this afternoon and he noticed a dead calf on the Lazy W."

Tory's shoulders slumped a little. It was always difficult losing livestock, especially the young ones. But it wasn't unexpected; it happened more often than she would like to admit and it certainly didn't warrant Rex driving over to the main house after dark. There had to be something more. Something he didn't want to discuss in front of Trask. "And?"

Rex rubbed his hand over his neck. He looked meaningfully at Trask. "The calf was shot."

"What?" Tory stiffened.

"From the looks of it, I'd guess it was done by a twenty-two."

"Then you saw the calf?" Trask cut in, his entire body tensing as he leaned one shoulder against the arch between den and entryway.

"Yep."

"And you don't think it was an accident?" Tory guessed.

"It's not hunting season," the foreman pointed out, moving his gaze to Trask in silent accusation. "And there were three bullet holes in the carcass."

Tory swallowed against the sickening feeling over-taking her. First Trask with his anonymous letter and the threat of dredging up the past again and now evidence that someone was deliberately threatening her livestock. "Why?" she wondered aloud.

"Maybe kids…" Rex offered, shifting his gaze uneasily between Tory and Trask. "It's happened before."

"Hardly seems like a prank," Trask interjected. There were too many unfortunate coincidences to suit him. Trask wasn't a man who believed in coincidence or luck.

Rex shrugged, unwilling to discuss the situation with the man who had sent Calvin Wilson to prison. He didn't trust Trask McFadden and his brown eyes made it clear.

Once the initial shock had worn off, Tory became furious that someone would deliberately kill the livestock. "I'll call Paul Barnett's office when we get back," she said.

"Get back?"

"I want to see the calf." Her gray-green eyes gleamed in determination; she knew that Rex would try to protect her from the ugly sight.

"There's not much to see," Rex protested. "It's dark."

"And this is my ranch. If someone has been deliberately molesting the livestock, I want to know what I'm up against. Let's go."

Rex knew there was no deterring her once she had set her mind on a plan of action. In more ways than one, Victoria was Calvin's daughter. He looked inquiringly at Trask and without words asked, what about him?

"Trask was just leaving."

"Not yet," Trask argued. "I'll come with you."

"Forget it."

"Listen to me. I think that this might have something to do with what we were discussing."

The anonymous letter? Her father's imprisonment? The horse swindle of five years ago? "I don't see how—" she protested.

"It won't hurt for me to take a look."

He was so damned logical. Seeing no reasonable argument, and not wanting to make a scene in front of Rex, Tory reluctantly agreed. "I don't like this," she mumbled, reaching for her jacket that hung on a wooden peg near the door and bracing herself for the unpleasant scene in the fields near the Ross property.

"Neither do I."

The tone of Trask's voice sent a shiver of dread down Tory's spine.

Rex cast her a worried glance, forced his gray Stetson onto his head and started for the door. As Tory grabbed the keys to her pickup she wondered what was happening to her life. Everything seemed to be turning upside down. All because of Trask McFadden.

Chapter 3

Trask sat on the passenger side of the pickup, his eyes looking steadily forward, his pensive gaze was following the disappearing taillights of Rex's truck.

Tory's eyebrows were drawn together in concentration as she attempted to follow Rex. Her fingers curled around the steering wheel as she tried to maneuver the bouncing pickup down the rutted dirt road that ran the length of the Lazy W toward the mountains.

The tension within the darkened interior of the pickup was thick enough to cut with a knife. Silence stretched tautly between Tory and Trask and she had to bite her tongue to keep from screaming at him that she didn't want him forcing himself back into her life.

She downshifted and slowed to a stop near the property line separating the Lazy W from Len Ross's spread.

"Over here," Rex announced when she shut off the

engine, grabbed a flashlight out of the glove box and jumped from the cab of the truck. Trask held the strands of barbed wire, which surrounded the pastures, apart as she wrapped her skirt around her thighs, climbed through the fence and followed the beam of Rex's flashlight. Trask slid through the fence after her. Though he said nothing, she was conscious of his presence, his long legs taking one stride to every two of her smaller steps.

The first large drops of rain began to fall just as Tory approached the crumpled heap near a solitary pine tree. The beam of Rex's flashlight was trained on the lifeless white face of the calf. Dull eyes looked unseeingly skyward and a large pink tongue lolled out of the side of the heifer's mouth.

"Dear God," Tory whispered, bending over and touching the inert form. Her stomach lurched uncomfortably as she brushed the flies from the curly red coat of the lifeless animal. Living on the ranch as she had for most of her twenty-seven years, Tory was used to death. But she had never been able to accept the unnecessary wanton destruction of life that had taken the small Hereford. It was all so pointless. Her throat tightened as she patted the rough hide and then let her hands fall to her sides.

Rex ran his flashlight over the calf's body and Tory noticed the three darkened splotches on the heifer's abdomen. Dried blood had clotted over the red and white hairs. Tory closed her eyes for a second. Whoever had killed the calf hadn't even had the decency to make it a clean kill. The poor creature had probably suffered for several hours before dying beneath the solitary ponderosa pine tree.

"What about the cow—the mother of the calf?"

"I took care of her," Rex stated. "She's with the rest of the herd in the south pasture."

Tory nodded thoughtfully and cocked her head toward the dead calf. "Let's cover her up," she whispered. "I've got a tarp in the back of the truck."

"Why?" Rex asked, but Trask was already returning to the pickup for the tarp.

"I want someone from the sheriff's office to see the calf and I don't want to take a chance that some scavenger finds her. A coyote could clean the carcass by morning," Tory replied, as she stood and dusted off her skirt. In the darkness, her eyes glinted with determination. "Someone did this—" she pointed to the calf "—deliberately. I want that person found."

Rex sucked in his breath and shook his head. "Might not be that easy," he thought aloud.

"Well, we've got to do something. We can't just sit by and let it happen again."

Rex shook his head. "You're right, Tory. I can't argue with that. Whoever did this should have to pay, but I doubt if having someone from the sheriff's office come out will do any good."

"Maybe not, but at least we'll find out if any of the other ranchers have had similar problems."

Rex forced his hands into the pockets of his lightweight jacket and pulled his shoulders closer to his neck as the rain began to shower in earnest. "I'll check all the fields tomorrow, just to make sure that there are no other surprises."

"Good."

Rex glanced uneasily toward the trucks, where Trask was fetching the tarp. "There's something else you should know," the foreman said. His voice was low, as if he didn't want to be overheard.

Tory followed Rex's gaze. "What?"

"The fence...someone snipped it. Whoever did this—" he motioned toward the dead calf "—didn't bother to climb through the fence, or use the gate. No, sir. They clipped all four wires clean open."

Tory's heart froze. Whoever had killed the calf had done it blatantly, almost tauntingly. She felt her stomach quiver with premonition. Things had gone from bad to worse in the span of a few short hours.

"I patched it up as best I could," Rex was saying with a frown. "I'll need a couple of the hands out here tomorrow to do a decent job of it."

"You don't think this is the work of kids out for a few kicks," Tory guessed.

Rex shrugged and even in the darkness Tory could see him scowl distractedly. "I don't rightly know, but I doubt it."

"Great."

"You don't have anyone who bears you a grudge, do you?" Rex asked uncomfortably.

"Not that I know of."

"How about someone who still has it in for your pop? Now that he's gone, you'd be the most likely target." He thought for a minute, as if he was hesitant to bring up a sore subject. "Maybe someone who's out to make trouble because of the horse swindle?"

"I don't think so," Tory murmured. "It's been a long time...over five years."

"But McFadden is back. Stirring up trouble..." If Rex meant to say anything more, he didn't. Trask reappeared with the heavy tarp slung over his shoulder.

Without a word the two men covered the small calf and lashed the tarp down with rope and metal stakes that Trask had brought from the truck.

"That about does it," Rex said, wiping the accumulation of rain from the back of his neck once the unpleasant job had been completed. "It would take a grizzly to rip that open." He stretched his shoulders before adding, "Like I said, I'll check all the fences and the livestock myself, in the morning. I'll let you know if anything looks suspicious." Rex's concerned gaze studied Trask for a tense second and Tory saw the muscles in Trask's face tighten a bit.

"I'll talk to you in the morning," Tory replied.

"'Night," Rex mumbled as he turned toward his truck.

"Thanks for checking it out, Rex."

"No problem." Rex pushed his hat squarely over his head. "All part of the job."

"Above and beyond the call of duty at ten o'clock at night."

"All in a day's work," Rex called over his shoulder.

Tory stood beside Trask and watched the beam of Rex's flashlight as the foreman strode briskly back to the truck.

"Come on," Trask said, placing his arm familiarly around her shoulders. "You're getting soaked. Let's go."

Casting a final despairing look at the covered carcass, Tory walked back to the pickup with Trask and didn't object to the weight of his arm stretched over her shoulders. This night, when her whole world was falling apart, she felt the need of his strength. She supposed her contradictory feelings for him bordered on irony, but she really didn't care. She was too tired and emotionally drained to consider the consequences of her renewed acquaintance with him.

"I'll drive," Trask said.

"I can—"

"I'll drive," he stated again, more forcefully, and she reached into her pocket and handed him the keys, too weary to argue over anything so pointless. He knew the back roads of the Lazy W as well as anyone. He had driven them often during the short months of their passionate but traitorous love affair. How long ago that happy carefree time in her life seemed now as they jostled along the furrowed road.

Trask drove slowly back to the house. The old engine of the truck rumbled through the dark night, the wipers pushed aside the heavy raindrops on the windshield, and the tinny sound of static-filled country music from an all-night radio station drifted out of the speakers.

"Who do you think did it?" Trask asked as he stopped the truck near the front porch.

"I don't have any idea," Tory admitted with a worried frown. "I don't really understand what's going on. Yesterday everything was normal: the worst problem I had to deal with was a broken combine and a horse with laminitis. But now—" she raised her hands helplessly before reaching for the door handle of the pickup "—it seems that all hell has broken loose." She looked toward him and found his eyes searching the contours of her face.

"Tory—" He reached for her, and the seductive light in his eyes made her heartbeat quicken. His fingers brushed against the rain-dampened strands of her hair and his lips curved into a wistful smile. "I remember another time," he said, "when you and I were alone in this very pickup."

A passionate image scorched Tory's mind. Just by staring into Trask's intense gaze she could recall the feel of his hands against her breasts, the way her skin would quiver at his touch, the taste of his mouth over hers. "I think we'd better not talk or even think about that," she whispered.

His fingers lingered against her exposed neck, warming the wet skin near the base of her throat. "Can't we be together without fighting?" he asked, his voice low with undercurrents of restrained desire.

After all these years, Trask still wanted her; or at least he wanted her to think that he still cared for her—just a little. Maybe he did. "I...I don't know."

"Let's try."

"I don't think I want to," she admitted, but it was too late. She watched with mingled fascination and dread as his head lowered and his mouth closed over hers, just as his hand pressed against her shoulder, pulling her against his chest. She was caught up in the scent of him; the familiar odor of his skin was dampened with the rain and all of her senses reawakened with his touch.

The warmth of his arms enveloped her and started the trickle of desire running in her blood. Warm lips, filled with the smoldering lust of five long years, touched hers and the tip of his tongue pressed urgently against her teeth.

I can't let this happen, she thought wildly, pressing her palms against his shoulders and trying to pull out of his intimate embrace. When he lifted his head from hers, she let her forehead fall against his chin. Her hands remained against his shoulders and only her shallow breathing gave her conflicting emotions away. "We can't start all over, you know," she said at length, raising her head and gazing into his eyes. "It's not as if either of us can forget what happened and start over again."

"But we don't have to let what happened force us apart."

"Oh, Trask, come on. Think about it," Tory said snappishly, although a vital but irrational part of her mind wanted desperately to believe him.

"I have. For five years."

"There's no other way, Trask. You and I both know it." Before he could contradict her or the illogical side of her nature could argue with her, she opened the door of the truck and dashed through the rain and across the gravel drive to the house.

She was already in the den when Trask entered the room. He leaned insolently against the archway. The rain had darkened his hair to a deep brown and the shoulders of his wet shirt clung to his muscles. Standing against the pine wall, his arms crossed insolently over his chest, his brilliant eyes delving into hers, he looked more masculine than she ever would have imagined. Or wanted. "What are you running from?" he asked.

"You...me...us." She lifted her hands into the air helplessly before realizing how undignified her emotions appeared. Then, willing her pride back into place, she wrapped her arms around herself and settled into the chair behind her father's desk. She hoped that the large oak table would put distance between her body and his—give her time to get her conflicting emotions back into perspective.

Trask looked bone-weary as he sauntered around the den and, uninvited, poured himself a healthy drink from the mirrored bar near the fireplace. He lifted the bottle in silent offering, but Tory shook her head, preferring to keep her wits about her. Her reaction to Trask was overwhelming, unwelcome and had to be controlled. She couldn't let herself be duped again. What was it they always said? Once burned, twice shy? That's the way it had to be with Trask, she tried to convince herself. He'd used her once. Never again.

He strode over to the window, propping one booted foot against a small stool, sipping his drink and staring out at the starless night. Raindrops slid in twisted paths down the panes.

"This ever happened before?" Trask asked. He turned and leaned against the windowsill, one broad hand supporting most of his weight.

"What?"

"Some of your livestock being used for target practice."

Her eyes narrowed at the cruel analogy. "No."

Swirling the amber liquor in his glass, he stared at her. "Don't you think it's odd?"

"Of course."

Trask shook his head. "More than that, Tory. Not just odd. What I meant is that it seems like more than a coincidence. First this letter—" he pointed to the anonymous note still lying face up crumpled on a small table "—and now the calf."

Tory felt the prickling sensation of dread climb up her spine. "What are you getting at?"

"I think the dead calf is a warning, Tory."

"What!"

"Someone knows I'm here looking for the person that was unconvicted in the original trial for Jason's murder.

I've made no bones about the fact that I intended to visit you. The calf was a message to stay away from me."

Tory laughed nervously. "You're not serious…."

"Dead serious."

Tory felt the first stirrings of fear. "I think you've been in Washington too long, senator," she replied. "Too many subcommittees on underworld crime have got you jumping at shadows. This is Sinclair, Oregon, not New York City."

"I'm not kidding, Tory." His eyes glittered dangerously and he finished his drink with a scowl. "Someone's trying to scare you off."

"It was probably just a prank, like Rex said."

"Rex didn't believe that and neither do you."

"You know how kids are: they get an idea in their heads and just for kicks—"

"They slaughter a calf?" he finished ungraciously. Anger flashed in his eyes and was evident in the set of his shoulders. "Real funny: a heifer with three gunshot wounds. Some sense of humor."

"I didn't say it was meant to be funny."

His fist crashed violently into the windowsill. "Damn it, Tory, haven't you been listening to a word I've said? It's obvious to me that someone is trying to scare you off!"

"Then why not send me a letter…or phone me? Why something as obscure as a dead calf? If you ask me, you're grasping at straws, trying to tie one event to the other just so that I'll help you in this…this wild-goose chase!" Realizing that he only intended to continue the argument, she reached for the phone on the corner of the desk.

Trask's eyes were blazing and the cords in his neck

protruded. He was about to say something more, but
Tory shook her head, motioning for him to be silent
as she dialed the sheriff's office and cradled the receiver between her shoulder and her ear. "No, Trask,
what you're suggesting doesn't make any sense. None
whatsoever."

"Like hell! If you weren't so damned stubborn—"

"Deputy Smith?" Tory said aloud as a curt voice an-
swered the phone. "This is Tory Wilson at the Lazy W."
Tory held up her hand to silence the protests forming on
Trask's tongue. As quickly as possible, she explained
everything that had occurred from the time that Len
Ross's hands had noticed the dead animal.

"We'll have someone out in the morning," the deputy promised after telling her that no other rancher had
reported any disturbances in the past few weeks. Tory
replaced the phone with shaking hands. Her brows drew
together thoughtfully.

"You're beginning to believe me," Trask deduced. He
was still angry, but his rage was once again controlled.

"No—"

"You'd better think about it. Has anything else un-
usual happened around here?"

"No...wait a minute. There was the combine that
broke down unexpectedly and I do have a stallion with
laminitis, but they couldn't be connected...never mind."
*What was she thinking about? Governor's condition and
the broken machinery were all explainable problems of
running the Lazy W. The malicious incident involving
the calf—that was something else again.* She forced a
fragile smile. "Look, Trask, I think you'd better leave."

"What about the letter?" he demanded, picking up

the small piece of paper and waving it in her face. "Are you going to ignore it, too?"

"I wouldn't take it too seriously," she allowed, lifting her shoulders.

"No?"

"For God's sake, Trask, it isn't even signed. That doesn't make much sense to me. Why wouldn't the person who wrote it want to be identified, that is if he has a logical authentic complaint? If the man who wrote this note wanted you to do something, why didn't he bother to sign the damned thing?"

"Maybe because he or she is afraid. Maybe the person who was involved with the swindle and avoided justice got away because he's extremely powerful—"

"And maybe he just doesn't exist." She eyed the grayish sheet of paper disdainfully. "That could be a letter from anyone, and it doesn't necessarily mean it's true."

"Tory—" His eyes darkened at her obstinacy.

"As I said before, I think it's time you left."

He took a step nearer to her, but she held up her hand before motioning toward the letter. "I can't help you with this. I have enough tangible problems here on the ranch. I don't have time to deal with fantasies."

Trask watched as she forced the curtain of callous disinterest over her beautiful features. The emerald-green eyes, which had once been so innocent and loving, turned cold with determination. "Oh, God, Tory, is this what I did to you?" he asked in bewilderment. "Did what happened between us take away all your trust? All your willingness to help? Your concern for others as well as yourself?" He was slowly advancing upon her, his footsteps muffled by the braided rug.

Tory's heart pounded betrayingly at his approach. It

pulsed rapidly in the hollow of her throat and Trask's intense gaze rested on the revealing cleft.

"I've missed you," he whispered.

"No—"

"I didn't mean for everything between us to end the way it did."

"But it did. Nothing can change that. You sent my father to prison."

"But I only told the truth." He paused at the desk and hooked a leg over the corner as he stared down at her.

"Let's not go over this again. It's been too long, Trask. Too many wounds are still fresh." She swallowed with difficulty but managed to meet his stare boldly. "I've hated you a long time," she said, feeling her tongue trip over the lie she had held true for five unforgiving years.

"I don't believe it."

"You ruined me single-handedly."

"Your father did that." He leaned forward. He was close enough to touch her, but he stopped just short and stared down into her eyes. Eyes that had trusted him with her life five years earlier. "What did you expect me to do? Lie on the witness stand? Would you have preferred not knowing about your father?"

She couldn't stand it anymore; couldn't return his self-righteous stare. "He was innocent, damn it!" Her fists curled into knots of fury and she pushed herself up from the chair.

"Then why didn't he save himself, tell his side of the story?"

"I don't know." Her voice trembled slightly. "Don't you think I've asked myself just that question over and over again?" She felt his arms fold around her, draw her close, hold her body against his as he straightened from the desk. She heard the steady beating of his heart, felt the warmth of his breath caress her hair and she knew in a blinding flash of truth that she had never stopped loving him.

"If there were another man involved in the horse swindle, don't you want to see him accused of the crime?"

"So he could be put behind bars like my father."

"Oh, Tory," he said, releasing a sigh as his arms tightened around her. "How can you be so damned one-sided? You used to care what happened to people…"

"I still do."

"But not to the extent that you're willing to help me find out who was involved in my brother's murder and the Quarter Horse swindle."

She felt herself sag against him. *It would be so nice just to forget about what happened. Pretend that everything was just as it had been on the night she'd met Trask McFadden before her life had become irrevocably twisted with his.* "I just don't know if it will do any good. For all you know that letter could be phony, the work of someone who gets his jollies by stirring up trouble."

"Like the dead calf?"

Tory ran her fingers through her hair. "You don't know that the two incidents are related."

"But we won't find out unless we try." He held her closer and his breath whispered through her hair. "Just give it a chance, Tory. Trust me."

The same old words. Lies and deceit. Rolling as easily off his tongue as they had in the past. All the kindness in her heart withered and died.

She extracted herself from his embrace and impaled him with her indignant green-eyed stare. "I can't help you, Trask," she whispered. "You're on your own this time." She reached for the copy of the note and slowly wadded it into a tight ball before tossing the damning piece of paper into the blackened fireplace.

Trask watched her actions and his lips tightened menacingly. "I'm going to find out if there was any truth to that letter," he stated emphatically. "And I'm going to do it with or without your help."

Though her heart was pounding erratically, she looked him squarely in the eye. "Then I guess you're going to do it alone, aren't you, senator?"

Looking as if he had something further to say, Trask turned on his heel and walked out of the room. The front door slammed behind him and the engine of his pickup roared to life before fading in the distance.

"You bastard," Tory whispered, sagging against the windowsill. "Why can't I stop loving you?"

Chapter 4

For several hours after Trask had left the ranch, Tory sat on the window seat in her bedroom. Her chin rested on her knees as she stared into the dark night. Raindrops pelted against the panes, drizzling against the glass and blurring Tory's view of the lightning that sizzled across the sky to illuminate the countryside in its garish white light. To the west, thunder rolled ominously over the mountains.

So Trask had come back after all. Tory frowned to herself and squinted into the darkness. *But he hadn't come back for her,* as he had vowed he would five years past. This time he had returned to Sinclair and the Lazy W because he needed her help to prove that another man was part of the Quarter Horse swindle as well as involved in Jason McFadden's premeditated death.

With tense fingers she pushed the hair out of her

eyes. Seeing Trask again had brought back too many dangerous memories. Memories of a younger, more carefree and reckless period of her life. Memories of a love destined to die.

As she looked through the window into the black sky, Tory was reminded of a summer filled with hot sultry nights, the sweet scent of pine needles and the familiar feel of Trask's body pressed urgently against hers.

She had to rub her hands over her arms as she remembered the feel of Trask's hard muscles against her skin, the weight of his body pinning hers, the taste of his mouth…

"Stop it," she muttered aloud, pulling herself out of her wanton reverie. "He's the man that sent Dad to prison, for God's sake. Don't be a fool—not twice."

She walked over to the bed and tossed back the quilted coverlet before lying on the sheets and staring at the shadowed ceiling. Her feelings of love for Trask had been her Achilles' heel. She had trusted him with every breath of life in her body and he had used her. Worse than that he had probably planned the whole affair; staging it perfectly. And she'd been fool enough to fall for his act, hook, line and sinker. But not again.

With a disconsolate sigh, she rolled onto her side and stared at the nightstand. In the darkness she could barely make out the picture of her father.

"Oh, Dad," Tory moaned, twisting away from the picture. "I wish you were here." Calvin Wilson had been an incredibly strong man who had been able to stand up to any adversity. He had been able to deal with the loan officers of the local banks when the ranch was in obvious financial trouble. His calm gray eyes and soft-spoken manner had inspired the local bankers' confidence when the general ledgers of the Lazy W couldn't.

He had stood stoically at the grave site of his wife of fifteen years without so much as shedding a tear. While holding his children close he had mourned silently for the only woman he had truly loved, offering strength to his daughter and young son.

When he had faced sentencing for a crime he hadn't committed he hadn't blinked an eye. Nor had he so much as flinched when the sentence of thirty years in prison had been handed down. He had taken it all without the slightest trace of fear. When he'd found out that he was terminally ill with a malignant tumor, Calvin Wilson had been able to look death straight in the eye. Throughout his sixty-three years, he had been a strong man and a loving father. Tory knew in her heart that he couldn't have been involved in Jason McFadden's murder.

Then why didn't he stand up for himself at the trial?

If he had spoken out, told his side of the story, let the court hear the truth, even Trask's damning testimony would have been refuted and maybe Calvin Wilson would be alive now. And Trask wouldn't be back in Sinclair, digging up the past, searching for some elusive, maybe even phantom, conspirator in Jason's death.

And now Trask had returned, actually believing that someone else was involved in his brother's death.

So it all came back to Trask and the fact that Tory hadn't stopped loving him. She knew her feelings for him were crazy, considering everything they had been through. She loved him one minute, hated him the next and knew that she should never have seen him again. He could take his wild half-baked theories, anonymous letters and seductive smile straight back to Washington where they all belonged. Surely he had better things to do than bother her.

"Just leave me alone, Trask," Tory said with a sigh. "Go back to Washington and leave me alone… I don't want to love you any more… I can't…"

The next morning, after a restless night, Tory was making breakfast when Keith, more than slightly hung over, entered the kitchen. Without a word he walked to the refrigerator, poured himself a healthy glass of orange juice and drank it in one swallow. He then slumped into a chair at the kitchen table and glared up at Tory with red-rimmed eyes.

"Don't tell me you're dehydrated," Tory said, with a teasing lilt in her voice.

"Okay, I won't. Then you won't have to lecture me."

"Fair enough." From the looks of it Keith's hangover was punishment enough for his binge, Tory thought, and she had been the one who had insisted that he go into town last night. If he were suffering, which he obviously was, it was partially because of her insistence that he leave the ranch. She flipped the pancakes over and decided not to mention that Keith hadn't gotten home until after three. He was over twenty-one now, and she didn't have to mother him, though it was a hard habit to break considering that the past five years she had been father, mother and sister all rolled into one.

"How about some breakfast?" she suggested, stacking the pancakes on a plate near a pile of crisp bacon and placing the filled platter on the table.

"After a few answers."

"Okay." Tory slid into the chair facing him and poured syrup over her stack of hotcakes. "Shoot."

"What have to decided to do about McFadden?" Keith asked, forking a generous helping of bacon onto his plate.

"I don't know," Tory admitted. She took a bite from a strip of bacon. "Maybe there's nothing I can do."

"Like hell. You could leave."

"Not a chance, we went over this yesterday." She reached for the coffeepot and poured each of them a cup of coffee.

"McFadden will come here."

"He already has."

"What!" Keith's face lost all of its color. "When?"

"Last night. While you were in town."

Keith rubbed his palm over the reddish stubble on his chin. "Damn, I knew something like this would happen."

"It wasn't that big of a deal. We just talked."

Keith looked at his older sister as if she had lost her mind. "You did what?" he shouted, rising from the breakfast table.

"I said I talked with him. How else was I supposed to find out what he wanted?"

Keith's worried eyes studied her face. "So what happened to the woman who, just yesterday afternoon, was going to bodily throw Trask McFadden off her land if he set foot on it. You know, the lady with the ready rifle and deadly aim?"

"Now, wait a minute—" Tory's face lost all of its color and her eyes narrowed.

"Weren't you the one who suggested that we point a rifle at his head and tell him to get lost?"

"I was only joking…"

"Like hell!" Keith sputtered before truly seeing his sister for the first time that morning. A sinking realization hit him like a ton of bricks. "Tory, you're still in love with him, aren't you? I can't believe it! After what he did to you?" Keith stared at his sister incredulously before stalking over to the refrigerator and pouring himself a large glass of milk. "This isn't happening," he said, as if to console himself. "This is all just a bad dream…"

"I'm not in love with him, Keith," Tory said, tossing her hair over her shoulder and turning her face upward in order to meet Keith's disbelieving gaze.

"But you were once."

"Before he testified against Dad."

"Goddamn," Keith muttered as he sucked in his breath and got hold of himself. His large fist curled in frustration. "I knew he'd show up the minute I left the ranch. What did he want?"

"My help."

"Your what? I can't believe it. After what he put you through? The nerve of that bastard!" He took a long swig from his glass with one hand, then motioned to his sister. "Well, go on, go on, this is getting better by the minute."

"He thinks that there may have been someone else involved in Jason's murder and the horse swindle."

"Are you kiddin'?" Keith placed his empty glass on the counter and shook his head in disbelief. "After all this time? No way!"

"That's what I told him."

"But he didn't buy it?"

"I'd say not."

"Great! The dumb bastard will probably drag all of it up again. It'll be in the papers and everything." Keith paced between the table and the back door. He squinted against the bright morning sunshine streaming through the dusty windowpanes and looked toward the barn. "Dad's name is sure to come up."

"Sit down and eat your breakfast," Tory said, eyeing Keith's neglected plate.

Keith ignored her. "This is the last thing we need right now, you know. What with all the problems we're having with the bank…" He swore violently, balled one fist and smashed it into his other palm. "I should never have left you last night, I knew it, damn it, I knew it!" His temper threatened to explode completely for a minute before he finally managed to contain his fury. Slowly uncurling his fist, he regained his composure and added with false optimism, "Oh, well, maybe Mc-Fadden got whatever it was he wanted off his chest and now it's over."

Tory hated to burst Keith's bubble, but she had always been straight with her brother, telling him about the problems with the ranch when they occurred. There was no reason to change now. "I don't know that it's over."

"What's that supposed to mean?"

"I don't think Trask is going to let up on this. He seemed pretty determined to me." Tory had lost all interest in her breakfast and pushed her plate aside. Unconsciously she brushed the crumbs from the polished maple surface of the table.

"But why? What's got him all riled up after five years?" Keith wondered aloud. "His term as a senator isn't up for another couple of years, so he isn't looking for publicity..."

"He got a letter."

Keith froze. He turned incredulous gray eyes on his sister. "Wait a minute. The man must get a ton of mail. What kind of a letter got under his skin?"

"An anonymous one."

"So what?"

No time like the present to drop the bomb, she supposed. With a feeling of utter frustration she stood, picked up her plate and set it near the sink. "If you want to read it, there's a copy in the den, in the fireplace."

"In the fireplace! Wonderful," Keith muttered sarcastically as he headed through the archway that opened to the short hallway separating the living room, kitchen, dining room and den.

"Hey, what about this breakfast?" Tory called after him.

"I'm not hungry," Keith replied, from somewhere in the vicinity of the den.

"Great," Tory muttered under her breath as she put the uneaten pancakes and bacon on another plate. "Tomorrow morning it's cold cereal for you, brother dear." With a frown at the untouched food, she opened the door to the back porch and set the plate on the floorboards. Alex, the ranch's ancient Border collie, stood on slightly arthritic legs and wagged his tail before helping himself to Keith's breakfast.

"Serves him right," Tory told the old dog as she petted him fondly and scratched Alex's black ears. "I'm glad someone appreciates my cooking."

Tory heard Keith return to the kitchen. With a final pat to Alex's head, she straightened and walked into the house.

Keith was standing in the middle of the kitchen looking for all the world as if he would drop through the floor. He was holding the crumpled and now slightly blackened piece of paper in his hands and his face had paled beneath his tan. He set the paper on the table and smoothed out the creases in the letter. "Holy shit."

"My sentiments exactly."

"So how does he think you could help him?" Keith asked, his eyes narrowing in suspicion.

"I don't know. We never got that far."

"And this—" he pointed down at the paper "—is why he wanted to see you?"

"That's what he said."

Keith closed his eyes for a minute, trying to concentrate. "That's a relief, I guess."

Tory raised an inquisitive brow. "Meaning?"

Keith smiled sadly and shook his head. "That I don't want to see you hurt again."

"Don't worry, brother dear," she assured him with a slightly cynical smile, "I don't intend to be. But thanks anyway, for the concern."

"I don't want to be thanked, Tory. I just want you to avoid McFadden. He's trouble."

Tory couldn't argue the point. She turned on the tap and started hot water running into the sink. As the sink filled she began washing the dishes before she hit Keith with the other bad news. "Something else happened last night."

"I'm not sure I want to know what it is," Keith said, picking up his coffee cup and drinking some of the lukewarm liquid. With a scowl, he reached for the pot and added some hot coffee to the tepid fluid in his cup.

"You probably don't."

He poured more coffee into Tory's empty cup and set it on the wooden counter, near the sink. "So what happened?"

"There was some other nasty business yesterday," Tory said, ignoring the dishes for the moment and wiping her hands on a dish towel. As she picked up her cup she leaned her hips against the edge of the wooden counter and met Keith's worried gaze.

"What now?" he asked as he settled into the cane chair near the table and propped his boots on the seat of another chair.

"Someone clipped the barbed wire on the northwest side of the ranch, came in and shot one of the calves. Three times in the abdomen. A heifer. About four months old."

Keith's hand hesitated over the sugar bowl and his head snapped up. "You think it was done deliberately?"

"Had to be. I called the sheriff's office. They're sending a man out this morning. Rex is spending the morning going over all of the fence bordering the ranch and checking it for any other sings of destruction."

"Just what we need," Keith said, cynicism tightening the corners of his mouth. "Another crisis on the Lazy W. How'd you find out about it?"

"One of Len Ross's men noticed it yesterday evening. Len called Rex and he checked it out."

"What about the rest of the livestock?"

"As far as I know all present and accounted for."

"Son of a bitch!" Keith forgot about the sugar and took a swallow of his black coffee.

"Trask thinks it might be related to that." She pointed to the blackened letter.

"Trask thinks?" Keith repeated, his eyes narrowing. "How does he know about it?"

"He was here when Rex came over to tell me about it."

Keith looked physically pained. "Lord, Tory, I don't know how much more of your cheery morning news I can stand."

"That's the last of the surprises."

"Thank God," Keith said, pushing himself up from the table and glaring pointedly at his older sister. "You're on notice, Tory."

She had to chuckle. "For what?"

"From now on when I decide to stay on the ranch rather than checking out the action at the Branding Iron, I'm not going to let you talk me out of it."

"Is that so? And how would you have handled Trask when he showed up on the porch?"

"I would have taken your suggestion yesterday and met him with a rifle in my hands."

"This isn't 1840, you know."

"Doesn't matter."

"You can't threaten a United States senator, Keith."

"Just you watch," Keith said, reaching for his Stetson on the peg near the back door. "The next time Mc-Fadden trespasses, I'll be ready for him." With those final chilling words, he was out the back door of the house and heading for the barn. Tory watched him with worried eyes. Keith's temper had never had much of a fuse and Trask's presence seemed to have shortened it considerably.

It was her fault, she supposed. She should never have let Keith see the books. It didn't take a genius to see that the Lazy W was in pitiful financial shape, and dredging up the old scandal would only make it worse. But

Keith had asked to see the balance sheets, and Tory had let him review everything, inwardly pleased that he had grown up enough to care.

Deputy Woodward arrived shortly after ten. Tory had been in the den writing checks for the month-end bills when she had heard the sound of a vehicle approaching and had looked out the window to see the youngest of Paul Barnett's deputies getting out of his car. Slim, with a thin mustache, he had been hired in the past year and was one of the few deputies she had never met. Once, while in town, Keith had pointed the young man out to her.

When the chimes sounded, Tory put the checkbook into the top drawer of the desk and answered the door.

"Mornin'," Woodward said with a smile. "I'm looking for Victoria Wilson."

"You found her."

"Good. I'm Greg Woodward from the sheriff's office. From what I understand, you think someone's been taking potshots at your livestock."

Tory nodded. "Someone has. I've got a dead calf to prove it."

"Just one?"

"So far," Tory replied. "I thought maybe some of the other ranchers might have experienced some sort of vandalism like this on their ranches."

The young deputy shook his head. "Is that what you think it was? Vandalism?"

Tory thought about the dead calf and the clipped fence. "No, not really. I guess I was just hoping that the Lazy W hadn't been singled out."

Woodward offered an understanding grin. "Let's take a look at what happened."

Tory sat in the passenger seat of the deputy's car as he drove down the rutted road she had traveled with Trask less than twelve hours earlier. The grooves in the dirt road were muddy and slick from the rain, but Deputy Woodward's vehicle made it to the site of the clipped fence without any problem.

Rex was already working on restringing the barbed wire. He looked up when he saw Tory, frowned slightly and then straightened, adjusting the brim of his felt Stetson.

As Deputy Woodward studied the cut wire and corpse of the calf, he asked Tory to tell him what had happened. She, with Rex's help, explained about Len Ross's call and how she and Rex had subsequently discovered the damage to the fence and the calf's dead body.

"But no other livestock were affected?" Woodward asked, writing furiously on his report.

"No," Rex replied, "at least none that we know about."

"You've checked already?"

"I've got several men out looking right now," Rex said.

"What about other fences, the buildings, or the equipment for the farm?"

"We have a combine that broke down last week, but it was just a matter of age," Tory said.

Woodward seemed satisfied. He took one last look at the calf and scowled. "I'll file this report and check with some of the neighboring ranchers to see if anything like this has happened to anyone else." He looked meaningfully at Tory. "And you'll call, if you find anything else?"

"Of course," Tory said.

"Does anyone else know what happened here?" the young man asked, as he finished his report.

"Only two people other than the ranch hands," Tory replied. "Len Ross and Trask McFadden."

The young man's head jerked up. "Senator McFadden?"

Tory nodded and offered a confident smile she didn't feel. Greg Woodward was a local man. Though he had probably still been in high school at the time, he would have heard of Jason McFadden's murder and the conspiracy of horse swindlers who had been convicted. "Trask was visiting last night when Rex got the news from Len and came up to the house to tell me what had happened."

"Did he make any comments—being as he was here and all—or did he think it was vandalism?"

Tory's mind strayed to her conversation with Trask and his insistence that the animal's death was somehow related to the anonymous letter he had received. "I don't know," she hedged. "I suppose you'll have to ask him—"

"No reason to bother the senator," Rex interjected, his eyes traveling to Tory with an unspoken message. "He doesn't know any more than either of us."

Deputy Woodward caught the meaningful glance between rancher and foreman but didn't comment. He had enough sense to know that something wasn't right at the Lazy W and that Senator McFadden was more than a casual friend. On the drive back with Tory, Woodward silently speculated on the past scandal and what this recently divulged information could mean.

When the deputy deposited Tory back at the house,

she felt uneasy. Something in the young man's attitude had changed when she had mentioned that Trask had been on the ranch. *It's starting all over again,* she thought to herself. *Trask has only been in town two days and the trouble's starting all over again.* As if she and everyone connected with the Lazy W hadn't suffered enough from the scandal of five years past.

Tory parked the pickup on the street in front of the feed store in Sinclair. So far the entire day had been a waste. Deputy Woodward hadn't been able to ease her mind about the dead calf; in fact, if anything, the young man's reaction to the news that Trask knew of the incident only added to Tory's unease.

After Deputy Woodward had gone, Tory had attempted to do something, anything to keep her mind off Trask. But try as she might, she hadn't been able to concentrate on anything other than Trask and his ridiculous idea—no, make that conviction—that another person was involved in the Quarter Horse swindle as well as his brother's death.

He's jumping at shadows, she told herself as she stepped out of the pickup and into the dusty street, but she couldn't shake the image of Trask, his shoulders erect in controlled, but deadly determination as he had stood in her father's den the night before. She had witnessed the outrage in his blue eyes. *"He won't let up on this until he has an answer,"* she told herself with a frown.

She pushed her way into the feed store and made short work of ordering supplies for the Lazy W. The clerk, Alma Ray, had lived in Sinclair all her life and had worked at Rasmussen Feed for as long as Tory could remember. She was a woman in her middle to late fifties and wore her soft red hair piled on her head. She had always offered Tory a pleasant smile and thoughtful advice in the past, but this afternoon Alma's brown eyes were cold, her smile forced.

"Don't get paranoid," Tory cautioned herself in a whisper as she stepped out of the feed store and onto the sidewalk. "It's not as if this town is against you, for God's sake. Alma's just having a bad day—"

"Tory."

At the sound of her name, Tory turned to face Neva McFadden, Jason's widow. Neva was hurrying up the sidewalk in Tory's direction and Tory's heart sank. She saw the strain in Neva's even features, the worry in her doe-brown eyes. Images of the courtroom and Neva's proud face twisted in agony filled Tory's mind.

"Do you have a minute?" Neva asked, clutching a bag of groceries to her chest.

It was the first time Neva McFadden had spoken to Tory since the trial.

"Sure," Tory replied. She forced a smile, though the first traces of dread began to crawl up her spine. It couldn't be a coincidence that Neva wanted to talk to her the day after Trask had returned to the Lazy W. "Why don't we sit down?" She nodded in the direction of the local café, which was just across the street from the feed store.

"Great," Neva said with a faltering smile.

Once they were seated in a booth and had been served identical glasses of iced tea, Tory decided to take the offensive. "So, what's up?"

Neva stopped twirling the lemon in her glass. "I wanted to talk to you about Trask."

"I thought so. What about him?"

"I know that he went to see you last night and I have a good idea of what it was about," Neva stated. She hesitated slightly and frowned into her glass as if struggling with a weighty decision. "I don't see any reason to beat around the bush, Tory. I know about the letter Trask received. He showed me a copy of it."

"He showed it to me, too," Tory admitted, hiding her surprise. She had assumed that Trask hadn't spoken to anyone but her. It wouldn't take long for the gossip to start all over again.

"And what do you think about it?" Neva asked.

Tory lifted her shoulders. "I honestly don't know."

Neva let out a sigh and ignored her untouched drink. "Well, I do. It was a prank," Neva said firmly. "Just someone who wants to stir up the trouble all over again."

"Why would anyone want to do that?"

"I wish I knew," Neva admitted, shaking her head. The rays of the afternoon sun streamed through the window and reflected in the golden strands of her hair. Except for the lines of worry surrounding her eyes, Neva McFadden was an extremely attractive woman. "I wish to God I knew what was going on."

"So do I."

Neva's fingers touched Tory's forearm. She bit at her lower lip, as if the next words were awkward. "I know that you cared for Trask, Tory, and I know that you think he..."

"Used me?"

"Yes."

"It was more than that, Neva," Tory said, suddenly wanting this woman who had borne so much pain to understand. "Trask betrayed me and my family."

Neva stiffened and she withdrew her hand. "By taking care of his own."

"He lied, Neva."

Neva shook her head. "That's not the way it was. He just wanted justice for Jason's death."

"Justice or revenge?" Tory asked and could have kicked herself when she saw the anger flare in Neva's eyes.

"Does it matter?"

Tory shrugged and frowned. "I suppose not. It was a horrible thing that happened to Jason and you. And… and I'm sorry for…everything… I know it's been hard for you; harder than it's been for me." Her mouth suddenly dry, Tory took a long drink of the cold tea and still felt parched.

"It's over," Neva said. "Or it was until Trask came back with some wild ideas about another person being involved in Jason's death."

"So you think the letter was a prank."

"Of course it was."

"How can you be sure?"

Neva avoided Tory's direct gaze. "It's been five years, Tory. Five years without a husband or father to my son."

All the feelings of remorse Tory had felt during the trial overcame her as she watched the young woman battle against tears. "Neva, I'm sorry if my family had any part in the pain you and Nicholas have felt."

"Your father was involved with Linn Benton and George Henderson. I know you never believed that he was guilty, Tory, but the man didn't even stand up for himself at the trial."

Tory felt as if a knife, five years old and dull, had

been thrust into her heart. "I don't see any reason to talk about this, Neva. I've already apologized." Tory pushed herself up from the table. "I think I should go."

"Don't! Sit down, Tory," Neva pleaded. "Look, I didn't mean to start trouble. God knows that's the last thing I want. The reason I wanted to talk to you is because of Trask."

Tory felt her heart begin to pound. She took a seat on the edge of the booth, her back stiff. "So you said."

"Don't get involved with him again, Tory. Don't start believing that there was more to what happened than came out in the trial."

"I know there was more," Tory stated, feeling a need to defend her father.

"I don't think so. And even if there was, what would be the point of dredging it all up again? It won't bring Jason back to life, or your father. All it will do is bring the whole sordid scandal back into the public eye."

Tory leaned back and studied the blond woman. There was more to what Neva was suggesting than the woman had admitted. Tory could feel it. "But what if the letter Trask received contains part of the truth? Don't you want to find out?"

"No." Neva shook her head vehemently.

"I don't understand—"

"That's because you don't have a child, Tory. You don't have a six-year-old son who needs all the protection I can give him. It's bad enough that he doesn't have a father, but does he have to be reminded, taunted, teased about the fact that his dad was murdered by men in this town that he trusted?"

"Oh, Neva—"

"Think about it. Think long and hard about who is

going to win if Trask continues his wild-goose chase; no one. Not you, Tory. Not me. And especially not Nicholas. He's the loser!"

Tory chose her words carefully. "Don't you think your son deserves the truth?"

"Not if it costs him his peace of mind." Neva lifted her chin and her brown eyes grew cold. "I know that you don't want another scandal any more than I do. And as for Trask, well—" she lifted her palms upward and then dropped her hands "—I hope that, for both your sakes, you don't get involved with him again. Not just because of the letter. I don't think he could handle another love affair with you, Tory. The last time almost killed him." With her final remarks, Neva reached for her purse and sack of groceries and left the small café.

"So much for mending fences," Tory muttered as she paid the small tab and walked out of the restaurant. After crossing the street, she climbed into her pickup and headed back to the Lazy W. Though she had never been close to Neva, not even before Jason's death, Tory had hoped that someday the old wounds would heal and the scars become less visible. Now, with the threat of Trask opening up another investigation into his brother's death, that seemed impossible.

As Tory drove down the straight highway toward the ranch, her thoughts turned to the past. Maybe Neva was right. Maybe listening to Trask would only prove disastrous.

Five years before, after her father's conviction, Tory had been forced to give up her dream of graduate school to stay at the Lazy W and hold the ranch together. Not only had the ranch suffered financially, but her brother Keith, who was only sixteen at the time, needed her support and supervision. Her goal of becoming a veterinarian as well as her hopes of becoming Trask McFadden's wife had been shattered as easily as crystal against stone.

When Calvin had been sent to prison, Tory had stayed at the ranch and tried to raise a strong-willed younger brother as well as bring the Lazy W out of the pool of red ink. In the following five years Keith had grown up and become responsible, but the ranch was still losing money, though a little less each year.

Keith, at twenty-one, could, perhaps, run the ranch on his own. But it was too late for Tory. She could no more go back to school and become a veterinarian than she could become Trask McFadden's wife.

Chapter 5

The buildings of the Lazy W, made mostly of rough-hewn cedar and fir, stood proudly on the flat land comprising the ranch and were visible from the main highway. Tory wheeled the pickup onto the gravel lane that was lined with stately pines and aspen and led up to the house.

Purebred horses grazed in the fields surrounding the stables, whole spindly legged foals romped in the afternoon sunlight.

Tory's heart swelled with pride for the Lazy W. Three hundred acres of high plateau held together by barbed wire and red metal posts had been Tory's home for all of her twenty-seven years and suddenly it seemed that everyone wanted to take it away from her. Trask, with his damned investigation of the horse swindle of five years ago, was about to ruin her credibility as a Quarter Horse breeder by reminding the public of the shady dealings associated with the Lazy W.

Tall grass in the meadow ruffled in the summer breeze that blew across the mountains. White clouds clung to the jagged peaks of the Cascades, shadowing the grassland. This was the land she loved and Tory would fight tooth and nail to save it—even if it meant fighting Trask every step of the way. He couldn't just come marching back into her life and destroy everything she had worked for in the past five years!

Tory squinted against the late-afternoon sun as she drove the pickup into the parking lot near the barn and killed the engine. The warm westerly wind had removed any trace of the rainstorm that had occurred the night before and waves of summer heat shimmered in the distance, distorting the view of the craggy snow-covered mountains.

She pushed her keys into the pocket of her jeans and walked to the paddock where Governor was still separated from the rest of the horses. Eldon, one of the ranch hands, was dutifully walking the bay stallion.

"How's our patient?" Tory asked as she patted Governor on the withers and lifted his hoof. Governor snorted and flattened his ears against his head. "Steady, boy," Tory murmured softly.

"Still sore, I'd guess," the fortyish man said with a frown. His weathered face was knotted in concern.

"I'd say so," Tory agreed. "Has he been favoring it?"

"Some."

"What about his temperature?" Tory asked as she looked at the sensitive tissue within the hoof.

"Up a little."

She looked up and watched Governor's ribs, to determine if his breathing was accelerated, but it wasn't.

"I'll call the vet. Maybe Anna should have a look at it."

"Wouldn't hurt."

She released Governor's hoof and dusted her hands on her jeans. "I'll see if she can come by tomorrow; until then we'll just keep doing what we have been for the past two days."

"You got it."

Tory, with the intention of pouring a large glass of lemonade once she was inside the house, walked across the gravel parking area and then followed a worn path to the back porch. Alex was lying in the shady comfort of a juniper bush. He wagged his tail as she approached and Tory reached down to scratch the collie behind his ears before she opened the door to the kitchen.

"Tory? Is that you?" Keith yelled from the vicinity of the den when the screen door banged shut behind her.

"Who else?" she called back just as she heard his footsteps and Keith entered the homey kitchen from the hall. His young face was troubled and dusty. Sweat dampened his hair, darkening the strands that were plastered to his forehead. "You were expecting someone?" she teased while reaching into the refrigerator for a bag of lemons.

"Of course not. I was just waiting for you to get back."

"That sounds ominous," she said, slicing the lemons and squeezing them on the glass juicer. "I'm making lemonade, you want some?"

Keith seemed distracted. "Yeah. Sure," he replied before his gray eyes darkened. "What took you so long in town?"

Tory looked up sharply. Keith hadn't acted like himself since Trask was back in Oregon. "What is this, an inquisition?"

"Hardly." Keith ran a hand over his forehead, forcing his hair away from his face. "Rex and I were just talking...about what happened last night."

"You mean the calf?" she asked.

"Partially." Keith had taken the wooden salt shaker off the table and was pretending interest in it.

Tory felt her back stiffen slightly as she poured sugar and the lemon juice into a glass pitcher. "And the rest of your discussion with Rex centered on Trask, is that it?"

"Right."

At that moment Rex walked into the room. He fidgeted, removed his hat and worked the brim in his gnarled fingers.

"How about a glass of lemonade?" Tory asked, as much to change the direction of the conversation as to be hospitable.

"Sure," the foreman responded. A nervous smile hovered near the corners of his mouth but quickly faded as he passed a hand over his chin. "I thought you'd like to know that all of the horses and cattle are alive and accounted for."

Relief seeped through Tory's body. So the calf was an isolated incident—so much for Trask's conspiracy theories about vague and disturbing warnings in the form of dead livestock. "Good. What about any other signs of trouble?"

Rex shook his head thoughtfully. "None that I could see. None of the animals escaped through that hole in the fence, and we couldn't find any other places where the fence was cut or tampered with."

Tory was beginning to feel better by the minute. The

dark cloud of fear that had begun to settle over her the evening before was slowly beginning to dissipate. "And the fence that was damaged has been repaired?"

"Yep. Right after you brought the deputy out to look at the calf. Did it myself."

"Thanks, Rex."

"All part of the job," he muttered, avoiding her grateful glance.

"Well, then, I guess the fact that the rest of the livestock is okay is good news," Tory said, wincing a little as she remembered the unfortunate heifer. Neither man responded. "Now, I think we should take some precautions to see that this doesn't happen again."

Rex smiled slightly. "I'm open to suggestion."

"Wait a minute, Tory," Keith cut in abruptly as Tory turned back to the pitcher of lemonade and began adding ice water to the cloudy liquid. "Why are you avoiding the subject of McFadden?"

"Maybe I'm just tired of it," Tory said wearily. She had hoped to steer clear of another confrontation about Trask but knew the argument with her brother was inevitable. She poured the pale liquid into three glasses filled with ice and offered a glass to each of the men.

"McFadden's not going to just walk away from this, you know," Keith said.

"I know."

"Then for Pete's sake, Tory, we've got to come up with a plan to fight him."

"A plan?" Tory repeated incredulously. She had to laugh as she took a sip of her drink. "You're beginning to sound paranoid, Keith. A plan! People who make up plans are either suffering from overactive imaginations or are trying to hide something. Which are you?"

"Neither. I'm just trying to avoid another scandal, that's all," Keith responded, his eyes darkening. "And maybe save this ranch in the process. The last scandal nearly destroyed the Lazy W as well as killed Dad, or don't you remember?"

"I remember," Tory said, some of the old bitterness returning.

"Look, Sis," Keith pleaded, his voice softening a little. "I've studied the books and worked out some figures. The way I see it, the Lazy W has about six months to survive. Then the note with the bank is due, right?"

"Right," Tory said on a weary sigh.

"The only way the bank will renew it is if we can prove that we can run this place at a profit. Now you're close, Tory, damned close, but all it takes is for all the old rumors to start flying again. Once people are reminded of what Dad was supposedly involved in, we'll lose buyers as quickly as you can turn around, and there go the profits."

"You don't know that—"

"I sure as hell do."

Tory shifted and avoided Keith's direct stare. She knew what he was going to say before the words were out.

"The only way the Lazy W can stay in business is to sell those Quarter Horses you've been breeding. You know it as well as I do. And no one is going to touch those horses with a ten-foot pole if they think for one minute that the horses might be part of a fraud. The reputation of this ranch is…well, shady or at least it was, all because of the Quarter Horse scam five years ago. If all the publicity is thrown into the public eye again, your potential buyers are going to dry up quicker than Devil's Creek in a hot summer."

"And you think that's what will happen if Trask is allowed to investigate his anonymous letter?"

"You can count on it."

Tory's eyes moved from the stern set of Keith's jaw to Rex. "You've been awfully quiet. What do you think?"

"I think what I always have," Rex said, rubbing his chin. "McFadden is trouble. Plain and simple."

"There's no doubt about that," Tory thought aloud, "but I don't know what any of us can do about it."

"Maybe you can talk him out of dredging everything up again," Keith suggested. "However, I'd like it better if you had nothing to do with the son of a bitch."

Tory glared at her younger brother. "Let's leave reference to Trask's parentage and any other ridiculous insults out of this, okay? Now, how do you know he'll be back?"

"Oh, he'll be back all right. He's like a bad check; he just comes bouncing back. As sure as the sun comes up in the morning, McFadden will be back."

Tory shook her head and frowned into her glass. She swirled the liquid and stared at the melting ice. "So if he returns to the Lazy W, you want me to try and persuade him to ignore the letter and all this nonsense about another man being involved in the Quarter Horse swindle and Jason's death. Have I got it right?"

"Essentially," Keith said.

"Not exactly an intricate plan."

"But the only one we've got."

Tory set her glass on the counter and her eyes narrowed. "What if the letter is true, Keith? What if another person was involved in Jason's death, a man who could, perhaps, clear Dad's name?"

Keith smiled sadly, suddenly old beyond his years. "What's the chance of that happening?"

"'Bout one in a million, I'd guess," Rex said.

"Less than that," Keith said decisively, "considering that McFadden wouldn't be trying to clear Dad's name. He's the guy who put Dad in the prison in the first place, remember? I just can't believe that you're falling for his line again, Sis."

Tory paled slightly. "I'm not."

"Give me a break. You're softening to McFadden and you've only seen him once."

"Maybe I'm just tired of everyone trying to manipulate me," Tory said hotly. She stalked across the room and settled into one of the chairs near the table. "This whole thing is starting to reek of a conspiracy or at the very least a cover-up!"

"What do you mean?" Keith seemed thoroughly perplexed. Rex avoided Tory's gaze and stared out the window toward the road.

"I mean that I ran into Neva McFadden at the feed store. She wanted to talk to me, for crying out loud! Good Lord, the woman hasn't breathed a word to me since the trial and today she wanted to talk things over. Can you believe it?"

"'Things' being Trask?" Keith guessed.

"Right." Tory smiled grimly at the irony of it all. Neva McFadden was the last person Tory would have expected to beg her to stay away from Trask and his wild theories.

"You know that she's in love with him, don't you?" Keith said and noticed the paling of Tory's tanned skin. Whether his sister denied it or not, Tory was still holding a torch for McFadden. That thought alone made Keith's blood boil.

"She didn't say so."

"I doubt if she would: at least not to you."

"Maybe not," Tory whispered.

"So anyway, what did she want to talk about?"

"About the same thing you're preaching right now. That Trask's anonymous letter was just a prank, that we should leave the past alone, that her son would suffer if the scandal was brought to the public's attention again. She thought it would be wise if I didn't see Trask again."

"Too late for that," Rex said, removing his hat and running his fingers through his sweaty silver hair as he stared through the window. His thick shoulders slumped and his amiable smile fell from his face. "He's coming down the drive right now."

"Great," Keith muttered.

Tory's heart began to pound with dread. "Maybe we should tell him everything we discussed just now."

"That would be suicide, Tory. Our best bet is to convince him that his letter was nothing more than a phony—"

A loud rap on the door announced Trask's arrival. Keith let out a long breath of air. "Okay, Sis, you're on."

Tory's lips twisted cynically. "If you're looking for an Oscar-winning performance, you're going to be disappointed."

"What's that supposed to mean?" Keith asked warily.

"Haven't you ever heard the expression 'You catch more flies with honey than with vinegar'?" Without further explanation, she walked down the short corridor, ignored the round of swearing she heard in the kitchen and opened the front door.

Trask was about to knock again. His fist was lifted to his shoulder and his jaw was set angrily. At the sight of Tory, her gray-green eyes sparkling with a private joke, he was forced to smile and his angular features softened irresistibly. When Senator McFadden decided to turn on the charm, the effect was devastating to Tory's senses, even though she knew she couldn't trust him.

"I thought maybe you were trying to give me a not-so-subtle hint," Trask said.

Tory shook her head and laughed. "Not me, senator. I'm not afraid to speak my mind and tell you you're not welcome."

"I already knew that."

"But you're back." She leaned against the door, not bothering to invite him inside, and studied the male contours of his face. Yes sir, the senator was definitely a handsome man, she thought. Five years hadn't done him any harm—if anything, the added maturity was a plus to his appearance.

"I hoped that maybe you'd reconsidered your position and thought about what I had to say."

"Oh, I've thought about it a lot," Tory replied. "No one around here will let me forget it."

"And what have you decided?" Cobalt-blue eyes searched her face, as if seeing it for the first time. Tory's heart nearly missed a beat.

"Why don't you come inside and we'll talk about it?" Tory stepped away from the door, allowing him to pass. Keith and Rex were already in the den and when Trask walked through the archway, the tension in the room was nearly visible.

"It takes a lot of guts for you to come back here," Keith said. He walked over to the bar and poured himself a stiff drink.

"I said I would," Trask responded. A confident grin contrasted with the fierce intensity of his gaze.

"But I can't believe that you honestly expect Tory or

anyone at the Lazy W to help you on...this wild-goose chase of yours."

"I just want to look into it."

"Why?" Keith demanded, replacing the bottle and lifting the full glass to his lips.

Trask crossed his arms over his chest. "I want to know the truth about my brother's death."

Keith shook his head. "So all of a sudden the testimony at the trial wasn't enough. The scandal wasn't enough. Sending an innocent man to jail wasn't enough. You want more."

"Only the truth."

Keith's jaw jutted forward. "It's a little too late, don't ya think, McFadden? You should have been more interested in the truth before taking that witness stand and testifying against Calvin Wilson."

"If your father would have told his side of the story, maybe I wouldn't be here right now."

"Too late for second-guessing, McFadden," Keith said, his voice slightly uneven. "The man's dead."

An uncomfortable silence filled the room. Rex shifted restlessly and pushed his Stetson over his eyes. "I've got to get home," he said. "Belinda will be looking for me." He headed toward the door and paused near the outer hallway. "I'll see ya in the morning."

"Good night, Rex," Tory said just as the sound of the front door slamming shut rattled through the building.

"I think maybe you should leave, too," Keith said, taking a drink of his Scotch and leaning insolently against the rocks of the fireplace. He glared angrily at Trask and didn't bother to hide his contempt. "We're not interested in hearing what you have to say. You said plenty five years ago."

"I didn't perjure myself, if that's what you're insinuating."

"I'm not insinuating anything, McFadden. I believe in telling it straight out."

"So do I."

"Then you'll understand when I ask you to leave and tell you that we don't want any part of your plans to drag up all the scandal about the horse swindle again. It won't do anyone a bit of good, least of all the people on this ranch. You'll have to find another way to get elected this time, senator."

Trask leaned a hip against the back of a couch and turned his attention away from Keith to Tory. His blue eyes pierced hers. "Is that how you feel?" he demanded.

Tory looked at Trask's ruggedly handsome face and tried to convince herself that Trask had used her, betrayed her, destroyed everything she had ever loved, but she couldn't hide from the honesty in his cold blue stare. He was dangerous. As dangerous as he had ever been, and still Tory's heart raced at the sight of him. She knew her fascination for the man bordered on lunacy. "I agree with Keith," she said at last. "I can't see that opening up this whole can of worms will accomplish anything."

"Except make sure that a guilty party is punished."

"So you're still looking for retribution," she whispered, shaking her head. "It's been five years. Nothing is going to change what happened. Neva's right. Nothing you can do or say will bring Jason back."

"Neva?" Trask repeated. "You've been talking to her?" His features froze and the intensity of his stare cut Tory to the bone.

"Today, she ran into me on the street."

"And the conversation just happened to turn to me."
The corners of his mouth pulled down.

Tory's head snapped upward and her chin angled
forward defiantly. "She's worried about you, senator,
as well as about her son. She thinks you're on a personal vendetta that will do nothing more than open
up all the old wounds again, cause more pain, stir up
more trouble."

Trask winced slightly and let out a disgusted sound.
"I'm going to follow this through, Tory. I think you can
understand. It's my duty to my brother. He was murdered, for God's sake! Murdered! And one of the men
responsible might still be free!

"The way I see it, you have two options: you can be
with me or against me, but I'd strongly suggest that you
think about all of the alternatives. If your father was
innocent, as you so self-righteously claim, you've just
gotten the opportunity to prove it."

"You would help me?" she asked skeptically.

"Don't believe him, Tory," Keith insisted, walking
between Tory and Trask and sending his sister pleading glances. "You trusted him once before and all he
did was spit on you."

Trask's eyes narrowed as he focused on Tory's
younger brother. "Maybe you'd better just stay out of
this one, Keith," he suggested calmly. "This is between
your sister and me."

"I don't think—"

"I can handle it," Tory stated, her gaze shifting from
Trask to Keith and back again. Her shoulders were
squared, her lips pressed together in determination.
Fire sparked in her eyes.

Keith understood the unspoken message. Tory would

handle Trask in her own way. "All right. I've said everything I needed to say anyway." He pointed a long finger at Trask. "But as far as I'm concerned, McFadden, you have no business here." Keith strode out of the room, grabbed his hat off the wooden peg in the entry hall, jerked open the front door and slammed it shut behind him.

Trask watched Keith leave with more than a little concern. "He's got more of a temper than you did at that age."

"He hates you," Tory said simply.

Trask smiled wryly and pushed his fingers through his hair. "Can't say as I blame him."

"I hate you, too," Tory lied.

"No, no, you don't." He saw that she was about to protest and waved off her arguments before they could be voiced. "Oh, you hate what I did all right. And, maybe a few years back, you did hate me, or thought that you did. But now you know better."

"I don't know anything of the kind."

"Sure you do. You know that I haven't come back here to hurt you and you know that I only did what I did five years ago because I couldn't lie on the witness stand. The last thing I wanted to do was send your dad to prison—"

Tory desperately held up a palm. "Stop!" she demanded, unable to listen to his lies any longer. "I—I don't want to hear any more of your excuses or rationalizations—"

"It's easier to hate me, is that it?"

"No—yes! God, yes. I can't have you come in here and confuse me and I don't want to be a part of this... investigation or whatever you want to call it. I don't care about anonymous letters."

"Or dead calves?"

"One has nothing to do with the other," she said firmly, though she had to fight to keep her voice from trembling.

Trask studied his hands before lifting his eyes to meet her angry gaze. "I think you're wrong, Tory. Doesn't it strike you odd that everyone you know wants you to avoid me?"

She shook her head and looked at the ceiling. "Not after the hell you put me through five years ago," she whispered.

"You mean that it hasn't crossed your mind that someone is deliberately trying to keep you out of this investigation for a reason?"

"Such as?"

"Such as hiding the guilty person's identity."

"I can't be involved in this," Tory said, as if to convince herself. She had to get away from Trask and his damned logic. When she was around him, he turned her mind around. She began walking toward the door but stopped dead in her tracks when he spoke.

"Are you afraid of the truth?"

"Of course not!" She turned and faced him.

He pushed himself away from the couch. "Then maybe it's me."

"Don't be ridiculous," she said, but as he advanced upon her, she saw the steadfastness of his gaze. It dropped from her eyes to her mouth and settled on the rising swell of her breasts. "I'm not afraid of you, Trask. I never have been. Not even after what you did to me."

He stopped when he was near her and his eyes silently accused her of attempting to deceive him. When he reached forward to brush a wayward strand of hair away from her face, his fingertip touched her cheek, but she didn't flinch. "Then maybe you're afraid of yourself."

"That's nonsense."

"I don't think so." His fingers wrapped around her nape and tilted her head upward as he lowered his head and captured her lips with his. His mouth was warm and gentle, his tongue quick to invade her parted lips. Memories of hot summer nights, star-studded skies and bodies glistening with the sheen of perfect afterglow filled her mind. How easily she could slip backward...

The groan from deep in his throat brought her crashing back to a reality as barren as the desert. He didn't love her, had never loved her, but was attempting once again to use her. As common sense overtook her, Tory tried to step backward but the arms surrounding her tightened, forcing her body close.

"Let go of me," she said, her eyes challenging.

"I don't think so. Letting you go was the biggest mistake I've ever made and believe me, I've made my share. I'm not about to make the same mistake twice."

"You may have made a lot of mistakes, Trask, but you didn't have a choice where I was concerned. I swore that I'd never let you hurt me again, and it's a promise to myself that I intend to keep."

The warm hands at the base of her spine refused to release her. Instead they began to slowly massage her, and through the thin fabric of her cotton blouse, she could feel Trask's heat. It seeped through the cloth and warmed her skin, just as it had in the past.

His lips caressed her face, touching the sensitive skin of her eyelids and cheeks.

"I can't let this happen," she whispered, knowing that she was unable to stop herself.

Her skin began to flush and the yearnings she had vowed dead reawakened as his mouth slid down her throat and his hands came around to unbutton her blouse. As the fabric parted Tory could feel his lips touching the hollow of her throat and the swell of her breasts.

"Trask, please...don't," she said, swallowing against the desire running wildly in her blood.

His tongue circled the delicate ring of bones at the base of her throat while his hands opened her blouse and pushed it gently off her shoulders. "I've always loved you, Tory," he said as he watched her white breasts rise and fall with the tempo of her breathing.

Her rosy nipples peeked seductively through the sheer pink lace of her bra and the swelling in his loins made him say things he would have preferred to remain secret. "Love me," he pleaded, lifting his gaze to her green eyes.

"I...I did, Trask," she replied, trying to think rationally. She reached for the blouse that had fallen to the floor, but his hand took hold of her wrist. "I loved you more than any woman should love a man and...and I paid for that love. I will never, never make that mistake again!"

The fingers over her wrist tightened and he jerked her close to his taut body. With his free hand he tilted her face upward so that she was forced to stare into his intense blue eyes. "You can come up with all the reasons and excuses you want, lady, but they're all a pack of lies."

"You should know, senator. You wrote the book on deceit."

His jaw whitened and his lips twisted cynically. "Why don't you look in the mirror, Tory, and see the kind of woman you've become: a woman who's afraid of the truth. You won't face the truth about your father and you won't admit that you still care for me."

"There's a big difference between love and lust."

"Is there?" He cocked a thick brow dubiously and ran his finger down her throat, along her breastbone to the front clasp of her bra. "What we felt for each other five years ago, what would you call that?"

"All those emotions were tangled in a web of lies, Trask, each one a little bigger than the last. That's how I've come to think of what we shared: yesterday's lies." He released her slowly and didn't protest when she reached for her blouse and slipped it on.

"Then maybe it's time to start searching for the truth."

"By reopening the investigation into your brother's death?"

"Yes. Maybe if we set the past to rest, we could think about the future."

Tory let out a disgusted sound. "No way, senator. You know what they say, 'You can never go back.' Well, I believe it. Don't bother to tease me with vague promises about a future together, because I don't buy it. Not anymore. I've learned my lesson where you're concerned. I'm not as gullible as I used to be, thank God." She stepped away from him and finished buttoning her blouse.

His lips tightened and he pinched the bridge of his nose with his fingers, as if trying to thwart a potential headache. "Okay, Tory, so you aren't interested in a relationship with me—the least you can do is help me a little. If you really believe your father's name can be cleared, I'm offering you the means to do it."

"How?"

"I want to go up to Devil's Ridge tomorrow."

The request made her heart stop beating. Devil's

Ridge was a piece of land not far from the Lazy W. It had once been owned by her father and Calvin had willed the forty acre tract in the foothills of the Cascades to Keith. Devil's Ridge was the parcel of land where the Quarter Horses were switched during the swindle; the piece of land that had proved Calvin Wilson's involvement in the scam.

"Tory, did you hear me?"

"Yes."

"Will you come with me?"

No! I can't face all of the scandal again. "If you promise that no one else will know about it." Tory saw the questions in his eyes and hastened to explain. "I don't want any publicity about this, until you're sure of your facts, senator."

"Fair enough." He studied her face for a minute. "Are you with me on this, Tory?"

"No, but I won't hinder you either," she said, tired of arguing with Trask, Keith, Neva and the whole damned world. "If you want permission to wander around Devil's Ridge, you've got it. And I'll go with you."

"Why?"

"Because I want to keep my eye on you, senator."

"You still don't trust me, do you?" he asked.

"I can't let myself." *It's my way of protecting myself against you.*

A cloud of anguish darkened his eyes but was quickly dispersed. "Then I'll be here around noon tomorrow."

"I'll be waiting."

He had started toward the door, but turned at the bittersweet words. "If only I could believe that," he said before opening the door and disappearing through it.

Tory watched his retreating figure through the glass.

The late-afternoon sun was already casting lengthening shadows over the plains of the Lazy W as Trask strode to his pickup and, without looking backward, drove away.

"What business is it of yours?" Trask demanded of his sister-in-law. She was putting the finishing touches on a birthday cake for Nicholas, swirling the white frosting over the cake as if her brother-in-law's tirade was of little, if any, concern. "Why did you confront Tory?"

"It is my business," Neva threw back coolly as she surveyed her artwork and placed the knife in the empty bowl. When she turned to face Trask, her small chin was jutted in determination. "We're talking about the death of *my* husband, for God's sake. And you're the one who brought me into it when you started waving that god-awful note around here yesterday afternoon."

"But why did you try to convince Tory to stay out of it? She could help me."

Neva turned world-weary brown eyes on her brother-in-law. "Because I thought she might be able to get through to you. You don't listen to many people, Trask. Not me. Not your advisors in Washington. No one. I thought maybe there was a chance that Tory might beat some common sense into that thick skull of yours."

"She tried," Trask admitted.

"But failed, I assume."

"This is something I have to do, Neva." Trask placed his large hands on Neva's slim shoulders, as if by touching he could make her understand.

With difficulty, Neva ignored the warmth of Trask's fingers. "And damn the consequences, right? Your integrity come hell or high water." She wrestled free of his grip.

"You're blowing this way out of proportion."

"Me?" she screamed. "What about you? You get one crank letter and you're ready to tear this town apart, dig up five-year-old dirt and start battling a new crusade." She smiled sadly at the tense man before her. "Only this time I'm afraid you'll get hurt, Don Quixote; the windmills might fight back and hurt you as well as your Dulcinea."

"Whom?"

"Dulcinea del Toboso, the country girl whom Don Quixote selects as the lady of his knightly devotion. In this case, Victoria Wilson."

"You read too much," he said.

"Impossible."

Trask laughed despite the seriousness of Neva's stare. "Then you worry too much."

"It comes with the territory of being a mother," she said, picking up a frosting-laden beater and offering it to him. "Someone needs to worry about you."

He declined the beater. "I get by."

She studied the furrows of his brow. "I don't know, Trask. I just don't know."

"Just trust me, Neva."

The smile left her face and all of the emotions she had been battling for five long years tore at her heart. "I'd trust you with my life, Trask. You know that."

"Neva—" He took a step closer to her but she walked past him to the kitchen window. Outside she could watch Nicholas romp with the puppy Trask had given him for his birthday.

"But I can't trust you with Nicholas's life," she whispered, knotting her fingers in the corner of her apron. "I just can't do that and you have no right to ask me." Tears began to gather in her large eyes and she brushed them aside angrily.

Trask let out a heavy sigh. "I'm going up to Devil's Ridge tomorrow."

"Oh, God, no." Neva closed her eyes. "Trask, don't—"

"This is something I have to do," he repeated.

"Then maybe you'd better leave," she said, her voice nearly failing her. Trask was as close to a father to Nicholas as he could be, considering the separation of more than half a continent. If she threw Trask out, Nicholas would never forgive her. "Do what you have to do."

"What I have to do is stay here for Nicholas's birthday party."

Neva smiled through her tears. "You're a bastard, you know, McFadden; but a charming one nonetheless."

"This is all going to work out."

"God, I hope so," she whispered, once again sneaking a glance at her dark-haired son and the fluff of tan fur with the beguiling black eyes. "Nicholas worships the ground you walk on, you know."

Trask laughed mirthlessly. "Well, if he does, he's the only one in town. There's no doubt about it, I wouldn't win any popularity contests in Sinclair right now."

"Oh, I don't know, you seem to have been able to worm your way back into Tory's heart."

"I don't think so."

"We'll see, senator," Neva mused. "I think Victoria Wilson has never gotten you out of her system."

Chapter 6

Anna Hutton lifted Governor's hoof and examined it carefully. Her expert fingers gently touched the swollen tissues and the bay stallion, glistening with nervous sweat, snorted impatiently. "Steady, there," she murmured to the horse before lifting her eyes to meet Tory's worried gaze. "I'd say your diagnosis was right on the money, Tory," Anna remarked, as she slowly let the horse's foot return to the floor of his stall. "Our boy here has a case of acute laminitis. You know, girl, you should have been a vet." She offered Tory a small grin as she reached for her leather bag and once again lifted Governor's hoof and started cleaning the affected area.

"I guess I got sidetracked," Tory said. "So I'll have to rely on your expertise."

Anna smiled knowingly at her friend before continuing to work with Governor's hoof. The two women had once planned to go to graduate school together, but that was before Tory became involved with Trask McFadden and all of the bad press about Calvin Wilson and the Lazy W had come to light.

Tory's eyes were trained on Anna's hands, but her thoughts were far away, in a time when she had been filled with the anticipation of becoming Trask's wife. How willingly she had given up her career for him…

Glancing up, Anna noticed Tory's clouded expression and tactfully turned the conversation back to the horse as she finished cleaning the affected area. Governor flattened his dark ears to his head and shifted away from the young woman with the short blue-black hair and probing fingers. "You might want to put him in a special shoe, either a bar shoe or a saucer; and keep walking him. Have you applied any hot or cold poultices or put his hoof in ice water?"

"Yes, cold."

"Good, keep doing that," Anna suggested, her eyes narrowing as she studied the stallion. "I want to wait another day and see how he's doing tomorrow, before I consider giving him adrenaline or antihistamines."

"A woman from the old school, huh?"

"You know me, I believe the less drugs the better." She patted the horse on the shoulder. "He's a good-looking stallion, Tory."

"The best," Tory replied, glancing affectionately at the bay. "We're counting on him."

"As a stud?"

"Uh-huh. His first foals were born this spring."

"And you're happy with them?"

Tory nodded and smiled as she held open the stall gate for her friend. "I've always loved working with the horses, especially the foals."

Anna chuckled and shook her head in amazement as the two women walked out of the stallion barn and into the glare of the brilliant morning sun. "So you decided to breed Quarter Horses again, even after what happened with your father. You're a braver woman than I am, Victoria Wilson."

"Or a fool."

"That, I doubt."

"Keith thought raising horses again was a big mistake."

"So what does he know?"

"I'll tell him you said that."

"Go ahead. I think it takes guts to start over after the trial and all the bad publicity…"

"That was all a horrible mistake."

Anna placed her hand on Tory's arm. "I know, but I just thought that you wouldn't want to do anything that might…you know, encourage all the old rumors to start up again. I wouldn't."

"You can't run away from your past."

"Especially when our illustrious Senator McFadden comes charging back to town, stirring it all up again."

Tory felt her back stiffen but she managed a tight smile as they walked slowly across the gravel parking lot. "Everyone has to do what they have to do. Trask seems to think it's his duty to dig it all up again… because of Jason."

One of Anna's dark brows rose slightly. "So now you're defending him?"

"Of course not!" Tory said too quickly and then laughed at her own reaction. "It's just that Trask's been here a couple of times already," she admitted, "and, well, just about everyone I know seems to think that I shouldn't even talk to him."

"Maybe that's because you've led everyone to believe that you never wanted to see him again. After all, he did—"

"Betray me?"

"Whatever you want to call it." Anna hesitated a moment, biting her lips as if contemplating the worth of her words. "Look, Tory. After the trial, you were pretty messed up, bitter. It's no wonder people want to protect you from that kind of hurt again."

"I'm a grown woman."

"And now you've changed your mind about Trask?"

Tory shook her head and deep lines of worry were etched across her brow. "It's just that—"

"You just can't resist the guy."

"Anna!"

"Oh, don't look so shocked, Tory. In my business it's best to say the truth straight out. You know that I always liked Trask, but that was before he nearly destroyed my best friend."

"I wasn't destroyed."

"Close enough. And now, just when it looks like you're back on your feet again, he comes waltzing back to Sinclair, stirring up the proverbial hornet's nest, digging up dead corpses and not giving a damn about who gets hurt, including you and Neva. It tends to make my blood boil a bit."

"So you don't think I should see him."

Anna smiled cynically. She stopped to lean against the fence and gaze at the network of paddocks comprising the central core of the Lazy W. "Unfortunately what I think isn't worth a damn, unless it's about your livestock. I'm not exactly the best person to give advice about relationships, considering the fact that I've been divorced for almost a year myself." She hit the top rail of the fence with new resolve. "Anyway, you didn't ask me here to talk about Trask, and I've got work to do."

"Can't you stay for a cup of coffee?" Anna was one of Tory's closest friends; one of the few people in Sinclair who had stood by Tory and her father during Calvin's trial.

Anna squinted at the sun and cocked her wrist to check her watch. "I wish I could, but I'm late as it is." She started walking to her van before turning and facing Tory. Concern darkened her brown eyes. "What's this I hear about a calf being shot out here?"

"So that's going around town, too."

Anna nodded and shrugged. "Face it, girl. Right now, with McFadden back in town, you're big news in Sinclair."

"Great," Tory replied sarcastically.

"So, what happened with the calf?"

"I wish I knew. One of Len Ross's hands saw the hole in the fence and discovered the calf. We don't know why it was shot or who did it."

"Kids, maybe?"

Tory lifted her shoulders. "Maybe," she said without conviction. "I called the sheriff and a deputy came out. He was going to see if any of the other ranchers had a similar problem."

"I hope not," Anna said, her dark eyes hardening. "I don't have much use for people who go around destroying animals."

"Neither do I."

Anna shook off her worried thoughts and climbed

into the van. The window was rolled down and she cast Tory one last smile. "You take care of yourself, okay?"

"I will."

"I'll be back tomorrow to see how old Governor's doing."

"And maybe then you'll have time for a cup of coffee."

"And serious conversation," Anna said with mock gravity. "Plan on it."

"I will!"

With a final wave to Tory, Anna put the van in gear and drove out of the parking lot toward the main road.

An hour later Tory sat in the center of the porch swing, slowly rocking on the worn slats, letting the warm summer breeze push her hair away from her face and bracing herself for the next few hours in which she would be alone with a man she alternately hated and loved.

Trask arrived promptly at noon. Fortunately, neither Keith nor Rex were at the house when Trask's Blazer ground to a halt near the front porch. Though Tory felt a slight twinge of conscience about sneaking around her brother's back, she didn't let it bother her. The only way to prove her father's innocence, as well as to satisfy Trask, was to go along with him. And Keith would never agree to work with Trask rather than against him.

What Tory hadn't expected or prepared herself for was the way her pulse jumped at the sight of Trask as he climbed out of the Blazer. No amount of mental chastising seemed to have had any effect on the feeling of anticipation racing through her blood when she watched him hop lithely to the ground and walk briskly in her direction. His strides were long and determined and his corduroy pants stretched over the muscles of his thighs and buttocks as he approached. A simple shirt with sleeves rolled over tanned forearms and a Stetson pushed back on his head completed his attire. *Nothing to write home about,* she thought, but when she gazed into his intense blue eyes she felt trapped and her heart refused to slow its uneven tempo.

"I thought maybe you would have changed your mind," Trask said. He mounted the steps and leaned against the rail of the porch, his long legs stretched out before him.

"Not me, senator. My word is as good as gold," she replied, but a defensive note had entered her voice; she heard it herself, as did Trask. His thick brows lifted a bit.

"Is it? Good as gold that is?" He smiled slightly at the sight of her. Her skin was tanned and a slight dusting of freckles bridged her nose. The reckless auburn curls had been restrained in a ponytail, and she was dressed as if ready for a long ride.

"Always has been." She rose from the swing and her intelligent eyes searched his face. "If you're ready—" She motioned to the Blazer.

"No time like the present, I suppose." Without further comment, he walked with her to his vehicle, opened the door of the Blazer and helped her climb inside.

"What happened to Neva's pickup?" Tory asked just as Trask put the Blazer in gear.

"I only used it yesterday because this was in the shop."

"And Neva let you borrow her truck?"

"Let's say I persuaded her. She wasn't too keen on the idea."

"I'll bet not." She tapped her fingers on the dash and a tense silence settled between them.

The road to Devil's Ridge was little more than twin ruts of red soil separated by dry blades of grass that scraped against the underside of the Blazer. Several times Trask's vehicle lurched as a wheel hit a pothole or large rock hidden by the sagebrush that was slowly encroaching along the road.

"I don't know what you hope to accomplish by coming up here," Tory finally said, breaking the smothering silence as she looked through the dusty windshield. She was forced to squint against the noonday glare of the sun that pierced through the tall long-needled ponderosa pines.

"It's a start. That's all." Trask frowned and downshifted as they approached a sharp turn in the road.

"What do you think you'll find?" Tory prodded.

"I don't know."

"But you're looking for something."

"I won't know what it is until I find it."

"There's no reason to be cryptic, y'know," she pointed out, disturbed by his lack of communication.

"I wasn't trying to be."

Tory pursed her lips and folded her arms across her chest as she looked at him. "You just think that you're going to find some five-year-old clue that will prove your theories."

"I hope so."

"It won't happen, senator. The insurance investigators and the police sifted through this place for weeks. And that was right after the indictments…" Her voice drifted off as she thought about those hellish days and nights after her father had been arrested. All the old feelings of love and hate, anger and betrayal began to haunt her anew. Though it was warm within the interior of the Blazer, Tory shivered.

"It doesn't hurt to look around," Trask insisted. He stepped on the throttle and urged the truck up the last half mile to the crest of the hill.

"So this is where it all started," Tory whispered, her eyes moving over the wooded land. She hadn't set step on Devil's Ridge since the scandal. Parched dry grass, dusty rocks and sagebrush covered the ground beneath the pine trees. The land appeared arid, dryer than it should have for late June.

"Or where it all ended, depending upon your point of view," Trask muttered. He parked the truck near a small group of dilapidated buildings, and pulled the key from the ignition. The Blazer rumbled quietly before dying. "If Jason hadn't come up here that night five years ago, he might not have been killed." The words were softly spoken but they cut through Tory's heart as easily as if they had been thin razors.

She had been reaching for the handle of the door but stopped. Her hand was poised over the handle and she couldn't hold back a weary sigh. "I'm sorry about your brother, Trask. You know that. And though I don't believe for a minute that Dad was responsible for your brother's death, I want to apologize for anything my father might have done that might have endangered Jason's life."

Trask's eyes softened. "I know, love," he said, before clearing his throat and looking away from her as if embarrassed at how easily an endearment was coaxed from his throat. "Come on, let's look around."

Tory stepped out of the Blazer and looked past the few graying buildings with broken windows and rotting timbers. Her gaze wandered past the small group of paddocks that had been used to hold the purebred Quarter Horses as well as their not-so-blue-blooded counterparts. Five years before, this small parcel of land had been the center of a horse swindle and insurance scam so large and intricate that it had become a statewide scandal. Now it was nothing more than a neglected, rather rocky, useless few acres of pine and sagebrush with a remarkable view. In the distance to the east, barely discernible to the naked eye were the outbuildings and main house of the Lazy W. From her viewpoint on the ridge, Tory could make out the gray house, the barn, toolshed and stables. Closer to the mountains she saw the spring-fed lake on the northwestern corner of the Lazy W. The green and gold grassland near the lake was dotted with grazing cattle.

"Hard to believe, isn't it?" Trask said.

Tory jerked her head around and found that he was staring at her. The vibrant intensity of his gaze made her heartbeat quicken. "What?"

"This." He gestured to the buildings and paddocks of the ridge with one hand before pushing his hat off his head and wiping an accumulation of sweat off his brow.

"It gives me the creeps," she admitted, hugging her arms around her breasts and frowning.

"Too many ghosts live here?"

"Something like that."

Trask smiled irreverently. His brown hair ruffled

in the wind. "I'll let you in on a secret," he said with a mysterious glint in his eyes.

"Oh?"

"This place gives me the creeps, too."

Tory laughed in spite of herself. If nothing else, Trask still knew how to charm her out of her fears. "You'd better be careful, senator," she teased. "Admitting something like that could ruin your public image."

Trask's smile widened into a affable slightly off-center grin that softened the square angle of his jaw. "I've done a lot of things that could ruin my public image." His gaze slid suggestively down her throat to the swell of her breasts. "And I imagine that I'll do a few more."

Oh, Trask, if only I could trust you, she thought as she caught the seductive glint in his eyes and her pulse continued to throb traitorously. She forced her eyes away from him and back to the ranch.

"I wish we could just forget all this, you know," she said, still staring at the cattle moving around the clear blue lake.

"Maybe we can."

"How?"

"If it turns out to be a prank."

"And how will you know?" she asked, turning to face him again.

He shook his head. "I've just got to play it by ear, Tory; try my best and then…"

"And then, what? If you don't find anything here today, which you won't, what will you do? Go to the sheriff?"

"Maybe."

"But?"

"Maybe I'll wait and see what happens."

That sounded encouraging, but she felt a small stab of disappointment touch her heart. "In Washington?"

"Probably."

She didn't reply. Though she knew he was studying her reaction, she tried to hide her feelings. That she wanted him to stay in Sinclair was more than foolish, it was downright stupid, she thought angrily. The man had sent her father to jail, for God's sake. And now that Calvin was dead, Trask was back looking for another innocent victim. As she walked toward the largest of the buildings Tory told herself over and over again that she hated Trask McFadden; that she had only accompanied him up here to get rid of him once and for all, and that she would never think of him again once he had returned to Washington, D.C. Unfortunately, she knew that all of her excuses were lies to herself. She still loved Trask as passionately and as blindly as she had on the bleak night he had left her to chase down, confront and condemn her father.

"It would help me if I knew what I was looking for," she said.

"Anything that you think looks out of place. We can start over here," he suggested, pointing to the largest of the three buildings. "This was used as the stables." Digging his boots into the dry ground, her pushed with his shoulder against the door and it creaked open on rusty hinges.

Tory walked inside the musty structure. Cobwebs hung from the exposed rafters and everything was covered with a thick layer of dust. Shovels, rakes, an ax and pick were pushed into one corner on the dirt floor. Other tools and extra fence posts leaned against the walls. The two windows were covered with dust and the dried carcasses of dead insects, letting only feeble light into the building. Tory's skin prickled with dread. Something about the abandoned barn didn't feel right and she had the uneasy sensation that she was trespassing. Maybe Trask was right; all the ghosts of the past seemed to reside on the hilly slopes of the ridge.

Trask walked over to the corner between the two windows and lifted an old bridle off the wall. The leather reins were stiff in his fingers and the bit had rusted. For the first time since receiving the anonymous letter he considered ignoring it. The brittle leather in his hands seemed to make it clear that all he was doing was bringing back to life a scandal that should remain dead and buried.

He saw the accusations in Tory's wide eyes. God, he hadn't been able to make conversation with her at all; they'd both been too tense and at each other's throats. Confronting the sins of the past had been harder than he'd imagined; but that was probably because of the woman involved. He couldn't seem to get Victoria Wilson out of his system, no matter how hard he tried, and though he'd told himself she was trouble, even an adversary, he kept coming back for more.

In the past five years Trask's need of her hadn't diminished, if anything it had become more passionate and persistent than before. Silently calling himself the worst kind of fool, he looked away from Tory's face and continued his inspection of the barn.

Once his inspection of the stable area had been accomplished, he surveyed a small shed, which, he surmised, must have been used for feed and supplies. Nothing.

The last building was little more than a lean-to of two small, dirty rooms. One room had served as observation post; from the single window there was a view of the road and the Lazy W far below. The other slightly larger room was for general use. An old army cot was still folded in the corner. Newspapers, now yellowed, littered the floor, the pipe for the wood stove had broken near the roof line and the few scraps of paper that were still in the building were old wrappers from processed food.

Tory watched as Trask went over the floor of the cabin inch by inch. She looked in every nook and cranny and found nothing of interest. Finally, tired and feeling as if the entire afternoon had been a total waste of time, she walked outside to the small porch near the single door of the shanty.

Leaning against one of the rough cedar posts, she stared down the hills, through the pines to the buildings of the Lazy W. Her home. Trask had single-handedly destroyed it once before—was she up here helping do the very same thing all over again? *History has a way of repeating itself,* she thought to herself and smiled cynically at her own stupidity for still caring about a man who would as soon use her as love her.

Trask's boots scraped against the floorboards and he came out to the porch. She didn't turn around but knew that he was standing directly behind her. The warmth of his breath fanned her hair. For one breathless instant she thought that his strong arms might encircle her waist.

"So what did you find, senator?" she asked, breaking the tense silence.

"Nothing," he replied.

The "I told you so" she wanted to flaunt in his face

died within her. When she turned to face him, Tory noticed that Trask suddenly looked older than his thirty-six years. The brackets near the corners of his mouth had become deep grooves.

"Go ahead, say it," he said, as if reading her mind.

She let out a disgusted breath of air. "I think we're both too old for those kinds of games, don't you?"

He leaned against the building and crossed his arms over his chest. "So the little girl has grown up."

"I wasn't a little girl," she protested. "I was twenty-two…"

"Going on fifteen."

"That's not nice, senator."

"Face it, Tory," he said softly. "You'd been to college, sure, and you'd worked on the ranch, but in a lot of ways—" he touched her lightly on the nape of her neck with one long familiar finger, her skin quivered beneath his touch "—you were an innocent."

She angled her head up defiantly. "Just because I hadn't known a lot of men," she began to argue.

"That wasn't it, and you know it," Trask said, his fingers stopping the teasing motion near her collar. "I was talking about the way you looked up to your father, the fact that you couldn't make a decision without him, your dependency on him."

"I respected my father, if that's what you mean."

"It went much further than that."

"Of course it did. I loved him." She took one step backward and folded her arms over her chest. "Maybe you don't understand that emotion very well, but I do. Simple no-holds-barred love."

"It went beyond simple love. You worshiped him, Tory; put the man on such a high pedestal that he was bound to fall; and when you discovered that he was human, that he did make mistakes, you couldn't face it. You still can't." His blue eyes delved into hers, forcing her to return their intense stare.

"I don't want to hear any of this, Trask. Not now."

"Not ever. You just can't face the truth, can you?"

A quiet anger had begun to invade her mind. It started to throb and pound behind her eyes. "I faced the truth a long time ago, senator," she said bitterly. "Only the man that I worshiped, the one that I placed on the pedestal and who eventually fell wasn't my father."

Trask's jaw tightened and his eyes darkened to a smoldering blue. "I did what I had to do, Tory."

"And damn the consequences?"

"And damn the truth."

There was a moment of tense silence while Tory glared at him. Even now, despite her anger, she was attracted to him. "I think we'd better go," she said. "I'm tired of arguing with you and getting nowhere. I promised to bring you up here so you could snoop around and I've kept my end of the bargain."

"That you have," he said, rubbing his hands together to shake off some of the dust. "Okay, so we found nothing in the buildings—I'd like to walk around the corral and along the road."

"I don't see why—"

"Humor me," he insisted. "Since we've already wasted most of the afternoon, I'd like to make sure that I don't miss anything." He saw the argument forming in her mind. "This way we won't have to come back."

And I won't have to make excuses to Keith or Rex, Tory thought. "All right, senator," she agreed. "You lead, I'll follow."

They spent the next few hours walking the perimeter of the land, studying the soil, the trails through the woods, the fence lines where it was still intact. Nothing seemed out of the ordinary to Tory and if Trask found anything of interest, he kept it to himself.

"I guess Neva was right," Trask said with a grimace.

"About what?"

"A lot of things, I suppose. But she thought coming up here would turn out to be nothing more than a wild-goose chase."

"So now you're willing to concede that your anonymous letter was nothing more than a prank?"

Trask pushed his hat back on his head and squinted thoughtfully up at the mountains. "I don't know. Maybe. But I can't imagine why."

"So you're not going to give it up," Tory guessed. "The diligent hard-working earnest Senator McFadden won't give up."

"Enough already," Trask said, chuckling at the sarcasm in Tory's voice. "Why don't we forget about the past for a while, what d'ya say?"

"Hard to do, considering the surroundings."

"Come on," Trask said, his anger having melted at the prospect of spending time alone with Tory now that what he had set out to do was accomplished. "I've got a picnic hamper that Neva packed; she'll kill me if we don't eat it."

"Neva put together the basket?" Tory asked, remembering Keith's comment to the effect that Neva was in love with Trask.

"Grudgingly," he admitted.

"I'll bet."

"Nicholas and I teamed up on her though."

"And she couldn't resist the charms of the McFadden men."

Trask laughed deep in his throat. "Something like that."

"This is probably a big mistake."

"But you'll indulge me?"

"Sure," she said easily. "Why not?" *A million reasons why not,* and she ignored all of them. The sun had just set behind the mountains and dusk had begun to shadow the foothills. An evening breeze carrying the heady scent of pine rustled through the trees.

After taking the cooler and a worn plaid blanket out of the back of the Blazer, Trask walked away from the buildings to a clearing in the trees near the edge of the ridge. From there, he and Tory were able to look down on the fields of the ranch. Cattle dotted the landscape and the lake had darkened to the mysterious purple hue of the sky.

"Bird's-eye view," she remarked, taking a seat near the edge of the blanket and helping Trask remove items from the cooler and arrange them on the blanket.

Trask sat next to her, leaning his back against a tree and stretching his legs in front of him. "Why did your father buy this piece of land?" he asked, while handing Tory a plate.

Tory shrugged. "I don't know. I think he intended to build a cabin for mother..." Her voice caught when she thought of her parents and the love they had shared. As much to avoid Trask's probing stare as anything, she began putting food onto her plate. "But that was a long time ago, when they were both young, before Mom was sick."

"And he could never force himself to sell it?"

"No, I suppose not. He and Mom had planned to retire here, where they still could see the ranch and be involved a little when Keith took over."

"Keith? What about you?"

She smiled sadly and pretended interest in her meal. "Oh, you know, senator. I was supposed to get married and have a dozen wonderful grandchildren for them to spoil..." Tory heard the desperation in her voice and cleared her throat before boldly meeting his gaze. "Well, things don't always turn out the way you plan, do they?"

Trask's jaw tightened and his eyes saddened a little. "No, I guess not. Not always."

Trask was silent as he leaned against the tree and ate the meal that Neva had prepared. The homebaked bread, fried chicken, fresh melon salad and peach pie were a credit to any woman and Trask wondered why it was that he couldn't leave Tory alone and take the love that Neva so willingly offered him. Maybe it was because she had been his brother's wife, or, more honestly, maybe it was because no other woman affected him the way Tory Wilson could with one subtle glance. To distract himself from his uncomfortable thoughts, he reached into the cooler.

"Damn!"

"What?"

Trask frowned as he pulled out a thermos of iced tea. "I told Neva to pack a bottle of wine."

Tory looked at the platters of food. "Maybe next time you should pack your own lunch. It looks like she did more than her share, especially considering how she feels about what you're doing." After taking the thermos from his hands, she poured them each a glass of tea.

Trask didn't seem consoled and ignored his drink.

"We don't need the wine," Tory pointed out. "Maybe Neva knew that it would be best if we kept our wits about us."

"Maybe." Trask eyed Tory speculatively, his gaze centering on the disturbing pout of her lips. "She thinks I've given you enough grief as it is."

"You have."

Trask took off his hat and studied the brim. "You're not about to let down a bit, are you?"

"What do you mean?"

"Just that you're going to keep the old barriers up, all the time."

"You're the one intent on digging up the past; I'm just trying to keep it in perspective."

"And have you?"

Tory's muscles went tense. She took a swallow of her tea before answering. "I'm trying, Trask. I'm trying damned hard. Everyone I know thinks I'm crazy to go along with your plans, and I'm inclined to believe them. But I thought that if you came up here, poked around, did your duty, so to speak, that you'd drop it and the fires of gossip in Sinclair would die before another scandal engulfed us. I knew that you wouldn't just let go of the idea that another person was involved in your brother's death, and I also realized that if I fought you, it would just drag everything out much longer and fuel the gossip fires."

He set his food aside and wrapped his arms around his knees while studying the intriguing angles of Tory's face. "And that's the only reason you came up here with me?"

"No."

He lifted his thick brows, encouraging her to continue. After setting her now empty plate on the top of the basket, she leaned back on her arms and stared at the countryside far below the ridge. "If by the slim chance you did find something, some clue to what had happened, I thought it might prove Dad's innocence."

"Oh, Tory..." He leaned toward her and touched her cheek. "I know you don't believe this, but if there were a way to show that Calvin had no part in the Quarter Horse swindle, or Jason's death, don't you think I'd be the first to do it?"

He sounded sincere and his deep blue eyes seemed to look through hers to search for her soul. God, but she wanted to believe him and trust in him again. He had been everything to her and the hand on her cheek was warm and encouraging. It conjured vivid images from a long-ago love. She had trouble finding her voice. The wind rustled restlessly through the branches overhead and Tory couldn't seem to concentrate on anything but the feel of Trask's fingers against her skin. "I...I don't know." She finished the cold tea and set her glass on the ground.

"My intention wasn't to crucify your father, only to tell my side of the story, in order that Jason's murderers were found out and brought to justice. If Calvin wasn't guilty, he should have stood up for himself—"

"But he didn't; and your testimony sent him to prison." She swallowed back the hot lump forming in her throat.

"Would it help you to know that I never, never meant to hurt you?" he asked, lowering his head and tenderly brushing his lips over hers.

"Trask—" The protest forming in her throat was cut off when his arms wrapped around her and he drew her close, the length of his body pressed urgently to hers.

"I've missed you, Tory," he admitted, his voice rough with emotions he would rather have denied.

"And I've missed you."

"But you still can't forgive me?"

She shook her head and for a moment she thought he would release her. He hesitated and stared into her pain-filled eyes. "Oh, hell," he muttered, once again pulling her close to him and claiming her lips with his.

His hands were warm against her back and through the fabric of her blouse she felt the heat of his fingers against her skin. Her legs were entwined with his and his hips pressed urgently to hers, pinning her to the ground as one of his hands moved slowly upward and removed the leather throng restraining her hair.

"God, you're beautiful," he whispered against her ear as he twined his fingers in her hair, watching the auburn-tinged curls frame her face in wild disarray. Slumberous green eyes rimmed with dark curling lashes stared up at him longingly. "I want you, Tory," he said, his breathing ragged, his heart thudding in his chest and the heat in his loins destroying rational thought. "I've wanted you for a long time."

"I don't know that wanting is enough, Trask," she whispered, thinking about the agonizing hours she had spent in the past five years wanting a man she couldn't have; wishing for a father who was already dead; desiring the life she had once had before fate had so cruelly ripped it from her.

"Just let me love you, Tory."

The words had barely been said when she felt Trask stiffen. He turned to look over his shoulder just as a shot from a rifle cracked through the still mountain air.

Tory's blood ran cold with fear and a scream died in

her throat. Trask flattened himself over her body, protectively covering her as the shot ricocheted through the trees and echoed down the hillside. *Dear God, what was happening? The sound was so close!*

With the speed and agility of an athlete, Trask scrambled to his feet while jerking her arm and pulling her to relative safety behind a large boulder.

Tory's heart was hammering erratically as adrenaline pumped through her veins. She pushed her hair out of her eyes and discovered that her hands were shaking. "Oh, God," she whispered in desperate prayer.

"Are you okay?" His eyes scanned her face and body.

Her voice failed her but she managed to nod her head.

"You're sure?"

"Yes!"

"Who knows we're here?" Trask demanded, his hushed voice harsh, his eyes darting through the trees.

"No one—I didn't tell anyone," she replied.

"Well, someone sure as hell knows we were here!"

"But—"

"Shh!" He clamped his hand over her mouth and raised a finger to his lips as he strained to hear any noise that might indicate the whereabouts of the assailant. Far down the hillside, the sound of hurried footsteps crackled through the brush. Tory's skin prickled with fear and her eyes widened until she realized that the footsteps were retreating, the sound of snapping branches becoming more distant.

Trask moved away from the protection of the boulder as if intent on tracking the assailant.

"Trask! No!" Tory screamed, clutching at his arm. "Leave it alone."

He tried to shake her off and turned to face her. "Someone's taking shots at us and I'm going to find out who."

"No wait! He has a rifle, you…you can't go. You don't have any way of protecting yourself!"

"Tory!"

"Damn it, Trask, I'm scared!" she admitted, holding his gaze as well as his arm. Her lower lip trembled and she had to fight the tears forming in her eyes. "You can't die, too," she whispered. "I won't let you!" He stood frozen to the spot. "I love you, Trask," Tory admitted. "Please, please, don't get yourself killed. It's not worth it. Nothing is!" Tory felt near hysteria as she clutched at his arm.

Trask stood stock still, Tory's words restraining him. "You love me?" he repeated.

"Yes!" Her voice broke. "Oh, God, yes."

"But you've been denying—"

"I know, I know. It's just that I don't want to love you."

"Because of the past."

"Yes."

"Then we have to find out the truth," he decided.

"It's not worth getting killed."

Trask's eyes followed the sound of the retreating footsteps and the skin whitened over his cheekbones as he squinted into the encroaching night. His one chance at finding the accomplice in Jason's murder had just slipped through his fingers. When silence once again settled on the ridge, he turned his furious gaze on Tory. His grip on her shoulders, once gentle, was now fierce.

"Who did you tell that we were here?" he demanded.

"No one!"

"But your brother and that foreman, Rex Engels, they knew we would be here this afternoon."

Tory shook her head and her green eyes blazed indignantly. She jerked away from his fingers and scooted backward on the ground. "I didn't tell anyone, Trask. Not even Keith or Rex; they…neither one of them would have approved. As far as I know the only person who knew we were coming here today was Neva!"

The corners of Trask's mouth tightened and he glared murderously at Tory. "Someone set us up."

"And you think it was me?"

"Of course not. But it sure as hell wasn't Neva!"

"Why not? She didn't want you coming up here, did she? She doesn't want you to look into Jason's death, does she? Why wouldn't she do something to sabotage you?"

He walked away a few steps and rubbed the back of his neck. "That just doesn't make any sense."

"Well nothing else does either. The anonymous note, the dead calf and now this—" She raised her hands over her head. "Nothing is making any sense, Trask. Ever since you came back to the Lazy W, there's been nothing but trouble!"

"That's exactly the point, isn't it?" he said quietly, his mouth compressing into an angry line. "Someone's trying to scare you; warn you to stay away from me."

"If that's his intention, whoever he is, he's succeeded! I'm scared right out of my mind," she admitted while letting her head fall into her palm.

"What about the rest, Tory? That shot a few minutes ago was a warning to you to stay away from me!" He looked over his shoulder one last time.

"If that's what it was—"

"That's exactly what it was," he interjected. "Let's go, before someone decides to take another potshot at us."

"You think that's what they were trying to do?"

"I'm certain of it."

"But maybe someone saw a rattlesnake, or was hunting."

"It's not deer season."

"Maybe rabbits—" She saw the look of disbelief on his face. "Or maybe the guy was a poacher...or someone out for target practice."

"It's nearly dark, Tory. I don't know about you, but I don't like being the bull's-eye."

From the look on Trask's rugged features, Tory could tell that he didn't believe her excuses any more than she did. He walked over to her and placed his hands upon her shoulders, drawing her close, holding her as he started walking back to the Blazer. "I'd like to believe all those pitiful reasons, too," he admitted.

"But you can't."

"Nope." He opened the door of the Blazer for her, helped her inside and climbed into the driver's seat. "No, Tory," he said, his voice cold. "Someone's trying to keep us apart, by scaring us with dead cattle and rifle shots."

"And that means there must be some truth to the letter," she finished for him.

"Exactly." He smiled a little remembering Tory's confession of love, started the Blazer, circled around the parking lot and started driving down the rutted lane back to the Lazy W.

Chapter 7

"So where is everyone?" Trask asked as he parked the truck near the barn.

"I don't know," Tory admitted uneasily. She got out of the Blazer and started walking toward the back of the dark house. The only illumination came from a pale moon and the security lamps surrounding the buildings of the ranch.

Trask was on Tory's heels, his footsteps quickening so that he could catch up with her. "What about your brother, where is he?"

If only I knew. "He and Rex were working on the broken combine this afternoon," she thought aloud, trying to understand why the ranch was deserted. "They probably went into town for a part, got held up and decided to stay for dinner..."

"Or he was up on the ridge with a rifle?" Trask suggested.

Tory turned quickly and couldn't disguise the flush of anger on her cheeks. "Don't start in about Keith, okay? He would never do anything that might jeopardize my life."

"You're sure about that?"

"As sure as I am about anything." Tory turned toward the house, dashed up the steps to the porch and unlocked the back door. She had trouble keeping her fingers steady as she worked with the lock. What was it Keith had said just yesterday? His words came back to her in chilling clarity.

"I would have met McFadden with a rifle in my hands...the next time McFadden trespasses, I'll be ready for him."

Tory's stomach knotted with dread and disgust. Trask had her thoughts so twisted that now she was doubting her own brother; the boy she had helped rear since their mother's death. Ignoring the hideous doubts crowding her mind, she flipped on the light and walked into the kitchen.

"What about the foreman?"

"Rex?"

"Yeah."

Tory almost laughed at the absurdity of Trask's insinuation. "You've got to be kidding! I've known Rex since I was a little girl—he'd do anything for the ranch. It's been his life. Dad hired him when Rex was down and out, when no other rancher in this state would touch him. Besides, neither Rex nor Keith knew where I was this afternoon."

Trask leaned against the cupboards, supporting his weight with his hands while Tory made a pot of coffee.

Deep furrows etched his brow. "Why wouldn't anyone hire Rex?"

"You want to see all of the skeletons in the closet, don't you?"

"Only if it helps me understand what's going on."

"Well, forget it. Rex was in trouble once, when he was younger—before I was born. Dad hired him."

"What kind of trouble?" Trask persisted.

Tory frowned as she tried to remember. "I don't really know. Dad never talked about it. But once, when I was about eleven and I was supposed to be studying, I overheard Dad talking to Rex. It was something to do with Rex's past. It had to do with his ex-wife, I can't remember her name, it was something like Marlene or…Marianne, maybe. Something like that. Anyway, there was some sort of trouble between them, talk of him drinking and becoming abusive. She left Rex and no one would hire him."

"Except your dad."

"Right. And Rex has been with the Lazy W ever since."

"Without any trouble."

"Right."

Trask bit at his lower lip pensively. "I thought he was married."

"He is. He married Belinda about seven years ago."

"So he's above suspicion."

"Of course he is. He was the one who showed us the dead calf in the first place, remember?" She tapped her fingers on the counter impatiently. "Look, I don't like the thoughts that are going through your head. You're more than willing to start pointing fingers at anyone associated with the ranch, but no one here knew where we were going."

"We could have been followed," he said, rubbing the back of his neck and watching her movements.

She was about to pull some mugs down from the shelf, but hesitated and her slim shoulders slumped. "God, you're as bad as Keith," she muttered.

"What's that supposed to mean?"

"Just that the both of you have overactive, extremely fertile imaginations when it comes to each other. If you'd just sit down and try to straighten all of this out like adults instead of going for each other's throat, we'd all be a lot better off."

"I agree."

Trask grabbed a chair from the table, placed it on the floor and straddled it. He folded his arms over the back of the chair and rested his chin on his arms as he studied Tory.

"You agree?" she repeated incredulously.

"Of course. It just makes sense that if we all work together we can accomplish much more in a shorter space of time."

"And then you could finish this business and fly back to Washington," she thought aloud. Suddenly the future seemed incredibly bleak.

"Don't you want me to go?" he asked.

Swallowing a lump in her throat, she pushed her burnished hair from her face. "It doesn't really matter what I want," she whispered. "You've got an important job in Washington, people depend on you. There was a time when I would have begged you to stay…"

"And now?"

She winced, but decided to put her cards on the table. As the coffee finished perking and filled the room with its warm scent, she leaned one hip against the counter and stared into his deep blue eyes. "And now I think we're all better off if you go back to the capital, senator. I fell in love with you once and I won't let it happen again. Ever."

"What about what you said on the ridge?" he asked softly.

"I was scared; nothing more. I didn't want you to do anything foolish!"

"Tory—" He stood, but she cut off his next words.

"I don't want to hear it, Trask. Here—" She quickly poured them each a cup of coffee and tried to think of a way, any way, to change the course of the conversation. "Take your coffee and we'll drink it in the den."

"You can't ignore or deny what's happening between us."

"What's happening is that I'm trying to help you figure out if that note you received is a phony. That's all." She turned away from him and walked down the hall, hoping that her hands and voice would remain steady.

Once in the den she snapped on two lamps and walked over to the window. *Where was Keith?* She needed him now. Being alone with Trask was more than foolhardy, it was downright dangerous and seductive. She stood in front of the window and sipped her coffee as she looked across the parking lot to the shadowy barns.

Trask entered the room. She heard rather than saw him and felt the weight of his stare. His eyes never left her as he crossed the room and propped one booted foot on the hearth. "What are you afraid of, Tory?"

"I already told you, I'm not afraid…just confused. Everything in my life seems upside-down right now."

"Because of me?"

She let out a long sigh. "Yes."

"It will be over soon," he said. "Then your life will be back to normal—if that's what you want."

My life will never be the same again, Trask. "Good. I…I just want all this…nonsense to be over." She took a long sip of her coffee and set the empty mug on the windowsill. Her fingers had stopped shaking. "It's late. I think maybe you should leave."

"Maybe," he agreed, cocking a dark brow. "But I think it's time we settled some things between us." He reached over and snapped off the lamp on an end table. With only the light from the small brass lamp on the desk, the corners of the room became shadowed, more intimate.

Bracing herself, she turned and faced him. "Such as?"

He leaned back against the rocks of the fireplace and all of his muscles seemed to slacken. Defeat darkened his eyes. "Such as the fact that I've never gotten over you—"

"I told you, I don't want to hear this," she said, walking away from the window and shaking her head. "The past is over and done—it can't be changed or repeated. What happened between us is over. *You* took care of that."

"I love you, Tory," he said slowly, his voice low.

Tory stopped dead in her tracks. How long had she waited, ached, to hear just those words? "You don't understand the first thing about love, Trask. You never have."

"And you're always quick to misjudge me."

"You can't expect me to trust you, Trask, not after what happened to my father. It was all because of you."

Trask's face hardened and a muscle in the back of his

jaw tightened. "Calvin is dead; I can't change that." He pushed away from the fireplace and crossed the room to stand before her. "Don't you think I wish he were alive? Don't you realize how many times I've punished myself, knowing that he died in prison, primarily because of my testimony?" His troubled eyes searched her face and he reached forward to grip her shoulders. "Damn it, woman, I'd have given my right arm to hear his side of the story—only the man wouldn't tell it. It was as if he'd taken this vow of silence as some sort of penance for his crimes!" Trask's voice was low and threatening. "I've been through hell and back because of that trial!"

The grip on her arms was punishing, the conviction on Trask's face enough to cut her to the bone. "God, Trask, I wish I could believe you," she admitted, her voice trembling.

"But you can't."

"You betrayed me!"

He gave her a shake. Her hair fell over her eyes. "I told the truth on the witness stand. Nothing less. Nothing more." His voice was rising with his anger. "And your father didn't do a damned thing to save himself! Don't you think I've lain awake at night wondering what really happened on the night Jason was killed?" His face contorted with his rage and agony.

"I…I don't know…"

"Damn it, Tory! Believe it or not, I'm human. If you cut me, I bleed." He released her arms and let out a disgusted breath of air. Blue eyes seared through hers. "And, lady, you've cut me to ribbons…"

She let her face fall into her hands. Her entire body was shaking and the tears she would rather have forced back filled her eyes to spill through her fingers. "God,

I wanted to trust you, Trask. I…I spent more than my share of sleepless nights wondering why did you use me? Why did you tell me you loved me? Why was I such a fool to believe all your lies…all your goddamned lies!" She began to sob and she felt the warmth of his arms surround her. "Let go of me," she pleaded.

"Never again." With one hand he snapped off the light on the desk. The room was suddenly shrouded in darkness. Only the pale light from a half-moon spilled through the windows. "Oh, love, I never used you. Never—"

"No… Trask…" His lips touched her hair, and his arms held her close. The heat of his body seemed to reach through her flesh and melt the ice in her heart. "I…I just loved you too much."

"Impossible."

"I know it's stupid," she conceded, letting the barriers that had held them apart slowly fall, "but I want to trust you again. God, I've wanted to be able to talk to you for so long; you don't know how many times I just wished that you were here, that I could talk to you."

"You should have called."

"I couldn't! Don't you see? You were my whole world once and you destroyed everything I'd ever loved. My father, my career, this ranch, and our love—everything."

"All because I told the truth."

"Your perception of the truth!"

"Tory, listen to me, you have to understand one thing: throughout it all I always loved you. I still do."

She felt the cold hatred within her begin to thaw and her knees went weak as she leaned against him, felt the strength of his arms, the comfort of his kiss. How many times had she dreamed and fantasized about being in

Trask's arms again? "You love me, Trask," she sniffed, slowly pulling out of his embrace and drying her eyes with her fingers, "when it's convenient for you. It was convenient for you five years ago when you were trying to help your brother with the horse swindle and it's convenient now, when you need my help." She stepped back and held his gaze. "I won't be used again, you know. Not by you."

"I wouldn't." His blue eyes were honest; the jut of his jaw firm with conviction. It was impossible not to believe him.

Tory cleared her throat. "Then what about Neva?"

"What about her?"

"Are you staying with her?" she asked, knowing the question was none of her business, but unable to help herself.

Trask's skin tightened over his cheekbones and his muscles tensed, but he didn't look away. "I did the first night. Since then, I've opened up the cabin on the Metolius River. It wasn't ready when I got into Sinclair," he began to explain and then let out an angry oath. "Hell, Tory, does it matter?" he demanded.

Her eyes turned cold. "Not really, I guess. I just like to know what or whom I'm up against. With you and that damned anonymous letter of yours, sometimes it's hard to tell."

"I'm not having an affair with my brother's widow, if that's what you want to know."

"It's none of my business."

"Like hell! Haven't you listened to a word I've said?" When she didn't respond, he curled a fist and slammed it into the wall near the desk, rattling a picture of an Indian war party. "Hell, woman, I'd be a liar to say that

I've spent that past five years celibate, but I'm not involved with anyone right now except for you!" Once again his fingers captured her, winding comfortably behind her neck.

"We're not involved!"

With her indignation, his anger dissipated into the intimate corners of the room. Trask's smile was lazy and confident. "That's where you're wrong. We've been involved since the first time I laid eyes on you. Where was it? Rafting on the Deschutes River!"

"That was a long time ago," she murmured, recalling the wild ride down the white water. Though she had gone with another man, Trask's eyes hadn't left her throughout the day. Even then she'd seen the spark of seduction in his incredible blue gaze. Sitting on the raft, his tanned skin tight over lean corded muscles, his wet hair shining brown-gold in the summer sun, he didn't bother to hide his interest in her. And she fell. Lord, she fell harder than any sane person had a right to fall. She had met him later that night and within two weeks they'd become lovers. The irony of it all was that she had thought she would spend the rest of her life with him. *Only it didn't work out that way.*

"Let's not talk about the past."

He let go of her, holding her only with his eyes. "We have to sort this out."

"What's the point? Nothing will come of it." She felt the urge to back away but stood her ground. "I'll admit that I loved you once, but it's over. It's been over for a long time."

"Liar." He reached for her, drawing her body close to his. When his lips touched hers, and she tasted him, her resistance fled. Familiar yearnings awoke within the most feminine part of her, causing a bittersweet ache that only he could salve. Instead of pushing him away, she was leaning closer to him, her body reacting to the sensual feel of his hands on her skin, her blood pulsing with need as it rushed through her veins. "You want me," he whispered against her ear.

"No..."

"Let me love you."

Desire was heating her blood, thundering in her head, and the touch of his lips on her face and neck only made the throbbing need within her more painful. "I don't think—" she tried to say, but his lips cut off the rest of her objection.

She felt the warm invasion of his tongue and returned his kiss without restraint. When his lips moved downward to touch her neck and then slid still lower, she could do nothing but wait in anticipation. His tongue rimmed the hollow of her throat and she was forced to swallow against the want of him.

Suddenly, Trask released her, and Tory wanted to cry out against the bereft feeling she was left with. She watched as he strode to the den door and locked it, then moved toward her quickly banishing the cold feeling.

Warm hands outlined her ribs before reaching upward to mold a swollen breast. She felt her nipple tighten against the feel of his fingers and she let out a low moan of desire.

Slowly he removed her blouse, slipping each button through its hole and letting the fabric part to display her rounded breasts, swollen and bound only by the sheer white lace of her bra. His fingers teased the hardened nipple, and Tory leaned closer to him, the ache within her spreading throughout her body.

A primal groan escaped from his lips as he lowered himself to his knees and licked first one rose-tipped breast before suckling the other. The lace of the bra became moist and Trask's warm breath fanned the sheer fabric to send sharp electric currents through Tory's body. She closed her eyes and was blind to everything but the hunger for him. Her fingers twined in his hair.

The warmth of his hands pressed against the small of her back, bringing her closer to him, pressing more of her breast into his mouth. He groaned with the savage urgency of his lust, sucking hungrily from the white mound.

Scorching feelings of desire once awakened in Tory were impossible to smother. With each touch of his hand, Tory lost ground to the urges of her flesh. With each stroke of his tongue, the ache within her throbbed more painfully. With the heated pressure of his body against hers, she felt the urge to arch against him, demanding more of his sensual touch.

Five years she had waited for the feel of him, denying her most secret dreams and now the pain of those long empty nights alone was about to be rewarded. The scent of him was strong in her nostrils and the sound of his breathing filled her ears.

Her fingers curled in his hair as he removed her bra and took her naked breast in his mouth. She cradled his head to her body, holding on to him for dear life, knowing that her love for this man would never be returned and not caring about the consequences. This night, for a few short hours, he was hers—alone.

She moaned his name when his fingers sought the front opening of her jeans and touched the sensitive skin of her abdomen.

"Trask, please," she whispered hoarsely as his tongue traced the delicate swirl of her navel and he pulled her jeans and underwear off her body. Slowly she was pressed to the floor by the weight of his body. The braided carpet felt coarse against her bare skin, but she didn't care.

She helped him remove his clothes and her fingers caressed the fluid muscles of his shoulders and chest. His body tensed beneath the tantalizing warmth of her touch.

Sweat dotted his brow; his restraint was obvious in the coil of his muscles. When Tory reached for the waistband of his pants, his abdominal muscles tightened. With all of the willpower he could muster, he stopped her by taking hold of her wrist and forced her chin upward with his other hand. His eyes searched hers. "I love you, Tory," he said, his voice rough. "I always have. But I want you to be sure about this…stop me now, if you have to, while it's still possible."

Closing her eyes against the flood of tears that threatened to spill, she tried to speak, to tell him how much she wanted him. Her lips quivered, but all the words she thought she should say wouldn't come.

Trask kissed her softly and wound his fingers in the thick auburn strands of her tousled hair. "If only I could make you happy," he murmured before capturing her lips in his and shifting his weight so that his body covered hers in a protective embrace.

As his flesh touched hers, his body heated until it glistened in a film of sweat. Her arms wound around his back and she clung to him as he became one with her, moving gently at first and then more quickly as her body responded to the familiarity of his touch. His hands massaged her breasts in the rhythm of his lovemaking.

"Oh, God," he whispered against her ear as the heat within her seemed to burst and he, too, surrendered. "Tory," he called, his voice raspy. "Just love me again." And then he fell against her, his weight a welcome burden.

The tears that had been welling beneath her lids began to stream down her cheeks. "Shh," he whispered, "everything will be okay."

Slowly Trask rolled to his side and held her close to him. He kissed her and tasted the salt of her tears. For several minutes, they clung to each other in silence and Tory, her head pressed against his chest, listened to the steady beating of Trask's heart. Surrounded by his strength, she was lost in her feelings of love and despair for this man.

"Regrets?" he asked, once his breathing had slowed. Tenderly he brushed a tear from the corner of her eye.

"No…"

"But?"

Her voice trembled slightly. "I'm not sure that getting involved again is the smartest thing to do. But then I've made a lot of questionable decisions lately."

He propped himself on one elbow and stared down at her. His face was shadowed but even in the darkness Tory could see the seductive slash of his smile.

"Why not…get involved, that is?"

"I only agreed to see you because of the letter…and, well, having an affair with you now will only complicate things."

His grin slowly faded, and his hands caressed her

bare shoulders. "I think you'd better say what you mean and quit beating around the bush."

Tory gathered her courage. The next words were difficult, but necessary. She couldn't continue to live in a crystal dreamworld that could shatter so easily. "All right, senator. What I'm trying to say is that I'm not comfortable with short-term affairs. You and I both know that when all of this…note business is cleared up, you'll be returning to Washington."

"You don't like dead-end relationships?"

"Exactly."

"You could come to Washington with me," he suggested. His arms tightened around her, holding her close to the contours of his body.

Tory almost laughed. She reached for her jeans. "And what would you do if I took you up on your offer?" she said. "I'm no more ready for the Washington social scene than you are to explain a mistress from Oregon."

"I was talking about a wife, not a mistress."

Tory's heart missed a beat and pain darkened her eyes. "Oh, Trask. Don't—"

"I asked you to marry me five years ago—remember?"

"That was before the trial."

"Forget the trial!" He jerked her roughly to him and she was forced to gaze into the intensity of his eyes.

"How can I? You're here, looking for another conspirator in your brother's death, for crying out loud!" She jerked on her jeans and reached for her blouse as all of the old bitterness returned to her heart. "And don't think that just because we made love you have to dangle a wedding ring in front of my nose. I fell for that trick once before—"

Trask's patience snapped. He took hold of her upper

arms and refused to let go. "You're so damned self-righteous. I don't know how to make it any clearer to you that I love you. Asking you to marry me isn't a smoke screen for some dark ulterior motive. It's a proposal, plain and simple. I want you to be my wife and I was hoping that you could rise above the past and come to terms with your feelings as a mature adult woman!"

"I can."

He let go of her arms. "And?"

The lump in her throat swelled uncomfortably. "I love you even though I've been denying it, even to myself," she whispered. "I love you very much, but...but I'm not sure that I *like* you sometimes. As for marriage—we're a long way from making a decision like that."

Trask's back teeth ground together. "Have you been seeing someone else?"

Tory let out a disgusted sigh. "No. Not seriously."

"I heard that you were going to be married a couple of years back to some schoolteacher."

Tory smiled sadly with her confession. "It didn't work out." She turned away from him and began dressing. He watched as she slid her arms through the sleeves of her blouse.

"Why?"

Wasn't it obvious? "Because of you. As crazy as it sounds, senator, you're a hard act to follow." She smiled sadly at her own admission. How many times had she tried to deny, even to herself, that she still loved him?

"That's some consolation," he said, relief evident on his face. He had pulled on his cords, and pushed his arms through his shirt, but it was still gaping open, displaying in erotic detail, the muscles of his chest and abdomen. "I want you to consider my proposal."

"I think it's five years too late."

One dark brow quirked. "Better late than never, isn't that what they say?"

"'They' aren't always right."

Trask smiled cynically as he helped her to her feet. "Marry me, Tory. I need you."

"Not now, don't ask—"

"We put it off too long once before."

"I can't make a decision like this; not now, anyway. We've got too many things hanging over our heads. I...I need time, and so do you."

"You think that I'm caught up in the moment."

Her head snapped up. "I wouldn't be surprised."

"What would it take to convince you?"

"Time—enough time to put all of what happened behind us."

"Five years isn't enough?"

Tory smiled sadly. "Not when one party is interested in dredging it all up again."

He leaned forward, pushing his forehead against hers and locking his hands behind her shoulders. "I love you and I'm worried about you."

"I'm fine," she tried to assure him.

"Yeah, I can tell." He patted her gently on the buttocks. "So who would want to fill that gorgeous skin of yours full of buckshot?" he asked.

"No one was shooting at me."

His face became stern. "Whoever shot the calf wasn't playing around."

"I'm okay," she insisted but he didn't seem convinced. *"Really."*

"I think you should come and stay with me at the cabin. You'd be safer."

"I can't."

He rubbed his chin in frustration. "Look, Tory, I dragged you into this mess and now it seems to be getting dangerous. I feel responsible."

"You don't have to. I can look after myself."

"If another person was involved in the Quarter Horse swindle, he's also involved in murder, Tory. Jason's murder. There's no telling to what lengths he might go to protect himself. The dead calf and the potshot taken at us today are serious."

"Don't try to scare me; I'm already scared."

"Then?"

"I told you, I can handle it."

Impatiently Trask raked his fingers through his hair. "I want to keep an eye on you, but I have to go to Salem, to the penitentiary, tomorrow."

"To talk to George Henderson?"

"And Linn Benton."

Tory felt her throat constrict at the mention of her father's two "partners" in the horse swindle. "Do you think that's smart?"

Trask's eyes narrowed and in the darkness Tory could see the hardening of his jaw. "If someone else was involved, they'd know about it."

"And what makes you so sure they'd talk to you?"

"I already set up the meeting through the warden. Henderson and Benton are both up for parole in the next couple of years—your dad took most of the blame, you know. While he was handed down thirty years, they plea bargained for shorter sentences."

"It was never fair," she whispered.

"Because Calvin didn't even try to defend himself!" When she blanched he touched her lovingly on the chin.

"Look, knowing the likes of Benton and Henderson, they won't want to stir up any trouble that might foul up their chances for parole."

"And you intend to throw your weight around, now that you're a senator and all."

"That's about the size of it."

"Isn't that unethical?"

"But effective."

She couldn't argue with his logic, though she didn't like the idea of involving Henderson and Benton. A small feeling of dread skittered down her spine. "When will you be back?"

"Tomorrow night. I'll come by here and let you know what happened."

"Good."

"Are you sure you won't come with me to the cabin?" he asked, pushing a wisp of hair out of her eyes. "It might be safer." Once again his eyes had darkened seductively.

"That depends upon what you call safe, senator," she said teasingly, trying to push aside her fears. "Besides, the Lazy W is home. I feel safer on this ranch than I do anywhere in the world. I've managed to make it by myself for five years. I think I'll be okay for the next twenty-four hours." She winked conspiratorially at him and he couldn't resist kissing her provocative pout.

Trask realized that there was no point in arguing further with Tory. Short of bodily carrying her to the Blazer and taking her hostage, there was no way of getting her to leave the ranch. "Just remember that I love you and that I expect you to take care of yourself."

She couldn't hide the catch in her voice. "I will."

He reached for his hat and forced it onto his head before kissing her once more and striding out of the house. Tory watched him from the window and smiled when she saw him tuck his shirttails into his cords. Then he climbed into the Blazer and roared down the lane.

"It's too easy to love you," she whispered as she mounted the stairs and headed to her bed…alone.

Trask drove like a madman. His fingers were clenched around the steering wheel of the Blazer and the stream of oaths that came from his mouth were aimed at his own stupidity.

He skidded to a stop at the main intersection in town and slammed his fist into the steering wheel. He was furious with himself. Inadvertently, because of his own damned impatience, he had placed Tory in danger.

"Damn it all to hell," he muttered, stripping the gears of the Blazer as he pushed the throttle and maneuvered through town. He drove without conscious thought to Neva's house. After parking the Blazer in the driveway, Trask strode to the front door and let himself in with his own key.

"Trask?" Neva called anxiously from her room. She tossed on her robe and hurried into the hallway. Trask was standing in the living room, looking as if he'd like to break someone's neck. "What are you doing here at this time of night?"

"I need to use your phone. There isn't one at the cabin."

"Go ahead." She pushed the blond hair away from her face and stared at the disheveled state of Trask's clothes and the stern set of his jaw. "You nearly scared me to death, you know."

"Sorry," he said without regret and paced between the living room and hallway. "I should have called."

"It's okay." She sighed and looked upward to the loft where her son was sleeping. "At least you didn't wake Nicholas...yet." She folded her arms over her chest and studied Trask's worried expression. "Are you going to tell me what's wrong or do I have to guess?"

"I'm really not sure."

"Don't tell me, Tory didn't go along with your plan."

"That wasn't it, no thanks to you." He frowned. In the past he'd been able to confide everything to Neva, but now things had changed; he sensed it. "Look, let me use the phone in the den and then we can talk."

"Okay. How about a cup of coffee?"

"How about a beer?"

Neva's brows shot upward. "That bad?"

"I don't know, Neva." He shook his head and the lines of worry near the corners of his eyes were more evident than they had been. "I just don't know." He walked through the kitchen to the small office where his brother had once planned to expose the biggest horse swindle in the Pacific Northwest.

Trask closed the door to the den and stared at the memorabilia that Neva had never managed to put away. A picture of Jason holding a newborn Nicholas was propped up on the desk. Jason's favorite softball glove and a ball autographed by Pete Rose sat on a bookcase next to all of the paperback thrillers Jason had intended, but never had time, to read. A plaque on the wall complimented the trophies in the bookcase; mementos of a life cut off much too early.

The desk chair groaned as Trask sat down, picked up the phone and punched out the number of the sheriff's department. After two rings the call was answered and

Trask was told that Paul Barnett wasn't in the office, but would return in the morning.

"Great," Trask muttered. Rather than leave his name with the dispatcher, Trask hung up and drummed his fingers on the desk as he considered his alternatives. *You've been a fool,* he thought as he leaned back in the chair and put his fingers together tent style. *How could you have been so stupid?*

It was one thing to come back to Sinclair and start a quiet investigation; quite another to come back and flaunt the reasons for his return. Although he hadn't told anyone other than Neva and Tory about the anonymous letter, he hadn't hidden the fact that he was back in Sinclair for the express purpose of seeing Tory again. By now, half the town knew his intentions. The guilty persons could certainly put two and two together.

And so Tory was in danger, because of him. Trask took off his hat and threw it onto the worn leather couch. His mouth felt dry for the need of a drink.

The trouble was, Trask wasn't cut out for this cloak-and-dagger business. Never had been. Even the back-scratching and closed-door deals in Washington rubbed him the wrong way. As a junior senator, he'd already ruffled more than his share of congressional feathers.

With a grimace he pulled a copy of the anonymous letter out of his wallet and laid it on the desk while he dialed Paul Barnett's home number and waited. It took several rings, but a groggy-voiced Barnett finally answered.

The conversation was short and one-sided as Trask explained why he was in Sinclair and what had happened.

"I'll need to see the original note," Barnett said, once

Trask had finished his story. All the sleep was out of the sheriff's voice. "I already sent one of my men out to check out the dead calf. As far as we can tell, it was an isolated incident."

"A warning," Trask corrected.

"Possibly."

"The same as the rifle shot this evening."

"I'll check into it, do what I can."

"Good. Tory's not going to like the fact that I called you. She wanted to keep things under wraps until we'd found what we were looking for."

"That's foolish of course, but I can't say as I blame her, considering what happened to her pa and the reputation of that ranch."

"What happened to Calvin and the ranch aren't important. Right now she needs protection. Whether she knows it or not," he added grimly.

"I don't have the manpower to have someone cover the Lazy W day and night, you know."

"I'll take care of that end. John Davis, a private investigator in Bend, owes me a favor—a big one."

"And you've called him?"

"I will."

"Good. And the note?"

"I'll bring it over within the hour."

"I'll be waiting."

Just as Trask hung up the phone, Neva knocked quietly on the door and entered the den. She offered Trask a mug filled with coffee. "We were out of beer," she lied.

Trask grinned at the obvious deception. "I don't need a mother, you know."

Neva leaned against the doorjamb and eyed him sadly. "Sometimes I wonder."

"I do all right."

"I read the papers, Trask. What do they call you? 'The young rogue senator from Oregon'?"

"Sometimes." He took a sip from the cup and let the warm liquid salve his nerves. "When are you going to take all this stuff—" he motioned to Jason's softball trophies and plaques "—down and put it away?"

"Maybe never."

Trask frowned and shook his head. "You're a young beautiful woman, Neva—"

"With a six-year-old son who needs to know about his father."

"Maybe he needs a new one."

Neva looked shocked. "He's a McFadden, Trask. Your brother's son. You want some stranger to raise him?"

"He'll always be a McFadden; but he could use some male influence."

"He has you," she said softly.

"I live in Washington."

"Until you don't get reelected."

Trask nearly choked on his coffee. "That's what I like to hear: confidence." Trask's eyes darted around the room and his smile faded. "You can't live in the past, Neva."

"I was going to say exactly the same thing to you."

Trask caught her meaningful glance and frowned into his cup before finishing his coffee in one swallow and setting the empty mug on the desk. "I've got to go."

"You could stay," she suggested, her cheeks coloring slightly. "Nicholas would be thrilled."

Trask shook his head, stood up, grabbed his hat and

kissed Neva on the forehead. "Can't do it. I've got things to do tonight."

"And tomorrow?"

"I'll be in Salem."

Neva paled and sank into the nearest chair. Her fingers nervously gripped her cup. "I knew it," she said with a sigh. "You're going to see Linn Benton and George Henderson in the pen, aren't you?"

"Yes."

"Oh, Trask, why?" Doe-soft eyes beseeched him.

"It's important." He saw the tears of frustration fill her large eyes and he felt the urge to comfort her. "Look, Neva—"

She sniffed the tears aside and met his gaze. "It's all right, Trask. I'll manage. And when Nicholas wonders why all of his friends are pointing fingers at him and whispering behind his back, I'll tell him." Using the sleeve of her robe to dry her cheeks, she forced a frail smile. "Do what you have to do, senator. Don't worry about how it affects a six-year-old boy who worships the ground you walk on."

"You're not making this easy—"

"Damn it, Trask, I'm not trying to! I'd do anything I could to talk you out of this…madness."

Trask's eyes became incredibly cold. "How far would you go to protect your child?"

"As far as I had to."

"Regardless?"

"Nicholas's health, safety and well-being are my first concerns."

"And what about your health and safety?"

Neva smiled cynically. "I can't wait until you have a child, Trask. Then I'll ask you the same question."

"I just think you should put yourself first occasionally."

"Pearls of wisdom, senator. I'll think about them."

Trask paused at the door. "By the way, thanks for the picnic lunch today."

"You're welcome, I guess. Did you bring the cooler in?"

A picture of the empty cooler, scattered dishes and rumpled blanket filled his mind. In the urgency of the moment after the rifle shot had pierced the air, he had forgotten to retrieve anything. "No, uh, Tory wanted to clean it. I'll pick it up tomorrow and bring it back."

A spark of interest flickered in Neva's dark eyes. "So the picnic went well?"

For a reason he didn't understand, Trask lied to his sister-in-law for the first time in his life. No need to worry her, he thought, but he knew there was more to his evasive answer than he would acknowledge. "It was fine."

"And what did you find on Devil's Ridge?"

"Absolutely nothing." *Except a potential assassin.*

"But you're still going to Salem tomorrow," she said with a sigh. "You just can't let it drop, can you?"

"Not this time."

"Well go on." She waved him off with a limp hand. "You've got things to do, remember? Just be careful. Linn Benton, whether he's in prison or not, is still very powerful. He may have been stripped of his judicial robes, but he's still a wealthy and influential man with more than his share of friends, all of whom haven't forgotten that your testimony was instrumental in sending him to prison."

"Good night, Neva," Trask said, without waiting for a reply. There was none. He walked out the front door.

As he stepped off the porch and headed for the Blazer, he heard a noise and turned. Before he could see his assailant, Trask felt the thud of a heavy object strike the back of his head. Blinding lights flashed behind his eyes just as a knee caught him in the stomach and he fell forward onto the dry ground. Before he lost consciousness he heard a male voice that was vaguely familiar.

"Leave it alone, McFadden," it warned gruffly. Trask tried to stand, but was rewarded with another sharp kick in the abdomen. "You're out of your league, senator."

Chapter 8

The first thing Trask remembered were hands, incredibly soft hands, holding his head. A woman's voice, filled with anguish and fear, was calling to him from a distance and there was pain, a pain so intense it felt as if it was splintering his head into a thousand fragments.

"Trask… Oh, dear God…" the woman cried out, nearly screaming with terror as she looked down on him. Moonlight caught in her silver hair, but the features of her face were blurred and indistinct. *"Trask!"*

His mouth felt cotton-dry and when he tried to speak the voice that he heard didn't sound like his own. "Neva?" He reached forward and his fingers touched her hair before his hand dropped to the ground. A blinding stab of pain shot through his brain when he tried to lift his head.

"Oh, God, Trask…are you all right?" Her fingers

were exploring the lump on the back of his head and tears gathered in her large eyes. "I was afraid something like this might happen, but I just couldn't believe…"

He opened his eyes and tried to focus. It was dark, but the woman's face was definitely that of his sister-in-law. Propping himself on one elbow, he tried to push his body upright to stand, but the jarring pain in his ribs and abdomen made him suck in his breath and remain on the hard ground.

"What happened?" Neva demanded, looking at the beaten man with pitying eyes.

As if she could have prevented what happened, Trask thought dizzily and then discarded his annoying thought. Neva's head moved quickly from side to side, her eyes darting from one shadowed tree to another as if she half expected to discover the man who had attacked him lurking in the still night.

"Someone jumped me—" Trask began to explain.

"I knew it!" Her attention swung back to the injured man. "I knew that something like this would happen!" She let out a breath of despair and her shoulders slumped in resignation. As if finding an answer to an inner struggle, Neva clenched her fist in determination. "I'm going to call the police and then I'll get an ambulance for you."

"Hold on a minute," Trask ground out, again leveling himself up on one elbow. Sweat had broken out on his forehead and chest and several buttons were missing from his shirt. "I don't need an ambulance or the police…"

"You've been beaten, for God's sake!" she shrieked.

"Neva, get hold of yourself," he insisted as his groggy mind began to clear. *Tory! If anything had happened to her…*

With one hand he reached forward and held on to Neva's arm. "I've got to get into the house—to a phone," he stated. Disjointed but brutally clear images of Tory and what might have happened to her began to haunt him.

"You need a doctor."

"You're a nurse. Can't you just fix me up?"

She eyed him severely. "No. You need X-rays. And an examination by a doctor. You might have a concussion, maybe cracked ribs and God only knows what else." Gingerly she touched the deep cut along his jaw where his chin had crashed into the ground.

"I'll be fine," Trask said angrily, mentally cursing himself for not being more careful with Tory's safety. "Just help me up and get me into the house. Whoever did this to me may have gone after Tory."

"Tory?" Neva repeated, freezing.

"I don't have time to talk, damn it!" A dozen hideous scenarios with Tory as the unwitting victim filled his mind.

"Yes, sir," Neva snapped back at him, offering her body as support as he rose unsteadily. With her arm around his torso to brace him, Neva forced Trask to lean on her as they walked up the steps to the front door. "Before you do anything else, I expect you to tell me exactly what happened."

"Later."

Once inside the house, she examined his head and offered him an ice pack. "Lucky for you you've got a thick skull," she murmured tenderly. "Now, what else?"

He motioned to his side. She took off his shirt and frowned at the purple bruise already discoloring his ribs. "Someone doesn't like you poking around," she decided.

"No one likes me poking around," he said with what was an attempt at a smile. "Not even you."

"Maybe you should take this warning seriously," she suggested.

"Can't do it, Neva."

"Oh, Trask, why not?"

"I'll explain once I make a few calls—"

"Mom?" Nicholas was standing on the landing of the stairs to the loft. His blue eyes rounded at the disheveled and battered sight of Trask sprawled over the couch in the living room.

"Nick, I thought you were asleep." Neva's eyes flickered with fear before darting from Trask to her son and back again. Her gaze silently implored Trask to keep the truth from Nicholas.

The young boy ignored his mother and his eyes clouded with worry. "What happened, Uncle Trask?"

"Would you believe a barroom brawl?" Trask asked, forcing a painful grin.

"Naw." Nicholas stuck out his lower lip pensively and looked at his mother. "Is that really what happened?"

Neva shrugged.

"Sort of," Trask intervened, sensing Neva's discomfiture. "We good guys always have to be on the lookout, you know."

Nicholas came down the last few steps. The boy's eyes were round with excitement and hero worship for his uncle. "Mom? Did Uncle Trask get into a fight?"

"I don't really know," Neva said nervously.

"So where's the other guy?"

"He took off," Trask said, attempting levity. "He'd had enough I guess."

"Because you beat him?" Nicholas sat on the edge of the couch.

Trask had to laugh and the pain in his ribs seared through his body. "Unfortunately the other guy got the better of me."

Nicholas frowned petulantly while stepping closer to the couch and surveying his uncle. "But the good guys are always supposed to win."

"Only on television," Trask replied, ruffling the boy's coarse hair. "Or if they get help from their friends." Trask's eyes moved from Nicholas to Neva. She paled slightly and tried to avoid his gaze.

"Come on, Nick. You can have a piece of pie and a glass of milk. Then you've got to go back to bed. Uncle Trask has to make some phone calls." She placed the telephone on the coffee table and carefully stepped over the cord. "Here, take these," she said to Trask, offering him aspirin and a glass of water.

"Thanks."

"But I want to stay up." Nicholas turned pleading eyes on his uncle.

"You'd better do what your mom says," Trask suggested.

"But it's not fair!"

"Nothing ever is," Neva replied softly, thinking of Jason's early death and the men who were responsible for his murder as she guided Nicholas into the kitchen and waited while he ate his pie.

When Nicholas had finished eating, over his loud protests, Neva put him back into bed. She watched the boy until his breathing became regular and he fell asleep with one arm tossed around the neck of the puppy Trask had given him for his birthday. Her throat tightened at the sight of her tousle-headed son sleeping so blissfully unaware of any of the suffering or malice in the world. How desperately she wanted to protect him.

As Nicholas started to snore, Neva could hear Trask talking on the phone in the living room though most of the one-sided conversation was muffled.

"Damn!" Trask muttered as he slammed the receiver of the telephone back into the cradle. He had tried calling Tory twice, but no one at the Lazy W had bothered to answer the phone. Fortunately his other calls had gotten through. He ran his fingers through his hair and swung his feet over the edge of the couch.

"This has gone on long enough," Neva said tightly as she came down the stairs and took a seat in her favorite rocker. "The next time someone attacks you, it might be your life, senator...or maybe someone else's." Her voice cracked and her hands worked nervously in her lap. "I think you should call the sheriff. Let Paul Barnett do his job and wash your hands of this accomplice to the conspiracy theory right now."

"I already have," he said slowly as he watched her. For the first time since he had returned to Sinclair, Trask had an inkling of Neva's true fears and he finally understood her odd behavior.

With a groan, he stood. Neva started. "You should be lying down—in the guest room."

Trask walked over to her and, placing both hands on either arm of the wooden rocker, he imprisoned her in the chair. "Why don't you tell me what's really going on, Neva, what you're really afraid of?" he suggested, his voice cold. "Come on, level with me." His blue eyes pierced into hers.

"I'm afraid for you," she whispered.

"Not good enough."

"And for Nicholas." She rubbed her chin nervously and tried to avoid his stare. It was impossible as his face was only inches from hers.

"That's better."

Tears started to pool in her eyes. "The kids at school—"

"Are not what you're afraid of, are they? Someone's been threatening you and Nicholas."

"No…oh, God, no," she cried, desperation and fear contorting her face.

He placed one hand over hers. "Neva?"

There was silence, tense unbearable silence. Only the sound of the clock ticking over the mantel disturbed the quiet.

"Look, it's obvious that someone got to you and used Nicholas's safety as part of a threat. I just want a name, Neva."

"I don't know…"

Trask's fist coiled over her fingers. "Just one name!"

"Oh, Trask," she whispered, closing her eyes and slumping in the chair. "There is no name…." Her voice was shaking and she let her head drop into her hands. "Oh, God, Trask, I'm so scared," she whispered. He placed his arms around her and she tried in vain to stem the flow of her tears. Instead she began to sob against his shoulder. "I've been getting these calls— horrible calls—"

"From whom?"

"I don't know. Some man. He threatened me. Told me that if I didn't convince you to forget about the horse swapping swindle that…that…he'd take Nicholas from me…hurt him." She was shaking violently. "I was afraid to tell anyone."

White-hot rage raced through Trask's blood and all of his muscles tensed. "You should have told me," he ground out, pushing away from the chair.

"Probably," she admitted. "For the first time in my life I didn't know what to do. And the man insisted that I wasn't to tell you anything, or—" her anguished eyes searched Trask's bruised face "—or one of us would be hurt. And now look at you…look what he did…."

"Nothing's going to happen to Nicholas," Trask swore.

"How can you be sure—look what happened to you!"

Trask's eyes sparked blue fire. "I'll see to it that you're safe. Not only are we going to call Paul Barnett and tell him what's going on, I've got a friend, a private investigator, who'll put a twenty-four hour watch on you and Nicholas." He checked his watch. "Paul's probably already on his way to the Lazy W." Quickly he punched out the number of the sheriff's department and got hold of Deputy Woodward, who promised to come directly to Neva's house.

"I don't need to be watched," Neva stated, gathering her courage as Trask hung up and immediately redialed the phone.

"Don't argue with me, Neva," Trask nearly shouted just as the groggy voice of John Davis answered the phone. Again, Trask told his story and John promised to send a detective to Neva's home as well as have someone survey the comings and goings at the Lazy W.

"What are you planning?" Neva asked, once Trask had hung up the phone and was slipping his arms through his shirt.

"A deputy from the sheriff's department, a man by the name of Greg Woodward is coming over here tonight."

"No."

"Just listen to me, damn it. Woodward is going to take your statement and wait until one of John Davis's men arrives. Then he's going to meet me and Sheriff Barnett at the Lazy W."

"You're going back to see Tory?"

Trask's face hardened and his eyes darkened murderously. "If someone is dead set on discouraging me, I'd be willing to bet that the next person they'll approach is Tory."

Neva's mouth went dry. "What do you mean?"

"I mean simply that I'm worried about her. While we were at Devil's Ridge, someone took a shot at us."

"No!" Neva looked half-crazed with fear. Her face went deathly white and she glanced from Trask to the loft where Nicholas was sleeping so peacefully and back again. "I can't believe this is happening. All because of some damned note!"

"Believe it."

"Oh, dear Lord," she whispered.

There was a sharp knock at the door and Trask opened it to find Deputy Woodward on the doorstep. After assuring himself that Woodward had contacted the sheriff and was following Barnett's orders, Trask half ran to the Blazer, shoved the truck into gear and drove toward the Lazy W.

A thunderous noise awakened Tory. She sat bolt upright in bed until her groggy thoughts began to make sense and she realized that someone was pounding urgently at the front door. Probably Keith. He had a habit of losing his key....

She tossed on a robe and hurried down the stairs. "I'm coming, I'm coming," she called. "Hold your horses."

"Thank God," she heard a male voice say and grinned when she realized it belonged to Trask.

Jerking the door open, she felt her smile widen for the man she loved. "Well, Senator McFadden, what brings you back to the Lazy W at this hour?"

As she stepped onto the front porch, she was swept into Trask's arms as he crushed her desperately to him. "Thank God, you're all right," he whispered against her wet hair. "If I ever lost you again..." His voice caught and the arms around her held on as if he expected her to disappear. "Where were you?" he demanded.

"When?"

"About twenty minutes ago." Still he held her tightly, almost deliberately.

"I was here."

"But I called. No one answered."

"I was here," she repeated. "Maybe you caught me when I was in the shower. I thought I heard the phone ring, but by the time I got to it, no one was there."

"Lord, Tory," he whispered, closing his eyes. "You had me half out of my mind with fear." He slowly pulled his head back and stared into her eyes. "Where's Paul Barnett?"

"The sheriff?" she asked incredulously. "Trask, what's going on? Do you have any idea what time it is? Why would Paul Barnett be here?"

"Because I asked him to come. He's supposed to be here, damn it!"

"Slow down, will you? You're talking like a lunatic!"

The light from the hallway spilled onto the front porch and for the first time she noticed that his clothes were ripped and dirty and there were cuts below his right eye and on his chin. "Wait a minute," she said, drawing away and gently touching his beard-darkened jaw. "What in God's name happened to you?"

Trask's eyes fell on her face and then looked past her to the interior of the house. It was then she noticed his haggard expression and the fact that he walked with a slight limp. Worry crept into her voice. "Trask? What's going on?"

"Are you okay?"

"Looks like I should be asking you that one," she observed, concern making her voice rough. "Trask, what happened?"

"Our friend from the ridge caught up with me."

"What?"

Trask walked into the entry hall and began snapping on lights before he started looking into the corners of the rooms on the ground floor. Once a quick, but complete search of the lower level was accomplished, he started up the stairs and Tory followed him. "I was worried about you," he finally explained, once all the rooms and closets were searched. "Are you alone?"

"Yes. You could have asked me, y'know, instead of walking in here and tearing the place apart like some kind of madman."

He ignored her sarcasm. "Where's Keith?"

"I don't know," she admitted. "Sometimes he stays out late—"

"Son-of-a-bitch!" Trask stalked into the den. All of his muscles became instantly tense.

"Oh, no, Trask," Tory whispered, following him into

the study and understanding his anger. She tried to ignore the tiny finger of dread slowly creeping up her spine. "You're not seriously trying to blame Keith for this—" she pointed at the disheveled state of his appearance "—are you?"

"I was hoping that he had an alibi."

Tory's eyes widened in horror. "You think Keith did this to you?"

"Maybe."

"Oh, Trask, no! You can't be serious!" she said, her voice shaking as she clamped a hand over her mouth and tried to pull herself together. Reading the anger in his eyes she slowly let her hands fall to her side. "But you're just guessing, aren't you? I take it you didn't see who attacked you?"

"Didn't have time. It was dark."

Tory felt a little sense of relief. This was all a big mistake. Keith wouldn't rough somebody up, not even Trask McFadden. "Have you seen a doctor?"

"Neva examined me."

"Neva! Good Lord, have you been there, too?" Tory pushed her damp hair out of her eyes.

"That's where it happened."

Tory's eyes turned cold. Too much was happening and she couldn't think straight. "Wait a minute, slow down. Come into the kitchen and tell me exactly what happened and when and where and why." She started down the hallway, Trask right behind her.

"Why? That's the kicker, isn't it?"

Tory frowned as she took down two cups and made a pot of tea. Forcing her hands to remain steady, she poured the tea into the cups. "So tell me, what did Neva say?"

"Other than that I should be more careful?" Tory didn't crack a smile. "She thinks I'll live."

"Some consolation." She handed him a cup of tea and tried to force a grin as her eyes slid down his slightly bruised chin to the torn shirt that displayed all too vividly his muscled chest and discolored abdomen. "You look awful."

"That's a cut above the way I feel."

"I really think you should go to the emergency room, and get some X-rays."

"Later." He set down his cup and his eyes took her in; the tousled damp hair that hung in springy curls around a fresh face devoid of makeup, the gorgeous green eyes now dark with concern, and the soft heather-colored robe clinched loosely over her small waist. "God, I was worried about you," he admitted, rubbing his hand over his unshaven jaw.

"It looks like I should have been the one worrying."

He took the cup from her hands and pulled her toward him. Lowering his head, he caught her lips with his and let the fresh feminine scent of her fill his nostrils and flood his senses. "From now on, I'm not letting you out of my sight," he vowed against her ear before reluctantly releasing her.

"Is that a promise or a threat?"

His uneven, incredibly charming grin flashed white against his dark skin. "However you want to take it."

"I'll think about it and let you know what I decide."

Trask's face sobered and his fingers toyed with the lapel of her plush robe. "As much as I find the thought distasteful," he said with a frown as he kissed her forehead, "I think you should get dressed. I asked Sheriff Barnett to meet us here."

"Tonight?"

"Yeah." He stepped away from her and patted her firmly on the behind. "Look, I'll explain everything when Paul gets here, just go put on something—" he lifted his palms upward as he looked at her soft terry robe and the white silk gown that was visible when she walked "—something less erotic."

"I've never heard of a terry-cloth bathrobe being called erotic."

"Only because I've never seen you in one before."

Tory laughed and shook her head. Against her better judgment she walked upstairs and changed into a pair of cords and a sweater. She was braiding her hair into a single plait as she stood on the landing when she heard the knock at the front door.

"I'll get it," Trask said. He'd positioned himself at the bottom of the stairs and was watching with interest as Tory wrapped the rubber band around the tip of her braid.

"Suit yourself."

His teasing expression turned grim. "And I think you'd better try and track down your brother. There are a few questions he'll have to answer." With one last glance upward in her direction Trask opened the door.

Paul Barnett and Detective Woodward were standing on the front porch. Tory's fingers curled around the banister as she walked slowly down the stairs and faced all three men.

"Come in, sheriff... Deputy Woodward." She inclined her head toward each man and wondered if it was obvious to them how nervous she felt. Not since the trial had she been uncomfortable with the police, but this night, with Trask beaten and Keith missing, she felt a nervous sweat break out between her shoulder blades. "I was going to make a pot of coffee. I'll bring it into the den."

Barnett pursed his lips and nodded his agreement. He was a slightly paunchy man with wire-rimmed glasses, cold eyes and a hard cynical smile. "Anyone else here?"

"No."

"No hands on the ranch?"

"Not tonight."

"What about that kid brother of yours?" the sheriff pressed, his graying bushy eyebrows lifting with each of her negative responses.

Tory felt herself stiffen. "Keith isn't home. He's in town, I think."

"But you don't know?"

"No. Not for sure."

Barnett pressed his thin lips tightly together but didn't comment. When the three men went into the den, Tory escaped to the kitchen and put on a pot of coffee. She tried to ignore the fact that her hands as well as her entire body were trembling.

Where was Keith? Everyone wanted to talk to her brother and she had no idea where he was. It was late, damned late and unlike her brother to be out on a weeknight.

The grandfather clock in the entry hall chimed one o'clock. The hollow notes added to Tory's growing paranoia.

Drumming her fingers on the counter as the coffee perked, she considered using the phone and trying to track down her brother, but discarded the idea. He was twenty-one and able to make his own decisions. Or so she silently prayed.

The murmur of voices from the den caught her attention and her heart began to pound with dread. Quickly grabbing the glass carafe, four mugs, the sugar bowl and creamer, she set everything onto a woven straw tray and carried it into the den. Trask looked up from his position in her father's leather recliner and smiled reassuringly.

"Okay, now let me get this straight," Barnett was saying, his graying mustache working as he spoke. "You two went up on Devil's Ridge looking for some sort of clue that might lead you to the fourth man who was supposedly involved in the Quarter Horse swindle. Right?"

"Right," Trask replied.

Tory caught Barnett's inquisitive stare and nodded curtly to his unspoken question. "However, it could be a three-man conspiracy," she said. "I still don't believe that my father was involved."

"Be that as it may, Ms Wilson, your father was tried and convicted, so we'll have to assume that he was in on the swindle," Barnett said slowly before turning to Trask. "So, you believe the fourth man theory because of this piece of paper." He held up the anonymous letter, without waiting for a response. "And, you think that because you've been poking around looking for some proof to support the fourth man theory, one of the calves from the Lazy W was shot, and someone tried to shoot you as well, this afternoon—"

"I'm not sure they were shooting at us, maybe just trying to scare us," Trask interjected.

"Nevertheless, a shot was fired in your general direction."

"Yes."

"And when that didn't work, whoever it was that

fired the rifle followed you to Neva McFadden's place and beat the tar out of you."

Trask frowned, nodded his head and rubbed his jaw pensively. "That's why I think it was a warning. If they had wanted me dead, I would have been. I had to have been an easy target coming out of Neva's house."

"So that's all of your story?"

"Except that someone's been calling Neva and harassing her, making threats against her son," Deputy Woodward added.

"What!" Tory's face drained of color and she almost dropped her coffee. She turned her wide eyes on Trask. "No—"

Trask's jaw hardened and his eyes turned as cold as blue ice. "That's why Neva tried to talk both me and you out of the investigation. She was afraid for Nicholas's life."

"This has gotten completely out of hand," Tory whispered, leaning against the pine-paneled wall.

"You should have called me," Barnett said, leveling his gaze at Trask, "instead of trying to investigate something like this on your own. Could have saved yourself a lot of grief as well as a beating."

"I was just trying to keep it quiet."

Barnett frowned. "We could have done a better job. In case you've forgotten, that's what my department gets paid to do. As it is, you've made one helluva mess of it."

Trask's lips twisted wryly. "Thanks."

After asking Tory questions that confirmed Trask's story about what happened on the ridge, the sheriff and his deputy finished their coffee, grabbed their notes and left.

"It gets worse by the minute," Tory confided, once she was alone with Trask.

"Barnett's right. I should have gone to the police in the beginning."

"And then the police would have flocked back here, the press would have found out about it and the scandal would have been plastered on the front pages of the local papers all over again."

"Looks like it's going to end up that way regardless."

"Nothing we can do about it now," she said with a sigh. Walking toward the recliner Tory searched Trask's face. His jaw was still strong, jutted in determination, but pain shadowed his blue eyes. The cuts on his face, though shallow, were slightly swollen and raw. "Are you okay? I could take you into Bend to the hospital."

"Not now."

"But your head—"

"It's fine. It'll wait until morning."

"Oh, senator," she said with a sad smile. "What am I going to do with you?"

His eyes slid seductively up her body to rest on the worried pout of her lips. "I can think of a dozen things…"

"Be serious."

"I am."

"Well, I'm not about to have you risk further injury." She glanced out the window and back at the clock. *Two-fifteen, and still no sign of Keith.* "Besides, it's late."

"Are you trying to give me a less than subtle hint?"

"I'm tired." She touched his head fondly. "You should be, too."

"I'm okay. Go to bed."

"And what about you?"

"I'm staying here."

"You can't—"

"Watch." He settled into the recliner and folded his hands over his chest.

"Trask. Think about it. You can't stay here. Keith will be home soon."

"That's who I'm waiting for."

"Oh, Trask." The rest of her response was cut off by the sound of an engine roaring up the driveway and the spray of gravel hitting the sides of the barn as the pickup ground to an abrupt halt.

"About time," Trask said, pushing himself upward.

Tory's heart was beating double time by the time that Keith opened the front door and strode into the den. His young face was set with fierce determination and he scowled at the sight of Trask.

"What's he doin' here?" Keith demanded of Tory, as he cocked an insolent thumb in Trask's direction.

"Why don't you ask me?" Trask cut in.

Turning, Keith faced Trask for the first time. It was then that he noticed the bruise on Trask's chin and his rumpled dirty clothing. "What the hell happened to you?"

"Why don't you tell me?" Trask hooked his thumbs in the belt loops of his jeans and leaned his shoulders against the fireplace. His intense gaze bored into Keith's worried face.

Keith immediately sobered. "What're you talking about?"

Trask's eyes narrowed. "Someone followed Tory and me up to Devil's Ridge this afternoon. Not only did this guy have a rifle, but he decided to use it by taking a shot at us."

"What?" Keith spun and faced his sister. "What's he

talking about? Why would you go up to the ridge with him after what he did to you?" Keith became frantic and began pacing from the den to the hallway and back again. "I knew that McFadden couldn't wait to bring up all the dirt again!" He glanced over his shoulder at Trask. "What's he talking about—someone shooting at you? He's not serious—"

"Dead serious," Trask said tonelessly. "Then later, at Neva's place, someone decided to use the back of my head for batting practice."

Keith's face lost all of its color and his cocky attitude faded with his tan. "You're not kiddin', are ya?"

"Hardly," Trask said dryly, approaching the younger man in long sure strides. "And that same person has been calling my sister-in-law, threatening her to get me to stop this investigation." Keith looked as if he wanted to drop through the floor. "I don't suppose you know anything about that, do you?"

"I...I don't know anything."

"So where were you tonight?" Trask ground out.

"Tonight? You think I did it?" Keith seemed genuinely astounded. He looked pleadingly at Tory before stiffening at the sound of Trask's voice.

"Where were you?"

"I've been in town."

"Until two in the morning?"

"Yeah. Rex and I went into town, looking for a part for the combine. When we couldn't get it, I stayed at the Branding Iron for dinner and a few beers. Later I went over to Rex's place. He and several of the hands had a poker game going."

"And someone was with you all night?"

"For most of it." Keith's indignation flashed in his

eyes. "Look, McFadden, I've done a lot of things in my life that I'm not particularly proud of, but what happened to you and Tory today has nothing to do with me."

"Why do I have difficulty believing you?"

"Because I've made no bones about the fact that I hate your guts." He pointed a condemning finger at Trask. "You nearly single-handedly destroyed everything my dad worked all of his life to achieve; you not only sent him to prison, but you took away all of his respectability by using his daughter and publicly humiliating her."

Trask's face hardened. A muscle worked in the corner of his jaw and his eyes narrowed fractionally. "I've made my share of mistakes," he admitted.

"Too many, McFadden. Too damned many! And tonight is just one more in the string. I didn't have anything to do with what happened to you tonight." He was shaking with rage. "Now I think it's about time you left."

Trask's eyes glittered with determination. "I'm not going anywhere, Wilson." He sat down in one of the chairs and propped the heels of his boots on the corner of the coffee table. "As a matter of fact, I intend to spend the rest of the night right here."

"Get out!"

"Not on your life."

Keith glared at his sister. "He's your problem," he spat out before stomping out of the den and treading heavily up the stairs to his room.

Tory took a seat on the arm of Trask's chair. "You were too hard on him, y'know," she reprimanded, her brow knotted in concern. "He's not involved in this."

"So he claims."

"You don't believe him," she said with a sigh.

"I don't believe anyone—" he looked into her worried eyes and smiled slightly "—except for you."

"Not too long ago you didn't trust me."

"Not you, lady; just your motives."

"Same thing."

Trask took her hand and pressed her fingers to his lips. "Not at all. But sometimes I think you'd lie to protect those closest to you."

She shook her head and smiled sadly. "Wrong, senator. Maybe I should have five years ago. Since Dad wouldn't say what happened, maybe I should have covered for him." She picked up a crystal paperweight from the desk and ran her fingers over the cut glass. "Maybe then he'd still be alive."

"And you'd be the criminal for perjuring yourself."

She frowned at her distorted reflection in the glass. "I guess there are no easy answers," she said, as she placed the paperweight on the corner of the desk. "You really don't have to stay, you know."

"Wouldn't have it any other way."

"It's ridiculous. Keith's here."

"Precisely my point." He looked up at her and wrapped his hand around her neck, drawing her lips to his. "I'm not taking any chances with your life."

"What about Neva and Nicholas?"

"A private investigator is with them."

"And you've assigned yourself to me as my personal bodyguard, is that it?"

"Um-hm." He rubbed his lips gently against hers, then murmured, "I'm going to stick to you like glue."

"I just can't believe that anyone would want to hurt Nicholas or you."

He smiled wryly. "Believe it."

He pulled on her hand and she tumbled into the chair with him. Though he let out a sharp breath as her weight fell against his ribs, he grinned wickedly. "Maybe it would be best if I came to bed with you," he suggested, his breath touching her hair.

"I don't think so."

"Are you worried about what Keith and the rest of the hands will think?"

She shrugged. "A little, I guess."

"Hypocrite." He nuzzled her neck and she felt her blood begin to warm.

"There's nothing hypocritical about it, I'm just trying to use my head. We both need sleep. You can stay in the guest room. It's only a couple of doors down the hall from mine."

"I remember," he said softly, his voice intimate.

Tory had to look away from him to ignore the obvious desire smoldering in his eyes. *Who was she kidding? How many times had he stolen into her room in the past? He knew the ranch house like the back of his hand.*

"Where does Keith sleep?"

"He, uh, moved into Dad's room when Dad passed away."

"And the rest of the hands?"

"Usually go home. Once in a while someone will stay in the bunkhouse, but that's pretty rare these days."

"What about tonight or, say, the past week?"

"No one is staying on the ranch except Keith and myself."

"And Rex?"

"He has his own place, just north of Len Ross's spread. He and Belinda have lived there for over five years." *Five years!* Once again, Tory was reminded of the time when she was free to love Trask with all her heart. But that was before her world was destroyed by the horse swapping scam, Jason's murder and the trial.

She stood up and tugged on Trask's arm, hoping to break the intimacy that memories of the past had inspired. "Come on, mister, let me help you up the stairs." As he stood, she eyed him speculatively. "If you give me your clothes, I'll throw them in the wash so that you have something clean in the morning."

"Gladly," he agreed as they mounted the stairs.

"Just leave them in the hall outside your door."

"Whatever you say," he whispered seductively and a shiver of desire raced down her spine.

"What I say is that we both need some time to think about what happened today. Maybe then we can make some sense of it."

Trask's smile slid off his face. "None of this makes any sense," he admitted, grimacing against a sudden stab of pain.

A few minutes later Trask was in the guest room, his clothes were in the washer and Tory was lying on her bed wondering if she would ever get to sleep, knowing that Trask was only two doors down the hall.

Chapter 9

Pale light had just begun to stream into the bedroom when Tory heard the door whisper open. She rolled over to face the sound and focused her eyes on Trask as he approached the bed. He was wearing only a towel draped over his hips. A dark bruise discolored the otherwise hard muscles of his chest and the cut on his chin was partially hidden by his dark growth of beard. As he walked the towel gaped to display the firm muscles of his thighs moving fluidly with his silent strides.

"What're you doing?" she whispered, lifting her head off the pillow and rubbing her eyes.

"Guess."

The sight of him in the predawn light, a mischievous twinkle dancing in his blue eyes, his brown hair disheveled from recent slumber, made Tory's blood begin to race with anticipation.

But the purple bruise on his abdomen put everything into stark perspective. Someone didn't want Trask digging into the past and that person was willing to resort to brutal violence to stop Trask's investigation.

"What time is it?" she asked, pushing the disturbing thought aside.

"Five." He stopped near the bed and looked down at her, his gaze caressing the flush in her cheeks then meeting her questioning eyes. "I couldn't sleep very well," he admitted, his fingers working the knot on his towel. "Knowing you were in the same house with me has been driving me crazy."

"You're absolutely indefatigable…or is it insufferable? It's too early to decide which," she murmured, gazing up at him affectionately. "Last night someone tried to beat the living daylights out of you. There's a good chance you could have been killed and here you are—"

"Intent on seducing the woman I'm supposed to protect." He let the towel slide to the floor and sat on the edge of the bed. Bending slightly, he pushed the tousled auburn hair from her eyes and gently kissed her forehead. "Any complaints?"

"None, senator," she replied as he threw back the covers and settled into the bed, his naked body pressing urgently against the softer contours of hers.

"I could get used to a job like this," he said as he held her face in his hands and gazed into her slumberous eyes.

Happiness wrapped around Tory's heart. A cool morning breeze carrying the faint scent of new-mown hay ruffled the curtains as it passed through the open window. Morning birds had begun to chirp and from far in the distance came the familiar sound of lowing cattle. Lying with Trask in her bed as the first silvery rays of dawn seeped into the room seemed the most natural thing in the world. There was a peaceful solitude about dawn and Tory loved sharing that feeling with the only man she had ever loved.

His arms wrapped around her, pulling her close to him. The warmth and strength of his body was welcome protection. It felt good to lean on him again, she thought. Maybe there was a chance they could forget the pain of the past and live for the future. Looking into his eyes, Tory felt that there was nothing in the world that could possibly go wrong as long as he was beside her.

"God, I love you," he whispered as he lowered his head and kissed her almost brutally.

Through the sheer nylon nightgown, she felt his hands caress her skin. Deft fingers outlined each rib as they moved upward to mold around her breasts and Tory gasped at the raw desire laboring within her.

Her breast ached with the want of him, straining to be caressed by his gentle fingers. As he found one nipple and teased it to ripe anticipation, Tory moaned. The exquisite torment deep within her became white-hot as he lifted the nightgown over her head and slowly lowered himself alongside of her. His hands pressed against the small of her back as he took first one hard nipple into his mouth and after suckling hungrily for a time, he turned his attention to the other ripe bud and feasted again.

Tory's blood was pulsing through her veins, throbbing at her temples in an erratic cadence. Sweat moistened her body where Trask's flesh molded to hers. She could feel the muscles of Trask's solid thighs straining against hers and the soft hair on his legs rubbed her calves erotically, promising more of the impassioned bittersweet torment.

"I love you," she cried, all of her doubts erased by the pleasure of his body straining against hers. Painful emotions were easily forgotten with the want of him. Her fist clenched with forced restraint and her throat ached to shout his name as he slid lower and kissed the soft flesh of her abdomen, leaving a dewy trail from her breasts to her navel.

"I'm never going to let you go again," Trask vowed, his breath fanning her abdomen, his hands kneading the soft muscles of her back and buttocks as she lifted upward, offering herself to him. "Don't ever leave me, Tory."

"Never," she cried, the fires within her all-consuming in the need to be fulfilled, to become one, to surrender to her rampant desire for this one, proud man.

Slowly he drew himself upward and his hands twined in the wanton curls framing her face. His moist skin slid seductively over hers. "I'll keep you to that promise," he said, his voice rough and his blue eyes dark with passion. "Make love to me."

As she stared into his eyes, she reached forward, her arms tightening around his muscular torso. The warm mat of hair on his chest crushed her breasts as he rolled over her and his knees gently prodded her legs apart. "I want every morning to be like this one," he said as he lowered himself over her. His lips once again touched hers and she felt the warm invasion of his tongue just as he pushed against her and began the slow rhythmic dance of love.

Closing her eyes, Tory held him tightly, her fingers

digging into the hard muscles of his back and shoulders as he moved over her in ever more rapid strokes. Her heart was thudding wildly in her rib cage. The warmth within her expanded around him and her breathing came in short gasps as Trask pushed her to the brink of ecstasy time and time again before the rippling tide of sweet fulfillment rushed over her and she felt his answering surrender.

Sweat dampened her curls as the warmth of afterglow caressed her. With Trask's strong arms wrapped around her, Tory felt there was nothing that they couldn't do, as long as they did it together.

She snuggled closer to him and Trask kissed her hair. "I meant it, you know," he insisted, his voice low. "About never letting you go."

"Good, because I'm going to hold you to it."

Silently they watched as the pale gray light of dawn faded with the rising sun. Clear blue sky replaced the early-morning haze.

Tory looked at the clock and groaned. "I've got to get up, senator. Rex usually gets here between six-thirty and seven."

"Why don't you call him and tell him to take the day off?"

Laughing at the absurdity of his request, she wiggled out of his arms. "It's easier to get a straight answer out of a politician than it is to get Rex to take a day off," she said teasingly.

"You're feeling particularly wicked this morning, aren't you?" But he was forced to chuckle.

"And what about you? Are you going to take the day off and forget about going to visit Linn Benton and George Henderson in the pen?"

His voice became stern. "Not on your life."

"That's what I was afraid of." Concern clouded her eyes as she rolled off the bed and reached for the robe draped over a bedpost at the foot of the bed. "It wouldn't surprise me if they were behind what happened to you last night."

Tenderly rubbing his jaw, Trask shook his head. "They're in prison, remember?"

"Yeah, but Linn Benton's got more than his share of friends." She shivered involuntarily and cinched the belt of her robe more tightly around her waist.

"So do I."

"I don't think friends in Washington count. They can't help you here," she thought aloud. Mentally shaking herself, she then tried to rise above the worries that had been with her ever since Trask had forced himself back in her life with his damned anonymous letter.

As she stared at the man she loved, she had to smile. His brown hair was tousled, his naked body was only partially hidden by the navy-blue sheet and patchwork quilt and his seductive blue eyes were still filled with passion. "I'll go throw your clothes in the dryer."

"Don't bother. I already did. They're probably dry by now."

"You mean that you went creeping around this house this morning with only a towel around you?"

"I wasn't creeping. And the only people here are you and Keith." His grin widened and amusement sparked in his eyes. "Besides I know where the utility room is. Believe it or not, I have done my own laundry on occasion."

"Hmph. I suppose you have." With a shake of her head, Tory went downstairs and into the kitchen. After starting the coffee, she walked into the adjoining utility room and removed Trask's clothes from the dryer. As he had predicted, the jeans and shirt were warm and dry. She draped them over her arm, climbed the stairs and returned to her room.

Trask was still lying on the four-poster, his head propped up with both pillows, a bemused grin making his bold features appear boyishly captivating. Tory's heart beat more quickly just at the sight of him.

"There you go, senator," she said, tossing the clothes to him.

"Can't I persuade you to come back to bed?"

"Not this morning. I'm a working woman, remember?"

"Excuses, excuses," he mumbled, but reached for his clothes. She sat on the edge of the bed while he pulled on his jeans and slipped his arms through the sleeves of his shirt.

"So tell me," she suggested, eyeing his bruised ribs and the cut on his chin. "Have you got any theories about who decided to use you as a punching bag?"

He looked up from buttoning his shirt. "A few."

"Care to share them?"

"Not just yet."

"Why not?"

"No proof."

"So what else is new?" she asked, leaning back against the headboard of the bed and frowning. Here, lying with Trask in the small room decorated in cream-colored lace, patchwork and maple, she had felt warm and secure. The worries of the night had faded but were now thrown back in her face, quietly looming more deadly than ever.

Trask stood and tucked in the tails of his shirt. "What's new?" he repeated. "Maybe a lot."

"This is no time to be mysterious."

"Maybe not," he agreed while cocking his wrist and looking at his watch. "But I've got to get out of here. I want to check on Neva and Nicholas, change clothes at the cabin and be in Salem by ten."

The thought of Trask leaving the ranch was difficult for Tory to accept. In a few short days, she had gotten used to his presence and looked forward to the hours she spent with him. The fact that he was leaving to face two of the men responsible for his brother's death made Tory uneasy. Though she knew that her father had been innocent, the ex-judge Linn Benton and his accomplice, George Henderson, had been and, in her opinion, still were ruthless men more than capable of murder.

"Look," he was saying as he walked to the door. "I want you to be careful, okay? I'll check with John Davis and make sure he has a man assigned to the Lazy W."

"I don't think that's necessary."

Trask's eyes glittered dangerously. "I hope not, but I'm a firm believer in the better-safe-than-sorry theory."

"Oh, yeah?" She stared pointedly at the cut on his chin and the bruise peeking out of his shirt. "Look where it's gotten you. And now you're going to talk to your brother's murderers!"

He frowned and crossed the room to hold her in his arms. Placing a soft kiss on the crown of her head he let out a long weary sigh. "Believe me, lady, someday this will all be behind us."

"You hope."

"I promise."

"Just don't tell me that in twenty years I'll look back

at what we're going through now and laugh, 'cause I won't!"

He chuckled and hugged her fiercely. "Okay, I won't lie to you, but I will promise you that we'll have plenty of stories that will entertain our grandchildren."

"That's a promise?" *Grandchildren and children. Trask's children.* At this point the possibility of marrying Trask and having his children seemed only a distant dream; a fantasy that she couldn't dare believe would come true.

"One I won't let you get out of." He lowered his head and captured her lips with his. "The sooner we get all of this mess behind us, the better. Then we can concentrate on getting married and filling the house with kids."

"Slow down, senator," she said, her love shining in her eyes. "First things first, don't you think? Oh, and if you want a cup of coffee, I'm sure it's perked."

He shook his head. "Haven't got time. I'll be back this afternoon."

"I'm counting on it."

"Maybe then I'll get a chance to talk to your foreman, Rex Engels."

Tory stiffened slightly. "Are you going to put him through the third degree, too?"

"Nothing so drastic," Trask promised. "I just want to ask him a few questions."

"About last night?"

"Among other things."

"You don't trust anyone, do you?"

"Just you," he said.

"Hmph," she muttered ungraciously and crossed her arms over her chest. "I'll tell Rex that you want to talk to him."

"Thanks." With a broad wink, he opened the door of her room and disappeared. She watched from the window as he walked out of the house, got into his Blazer and drove down the lane. A plume of gray dust followed in his wake and disturbed the tranquility of the morning. As the Blazer roared by the pasture, curious foals lifted their heads, pricking their ears forward at the noise while the mares continued to graze.

"When will it ever end?" Tory wondered aloud, taking one final look at the dew-covered grass and the rolling green pastures and dusty paddocks. With a thoughtful frown she turned away from the window and headed for the shower.

Tory was in the den balancing the checkbook when she heard Keith come down the stairs. He walked by the study without looking inside and continued down the hall to the kitchen.

"I'm in here," Tory called. When she didn't get a response, she shrugged and continued sorting through the previous month's checks. A few minutes later, Keith strode into the room, sipping from a cup of coffee.

He frowned as if remembering an unpleasant thought. "So where's our guest?"

"Trask already left for Salem."

Keith tensed. "Salem? Why?" His eyes narrowed and he lifted a hand. "Don't tell me: he plans on visiting Linn Benton and George Henderson in prison."

"That's the idea."

"He just won't let up on this, will he?"

"I doubt it. And now that the sheriff's department is involved, I would expect that Paul Barnett or one of his deputies will be out later to ask you questions."

"Just what I need," Keith said grimly and then changed the subject. "So how're you this morning?" He threw a leg over one of the arms of the recliner, leaned back and studied his sister.

"As well as can be expected after last night."

Keith scowled into his cup. The lines of worry deepened around his eyes. "What McFadden said, about you being shot at, was it true?"

Tory let out a long breath. "Unfortunately, yes."

Keith's eyes clouded as he looked away from his sister. "And you think it has something to do with this anonymous note business, right?"

"I don't know," she admitted, taking off her reading glasses and setting them on the corner of the desk as she stared at her brother. "But it seems to me that it's more than a coincidence that the minute Trask comes into town, all the trouble begins."

"Has it ever occurred to you that Trask may have initiated all this hoopla just to get his name in the papers? You know, remind the voters that he's a hero."

"I don't think he hired someone to beat him up, if that's what you mean. And I don't think that he would let someone terrorize Neva or Nicholas—do you?"

Keith squirmed uncomfortably. "Maybe not."

"So how do you explain it?"

He looked straight into her eyes. "I can't, Sis. I don't have any clue as to why someone would take a shot at you or want to hurt Neva. And it scares me, it scares the hell out of me!"

"But maybe someone was just interested in hurting Trask?" she said. "The rest of us might just have gotten in the way. After all, he was the one that took the punches last night."

Keith's head snapped upward and his jaw tightened. "I hate the bastard. It's no secret. You know it and so does he." Keith's voice faded slightly and he hesitated before adding, "And I hate the fact that he's back here, getting you all messed up again, but I wouldn't beat him up or shoot at him, for crying out loud."

Tory tapped her pencil nervously on the desk. What she was about to say was difficult. "I'm sorry, Keith. But I can't seem to forget that the first day Trask came into town you were in a panic. You came out to the paddock to tell me about it, remember?" Tory's heart was hammering in her chest. She didn't like the role of inquisitor, especially not with Keith.

"I remember."

"And later you said something about pointing a gun at him if Trask tried to trespass."

Keith squeezed his eyes shut and rubbed the stiffness out of his neck. "That was all talk, Tory." He leaned back in the chair. "I just wish he'd leave us alone." After finishing his coffee, Keith stood. "I don't want to see you get hurt again. Everything that's happening scares me."

"I'm a big girl, Keith. I can take care of myself."

Keith offered his most disarming smile. "Then I'll try not to worry about you too much."

"Good." She let out a sigh of relief and felt the tension in her tight muscles ease. She believed everything Keith had told her and wondered why she had ever doubted him. "Oh, by the way, how did you do in the poker game last night?"

Keith's grin widened and he pulled out his wallet. When he opened it, he exposed a thick roll of bills tucked neatly in the side pocket. "I cleaned everyone's clock."

"That's a switch."

"Thanks for the vote of confidence."

"So how'd you get so lucky?"

Keith took his hat off a peg near the entry hall and jammed it onto his head. "Haven't you ever heard that poker is a game of skill, not luck?"

"Only from the winners."

Keith laughed as he walked out the front door. "I'll be on the west end of the ranch helping Rex clear out some brush."

"Will you be back for lunch?"

"Naw, I'll grab something later."

Keith left and Tory began drumming her fingers on the desk. Her brother had never won at poker in his life. Just when she was beginning to trust him, something he did seemed out of character. It worried her. It worried her a lot.

"Cut it out," she told herself, pushing her glasses onto her nose and studying the bank statement. "Trask's got you jumping at shadows." But she couldn't shake the unease that had settled in her mind.

It was nearly one-thirty when Tory heard the sound of a vehicle coming down the drive. She had been leaning over the fence and watching the foals and mares as they grazed in the pasture. Shading her eyes against the glare of the afternoon sun, she smiled when she recognized Anna Hutton's white van.

Dusting her hands on her jeans, Tory met the van just as Anna parked it near the stables.

"How's our boy doing?" Anna asked as she hopped out of the van and grabbed her veterinary bag.

"Better than I'd expected. I took your advice about the cold poultices and he's even putting a little weight on the leg this morning."

"Good." Anna grinned broadly. "See, I told you. Sometimes we don't have to resort to drugs."

"He's in the paddock around back," Tory said, leading Anna past the stables to the small enclosure where Governor was being walked by Eldon.

The stallion snorted his disapproval when he saw the two women and his black ears flattened to his head.

"So walking him hasn't proven too painful for him?" Anna asked, carefully studying the nervous horse.

"I don't think so," Tory replied. "Eldon?"

The ranch hand shook his head and his weathered face knotted in concentration. "He's been doin' fine. If I thought walkin' him was causing him too much pain, I wouldn't have done it, no matter what you said."

"It's great to have employees who trust your judgment," Tory commented when she read the amusement in Eldon's eyes.

Anna seemed satisfied. "Let's take a look at you," she said to the horse as she slid through the gate, patted Governor's dark shoulders and gently prodded his hoof from the ground. "Come on, boy," she coaxed. "You should be used to all of this attention by now."

After carefully examining Governor's hoof Anna released the horse's leg. "He looks good," she said to Tory. "Just keep doing what you have with the poultices. Keep walking him and consider that special shoe. I'll look in on him in another week."

"That's the best news I've had in two days," Tory

admitted as Anna slipped through the gate and they began walking toward the house.

"I heard about what happened yesterday on Devil's Ridge," Anna commented.

Tory stopped dead in her tracks. "What? But how?"

With an encouraging smile, Anna met her friend's questioning stare. "You'd better be sure that your backbone is strong, Tory. All sorts of rumors are flying around Sinclair."

"Already? I don't see how—"

Anna placed her hand over Tory's arm. "Trask McFadden, excuse me, *Senator* McFadden is a famous man around these parts. What he does is news—big news. When someone attacks a man of his stature, it isn't long before the gossip mill gets wind of it and starts grinding out the information, indiscriminately mixing fact with fiction to distort the truth."

"But it only happened last night," Tory argued.

"And how many people knew about it?"

Tory smiled wryly and continued walking across the parking lot. "Too many," she admitted, thinking about Trask, Neva, Keith, the private investigator... The list seemed nearly endless.

"Then brace yourself; no doubt the press will be more than anxious to report what happened and how it relates to the horse swindle of five years ago as well as Jason McFadden's murder." Anna's voice was soft and consoling. "Your father's name, and his involvement in the scam, whether true or not, is bound to come up."

Tory let out a long breath of air. "That's just what I was trying to avoid." The afternoon sun felt hot on the back of her neck and the reddish dust beneath the gravel was stirred up by the easterly breeze.

"Too late. The handwriting's on the wall."

Tory lifted her chin and her eyes hardened. Involuntarily her slim shoulders squared. "Well, what's done is done, I suppose. At least you've given me fair warning. Now, how about staying for a late lunch?"

"It sounds heavenly," Anna admitted, pleased that Tory had seemed to buck up a little and was ready to face the challenge of the future. "I thought you'd never ask!"

Tory laughed and found that she looked forward to Anna's company and sarcastic wit. She needed to think about something other than the mysterious happenings on the ranch and it had been a long time since she and Anna had really had a chance to talk.

"That was delicious," Anna stated, rolling her eyes as she finished her strawberry pie. "Denver omelet, spinach salad and pie to boot. Whenever you give up ranching, you could become a chef. It's a good thing I don't eat here more often or I'd gain twenty pounds."

"I doubt that," Tory said, pleased with the compliment nonetheless. "You'll never gain weight, not with the work schedule you demand of yourself."

"That's my secret," Anna said. "I never have time to eat."

Chuckling softly the two women cleared the dishes from the table and set them in the sink. "So we've talked about what happened here yesterday, and about my plans for the ranch, and about Governor's condition. Now, tell me about you. How're you doin'?"

Anna's dark eyes clouded. "Things have been different since Jim moved out." She held up a strong finger, as if to remind herself. "However, despite it all, I've survived."

"If you don't want to talk about it…"

Anna forced a sad smile. "There's nothing much to talk about. I was involved with starting my own veterinary practice. I worked long hours and was exhausted when I got home. I resented the fact that he expected me to be the perfect wife, housekeeper, you-name-it, and he got bored with listening to my dreams, I guess. I kind of ignored him and I guess he needed a woman. So I really can't blame him for taking up with someone else, can I?"

"I would," Tory said firmly. "It seems to me that if two people love each other, they can work things out."

"It's not always that easy."

Tory thought of her own situation with Trask. The love they shared had always been shrouded in deceit. "Maybe you're right," she finally admitted. "But I don't see why you should have to go around carrying all this guilt with you."

Frowning thoughtfully, Anna rubbed her thumb over her index finger. "Maybe I carry it because I was brought up to believe that a woman's place is in the home, having babies, washing dishes, enjoying being her husband's best friend." She leaned against the counter and stared out the window. "But I got greedy. I wanted it all: husband, home, children and a fascinating career. I didn't mean to, but somehow I lost Jim in the shuffle."

"Easy to do—"

"Too easy. But I've learned from my mistakes, thank you, and you should, too."

"What's that supposed to mean?"

Anna laughed grimly. "That I'm about to poke my nose in where it doesn't belong."

"Oh?"

"Look, Tory. I know you never got over Trask." Anna saw the protest forming on Tory's lips and she warded it off with a flip of her wrist. "There's no use denying it; you love him and you always have, regardless of all that mess with your dad. It's written all over your face.

"And, despite what happened in the past, I think Trask's basically a decent man who loves you very much. What happened with your dad was unfortunate and I was as sad as anyone when Trask took the stand against Calvin. But that was five years ago and it's over." She took a deep breath. "So, if Trask is the man you love, then you'd better do your damnedest to let him know it."

Tory couldn't hide the stunned expression on her face. "That's the last piece of advice I would have expected from you," she replied.

"I had a chance to think about it last night. Let me tell you, if fate dealt me another chance with Jim, I'd make sure that I held on to him."

"How? By giving up your practice and independence?"

Anna shook her head. "Of course not. By just being a little less stubborn and self-righteous. I still believe that you can have everything, if you work at it. But you have to give a little instead of taking all the time."

"But that works two ways," Tory thought aloud.

"Of course. But if you're both willing, it should be possible." Anna looked up at the clock on the wall and nearly jumped out of her skin. "Geez, is it really three? Look, Tory, I've got to cut this session short, if you don't mind. I'm supposed to be in Bend at four."

"I'm just glad you stopped by."

"Anytime you're willing to cook, I'm ready to eat. Thanks for lunch!" Anna was out the back door in a flash and nearly bumped into Keith as he was walking through the door to the back porch.

"Excuse me," Anna called over her shoulder, while running down the two wooden steps to the path that led to the front of the house.

Keith, his eyes still fastened on Anna's retreating back came into the kitchen and threw the mail down on the table. Dust covered him from head to foot and sweat darkened the strands of his hair. Only the creases near his eyes escaped the reddish-brown dust. He placed his hat on the peg near the back door and wiped the back of his hand over his face, streaking the brown film. "I suppose I missed lunch," he said, eyeing the dishes in the sink.

"I suppose you did," Tory replied. "Anna and I just finished."

"I saw her take off." He stretched the knots out of his back. "I have to go into town and pick up the part for the combine. Then I'll go talk to Paul Barnett—you did say that he wanted to see me?"

Tory nodded.

"After that I'll probably stay in town for a couple of hours and have a few beers at the Branding Iron. Do you think I could con you into making me a sandwich or something while I get cleaned up?"

"Do I look like a short order cook?" she asked testily. "Didn't I ask you if you'd be back for lunch this morning before you left?"

"Please?"

Keith could be so damned charming when he chose

to be, Tory thought defensively. She managed a stiff smile. "Okay, brother dear, I'll see what I can scrape together, but I'm not promising gourmet."

"At this point I'd be thrilled with peanut butter and jelly," Keith admitted as he sauntered out of the kitchen and up the steps. In a few minutes, Tory could hear the sounds of running water in the shower upstairs.

By the time that Keith returned to the kitchen, some twenty minutes later, he'd showered, shaved and changed into clean clothes.

"I hardly recognized you," Tory said teasingly. She placed a platter of ham sandwiches next to a glass of milk on the table. It was then she saw the mail. Quickly pushing aside the magazines and catalog offers, she picked up the stack of envelopes and began to thumb through them.

"Bills, bills and more...what's this?" Tory stopped at the fifth envelope. The small white packet was addressed to her in handwriting she didn't recognize. There was no return address on the envelope but the letter was postmarked in Sinclair. Without much thought, she tore open the envelope. A single piece of paper was enclosed. On it, in the same unfamiliar handwriting that graced the envelope was a simple message:

STAY AWAY FROM MCFADDEN

"Oh, dear God!" Tory whispered, letting the thin white paper fall from her hands onto the table.

"What?" Keith set down his sandwich and grabbed the letter before staring at the threat in disbelief. As the message began to sink in, his anger ignited and his face became flushed. He tossed the letter onto the table. "That does it, Tory, I'm not going to listen to any more of your excuses. When McFadden gets back here you tell him that you're out of this investigation of his!"

"I think it's too late for that." She was shaken but some of her color had returned.

"The hell it is! Damn it, Tory. He was beaten. Neva's been getting threatening phone calls. You were shot at, for crying out loud! Shot at with a rifle! What does it take to get it through your thick head that whoever is behind this—" he pointed emphatically at the letter "—is playing for keeps!"

"We can't back out, the police are involved and the whole town knows what's happening."

"Who gives a rip? We're talking about our lives, for God's sake!" His fist curled angrily and the muscles of his forearms flexed with rage. "All of this has got to stop!" Pounding the table and making the dishes rattle, Keith pushed his chair backward and stood beside the door. Leaning heavily against the frame he turned pleading gray eyes on his sister. "You can make him stop, y'know. You're the only one he'll listen to."

"Not when he's set his mind to something."

"Then unset it, Tory!" He turned his palms upward and shook his hands. "What does it take to get through to you?"

Tory looked down at the note lying face up on the table and she trembled. For a moment she considered Keith's suggestion, but slowly her fear gave way to anger. "I won't be threatened," she said, "or compromised. Whoever sent this must have a lot to lose. I wonder what it is?"

"Well, I don't!" Keith nervously pushed his hair away

from his face. "I wish this whole nightmare would just end."

"But it won't. Not unless we find the truth," she said.

"Oh, God, Tory, you're such a dreamer. You always have been. That's how McFadden tricked you the first time and now you've let him do it to you again. You're so caught up in your romantic fantasies about him that you don't see the truth when it hits you in the face!"

Tory leaned against the refrigerator. "Then maybe you'll be so kind as to spell it out for me."

"He's using you, Tory. All over again. I just never thought you'd be dumb enough to fall for it!"

With his final angry words tossed over his shoulder, Keith stalked out of the room leaving Tory feeling numb. Within a few moments, she heard the sound of the pickup as it roared down the lane before squealing around the corner to the open highway.

For the rest of the afternoon, Tory waited for Trask to return as he had promised. She tried to make herself busy around the house, her anxiety increasing with each hour that passed without word from him. As the day darkened with the coming of night, Tory began to worry. What, if anything, had he found out from Linn Benton and George Henderson?

Both men had to hate him. Trask's testimony had sealed their fate and sent them both to prison. What if they were somehow involved in his beating and the threatening calls to Neva?

When the phone rang at ten o'clock, Tory felt relief wash over her. It had to be Trask.

She answered the telephone breathlessly. "Hello?"

"Tory? It's Neva." Tory's heart fell through the floor.

"I was wondering—actually hoping—that you'd heard from Trask." All of Tory's fears began to crystallize.

"I haven't seen him since this morning," she admitted.

"I see." There was a stilted silence. "Do you know if he went to Salem?"

"That's where he was headed when he left here."

"Damn." Neva waited a second before continuing.

"Maybe he went to the cabin," Tory suggested hopefully, though she already guessed the answer.

"I was already there, about an hour ago. His Blazer's gone and no one answered the door. I have a key and let myself in. I'm sure he hasn't been there since early this morning."

Tory's heart began to pound with worry. "And I assume that he hasn't called you?"

"No."

"Have you called the sheriff?"

"Not yet."

"What about the investigator, John what's-his-name?"

"Davis," Neva supplied. "He knows I'm worried. He's already contacted a couple of his men."

Tory slid into a nearby chair and felt the deadweight of fear slumping her shoulders. "So what do we do now?"

"Nothing to do but wait," Neva replied. "You'll call if you hear from him?"

"Of course." Tory hung up the phone and a dark feeling of dread seemed to seep in through the windows and settle in her heart. Where was Trask? The question began to haunt her.

Dear God, please let him be all right!

Chapter 10

The road from the Willamette Valley was narrow. It twisted upward through the Cascades like some great writhing serpent intent on following the natural chasm made by the Santiam River. With sheer rock on one side of the road and the deep ravine ending with rushing white water on the other, the two lane highway cut across the mountains from the Willamette Valley to central Oregon.

At two in the morning, with only the beams from the headlights of the jeep to guide him, Trask was at the wheel of his Blazer heading east. And he was dead-tired. He had spent all of the morning and most of the after-noon at the penitentiary asking questions and getting only vague answers from the low-lifes Henderson and Benton.

Trask's hands tightened over the steering wheel as he thought about the ex-judge's fleshy round face. Even stripped of his judicial robes and garbed in state-issued prison clothes, Linn Benton exuded a smug untouchable air that got under Trask's skin.

Linn Benton had been openly sarcastic and when Trask had asked him about another person being involved in the horse swindle, the judge-turned-inmate had actually had the audacity to laugh outright. Trask's slightly battered condition and obvious concern about what had happened five years past seemed to be a source of amusement to the ex-judge. Trask had gotten nowhere with the man, but was more convinced than ever that somehow Linn Benton was pulling the strings from inside the thick penitentiary walls. But who was the puppet on the outside?

George Henderson had been easier to question. The ex-vet had been shaking in his boots at the thought of being questioned by a man whose brother he had helped kill. But whether Henderson's obvious anxiety had been because of Trask's stature as a senator, or because of previous threats he may have received from his prison mate, Linn Benton, Trask couldn't determine.

With an oath, Trask downshifted and the Blazer climbed upward toward Santiam Pass.

All in all, the trip hadn't been a complete waste of time, Trask attempted to console himself. For the first time he was certain that Linn Benton was still hiding something. And it had to be something that he didn't expect Trask to uncover, or the rotund prisoner wouldn't have smirked so openly at his adversary. It was as if Benton were privy to some private irony; an irony Trask couldn't begin to fathom.

"But I will." Trask squinted into the darkness and made a silent vow to get even with the men who had killed his brother. If another person was involved in

Jason's death, Trask was determined to find out about it and see to it that the person responsible would pay.

For over six hours, Trask had been in the Multnomah County Library in Portland. He had searched out and microfilmed copies of all of the newspaper clippings about the horse swindle and Jason's murder, hoping to find something, anything that would give him a hint of what was happening and who was behind the series of events starting with the anonymous letter. If only the person who had written the letter would show his face…tell his side of the story…let the truth be known once and for all…then justice could be served and Trask could put the past behind and concentrate on a future with Tory.

The night seemed to have no end. Tory heard Keith come in sometime after midnight. She tossed and turned restlessly on the bed, alternately looking at the clock and staring out the window into the dark night sky. *What could have happened to Trask?* she wondered for what had to be the thousandth time. *Where was he? Why hadn't he called?*

She finally slept although fitfully and when the first streaks of dawn began to lighten the room, Tory was relieved to have an excuse to get out of bed and start the morning chores. If she had had to spend another hour in bed staring at the clock, she would have gone out of her mind with worry about Trask.

She had changed, showered and started breakfast before she heard Keith moving around in his room upstairs.

Coffee was perking and the apple muffins were already out of the oven when Keith sauntered into the kitchen. She turned to face her brother and he lifted his hands into the air as if to ward off a blow. "Truce, Sis?" he asked, grinning somewhat sheepishly.

The corners of Tory's lips curved upward and her round eyes sparkled with affection for her brother. "You know I don't hold a grudge. Well, at least not against you."

"Or Trask McFadden," he pointed out, walking to the stove and pouring them each a cup of coffee.

"I think five years was enough," Tory said.

"For sending Dad to prison where he died? Give me a break!" He offered her a mug of steaming coffee, which she accepted, but she felt her smile disintegrate.

Tory set the basket of muffins on the table and tried to ignore Keith's open hostility toward Trask. "Did you say something about a truce?"

"A truce between you and me. Not with McFadden!" Keith frowned, sat down in his regular chair and reached for a muffin. "By the way, where is he this morning?"

"I don't know," she admitted, biting nervously at her lower lip and trying to hide the fact that she was worried sick about him. She glanced nervously at the clock. It was nearly seven.

"Did he visit Benton and Henderson yesterday?" Keith had his knife poised over the butter, but his eyes never left his sister's anxious face. It was evident from the circles under her eyes and the lines near the corners of her mouth that she hadn't been able to sleep.

"I don't know that either. No one's seen or heard from him since he left here yesterday morning."

Keith set the knife aside. "So you're worried about him, right?"

"A little."

"He can handle himself."

"I wish I could believe that," Tory said.

"But you can't? Why not?"

"Think about it," Tory said with a sigh. "His brother was murdered for what he knew, Trask was beaten up the night before last and someone shot at him on Devil's Ridge." Her voice trembled slightly and she took a long swallow of coffee. "I think I have a reason to be worried." She glanced nervously out the window before taking a seat at the table. "If I don't hear from him this morning, I'm calling Paul Barnett."

"Maybe Trask's with Neva," Keith said as gently as he could.

Tory felt the sting of Keith's remark and she paled slightly. "He wasn't with Neva," she whispered. "Neva called here last night. She's worried, too."

"Look, Tory," Keith cajoled. "A United States senator doesn't just vanish off the face of the earth. He'll be back flashing that politician's smile of his. The man's a survivor, for crying out loud."

Tory didn't answer. She swirled the coffee in her mug and silently prayed that this time Keith was right.

The sound of Rex's pickup caught her attention. Still wrapped in her own worried thoughts, Tory poured the foreman a cup of coffee without really thinking about it. By the time that Rex came in through the back door, she had already added a teaspoon of sugar to the cup.

"'Mornin'," Rex greeted, noting the lines of worry disturbing the smooth skin of Tory's brow.

"How about some breakfast?" Tory asked.

Rex eyed the muffins and the sliced fruit on the table. "Looks good, but no thanks." He patted his flat abdomen. "Already ate with Belinda." He paused for a moment and shook his head. "I just wanted to let you know that I fixed the combine late yesterday afternoon and that I'm planning to cut the yearling calves from the herd today. There's a rancher who lives in Sisters and he's interested in about thirty head. He'll be here around eleven." Rex pushed the brim of his hat farther up on his forehead as he accepted the cup of coffee Tory offered. He warmed his gnarled fingers around the ceramic mug. "He might want to look at the horses, too."

Tory managed a smile. "Good. You can show him the mares and the foals as well as the yearlings."

Keith didn't bother to hide his surprise. He frowned, causing a deep groove in his forehead between his eyebrows. "You plan on selling some of the mares?"

"Maybe. If the price is right."

Her brother leaned back in his chair and his eyes narrowed thoughtfully. "Because you know that once this scandal hits the papers no one, even if his life depends on it, will buy a Quarter Horse from the Lazy W."

"That's exaggerating a little, I think. But the note from the bank is due soon and we'll need all the cash we can get."

"Don't remind me."

"I'll try not."

"Okay," Rex said, noticing the simmering hostility between brother and sister. "I'll show the man from Sisters around, see if I can get him interested in any of the horses."

"I thought you wanted to keep the mares another year at least and wait until the foals were born," Keith persisted.

Tory pursed her lips and shook her head. "I think we'd better go with the bird in the hand theory." She leveled her concerned eyes at Rex. "If the buyer wants any of the mares, they're for sale."

"What about stallions?" Rex asked.

Tory clenched her teeth. "They're for sale, too. For the right price."

"Even Governor?" Rex asked.

"All of them," Tory whispered.

"Tory, I can't let you do this—" Keith began to interrupt and looked as if he wanted to say more, but Tory cut him off.

"I don't think we've got a choice. I have a meeting with the bank scheduled for the end of next week, and for once I'd like to show that the Lazy W has a positive cash flow. You were right when you first told me we'd have to sell—it just took a while for it to sink in. Selling some of the cattle and a few horses might get us out of the red for the month of June. Even if it's only one month, it would say a lot and help me convince the loan officer to lend us more operating capital."

"Hmph! How was I to know you'd listen to me for once?" Keith replied. Then, not having an argument against her logic, but worried just the same, Keith set down his empty coffee cup, got up from the table and explained that he would be working with some of the men who were cutting hay.

Rex and Keith walked out of the house together. Tory was left alone with the dirty dishes as well as her worries about what may have happened to Trask.

Two hours later, as she was finishing feeding the horses and wondering which, if any of the stock, would sell to the buyer from Sisters, she heard the sound of Trask's Blazer rumbling down the drive. Her heart seemed to leap inside her. She looked out the dusty window of the stables to confirm what her ears had told her and a smile grew from one side of her face to the other as she watched Trask's vehicle stop near the house. He got out of the Blazer and stretched, lifting his hands over his head, and making his flat abdomen appear almost concave with the unconscious, but erotic movement. He was dressed in worn cords and a shirt with the sleeves pushed up to his elbows. The sight of him brought tears of relief to Tory's eyes.

He started for the house, but she pounded on the window of the stables. Trask turned, squinted against the sun and his wonderful slightly crooked smile stole over his jaw when he noticed her. That was all the encouragement she needed. Without caring that they might be seen, Tory ran out of the stables and straight into his arms. He held her so tightly that her feet were pulled from the ground as he spun her around.

Bending his head, Trask kissed her passionately, sending warm bursts to every point in her body.

"What happened to you?" she asked breathlessly, once the lingering kiss was over. His arms were still around her, locking her body next to his, pressing her curves against the hard muscles of his thighs and torso. "I was worried to death!"

"I should have called," he admitted, kissing her forehead and letting the faint scent of lilacs from her hair fill his nostrils. All of the frustrations that had knotted the muscles in the back of his neck since visiting the penitentiary seemed to melt away just at the sight of Tory's enigmatic smile and the feel of her warm body pressed eagerly to his.

"At the very least you should have called! You had Neva and me out of our minds with worry."

"Neva, too, huh?" he asked with a frown.

"What did you expect would happen when you disappeared?"

"I had no idea I was so popular," he said with a smile and she laughed, her hands still clutching his shoulders. Through the light cotton fabric of his shirt, she could feel the corded strength of his muscles tightening around her as he kissed her once again before lifting his head. His blue eyes smoldered with aroused passion.

"Why didn't you come back last night?" she managed to ask, though her thoughts were centered on the feel of his body pressed tightly against her.

"It didn't cross my mind that it would take all day and half the night to finish what I'd set out to do. I didn't get back to the cabin until two-thirty and even if I had a phone there, I wouldn't have called. I thought you'd already be in bed." That thought brought a seductive curve to his lips.

"I was!" she retorted trying to sound angry and failing. She lovingly traced the rugged set of his jaw with a finger. "I was in bed tossing and turning and wondering what horrible fate had come to you." Unconsciously she touched the cut on his chin. "You don't have a great track record for keeping yourself safe, you know. I stared at the ceiling and the clock all night long."

"I'm sorry," he said, refusing to release her and grinning broadly. His blue eyes twinkled with the morning light and he kissed her finger when it strayed near his mouth. Her breath caught in her throat at the feel of his tongue on her fingertip. "You paint a very suggestive picture, y'know," he whispered hoarsely. "I would have done just about anything to be with you last night." Familiarly his hands slid up her back, drawing her still closer to him, letting her feel the need rising within him. Instantly her body began to react and as his head dipped again, she parted her lips, anxious for the taste of him. How right it felt to be held in his arms with the warmth of the morning sun at her back.

"Maybe we should make up for lost time," he suggested against her ear.

She had to clear her throat and force herself to think rationally. The feel of Trask's body pressed urgently against hers made it difficult to think logically. "Later, senator," she said, trying to ignore the sweet rush of desire flooding her veins. "I've got work to do and I want to hear everything you found out yesterday."

"Can't it wait?" His breath fanned her ear.

She swallowed with difficulty and the feel of his palms pressed against the small of her back made refusing him incredibly difficult. Tory was tempted to say "yes" but she couldn't forget the threatening letter she had received just the day before. "I don't think so," she replied, reluctantly slipping out of his embrace and taking his hand to lead him toward the house. "You're not the only one who has something to say."

For the first time he noticed the trace of worry in her gray-green eyes. "Something happened last night?"

They were approaching the path leading to the back of the house. Alex, who had been lying under his favorite juniper bush, tagged along behind them and slid through the screen door when Tory opened it.

"Yesterday," Tory clarified. She poured them both a cup of coffee, placed a plate of leftovers on the floor for

Alex's breakfast and retrieved the note from a drawer in her father's desk in the den.

Trask's eyes narrowed and glittered dangerously as she studied the single sheet of paper. "This has gone too far," he muttered. His fists clenched in frustrated rage and the muscles of his forearms flexed. "First Neva was threatened, and now you."

"Apparently someone has something to hide."

"And he'll go to just about any lengths to keep his secret hidden." Trask let out a long sigh and leaned against the counter. "Have you talked to the sheriff?"

"Not yet."

"What about any of John Davis's men?"

Tory shook her head. "The one man assigned to the ranch keeps a pretty low profile. He's only been inside the house a couple of times, but several of the hands have commented about his presence."

Trask's head snapped upward. "And what have you told them?"

"That I'm trying to prevent another one of the calves from being shot, you know, protecting the livestock."

"And they bought that story?" His dark brows raised suspiciously.

Tory shrugged. "I doubt it. The hands are too smart to be conned. They know when someone is trying to pull the wool over their eyes and can see through lies, just about any lie. Though they don't go poking around in my business, it's hard to ignore the fact that a United States senator showed up here, sporting a rather ugly cut on his chin. Especially since there was a scandal he was involved in a few years ago." She looked pointedly at Trask. "It hasn't helped that the rumors and gossip are already flying around Sinclair like vultures over a dying animal. So you see, it's really too much to expect the hands to think that the only reason a detective is on the ranch is to protect the cattle."

"I suppose so." He looked down at the letter again. "I don't like this, Tory."

She shuddered and took a sip of her coffee. "Neither do I."

Trask wearily pushed the hair from his face and began to pace across the kitchen floor.

"Cut that out," Tory admonished softly and then explained. "Pacing drives me nuts."

"You really are on edge, aren't you?"

"I think we both are. Why don't you call Neva and let her know that you're all right? Then you can sit down and tell me everything that happened yesterday with the judge and his accomplice."

Trask reluctantly agreed and while he was on the phone to Neva and Paul Barnett, Tory fixed him a breakfast of muffins, fresh fruit and scrambled eggs. She was just placing the eggs on a platter when Trask walked back into the kitchen.

"You're spoiling me," he accused with a devilish twinkle in his eyes.

"And you love it." She looked up and pointed at a chair near the table. "Now, sit, senator, and tell me everything there is to know about Linn Benton."

Trask slid into his chair and began eating. "Benton seemed to think it was a joke that I was there, but Henderson was scared spitless. I think Henderson would have talked, but he was afraid that Linn Benton would find out."

"So you didn't learn anything you didn't already know?"

"Nothing specific," Trask admitted. "But I've got

a gut feeling that somehow Linn Benton is involved in what's happening here. He was so amused by the whole thing, especially the fact that someone had beat the hell out of me." Puzzled lines etched across Trask's forehead.

"But you can't figure out exactly what he's doing or with whom, right?"

He looked away from her and his blue eyes grew as cold as the morning sky in winter. "I'm working on it. John Davis is checking out Benton's friends and the people that still work for him on his ranch near Bend, and after I was through at the penitentiary, I drove to Portland and did some research."

"What kind of research?"

"I made copies of all the newspaper accounts of what happened five years ago. Everything I could find on Jason's murder as well as the Quarter Horses and the swindle."

Tory felt her back stiffen. "But you were at the trial, heard and gave testimony. You already knew what happened; at least you thought you did."

"But I wanted to get a new perspective on the scam. I thought I could find it in the press accounts of the investigation and the trial."

"You must have read all those articles a hundred times," she whispered.

"I did five years ago under…a lot of stress and conflicting emotions," he said quietly. He finished his breakfast and again noticed the threatening letter. "So who do you think sent you this?" He pointed to the single white sheet of paper.

"I don't know."

"But surely you could hazard a guess," he coaxed.

"The only people I can think of are Linn Benton and George Henderson because we already know that they were involved. Benton has powerful allies outside of the penitentiary, people who are still on his payroll or owe him favors—"

The front door opened with a bang. "Tory?" Keith's anxious voice echoed through the house.

"In the kitchen," she called out to him.

"Thank God you're here," he said, striding to the back of the house and stopping short when he met Trask's cool stare. "I've got a bone to pick with you, McFadden."

Trask smiled wryly. "Another one?"

"Rex found another calf—shot just like the last one," Keith said, his face twisted with worry. He jerked his hat off his head, tossed it carelessly onto the counter and slid into the chair facing Trask.

Tory's slim shoulders slumped. Yesterday the note, today another calf…when would it end. "Where is it?" she asked.

"Rex found it on the south side of the pasture, near the lake. He's already taken care of the carcass."

"What was he doing in that pasture?" Trask asked.

"He works here, damn it!" Keith replied, his fist coiling angrily. "He was laying irrigation pipe—why the hell am I explaining all this to you?"

Tory held up her hands, forestalling the fight before it got started. "The calf was shot just like the other one?"

"Right. Near as we can tell, someone jumped the fence, picked out a victim and blasted it."

Tory felt her blood run cold. She looked at Trask and noticed that every muscle in his face had hardened.

"This all happened because of you," Keith pointed

out as he leaned against his elbows on the table and rubbed a dirty hand over his brow, leaving streaks of dust on his face. "Everything was going along okay until you started poking around here."

A muscle in the corner of Trask's jaw began to work convulsively and he set his coffee cup on the table. When he stood, he towered over Keith and felt older than his thirty-six years. "I know that because I returned to Sinclair, I've put the ranch in danger. Believe me, it wasn't intentional."

"Hmph." Keith stared insolently up at the man who was responsible for all of the pain in his life. Tory's brother had to close his eyes and shake the feeling of dread that had overtaken him in the last few days.

"You don't have to worry about what's happening—"

"Like hell!" Keith's head snapped upward. "Another calf's been killed and we got this…this threat, for crying out loud!"

"I'll take care of it."

"Like the way you took care of Dad?" Keith demanded.

Tory's stomach was in knots. "I don't think bringing up the past will help—"

"Hell, Tory, that's what this is all about—the past— or have you forgotten?"

"Of course not!"

"Maybe we should all just cool off," Trask suggested, staring pointedly at Keith.

The silence in the kitchen was so thick Tory could feel the weight of it upon her shoulders. When Rex came through the back door, she was glad for the excuse of pouring the foreman a cup of coffee.

"We lost another one," Rex stated, frowning slightly

at the sight of Trask in the house. He took off his Stetson and ran his hand over his forehead.

"Keith told us about it," Tory said.

"What are your theories about how it was killed?" Trask asked, leaning his elbows against the counter, stretching his legs in front of him before crossing his ankles and folding his arms over his chest. Though he tried to appear casual, Tory noticed the grim set of his jaw and the determination in his eyes.

Rex shrugged and accepted the cup of coffee Tory offered. "Don't really know."

"Surely you must have some thoughts about what happened?"

Rex stared at Trask over the rim of his cup. "All I know is that the trouble started when you arrived."

Trask's eyebrows cocked. "So you think it was more than a coincidence?"

"I'd stake my life on it."

"Tell me, Rex," Trask cajoled and Tory was reminded of the one time she had seen him working as a lawyer in the courtroom. Her blood chilled at the memory. It had been two or three months before the scandal involving her father had been discovered. Trask's country-boy charm and affable smile had won him the confidence of everyone in the courtroom, including a few of the prosecution's witnesses. He coaxed one woman, a witness for the prosecution, into saying something the D.A. would rather have remained secret. Dread began to knot in Tory's stomach as Trask began to question Rex in his soft drawl. "Tell me how long you've been with the Lazy W."

"More years than I'd want to count," Rex replied, returning Trask's stare without flinching. "What're you getting at, McFadden?"

Trask overlooked the question. "And why did Calvin hire you?"

Tory felt the air in the room become thick with suspicion. "Trask—"

"What's this got to do with anything?" Keith demanded.

The foreman disregarded Keith's interruption and drained his cup, never once taking his eyes off Trask. "Calvin needed help with the Lazy W, I guess. And I needed a job."

"And you've stayed all these years."

"Yep."

"Even after Calvin died." Trask made it sound as if Rex's loyalty were some sort of crime.

"I'm too old to jump from spread to spread."

"Trask," Tory interjected, her voice wavering slightly. "There's no need for this. Rex doesn't have to explain himself."

"Just a few friendly questions," Trask replied coldly.

Tory wondered what had happened to the warm caring man he had been only moments before.

"Well, let me ask you a few," Keith cut in. "You seem to be pointing fingers at nearly everyone you meet, McFadden. But what about you? How do we know that the letter you brought here isn't a phony? How do we know that you haven't been the one calling Neva, sending threatening letters to Tory or shooting the calves?"

If Trask was outraged, he managed to hide it. His lips twisted into a grim smile but his eyes became as cold as the deepest well at midnight.

"And you think I took a shot at myself, too?" Trask returned.

"You could have hired someone to fire a shot when you were up on Devil's Ridge. After all, you were the only one who knew you'd be up there. As for what happened to you—" Keith's palm flipped upward as he pointed to the discoloration under Trask's eye "—you could have hired that done as well, for authenticity's sake!"

"You know, Wilson, you have one hell of an imagination," Trask said with genuine amusement. "Why would I bother?"

"I think your motives are pretty obvious. Sure it looks like you're on the up and up; that way you could worm your way back into Tory's heart, not to mention the fact that you'd look good to the press. All the rumors and publicity that are bound to spring from your investigation aren't going to hurt your career, are they? And they'll serve to remind the voting public of the reason you were elected in the first place, proving beyond a shadow of a doubt that you're still the hard-nosed, filled-with-integrity candidate you were four years ago!"

"I just want to find out if another man was involved in Jason's death."

"You've got your vengeance and more," Keith said. "Because my father wasn't involved with Linn Benton or George Henderson."

"Then why didn't he say so, declare his innocence? He had his chance."

"I...I don't know," Keith said, his cocky attitude slipping a little.

"So we're back to square one, aren't we?" Trask thought aloud. "Well, not for long. I intend to figure

out what happened back then." Trask's eyes glittered so
fiercely that Tory felt a needle of fear pierce her heart.

"And what if your anonymous letter is a phony? How
about that?" Keith persisted. "Then you've brought us
all this trouble for no reason."

"I don't think so."

"Neither do I," Tory said with conviction as she
looked at the cut on Trask's face.

"Oh, God, Tory, you can't believe him, not again!"

"It sure takes a helluva a lot to convince you, Wilson," Trask said tiredly before returning his gaze to
Tory. The warmth returned to his eyes. "Look, I'm
going to be gone for a few days, do some checking
around. But I'll be back. And, while I'm gone, one of
John Davis's men will be here." He looked pointedly at
Rex and Keith before letting his gaze fall back on Tory.
"I think you should call Paul Barnett and report what
happened to the calf."

"I will," she promised.

"Here we go again," Keith muttered as he grabbed
his hat and walked out the door.

Rex shifted uncomfortably before wiping his hand
nervously over his brow. "I just want to clear the air,"
he said.

"About what?"

"The reasons I came to the Lazy W."

"Rex, you don't have to—"

"I've got nothing to hide, Tory. I couldn't get work
anywhere because of my first wife. She claimed that
I…that I'd get angry with her, drink too much and…
rough her up." Rex closed his eyes and sadly shook his
head. "Marianne swore that on several occasions I'd
beat her; but it just wasn't so. The only time I slapped

her was after a particularly bad fight and, well, she had a butcher knife, said she was going to use it on me if I came near her. I took the knife away from her and slapped her. She filed charges against me."

"Which were later dropped," Trask added.

"You knew all about it?" Rex asked with a grimace.

Trask nodded and Tory felt sick inside that Rex had been forced to bare his soul.

"Even though I was aquitted, no one would give me work."

"Except for Calvin Wilson."

Rex's chin jutted outward. "I've been here ever since." He set down his cup and started toward the door. "I'll be in the stables if you want me," he said to Tory. "The buyer from Sisters still wants thirty head of cattle."

Still slightly numb from the scene she had just witnessed, Tory found it difficult to concentrate on the work at hand. Her eyes offered Rex a silent apology. "What about horses?"

Rex frowned and shook his head. "He said he'll wait to decide about the horses, though he looked at a couple of yearlings that he liked." Forcing his hat onto his head, Rex walked out the back door. Tory didn't have to question him any further. She knew that the sale of the horses wasn't completed because of the Quarter Horse swindle her father was supposedly involved in five years ago. Even though it had happened long ago and her father was dead, people remembered, especially now that Trask was back. So the paranoia of the past had already started interfering with the future.

When she heard Trask move toward the door, she

impaled him with her eyes. "That was uncalled for, senator," she rebuked.

"What?"

"You didn't have to humiliate Rex. Especially since you knew all the answers anyway. That's called baiting, senator, and I don't like it. It might work in Washington, D.C., but I won't have it here, on the Lazy W, used against my employees."

"I just wanted to see if he would tell the truth."

Hot injustice colored Tory's cheeks. "And did he pass the test?" she demanded.

"With flying colors."

"Good. Then maybe you'll quit harassing everyone who works on this ranch and concentrate on Linn Benton or whoever else might have a grudge against your brother."

"I didn't mean to upset you," he said softly.

"You don't mean to do a lot of things, but you do them anyway, despite anyone else's feelings."

"Not true, Victoria," he countered, coming up to her and placing his hands over her shoulders, his blue eyes searching hers. His fingers gently massaged the tense muscles near the base of her neck, warming her skin. "I'm always concerned about you and what you feel."

"You weren't five years ago."

A shadow of pain crossed his eyes. "I only told what I thought was the truth and you still can't forgive me, can you?"

She closed her eyes against a sudden unwanted feeling that she would break down and cry. "It...it was very hard to sit by and know that Dad was dying...alone in some god-awful jail cell all because of what I told you."

"It's not your fault that you overheard Linn Benton discussing plans with your father."

"But it's my fault that you found out about it," she whispered.

Trask frowned and took her into her arms, but the response he got was cold and distant. "You can't keep blaming yourself."

She let out a tired sigh. "I try not to."

He hesitated a minute. "Are you okay?" She nodded mutely and took hold of her emotions to force the tears backward.

"Good." He kissed her softly on the forehead. "I've got to go. I'll be back in a couple of days."

"Where are you going?"

"I wish I knew," he admitted. "I'll start by visiting John Davis in Bend and showing him all these clippings. Maybe he can come up with something; a new angle. I'll be back...soon."

"I'm counting on it, senator," she whispered before he gathered her into his arms and kissed her with all of the passion that had fired his blood since the first time he had seen her. His tongue caressed and mated with hers and she leaned against him, her knees becoming soft. Once again she was caught up in the storm of emotions that raged within her each time she was near him, and when he finally released her, she felt empty inside.

Tory stood on the back porch and watched him leave. When his Blazer was out of sight, she tried to think of anything but Trask and his reasons for returning to the Lazy W.

Pouring hot coffee into her cup, she walked into the den and sat at the desk, intending to concentrate on preparing a financial statement to take to the bank later in the week.

But the numbers were meaningless and her mind wandered. She found her thoughts returning to the conversation she had overheard between her father and Linn Benton five years ago...in this very study.

The summer night had been breathlessly hot and humid. Tory had come downstairs for a glass of lemonade when she heard the muted whispers behind the closed doors to the study. Her father's den had never been off limits, but that night, the night that Linn Benton had stormed into the house, everything changed and the pieces of the argument that drifted to her ears caught her attention and made her hesitate on the lowest step.

"Don't be so goddamned sanctimonious," the judge had said in his high-pitched wheezing tone. "You're in this up to your neck, Wilson."

Tory slipped down the final step and stood frozen in the entry hall, eavesdropping on a conversation she wished later that she had never overheard.

"I should never have gotten involved with you," her father replied brusquely.

"Too late for second thoughts now."

"If it weren't for the kids..." Her father's voice had drifted off and her heart grew cold. Calvin was entangled with Linn Benton because of her brother and her. Her father was doing something he didn't believe in just to support his children! She reached for the door, but the self-satisfied laughter of Linn Benton made her withdraw her hand. Tory realized that it would be better if she waited until she could speak to her father alone before confronting him.

The rest of the angry conversation was muted and she only heard parts of it, just enough to know that whatever the two men were arguing about wasn't aboveboard. She silently worried in the outer hall before going upstairs and pacing the floorboards of her room.

When she heard the judge's car roar down the drive, she raced down the stairs, intent on confronting her father and begging him to abandon whatever it was that involved Linn Benton.

But Calvin was no longer in the study. The door to the den was open, and thick cigar smoke still lingered in the air. Two half-empty glasses of whisky sat neglected on the desk.

"Dad?" she called, starting for the kitchen and glancing out the window just in time to see her father reining his favorite gelding out of the stables and kicking the horse into a full gallop in the moonlight. Head bent against a mounting summer wind, Calvin Wilson raced through the pastures toward the mountains and Devil's Ridge.

Tory ran to the front door, jerked it open and let the hot dusty wind inside. *"Dad!"* she called again, this time screaming at the top of her lungs from the front porch. Either Calvin didn't hear her voice over the sound of his horse's racing hoofbeats and the whistling wind, or he chose to ignore her.

Tory was just about to follow him when Trask arrived. She was already leading a mare from the stables as his truck approached. Tory's nerves shattered with fear for her father's life and she quickly explained about the strange conversation she had overheard to the man she loved and trusted with all of her heart. Trask muttered an angry oath and his eyes blazed with angry lightning.

His jaw set with furious resolve and with only a few abrupt commands telling her to stay on the ranch and wait for his call, Trask wheeled his jeep around and followed Calvin through the open fields. Like a fool she had trusted him and obeyed, keeping her lonely vigil through the night, pacing in the den, praying that the phone would ring and end her fears.

Early the next morning, when Trask finally returned, she learned the horrible truth: Jason McFadden had been found dead—the result of a monstrous plot conceived by Linn Benton, George Henderson, and, according to Trask, her own father. Tory was numb with disbelief when she learned that Calvin Wilson had been charged with murder.

Chapter 11

Nearly two quiet weeks had passed when Trask found himself staring into the self-satisfied smile of the private investigator. Trask was sitting in one of the soft leather chairs near the desk, but his body had gone rigid.

"You found out *what*?" Trask demanded, staring at the private investigator in disbelief.

"Just what I told you," John Davis replied, settling back in his chair and casually lighting a cigarette. Behind him, through the second-story window of his office, was a bird's-eye view of the bustling downtown area of the city of Bend.

"Damn!" Trask's fist coiled and he slapped it into his other palm. His dark brows drew together.

"I thought you wanted the truth."

"I did. I did." Trask sounded as if he were trying to convince himself. "It's just that... Hell, I don't know."

His thoughts were jumbled and confused. The past couple of weeks had eased by in a regular routine. Fortunately there had been no more threatening letters, dead calves or violence. He had spent most of his time with Tory on the Lazy W. The days had been pleasant; the nights filled with passionate exhilaration. And now this unexpected news from John Davis was about to change all that. The damned thing was that it was exactly what he had been asking for.

"You're sure about this," Trask said, already knowing the answer as he stared at the damning report in John's hands.

The private investigator stubbed out his cigarette and studied his client through thick lenses. "Positive, and even if you're entertaining thoughts about keeping it quiet, I can't. I've got some responsibility to the law, y'know." He tossed the neatly typed report across the desk.

"As well as your clients."

"Doesn't matter. If you want to keep something the size of this quiet, Trask, you'll have to use every bit of senatorial pull you have in this state. Even that might not be enough."

"I didn't say I wanted to keep it quiet."

"Good. Now, if you're worried about your career once the truth is known..." The young man shrugged and smiled.

"I don't give a damn about my career!"

"Still the rogue senator, right?"

Trask's face tensed and his eyes dropped to the damning document lying on the polished mahogany of the desk. He picked it up and folded it neatly into the manila envelope John offered. "This is going to be one hell of a mess," he thought aloud.

"But it will be over," John replied. The investigator's voice sounded like a trumpet of doom.

"Yes, I suppose it will," Trask replied. "I guess I should thank you." He placed the thick envelope in his jacket pocket and tossed the coat over his arm.

"I guess maybe you should," John replied with a smile, though his eyes remained sober.

Trask strode out of the office feeling as if the weight of the world had been placed upon his shoulders. *So Tory had been right all along: Calvin Wilson had been innocent! But not so her younger brother, Keith.* And that news would destroy her. No doubt she would blame Trask.

Trask's blood began to boil with anger when he thought about how many times Keith had lied through his teeth, not only to Trask, but to Tory as well. Letting out a descriptive curse, Trask walked down the short flight of stairs to the ground floor. According to John Davis's report, which the investigator had double-checked, Keith Wilson and not Calvin Wilson had been involved in the Quarter Horse swindle five years past. All Trask's testimony at the original trial had been in error. Calvin Wilson had only been trying to protect his teenaged son from prosecution.

"Crazy old fool," Trask muttered as he walked out of the building and climbed into his Blazer. He threw the truck into gear and let out a stream of oaths against himself and the whole vile mess that Linn Benton had conceived. The aftermath of the ex-judge's illegal scam was ruining the lives of the only people he really cared about. Tory, Neva and Nicholas had all been innocent victims of a plot so malicious it had included the murder of his brother.

Trask's mouth twisted downward and he could feel his jaw clench at the stupidity of Keith Wilson. All of Tory's precious trust would be shattered when she found out the truth about her brother and that Trask had helped send her father, an innocent man, to prison. "Damn it, Wilson," he swore, as if Calvin were in the Blazer with him. "Why couldn't you have said something before being so goddamned noble!"

Tory walked out of the bank and into the blazing heat of midafternoon. Her head throbbed and the muscles in the back of her neck ached. For the past two hours she had explained the profit and loss statements, as well as going over the assets and liabilities of the Lazy W to a disinterested young loan officer.

"I'll let you know," the bored young man had said. "But I can't make any promises right now. Your loan application, along with the financial statements and a status report of your current note with the bank will have to be reviewed by the loan committee as well as by the president of the bank."

"I see," Tory had replied, forcing a discouraged smile. She knew, whether the young man admitted it or not, that he was peddling her nothing more than financial double-talk. The Lazy W didn't have a snowball's chance in hell of receiving more funds from this particular bank. "And how long will it take before I can expect an answer?" Tory had asked.

"The loan committee meets next Thursday."

"Fine." She had stood, shook the banker's soft hand and walked out of the building, certain that the Lazy

W would have to secure operating capital from another source.

After stopping by Rasmussen Feed for several sacks of oats and bran for the horses, Tory made her weekly visit to the grocery store and bought a local newspaper along with her week's supply of groceries. Once the sacks were loaded in the pickup, she glanced at the headlines on the front page of the paper.

The article was small, but located on page one. In five neatly typed paragraphs it reported that Senator Trask McFadden was back in Sinclair looking into the possibility that there may have been a fourth conspirator in his brother's death as well as the Quarter Horse swindle of five years past. The *Sinclair Weekly* promised a follow-up story the next week.

"Wonderful," Tory muttered with a groan, tossing the newspaper aside and heading back to the Lazy W.

The past two weeks had been quiet and Tory had ignored her earlier doubts about the past to the point that she had let herself fall completely and recklessly in love with Trask all over again. There had been no threats or violence and oftentimes Tory would allow herself to forget the reason that Trask had come back to Sinclair. She had even managed not to dwell on the fact that he would be leaving for Washington, D.C., very shortly.

Though she was still worried about the threats of violence that seemed to have accompanied him back to the Lazy W, Tory had thought less and less about them as Trask's wounds had healed and there hadn't been any further incidents. Unfortunately, the *Sinclair Weekly* decided to stir things up.

Just let me love him without the rest of the world intruding, she silently prayed.

Of course her hopes were in vain. With the article in the newspaper, everything came crashingly back to reality. No longer could she ignore the real reason Trask had returned to Sinclair. Nor could she forget that he would leave as soon as he had finished his investigation.

And then what? she asked herself. *What about all his words of love, promises of marriage? Is that what you want? To be married to a United States senator who lives in Washington, D.C.? And what if he isn't sincere? What if this has all been an adventure for him— nothing more. He left you once before. Nothing says he can't do it again.*

"But he won't," she said as she parked the pickup near the back door. "He won't leave me and he'll never betray me again!" Hearing her own voice argue against the doubts in her mind, she experienced a sudden premonition of dread.

Tory unpacked the groceries and after changing from the linen business suit she had worn to meet with the bank's loan officer, she drove the pickup to the stables, unloaded the heavy sacks of grain and stacked them in the feed bins against the wall.

Her eyes wandered lovingly over the clean wooden stalls, and she noted the shining buckets that were hung near the mangers. The smell of horses, leather and saddle soap combined with the sweet scent of oats and freshly cut hay. Tory gazed through the window. Against the backdrop of long-needled pines, Governor was grazing contentedly, his laminitis nearly cured. A distant sound caught his attention. He lifted his graceful dark head and pricked his ears forward, before pawing the ground impatiently and tossing his head to the sky. Tory's heart swelled with pride as she watched the magnificent stallion, a horse she had cared for since he was a fiery young colt.

She walked outside and closed the door of the stables behind her. Her eyes scanned the horizon and the rolling fields leading toward the craggy snowcapped mountains. What would she do if she lost the Lazy W? Leaning against the fence she could feel her brows draw together. The thought of losing the ranch was sobering and her small chin lifted in defiance against the fates that sought to steal her home and livelihood from her.

I can't, she thought to herself, slowly clenching her fists. *No matter what else happens, I can't lose this ranch.* Tory had always believed that where there was a will, there was a way. So it was with the Lazy W. She would find a way to keep the ranch, no matter what. Livestock could be sold, as well as pieces of machinery, if need be. And there were several parts of the ranch that could be parceled off without really affecting the day-to-day operations. The fields used for growing hay could be sold and she could buy the hay she needed from other ranchers. And there was always Devil's Ridge. Though Keith now owned that parcel, it could be sold or mortgaged.

She leaned on the fence and sighed. If things had gone differently, Devil's Ridge would now be where her father and mother would have retired and Keith would be running the ranch. Tory could have married Trask, and had several precious children to love…

"Stop it," she muttered to herself, slapping the fence post and dismissing her daydreams. "If wishes were horses, then beggars would ride."

Trying to shake the mood of desperation that had been with her since leaving the bank, Tory saddled her favorite palomino mare and mounted the spirited horse. After walking through the series of paddocks surrounding the stables, she urged the small horse into a gallop through the fields surrounding the main buildings of the ranch. Tory really didn't know where she was going, but she felt compelled to get away from the problems at the Lazy W.

The mare was eager to stretch her legs and Tory leaned forward in the saddle, encouraging the little horse. The only sounds she could hear were the thudding of the mare's hooves against the summer-hard ground and the pounding of her own heart. As the palomino raced toward the lake in the largest pasture, Tory felt the sting of the wind tangle her hair and force tears to her eyes. As if stolen by the wind, the pressures of running the ranch ebbed from Tory's mind and she gave herself up to the breathless exhilaration of the horse's sprint.

"You're just what I needed," she confided to the mare as she slowly reined the horse to a stop. Tory slid out of the saddle and let the horse drink from the clear lake. The late-afternoon sky reflected on the spring-fed pond and the scent of newly mown hay drifted over the land. *Her land.* The land both she and her father had worked to keep in the family.

While the mare grazed nearby, Tory propped her back against a solitary pine tree and stared at the horizon to the west. Misty white clouds clung to the uppermost peaks of the craggy snow-covered mountains in the distance. Closer, in the forested foothills, the distinct rocky spine of Devil's Ridge was visible.

Despite her earlier vows to herself, Tory's thoughts

centered on the ridge and the afternoon she had spent with Trask just a few short weeks before.

Trask. His image flitted seductively through her mind.

He was the one man she should hate but couldn't. Despite the deceit of the past and the uncertainty of the future, Tory loved him with all of her heart. The past few weeks even Keith seeemd to have thawed and for the first time Tory thought there was actually a chance of a future with the man she loved. She tossed a pebble into the lake and watched the ever-widening circles spread over the calm water.

So what about the anonymous note, the dead calves, the rifle shot on Devil's Ridge, the threats? her persistent mind nagged.

With lines of concern creasing her brow, Tory plucked a piece of grass from the ground and twirled it in her fingers. *When all of this is behind us,* she thought, envisioning Trask's face, *then there will be time for you and me. Alone. Without the doubts. Without the lies...*

The sound of an approaching horse caught Tory's attention. The mare lifted her head and nickered softly to the approaching horse and rider before grazing again.

Tory shielded her eyes from the sun with her hand and recognized a large buckskin gelding and the man astride the horse. A smile eased over her features at the sight of Trask riding the gelding. Dressed in jeans and a cotton shirt, bareheaded to the sun, he looked as comfortable in the saddle as he did in a Senate subcommittee.

Tory forced herself to her feet and dusted her hands together as Trask dismounted and tethered the gelding near Tory's mare. "I was just thinking about you," she admitted, her lips lifting into a welcoming smile. "How did you know where to find me?"

"One of the hands, Eldon—at least I think that's his name—" Tory nodded. "He saw you leave and told me which direction to take after saddling the buckskin for me."

"So much for privacy," she murmured.

"I didn't think you'd mind." He walked over to her and gently pulled her against him. Immediately she felt her body respond and the dormant stirrings of desire begin to waken deep in her soul.

"I don't, senator. Not much, anyway," she said teasingly, cocking her head upward to gaze at him. The late-afternoon sun caught in her hair, streaking the tangled auburn strands with fiery highlights of gold.

When she looked deep into his eyes she noticed the worry lingering in his gaze. The tautness of his skin as it stretched over his cheekbones and the furrow of his brow made her sense trouble. "Something's wrong," she said, feeling her throat constrict with dread.

He tried to pass off her fears with a patient smile, but his blue eyes remained intense, dark with a secret. "I was just thinking that it's about time we got married."

"What!" Though what he was saying was exactly what she wanted to hear, she couldn't hide the astonishment in her eyes.

"Don't look so shocked," he said coaxingly, kissing her tenderly on the forehead and squeezing his eyes shut against the possibility that he might never hold her again. "You know that it's something I've been talking about for the past three weeks."

"Wait a minute. What's going on? I thought we had an understanding that we had to get things settled between us. What about the note and the dead calves and your theory about another person being involved in the Quarter Horse swindle—"

"None of that will change." His voice was calm, his jaw hard with determination.

It was then that real fear gripped her throat. "You know something, don't you?" she asked, with the blinding realization that he was hiding something from her. She pulled away from his embrace and felt her heart thud with dread.

The pain in his eyes was nearly tangible and the lines near his mouth were grim with foreboding. "I want you to marry me, as soon as possible."

"But there has to be a reason."

"How about the fact that I can't live without you."

"Level with me, Trask."

"I am. I want to spend the rest of my life with you and I thought you wanted the same."

"I do…but something isn't right. I can see it in your eyes. What happened?" she demanded.

Trask pushed his hands through his hair and his broad shoulders slumped. "I just came from John Davis's office," he admitted.

John Davis. The private investigator. Tory's voice trembled slightly. "And?"

"And he came up with some answers for me."

"Answers that I'm not going to like," she surmised, taking in a deep breath.

"Yes."

"About Dad?"

"No."

Trask turned and met her confused gaze. "John Davis did some digging, thorough digging. He even went back to the penitentiary to double-check with George Henderson about what he'd discovered. George decided to come clean."

"About what?"

"Your father was innocent, Tory. Just as you believed."

So that was it! Trask's guilt for condemning an innocent man to prison was what was bothering him. Relief washed over her in a tidal wave and tears of happiness welled in her eyes. If only her father were still alive he could be a free man. "But that's wonderful news," she said, stepping closer to him.

The look he sent her could have cut through steel. "There's more. Your father wasn't involved with Linn Benton and George Henderson but someone else was."

She froze and the first inkling of what he was suggesting penetrated her mind. "Who?"

"Your brother, Tory. Keith was an integral part of the horse swindle."

Tory didn't move. She let the words sink in and felt as if her safe world was spinning crazily away from her. Cold desperation cloaked her heart. "But that's impossible. Keith was only sixteen. He didn't even know Judge Benton or…George…"

"He knew George Henderson, Tory. George was the local vet. He'd been out to the ranch more times than you can remember. He liked your brother. Keith had even gone hunting with him on occasion."

"But he was just a boy," she said, feeling numb inside. "It just doesn't make any sense, none of it."

"Why do you think Keith reacted so violently to my return to Sinclair?"

"He has reason to hate you."

"And fear me."

Tory's mind was clouded with worried thoughts, pieces of the puzzle that weren't fitting together. She walked away from Trask, pushed her hands into the back pockets of her jeans and stared into the lake, not noticing the vibrant hue of the water. The gentle afternoon breeze lifted her hair from her face. "I don't believe you," she whispered. "If Keith had been involved with Linn Benton and George Henderson, it all would have come out at the trial."

"Unless your father paid for your brother's crime."

"No!" She whirled to face him. Her eyes were wide with new understanding and fear.

"Why else wouldn't Calvin defend himself?" He reached forward and grabbed her upper arms, his fingers digging into the soft flesh. She was forced to stare past the anger of his eyes to the agony in his soul. "Your father sacrificed himself, Tory. So that your brother wouldn't have to go to some correctional institution or prison."

"No! I won't believe it!" A thousand emotions raged within her: love, hate, anger, fear and above all disbelief. "You're grasping at straws because that investigator found out that Dad was innocent."

"God, woman, do you think I made this up?" he asked, his voice cracking with emotion. "Do you think I enjoy watching you fall apart? Do you think I wanted to come out here and tell you that I was wrong, that I'd made some horrible mistake about your father and that your only living relative was the real criminal?"

She placed her head in her hands and closed her eyes. "I don't know, Trask."

"Marry me," he said, desperately trying to hold on to the love they had shared. "Don't think about anything else, just marry me."

"Oh, God, are you crazy?" she threw back at him, her chest so tight she could barely breath. "After what you just told me, you want to marry me." Her eyes became incredibly cold.

"I don't want to lose you again," he said, his fingers clutching her upper arms in a death grip.

Again she buried her face in her hands trying hopelessly to make some sense of what he was telling her, trying not to let her feelings of love for this man color her judgment. She swallowed with difficulty before lifting her eyes and meeting his stormy gaze. "I...I just can't believe any of this."

"Can't or won't?"

"Same thing," she pointed out, feeling suddenly alone in an alien world of lies and deception. "I won't believe it and I can't. Keith was with me at the trial, helped me here at the ranch. He's grown into a good man and now you're trying to make me believe that he was capable of swindling the public, being a part of a gruesome murder and letting my father go to prison in place of him? How would you feel if I'd just said the same thing to you?" Tory was shaking, visibly fighting to keep from breaking down.

"I don't know," he admitted, his voice harsh, "because I've lived the past five years without my brother."

"It's all happening again," Tory whispered, swallowing back the lump forming in her throat. "Just like before." She felt as if her heart was slowly being shredded by a destiny that allowed her to love a man who only wanted to hurt her. "And you're the one to blame." She shook her head and let the tears run freely. "I suppose you think that Keith beat you up, shot the calves and wrote threatening notes to both me and Neva?"

"I don't know," Trask said. "But I wouldn't rule it out."

"And what does your crackerjack ace detective think?" she asked, her voice filled with sarcasm.

"He knows he's found out the truth. He knows that some of the testimony of the original trial was faulty at best and maybe downright lies at the worst."

"Including yours?" she asked. Trask's jaw hardened and his eyes glittered dangerously, but Tory couldn't help the outrage overtaking her. *Keith. A criminal!* It couldn't be. She wouldn't sit still and let her only brother be given the same sentence as her innocent father. She had to fight back against the fates that were continually at odds with her happiness. "And I suppose Mr. Davis feels obligated to set the record straight."

"It's his job."

She smiled bitterly through her tears. "And what about you, senator? Is it your duty as well?"

"I've only wanted two things in my life: the truth and one other thing."

"I don't want to hear it," she whispered.

"You can't hide from it, Tory. I want you. All of you. No matter what else happens, I want you to be with me for the rest of my life." He lifted his head proudly and she realized just how difficult confronting her had been for him.

Her heart felt as if it were breaking into a thousand pieces. "Then why do you continue to try and ruin me?" she choked out, her eyes softening as she looked past the pain in his. "Must we always be so close and yet so distant?"

He reached for her, but she drew away. Her eyes were filled with tears and she didn't care that they ran down her cheeks and fell to her chest. "Please, just trust me," he asked so softly that she barely heard the words.

"I don't know if that's possible," she replied. She straightened her spine and attempted to tell herself that she could live without him. She had before. She would again, despite the gripping pain in her chest. "I...I think we should go back to the house." She turned toward the mare but the sound of his voice stopped her dead in her tracks.

"Victoria?" he said and she pivoted to face him. "I'll always love you."

She squeezed her eyes tightly shut, as if in so doing she could deny the painful words. *How desperately she had loved Trask and now she wished with all of her heart that she could hate him.*

They rode back to the house in silence, each wrapped in private and painful thoughts. Though dusk was gathering over the meadows, painting the countryside in vibrant lavender hues and promising a night filled with winking stars and pale light from a quarter moon, Tory didn't notice.

Keith's pickup was parked near the barn. Tory's heart began to race at the thought of the confrontation that was about to take place. She silently prayed that just this once Trask was dead wrong.

After Eldon offered to unsaddle and cool the horses, Tory walked with Trask back to the house. They didn't touch or speak and the tight feeling in Tory's chest refused to lessen.

"About time you showed up," Keith shouted down the stairs when he heard Tory walk into the house. "I'm starved." The knot in the bottom of her stomach tightened at the sight of her brother as he came down the stairs. His shirt was still gaping open and he was towel-drying his hair. "What say we go into Bend and catch a movie and then we'll go to dinner—my treat..." His voice faded when he saw Trask. He lowered the towel and smiled grimly. "I guess you probably have other plans." He stopped at the bottom step and noticed her pale face. "Hey, what's wrong?"

"There's something Trask wants to ask you about," Tory said, her voice quavering slightly.

"So what else is new?" Keith cast an unfriendly glance at Trask before striding into the kitchen.

"It's a little different this time," Trask remarked, following the younger man down the short hallway.

"Oh, yeah? Good." Keith chuckled mirthlessly to himself. "I'm tired of the same old questions." He seemed totally disinterested in Trask's presence and he rummaged in the refrigerator for the jug of milk.

Alex was whining at the back door and Keith let the old collie into the house. "What's the matter, boy?" he asked, scratching the dog behind the ears. "Hungry?"

The sight of her brother so innocently petting the dog's head tore at Tory's heart. "Keith—" Tory's words froze when she noticed Rex's pickup coming down the drive.

"What?"

"Maybe we should talk about this later," she said.

"Talk about what?" Keith poured a large glass of milk, then drank most of it in one swallow.

"About what happened five years ago," Trask stated.

"I thought you said you had come up with some new questions."

"I have." The edge to Trask's voice made Keith start.

"Not now—" Tory pleaded, desperation taking a

firm hold of her. She had already lost her father and the thought of losing Keith the same way was unbearable.

Though he felt his stomach tighten in concern as he studied the pale lines of Tory's face, Trask ignored her obvious dread, deciding that the truth had to be brought into the open. "No time like the present, I always say." He watched with narrowed eyes as the foreman climbed out of his pickup and started walking toward the house. "Besides, Rex should be part of this."

"Part of what?" For the first time Keith noticed the worry in his sister's eyes. "What's going on?" he insisted. "Don't tell me we got another one of those damned notes!"

"Not quite."

"Oh, Keith," Tory whispered, her voice cracking.

Rex rapped on the back door and entered the kitchen. His eyes shifted from Tory to her brother before settling on Trask and he felt the electric tension charging the air. "Maybe I should come back later—" he said, moving toward the door.

"No." Trask swung a chair around and straddled the back. "I think that you can help shed a little light on something I've discovered."

"You're still going at it, aren't you?" the foreman accused. He lifted his felt hat from his head and worked the wide brim between his gnarled fingers. "You're worse than a bullterrier once you get your teeth into something."

"Trask's private investigator has come up with another theory about what happened five years ago," Tory explained, her worried eyes moving to her brother.

Keith bristled. "What do you mean 'another theory'?"

"John Davis seems to think that your father was innocent," Trask said, silently gauging Keith's reaction.

"Big deal. We've been telling you that for years."

"But you wouldn't tell me who Calvin was protecting."

"What!" Keith's face slackened and lost all of its color. Tory felt as if her heart had just stopped beating.

"John Davis seems to think that your father was covering for you; that you were the man called 'Wilson' that was involved with Linn Benton and George Henderson."

"Wait a minute—" Rex cut in.

Tory's eyes locked with the foreman's anxious gaze. *Oh, my God, he knows what happened,* she realized with a sickening premonition of dread. Her chest felt tight and she had to grip the counter for support.

"What do you know about this?" Trask turned furious eyes on the foreman.

"Keith wasn't involved with the likes of Henderson and Benton," the foreman said, his face flushed, his grizzled chin working with emotion.

"Davis can prove it," Trask said flatly.

Dead silence.

"How?" Tory asked.

Trask took the envelope from his jacket and tossed it onto the table. "Someone, a man who worked for Linn Benton when he was judge, saw Keith. George Henderson verified the other guy's story."

"No!" Tory screamed, her voice catching on a sob. *Not Keith, too. She wouldn't, couldn't lose him.*

"Back off, McFadden," Rex threatened, his eyes darting to the rifle mounted over the door before returning to Trask.

Keith's shoulders slumped and he looked up at the ceiling. "No, Rex, don't. It's over—"

"Shut up!" the foreman snapped, his cold eyes drilling into Trask and his gnarled hands balling into threatening fists. "You just couldn't leave it alone, could you?"

"Why are you standing up for him? Were you involved, too?" Trask suggested.

"Save it, Rex," Keith said, his eyes locking with those of his sister. "He obviously knows everything." Keith's hands shook as he opened the envelope and skimmed through the contents of John Davis's report.

"Not everything. Maybe you can fill in a few of the missing blanks."

"Oh, God, Keith," Tory said, shaking her head, her voice strangling in her throat. "You don't have to say anything."

"It's time, Sis. I knew it the minute McFadden showed up here. I let Dad cover for me because I was young and scared. I don't have those excuses to hide behind any more."

"Please," she whispered.

"You promised your father," Rex reminded Keith.

"And it was a mistake. A mistake that you and I have had to live with for five years," Keith said. "I know what it's done to me and I can see what's happening to you."

"You were in on it, too?" Trask said, his voice stone-cold.

"No, he wasn't involved," Keith said.

"Wait a minute," Tory said, realizing that Keith was about to confess to a man who would ultimately want to see him sent to prison. "You don't have to say anything that might incriminate you—you should talk to a lawyer…."

"Forget it, Tory. It's time I said what's on my mind. Even if McFadden hadn't come back, I would have told the truth sooner or later. It wasn't fair for Dad to take the rap for me, or for Dad to expect Rex to protect me."

A deathly black void had invaded her heart and she felt as if her world was crumbling apart, brick by solid brick. *All because of Trask.*

"What happened?" Trask asked persistently. Every muscle in his body was tight from the strain of witnessing what this confrontation was doing to Tory. Maybe he'd been wrong all along he thought, maybe, as Keith and Neva had so often suggested, he should have forgotten it all and just fallen in love with Tory again. As it was, she was bound to hate him. He could read it in her cold gray-green eyes.

"George Henderson approached me," Keith was saying. "He asked me if I would help him with some horses he wanted hidden up on Devil's Ridge. All I had to do was keep quiet about it and make sure that no one went up to the ridge. I was stupid enough to agree. When I found out what was going on, how he and Linn Benton were switching expensive Quarter Horses for cheaper ones, I told George I wanted out. George might have gone for it, but the judge, he wouldn't let me out of the deal...told me I was an accomplice, even if an unwitting one. And he was right. No doubt about it, the judge knew the law from both sides. And I did know that something shady was going on. I just didn't realize how bad it was...or...or that it could mean a stiff jail sentence."

"So you were in over your head," Trask said without emotion.

Keith nodded and Tory's eyes locked with her brother's dull gaze before he looked ashamedly away from her.

"But you could have come to me or to Dad," Tory said, feeling dead inside. *First her father and now Keith!*

Her chest felt so tight she had to fight to stand on her feet. Closing her eyes, she leaned against the wall for support.

"No way could I have come to Dad or you. How could I let you know how bad I got suckered, or that I had let someone use our property to conduct illegal business? I was already a failure as far as Dad was concerned; you were the responsible one, Sis."

"We were a family, Keith," she moaned. "We could have helped you—"

"What about the horses? The ones from the Lazy W?" Trask cut in, knowing that he had to get this inquisition over fast before Keith could think twice about it. And Tory. God, he wished there was a way to protect and comfort her.

"I switched the horses," Keith admitted. "I figured that I was in too far to back out. If I didn't agree, Benton promised to tell Dad."

Trask's fingers rubbed together and a muscle in the back of his jaw clenched and unclenched in his barely concealed rage. "So what about my brother?" he asked, his voice low and cold.

"I had no idea that Jason was on to us," Keith said, his gray eyes filled with honesty. "I knew that Benton and Henderson were worried about being discovered but I didn't know anything about the insurance company investigation or your brother's role as an investigator."

"He's telling the truth," Rex admitted, wearily sliding into a chair and running his hands through his thinning hair.

"But what about the conversation that Tory overheard?"

Tory's disbelieving eyes focused on Rex.

"It was part of the ruse. Staged for your benefit," Rex said, returning Tory's discouraged stare. "Once Linn Benton approached your father and told him about Keith, Calvin was determined as hell to sacrifice himself instead of his boy. He had to make everyone, including you, Tory, believe that he had been a part of the swindle. He didn't know anything about the plot to kill Jason McFadden. That was Linn Benton's idea."

Tears had begun to stream down Tory's face. She swiped at them with the back of her hand, but couldn't stem the uneven flow from her eyes. She shuddered from an inner cold. "So Dad wouldn't testify on the stand because he wanted to protect Keith?"

"That's right," Keith said, tears clouding his vision. Angrily he sniffed them back.

"Your dad knew he was dying of cancer; it was an easy decision to sacrifice himself in order that his son go free," Rex explained.

"And you went along with it," Tory accused, feeling betrayed by every person she had ever loved.

"I owed your dad a favor—a big one."

Tory took in a shuddering breath. "I don't want to hear any more of this," she said with finality. "And I don't want to believe a word of it."

"We can't hide behind lies any longer," Keith said, squaring his shoulders. "I'll call Sheriff Barnett tonight."

"Wait!" Tory held up her hand. "Think about what you're doing, Keith. At least consider calling a lawyer before you do anything else!"

Keith came over to her and touched her shoulders. "I've thought about this too long as it is. It's time to do something—"

"Please…" she begged, clinging to her brother as if by holding on to him she could convince him of the folly of his actions.

Keith smiled sadly and patted her back. "If it makes you feel any better I'll call a lawyer, just as soon as I talk Barnett into coming out here and taking my statement."

"I wish you wouldn't—" Rex said.

"You're off the hook," Keith said, releasing his sister and walking from the kitchen and into the den. Tory sat in a chair near the doorway and refused to meet Trask's concerned gaze.

"So you were the one who shot the calves, right?" Trask asked the foreman once Keith had left the room.

Rex frowned and lifted his shoulders. He couldn't meet Tory's incredulous gaze. "I thought you would stop the damned investigation if you discovered any threats to Tory."

"So you sent the note?" Tory asked.

"I'm not proud of it," Rex admitted, "but it was all I could think of doing." His chin quivered before he raised his eyes to meet Tory's wretched stare. "I promised your old man, Tory. You have to believe I never meant to hurt you or the ranch… I…I just wanted to do right by your dad." His voice cracked and he had to clear his throat. "Your father hired me when no one else in this town would talk to me." He turned back to Trask. "I just wish it would've worked and you would've gone back to Washington where you belong instead of stirring up the lives of good decent people and making trouble."

Tory's head was swimming in confusion. So Keith had been involved in the Quarter Horse swindle and her father had only tried to protect his young son. And Rex, feeling some misguided loyalty to a dying man, had kept the secret of Keith's involvement. Even the foreman's fumbling attempts to deter Trask were in response to a debt that had been paid long ago.

"I reckon I'd better talk to the sheriff as well," Rex said, forcing his hat back on his head and walking down the hall to the den where the soft sound of Keith's voice could be heard.

Trask got out of the chair and walked over to Tory. He reached for her but she recoiled from him. Not only had Trask put her father in jail five years earlier, but now he was about to do the same to her brother.

"Tory—"

"Don't!" She squared her shoulders, stood, shook her head and looked away from him while her stomach twisted into painful knots. *How could this be happening?* "I don't want to hear reasons or excuses or anything!" Cringing away from him she backed into the kitchen counter.

"This had to come out, y'know."

"But you didn't have to do it, did you? You didn't have to drag it all out into the open and destroy everything that's mattered to me. First my father and now my brother. God, Trask, when you get your pound of flesh, you just don't stop, do you? You want blood and tears and more blood." Tears ran freely down her cheeks. "I hope to God you're satisfied!"

Trask flinched and the rugged lines of his face seemed more pronounced. He ran his fingers raggedly through his windblown hair and released a tired sigh. "I wish you'd believe that I only wanted to love you," he whispered.

"And I wish you'd go to hell," she replied. "I'd ask you if you intend to testify against my brother, but I already know the answer to that one, don't I?"

His lips tightened and the pain in his eyes was overcome by anger. "I had a brother once, too. Remember? And he was more than a brother. He was a husband and a father. And he was murdered. *Murdered*, Tory. Keith knew all about it. He just didn't have the guts to come clean."

"That's all changed now, hasn't it? Thanks to you."

"I didn't want it to end this way," he said, stepping closer to her, but she threw up her hands as if to protect herself. He stopped short.

"Then you should never have started it again. Face it, senator, if there was ever anything between us, you've destroyed it. Forever!"

"There are still a lot of unanswered questions," he reminded her.

"Well, just don't come around here asking for my help in answering them," she retorted. "I'm not a glutton for punishment. I've had enough to last me a lifetime, thanks to you."

Trask stood and stared at her. His blue eyes delved into her soul. "I won't come back, Tory," he warned. "The next move is yours."

"Just don't hold your breath, senator," she whispered through clenched teeth before turning away from him. For a moment there was silence and Tory could feel that he wanted to say something more to her. Then she heard the sound of his retreating footsteps. They echoed hollowly down the hallway. In a few moments she heard the front door slam shut and then the sound of Trask's Blazer roaring down the lane.

"Oh, God," she cried, before clamping a trembling hand over her mouth. Tears began streaming down her face. "I love you, Trask. Damn it all to hell, but I still love you." The sobs broke free of her body and she braced herself with the counter.

"Get hold of yourself," she said, but the tears continued to flow and her shoulders racked with the sobs she tried to still. "I never want to see him again," she whispered, thinking of Trask and knowing that despite her brave words she would always love him. "You're a fool," she chastised herself, lowering her head to the sink and splashing water over her face, "a blind lovesick fool!"

Knowing that she had another investigation to face this night, for surely Sheriff Barnett and his deputy would arrive shortly, she tried to pull herself together and failed miserably. She leaned heavily against the counter and stared into the dark night. Far in the distance she saw the flashing lights of an approaching police car.

"This is it," she said softly to herself. "The beginning of the end…"

Chapter 12

The courtroom was small and packed to capacity. An overworked air-conditioning system did little to stir the warm air within the room.

Tory sat behind Keith. She tried to console herself with the fact that Keith was doing what he wanted, but her heart went out to her brother. He hadn't been interested in hiring an attorney, in fact, he had petitioned the court to allow him to represent himself. Even the district attorney was unhappy with the situation, but Keith had been adamant.

He looks so young, Tory thought as she studied the square set of her slim brother's shoulders and the proud lift of his jaw. *Just the way Dad had faced his trial.* Tory had to look away from Keith and swallow against the thick lump that had formed in the back of her throat.

The district attorney had already called several witnesses to the stand, the most prominent being George Henderson, who had been accompanied by a guard, when he testified. Not only did George tell the court that Keith, not his father, Calvin, had been in on the Quarter Horse swindle, but he also explained that Linn Benton had blackmailed Calvin into admitting to be a part of the scam.

According to Henderson, Linn Benton had been interested in recruiting Keith as a naive partner in order to have some leverage over Calvin Wilson and the Lazy W. Linn Benton knew that Calvin would never let his son go to prison and a deal was made. Calvin would accept most of the guilt in order to keep Keith's name out of the scam.

"Then what you're suggesting, Mr. Henderson," the soft-spoken D.A. deduced, "is that Calvin Wilson's only crime was that of protecting his son."

"Yes, sir," an aged Henderson replied from the stand. He had thinned considerably in prison and looked haggard. While he continuously rubbed his hands together, a nervous twitch near his eyes worked noticeably.

"And that Linn Benton was blackmailing Calvin Wilson with his son's life."

"That's about the size of it."

"Then Keith Wilson knew about the horse swindle."

"Yes."

Tory cringed, but Keith didn't flinch. A murmur of disapproving whispers filtered through the hot room.

"And he was aware of the deal struck between his father and Judge Linn Benton?"

Henderson nodded.

"You'll have to speak up, Mr. Henderson. The court

reporter must be able to hear you. She can't record head movements," the elderly judge announced.

Henderson cleared his throat. "Yes, Keith Wilson knew about the blackmail and the deal," he rasped.

The district attorney paused and the courtroom became silent. "And did he know about the plan to kill Jason McFadden?"

George Henderson's wrinkled brow pulled into a scowl. "No."

"You're sure?"

"Yes," George answered firmly. He met Keith's stony gaze before looking away from him. "Benton did it all on his own. He only told me a few minutes before Jason McFadden's car exploded. By then it was too late to do anything about it." The old vet's shoulders slumped from the weight of five years of deceit.

"And why didn't you go to the police?"

"Because I was afraid," George admitted.

"Of being apprehended?"

"No." George shook his head and the twitch near his left eye became more pronounced. "I was afraid of crossing Linn Benton."

"I see," the district attorney said, sending a meaningful look to the jury. "No further questions."

Keith refused to cross-examine Henderson, as he had with all of the prosecution's witnesses. Tory felt sick inside. It was as if Keith had given up and was willing to accept his fate. For the past week, she had tried to get him to change his mind, hire an attorney and fight for his freedom, but her brother had been adamant, insisting that he was finally doing the "right" thing by his father.

"Don't worry about me," he had said just before the trial. "I'll be fine."

"I can't help but worry. You're acting like some sacrificial lamb—"

"That was Dad," Keith answered severely. "I'm just paying for what I did. It's my time."

"But I need you—"

"What you need is to run the ranch yourself, or better yet, make up with McFadden. Marry the guy."

"Are you out of your mind?" she had asked. "After everything he's done? I can't believe you, of all people, are suggesting this."

Keith just shook his head. "I did hate him, Tory, but that was because of fear and guilt. I knew, despite what I said, that Trask wasn't responsible for Dad being sent to prison and dying. It was my fault. All McFadden ever wanted was the truth about his brother and you can't really blame him for that."

"How can you feel this way?" she asked incredulously.

"It's easy. I've seen how you are when you're around him. Tory, face it, you were happier than you'd been in years when he came back to Sinclair." His gray eyes held those of his sister. "You deserve that happiness."

Tears had formed in her eyes. "What about you?"

"Me, are you kiddin'?" he had joked, then his voice cracked. "I'll be having the time of my life."

"Seriously—"

"Tory, this is something I've got to do and you won't change my mind. So take my advice and be happy... with McFadden."

"He's responsible—"

Keith lifted a finger to her lips. "*I'm* responsible and

it's time to pay up. Believe me, it's a relief that it's all nearly over."

Several other witnesses came to the stand, all painting the same picture that Keith was an ingrate of a son who had used his martyred father to protect himself.

When Trask was called to the stand, Tory felt her hands begin to shake. Until this point he had sat in the back of the courtroom and though Tory could feel his eyes upon her, she had never looked in his direction, preferring to stare straight ahead and watch the proceedings without having to face him or her conflicting emotions.

Trask seemed to have aged, Tory thought, her heart twisting painfully at the sight of him. He looked uncomfortable in his suit and tie. His rugged features seemed more pronounced, his cheeks slightly hollow, but the intensity of his vibrant blue eyes was still as bright as ever. When he sat behind the varnished rail of the witness stand, he looked past the district attorney and his eyes met Tory's to hold her transfixed. For several seconds their gazes locked and Tory felt as if Trask could see into her soul. Her throat tightened and her breath seemed trapped in her lungs.

"Senator McFadden," the D.A. was saying. "Would you describe in your own words why you came back to Sinclair and what you discovered?"

Trask tore his gaze away from Tory's and his voice was without inflection as he told the court about the series of events that had started with the anonymous letter he had received in Washington and had finally led to the arrest of Keith Wilson, as part of the Quarter Horse swindle that Trask's brother, Jason, was investigating when he was killed five years earlier.

Reporters were busy scribbling notes or drawing likenesses of the participants in the trial. The room was filled with faces of curious townspeople, many of whom Tory recognized. Anna Hutton sat with Tory, silently offering her support to her friend. Neva sat across the courtroom, her face white with strain. Several of the ranch hands were in the room, including Rex, who had already given his testimony. At Rex's side was his young wife, Belinda.

As Trask told his story, Tory sat transfixed. Though it was stifling hot in the old courtroom with the high ceilings, Tory shuddered and experienced the icy cold sensation of *deja vu*. Trask's shoulders slumped slightly and the smile and self-assurance that had always been with him had vanished.

This has been hard on him, Tory thought, realizing for the first time since Keith had confessed that Trask did care what happened to her. He was a man driven by principle and was forced to stalk anyone involved in the murder of his brother. And if the situation were reversed, and Keith had been the man murdered, wouldn't she, too, leave no stone unturned in the apprehension of the guilty parties?

She twisted her handkerchief in her lap and avoided Trask's stare.

"So tell me, senator, how you found out that the defendant was part of the horse swindle."

"I had a private investigator, a man by the name of John Davis, look into it."

"And what did Mr. Davis find out?"

"That Keith Wilson, and not his father, Calvin, was a partner to Linn Benton and George Henderson."

Tory felt sick inside as the questioning continued.

The D.A. opened his jacket and rocked back on his heels. "Did Mr. Davis find out who sent you the first anonymous letter to Washington?"

"Yes."

Tory's eyes snapped up and she felt her breath constrict in her throat. *Who was responsible for bringing Trask back to Oregon? Who knew about Keith's involvement and wanted to see him go to prison?*

"The letter came from Belinda Engels," Trask stated. Tory took in a sharp breath. "Belinda is the wife of Rex Engels, the foreman of the Lazy W."

"The same man who was sworn to secrecy by Calvin Wilson before he died?"

"Yes."

"Thank you, Senator McFadden. No more questions."

When Keith declined to cross-examine Trask, the senator was asked to step down. With his eyes fixed on Tory, Trask walked back to his seat, and Tory felt her heart start to pound wildly. Even now she couldn't look at him without realizing how desperately she loved him.

The district attorney called Belinda Engels to the stand and Tory watched in amazement as the young woman with the clear complexion and warm brown eyes explained that she had spent five years watching her husband's guilt eat at him until he became a shell of the man she had married.

"Then you knew about Keith Wilson's involvement in the horse swindle?"

"No," she said, looking pointedly at Keith. "I only knew that Rex was sure another man was involved. One night, not long after it happened, Rex woke from a horrible nightmare. Against his better judgment, he told me that he was covering for someone and that Calvin Wilson wasn't involved in the murder. I just assumed that the other man was someone connected to Linn Benton. I...I had no idea that he was Keith Wilson."

"And even though you knew that an innocent man was on trial five years ago, you didn't come forward with the information."

Belinda swallowed. "I...I thought that Rex might be charged with some sort of crime and I didn't think he'd be given a fair trial because of his past...with his ex-wife." Tory sitting silently, watched as the red-haired young woman struggled against tears.

"But you and your husband both knew that Calvin Wilson was innocent."

Belinda leveled her gaze at the district attorney. "My husband's a good honest man. He promised to keep Calvin's secret. I did the same."

Tory closed her eyes as she pictured her father and all of the suffering he had accepted for Keith's involvement with Linn Benton. Tears burned at the back of her eyes but she bravely pushed them aside.

The rest of the trial was a blur for Tory. She only remembered that Keith spoke in his own defense, explaining exactly what happened in the past and why. Since he had pleaded guilty to the charges, the only question was how stiff a sentence the judge would impose.

When Tory left the courtroom, her knees felt weak. She held her head high, but couldn't hide the slight droop of her shoulders or the shadows under her eyes. The past few weeks had been a strain. Not only had the trial loomed over her head, but she had been forced to deal with nosy reporters, concerned friends, and worst of all the absence of Trask in her life. She hadn't realized how difficult life would be without him. She had grown comfortable with him again in those first warm weeks of summer. Since he had discovered Keith's secret, there was a great emptiness within her heart, and life at the Lazy W alone was more than Tory could face at times.

Lifting her head over the whispers she heard in the outer hallway of the courthouse, she walked down the shiny linoleum-floored corridor, through the front doors and down the few concrete steps into the radiant heat of late July in central Oregon.

She stepped briskly, avoiding at all costs another confrontation with the press. At the parking lot, she stopped short. Trask was leaning against her pickup watching her with his harsh blue eyes.

After catching the breath that seemed to have been stolen from her lungs at the sight of him, Tory lifted her chin and advanced toward Trask. Her heart was pounding a staccato beat in her chest and her pulse jumped to the erratic rhythm, but she forced her face to remain emotionless.

Trask pushed his hands deep into his pockets, stretching his legs in front of him as he surveyed her. Dressed in a cool ivory linen suit, with her hair swept away from her face, Tory looked more like royalty or a sophisticated New York model than an Oregon rancher. He grimaced slightly when he noticed the coldness of her gaze as she approached. She stopped in front of him, her head slightly tilted to meet his gaze.

"Are you happy?" she asked, inwardly wincing at the cynicism in her words. She noticed him flinch.

His teeth clenched and a muscle worked in the corner of his jaw. The hot summer wind pushed his hair from his face, exposing the small lines etching his forehead.

The sadness in his eyes touched a very small, but vital part of Tory's heart.

"No."

"At least satisfied, I hope."

He frowned and let out a long sigh of frustration. "Tory, look. I just wanted to say goodbye."

She felt a sudden pain in her heart. "You're...you're leaving for Washington," she guessed, surprised at how hard it was to accept that he would be on the other side of the continent. *If only she could forget him, find another man to love, someone who wouldn't destroy all she had known in her life.*

"The day after tomorrow."

She stiffened. "I see. You wanted to stick around for the sentencing, is that it?"

His face hardened, but the agony in his blue eyes didn't diminish and her feelings of love for him continued to do battle in her heart. Rex and Keith had been right all along. Trask had used her to promote himself and his damned political career. Already the papers were doing feature articles about him; painting him as some sort of martyred hero who had come back home to capture his brother's killers. *Only Keith hadn't killed anyone!*

"I just hoped that we could..." He looked skyward as if seeking divine guidance.

"I hope that you're not going to suggest that we be friends, senator. That's a little too much to ask," she said, but the trembling of her chin gave away her real feelings.

"I wish that there was some way to prove to you that I only did what I had to do, and that I didn't intend to hurt you." He lifted a hand toward her and she instinctively stepped backward.

"Don't worry about it. It won't happen again. All my family is gone, Trask. There isn't anyone else you can send to prison." She walked around to the driver's side of the truck and reached for the door handle, but Trask was there before her. His hand took hold of hers and for a breathless instant, when their fingers entwined, Tory thought there was a chance that she could trust him again. God, how she still loved him. Her eyes searched his face before she had the strength to pull away. "I have to go."

"I just want you to be careful, some things still aren't clear yet."

She shook her head at her own folly of loving him. "Some things will never be clear. At least not to me."

"Listen… I thought you'd want to know that I've instructed John Davis to keep watching the ranch."

"What!"

"I think there still may be trouble."

"That's impossible. It's all over, Trask."

"I don't think so."

"Call him off."

"What?"

"You heard me!" She pointed an angry finger at Trask's chest. "Tell Davis that I don't need anyone patrolling the ranch. Furthermore, I don't want him there. I just want to forget about this whole damned nightmare!" Her final words were choked out and she felt the tears she had managed to dam all day begin to flow.

"Tory…" His voice was soft, soothing. His fingers wrapped possessively over her arm.

"Leave me alone," she whispered, unable to jerk away. "And tell that private investigator of yours to back off. Otherwise I'll have the sheriff arrest him for trespassing."

"I just want you to be safe."

"And I want you out of my life," she lied, finally pulling away and jerking open the door of the pickup. With tears blurring her vision, she started the truck and drove out of the parking lot, glancing in the rearview mirror only once to notice the defeat in Trask's shoulders.

Tory hadn't been back at the Lazy W very long before the telephone rang. She had just stepped out of the shower and considered not answering the phone, but decided she couldn't. The call could possibly be from Keith.

Gritting her teeth against the very distinct possibility that the call was from another reporter, she answered the phone sharply.

"Hello?"

"Ms. Wilson?" the caller inquired.

Tory grimaced at the unfamiliar voice. "This is Victoria Wilson."

"Good. Don Morris with Central Bank."

The young loan officer! Tory braced herself for more bad news. "Yes?"

"I just wanted to let you know that the loan committee has seen fit to grant you the funds you requested."

Tory felt as if she could fall through the floor. The last thing she expected from the bank was good news. Nervously she ran her fingers through her hair. "Thank you," she whispered.

"No problem at all," the loan officer said with a smile in his voice. "You can pick up the check the day after tomorrow."

"Can you tell me something, Mr. Morris?" Tory asked cautiously. She didn't want to press her luck, but the bank's agreement to her loan didn't seem quite right. She felt as if she were missing something.

"Certainly."

"The last time I came to see you, you insisted that I didn't have enough collateral for another loan with the bank. What happened to change your mind?"

"Pardon me?" She could almost hear the banker's surprise.

"You haven't had a change of policy, have you?"

"No."

"Well?"

The young banker sighed. "Senator McFadden agreed to cosign on your note."

Tory's eyes widened in surprise. "What does Senator McFadden have to do with this?"

"He talked with the president of the bank and insisted that we lend you the money. The senator owns quite a chunk of stock in the bank, you know. And the president is a personal friend of his. Anyway, he insisted that he cosign your note."

Blood money! "And you agreed to it?"

"You did want the loan, didn't you? Ms. Wilson?"

"Yes…yes. I'll clear things up with the senator," she replied, her blood rising in her anger as she slammed down the phone. "Bastard," she whispered between clenched teeth.

It occurred to her as she towel-dried her hair and pulled on her jeans that Trask might have cosigned on the note to the bank as a final way of saying goodbye to her. After all, he did appear sincere when he said he hadn't wanted to hurt her.

"Oh, God, Trask, why can't we just let it die?" she wondered aloud as she took a moment to look out the window and see the beauty of the spreading acres of the ranch. As August approached the countryside had turned golden-brown with only the dark pines to add color and contrast to the gold earth and the blue sky. And Trask had given her the chance to keep it. It wasn't something he had to do. It was a gift.

"And a way of easing his conscience," she said bitterly, trying desperately to hate him.

Without really considering her actions, she ran outside and hopped into the pickup with the intention of confronting Trask one last time.

Dusk had settled by the time that Tory reached Trask's cabin on the Metolius River. Even as she approached the single story cedar and rock building, she knew that Trask wasn't there. His Blazer was nowhere in sight and all of the windows and doors were boarded shut.

He'd already gone, Tory thought miserably, her heart seeming to tear into tiny ribbons. As she ran her fingers over the smooth wooden railing of the back porch, she couldn't help but remember the feel and texture of Trask's smooth muscles and she wondered if she would ever truly be free of him, or if she wanted that freedom.

With one last look at the small cabin nestled between the pines on the banks of the swift Metolius, Tory climbed back into her pickup and headed into Sinclair. On the outskirts of the small town, she turned down the road where Neva McFadden lived.

Trask's Blazer was parked in the driveway.

Maybe he had turned to Neva. Keith had said that

Neva was in love with him. A dull ache spread through her at the thought of Trask with another woman, any other woman.

With her heart thudding painfully, Tory walked up the sidewalk and pounded on the front door. Almost immediately, Neva answered her knock.

"Trask!" she shouted before seeing Tory. The color drained from Neva's face. "Tory?" she whispered, shaking her head. "I thought that you might be Trask..." The blond woman's voice cracked and she had to place a hand over her mouth.

Tory felt her blood turn to ice water. "What happened? Isn't he here?" She lifted her hand and pointed in the direction of the Blazer but Neva only shook her head.

"I guess you'd better come in."

Neva led Tory into the house. "Where's Trask?" Tory asked, her dread giving way to genuine fear.

"I don't know. He...he and John Davis and Sheriff Barnett are looking for Nicholas."

Tory stood stock-still. When Neva lifted her eyes, they were filled with tears. "Where is Nicholas?" Tory asked.

"I...I don't know. Trask and I assume that he's been kidnapped."

"Kidnapped?" Tory repeated, as she leaned against the wall. "Why?"

"Because of the trial. Trask thinks Linn Benton is behind it."

"But how—?"

"I don't know. George Henderson told everything he knew about the swindle and that included some pretty incriminating things against Linn Benton. The blackmailing alone will keep him in the pen several more years," Neva said.

"Wait a minute, slow down. What about your son?"

"I came back from the trial and he was gone. There was just a note saying that I hadn't kept Trask from digging up the past and I'd have to pay."

"And you're sure that Nicholas didn't go to a friend's house?"

"Yes." Neva could stand the suspense no longer. Her tears fell freely down her face and her small body was racked with the sobs.

Tory wrapped her arms around the woman and whispered words she didn't believe herself. "It's going to be all right, Neva," she said. "Trask will find your son."

"Oh, God, I hope so! He's all I have left."

Gently Tory led Neva to the couch. "I think you should lie down."

"I can't sleep."

"Shh. I know, but you're a nurse; you've got to realize that the best thing to do is lie still. I'll…I'll make you some tea."

Neva reluctantly agreed. She sat on the edge of the couch, staring at the clock and wringing her hands with worry.

Tory scrounged around in Neva's kitchen and found the tea bags. Within a few minutes, she brought two steaming cups back to the living room.

"Thank you," Neva whispered, when Tory offered her the cup. She took a sip of the tea and set it on the arm of the couch, letting the warm brew get cold.

"They're going to kill Nicholas," she said firmly and tears ran in earnest down her cheeks.

"Don't talk that way—"

"I should never have told Trask. Oh, God—" Neva buried her face in her hands. "I'll never forgive myself if they hurt my baby—"

The knock on the door made Neva leap from the couch. "Oh, God, it's got to be Nicholas," she whispered, racing to the door to discover Deputy Woodward on the front steps.

"What happened?" she cried.

The grim deputy looked from one woman to the next. "We've found your boy, Mrs. McFadden."

Neva looked as if she would faint in relief. "Thank God. Is he all right?"

"I think so. He's in the hospital in Bend, just for observation. He appears unharmed. I'd be happy to drive you there myself."

"Yes, please," Neva said, reaching for her purse.

"Where's Trask?" Tory asked.

"Senator McFadden is in the hospital, too."

Tory felt sick inside and she paled. *What if something had happened to Trask? What if she could never see him again? What if he were dead?* Tory couldn't live without him.

Neva turned and faced the young deputy. "What happened?"

"The senator got into a fist fight with the man who kidnapped your son. It looks as if this guy might be the one that knocked Senator McFadden out and beat him up a few weeks ago—the guy who was shooting at you on Devil's Ridge."

"Who is he?" Tory demanded, fear and anger mingling in her heart.

"A man by the name of Aaron Hughs. He's the foreman of Linn Benton's spread, just north of Bend."

"And Hughs still works for him?"

"Appears that way." The deputy turned his attention to Neva. "Anyway, if it hadn't been for the senator, your boy would probably be across the state line by now. According to the sheriff, McFadden should be awarded some sort of medal."

"Then he's all right?" Tory asked.

"I think so."

"Thank God."

"How did you know where to find Nicholas?" Tory asked.

"Senator McFadden, he thought your son had to be somewhere on Linn Benton's ranch. As it turns out, he was right. The kid was tied to a chair in the kitchen."

A small cry escaped from Neva's lips. "Come on, let's go."

The trip to the hospital seemed to take forever. Tory closed her eyes and imagined Trask lying in a stark, white-sheeted hospital bed, beaten beyond recognition. *Oh, God, I've been such a fool,* she thought, knowing for the first time since Keith had been arrested that she would always love Trask McFadden. The few fleeting minutes that she had thought he might be dead had been the worst of her life.

Deputy Woodward took them into the hospital and straight into the emergency ward. Nicholas was sitting up on a stretcher looking white, but otherwise none the worse for wear. At the sight of his mother, he smiled and let out a happy cry.

Neva raced into his small arms and lifted him off the portable bed. "Oh, Nicholas," she cried, her tears streaming down her face. "My baby. Are you all right?"

"I'm not a baby," the boy insisted.

Neva laughed at Nicholas's pout. "You'll always be my baby, whether you like it or not."

It was then that Tory noticed Trask. He was seated on a gurney, his legs dangling over the side. His hair was messed and there was a slight bruise on his chin, but other than that he appeared healthy.

Tory's heart leaped at the sight of him and tears of relief pooled in her eyes. Without hesitation, Tory walked up to him and stared into the intense blue of his eyes. She placed a hand lovingly against his face. "Thank God you're alive," she whispered, her voice husky with emotion.

"You thought my constituents might miss me?" he asked, trying to sound self-assured. The sight of her in the noisy emergency room had made his stomach knot with the need of her.

"It wasn't your constituents I was concerned about, senator. It was me. I'd miss you…more than you could ever imagine," she admitted.

He cracked a small smile. "How did you know I was here?"

"I came looking for you." She wrapped both of her arms around his neck.

His eyebrows shot up, encouraging her to continue. "Because you were going to beg me to marry you?"

"Not quite. I was going to give you hell about co-signing on my loan."

"Oh." He let out a long groan. "I thought maybe you'd finally come to your senses and realized what a catch I am."

Her smile broadened and the love she had tried to deny for many weeks lighted her eyes. "Now that you mention it, senator," she said, pressing her nose to his and gently touching the bruise on his jaw, "I think you're right. You need me around—just to make sure that you stay in one piece. Consider this a proposal of marriage."

"You're not serious?"

"Dead serious," she conceded. "I love you, Trask and though I hate to admit it, I suppose I always have. If you can see your way clear to forgive me for being bull-headed, I'd like to start over."

His arms wrapped around her slender waist and he held her as if he was afraid she would leave him again. "What about Keith?" he asked softly.

"That's difficult," she admitted. "But he made his own mistakes and he's willing to pay for them. I only hope that he doesn't get a long sentence. I can't say that I feel the same about Linn Benton."

"I've already taken care of that. There are enough charges filed against him including blackmail and kidnapping to keep him in the penitentiary for the rest of his life.

"As for Keith, I talked to the judge. He's a fair man and I think he realizes that Keith was manipulated. After all, he was only sixteen when the Quarter Horse swindle was in full swing. That he finally turned himself in and confessed speaks well for him and he was absolved in the murder. My guess is that he'll get an extremely light sentence, or, if he's lucky, probation."

"That would be wonderful," Tory said with a sigh.

Trask slid off the bed and looked longingly into her eyes.

"Are you supposed to do that? Don't you have to be examined or something?"

"Already done. Now, what do you say if I find a way

to get released from the hospital and you and I drive to Reno tonight and get married?"

"Tonight?" She eyed him teasingly. "Are you sure you're up to it?"

"A few cracked ribs won't slow me down." He nuzzled her neck. "Besides I'm not taking a chance that you might change your mind."

"Never," she vowed, placing her lips on his. "You're stuck with me for the rest of your life, senator."

"What about the Lazy W?"

"I guess I can bear to be away from it for a little while," she said. "Just as long as I know that we'll come back home after you've finished terrorizing Capitol Hill."

"That might be sooner than you know. I'm up for re-election pretty soon."

"And if I get lucky, you'll lose, right?"

Trask laughed and held her close. "If you get lucky, we'll be in Reno by morning," he whispered against her ear.

"Trask!" Neva, holding a tired Nicholas in her arms, ran up to her brother-in-law. "Thank you," she said, her joy and thanks in her eyes. Her smile trembled slightly. "Thank you for finding Nicholas."

Trask grinned at Nicholas and rumpled his hair. "Anytime," he said. "We good guys have to stick together, don't we?"

"Right, Uncle Trask. Come on, Mom, you promised me an ice-cream cone."

"That I did," Neva said, shaking her head. "Now all I have to do is find an all-night drive-in. Want to come along?"

"Please, Uncle Trask?" Nicholas's eyes were bright with anticipation.

Trask shook his head. "Another time, Nick." Trask looked meaningfully at Tory. "Tonight I've got other plans. Something that can't be put off any longer."

Neva's smile widened and she winked at Tory. "I'll see you later," she said. "Good luck." With her final remark, she packed her son out of the hospital.

"So now it's just you and me," Trask said. "The way it should have been five years ago."

"Senator McFadden?" A nurse called to him. "If you just sign here, you're free to go."

Trask signed the necessary forms with a flourish. "Let's get out of here," he whispered to Tory, gently pulling on her hand and leading her out of the building.

"You're sure about this, aren't you?" he asked, once they had crossed the parking lot and were seated in his Blazer.

"I've never been more sure of anything in my life," she vowed. "I've had a lot of time alone to think. And even though I tried to tell myself otherwise, even as late as this afternoon, I discovered that I loved you. There was a minute when I thought you were dead…and…I can't tell you how devastated I was. Thank God you're alive and we can be together."

He lifted his hands and held her face in both palms. "This is for life, you know. I won't ever let you go."

"And I won't be running, senator."

When his lips closed over hers. Tory gave herself up to the warmth of his caress, secure in the knowledge that she would never again be without the one man she loved with all her heart.

* * * * *

Delores Fossen, a *USA TODAY* bestselling author, has sold over fifty novels, with millions of copies of her books in print worldwide. She's received a Booksellers' Best Award and an RT Reviewers' Choice Best Book Award. She was also a finalist for a prestigious RITA® Award. You can contact the author through her website at deloresfossen.com.

Books by Delores Fossen

Harlequin Intrigue

The Lawmen of McCall Canyon

Cowboy Above the Law
Finger on the Trigger
Lawman with a Cause

Blue River Ranch

Always a Lawman
Gunfire on the Ranch
Lawman from Her Past
Roughshod Justice

The Lawmen of Silver Creek Ranch

Grayson
Dade
Nate
Kade
Gage
Mason
Josh
Sawyer
Landon
Holden

Visit the Author Profile page
at Harlequin.com for more titles.

GUNFIRE ON THE RANCH

Delores Fossen

Chapter 1

Theo Canton wished there was a better way to stop a killer. Anything other than coming here to the Beckett Ranch to disrupt wedding plans. But if his intel was right, there could be another murder—tonight.

Maybe Ivy Beckett's murder.

Hell, maybe her entire family and Theo's sister, since they would possibly all be under the same roof for the ceremony. A ceremony that was to take place tomorrow.

Theo definitely didn't want a repeat of what had happened ten years ago when two people died at the hands of a killer. Just the thought of it put a knot in his stomach, along with bringing back old memories. He had to shove those memories aside, though, because they would only cause him to lose focus.

He had enough Beckett blood on his hands without adding more.

Theo took the final turn to the ranch and spotted the decorations already on the pasture fences. Blue satin ribbon flapping in the hot May breeze. There were no ranch hands out and about. No signs of a killer, either, but the snake could already be there, waiting to strike.

His phone buzzed, and he saw the name flash on the screen. Wesley Sanford, a fellow DEA agent who'd alerted Theo that there could be a problem, that a killer could be headed to the ranch. Theo kept his attention on the road, on his surroundings, too, but he hit the answer button to put the call on speaker.

"Anything?" Wesley asked right away.

"No, not yet. How about you?"

"I'll be at the Blue River sheriff's office in just a couple of minutes. I'll tell the deputies what's going on. I might even get the chance to speak to Gabriel himself."

Gabriel, the sheriff of the ranching town of Blue River as well as Ivy's brother. Well, one of them, anyway. Her other brother, Jameson, was a Texas Ranger.

"But I'm guessing that the sheriff won't be working this late the night before his wedding?" Wesley added.

Theo had no idea. He hadn't kept up with news on the Becketts. They were more of those old memories, and wounds, that he hadn't wanted in his life. Besides, the Becketts wouldn't want him keeping up with them. Or even want him around, for that matter. They'd made that crystal clear ten years ago. Theo had had no choice but to come tonight, though. Once the danger was over, however, he'd get out of there as fast as he had a decade ago.

"If Gabriel is at his office," Theo told Wesley, "remember not to say anything in the police station. Take him outside to talk." If their criminal informant had been right, the killer could have managed to plant a bug in the building. And in the sheriff's house. "I don't want this clown to know we're onto him. I want to catch him."

Wesley hadn't especially needed that reminder, but the stakes were too high for either of them to make a mistake. The last time Theo had made a mistake with the Becketts, Ivy's parents had been murdered. Maybe by this same killer who was after them now.

Or maybe by Theo's own father.

But if his father had actually been the murderer ten years ago, then tonight Theo was dealing with a copycat. Because his father was miles away behind bars in a maximum-security prison. Still, a copycat could be just as lethal as the original one had been.

Too bad Theo couldn't just sound the alarm and alert Ivy's brothers and the ranch hands, but that possible bug in Gabriel's house meant the only secure way for Theo to contact the Becketts was outside, face-to-face.

"Whether the sheriff is here or not, I'll let someone know there might be a bug," Wesley assured him. "Call me when you can."

Theo hit the end-call button on his phone just as he reached the top of the hill, and the ranch house came into view. Well, one of the houses, anyway. From what he'd learned, there were now four on the grounds. One for Gabriel. Another belonging to Jameson. The third was one Gabriel's deputy and longtime friend, Cameron Doran, had built.

It was the fourth house, though, that contained the bad memories.

Because that was where Ivy's parents had been murdered. No one lived there and hadn't since, well, since that night.

According to the quick check Theo had done before he'd left for Blue River, Ivy's house was hours away in a rural area near Houston. Apparently, Theo wasn't the only one who'd left Blue River after the murders.

Other than her address, there hadn't been a lot of info to find on Ivy, though she had listed herself as widowed on the tax documents for her small ranch. So she'd not only moved on physically but also emotionally with another man she'd married and lost. Theo felt a hit of the jealousy before he quickly reined it in. Ivy wasn't his, hadn't been for a long time, so of course she had moved on. That's what normal people did.

Theo hadn't considered himself *normal* in a while now.

He stopped his truck beneath a cluster of trees only about twenty yards from Gabriel's house. Theo drew his gun and made his way to the side of the wraparound porch. There were plenty of shrubs where he could hide and have a line of sight to all four houses. However, he'd barely gotten into position when he heard something he didn't want to hear.

"Drop your gun," someone snapped.

Hell. How had a person managed to get so close without him noticing? And it wasn't just any ordinary someone, either. Theo recognized that voice even after all these years.

Ivy.

He turned, slowly, and he spotted her at the back corner of the house. Thanks to the light coming from one of the windows, he had no trouble seeing her face.

And the rifle she was pointing at him.

Apparently, she had no trouble seeing him, either,

because she whispered his name on a rise of breath. What she didn't do was lower her weapon.

Theo said her name, and it had far more emotion in it than he wanted. Of course, any drop of emotion was too much right now, since he didn't want their past playing into this. She was his ex-lover, emphasis on the *ex*. All he wanted now was to do his job and get the heck out of there.

Ivy didn't say anything else, but she started walking toward him. Her attention volleyed between his face and his gun, which he lowered to his side.

"I was getting something from Gabriel's office when I glanced out the window and saw you," she finally said. "We didn't expect you. Judging from the way you were sneaking around, you didn't want us to see you."

No, he hadn't wanted the killer to see him.

"I had to come," he told her. "I found out...something."

Ivy flinched a little and came even closer until she was only about a foot away from him. She hadn't changed much in the past ten years. She was almost thirty now and still had that thick, dark brown hair that fell just past her shoulders. Still had the same intense eyes. He couldn't see the color of them in the darkness, but he knew they were sapphire blue.

Despite Theo's not wanting to feel anything, he did. The old attraction that for some stupid reason felt just as strong as it always had. But he was also feeling something else. The anger. That's why he kept watch around them.

"I guess you heard about the wedding. Are you here to see your sister?" she asked.

"No." Best not to get into the fact that he hadn't seen his kid sister, Jodi, in a long time. Because that was a different set of bad memories. Not because he didn't love her. He did. But Jodi was a reminder that he'd failed her, too. She'd nearly gotten killed the same night as Ivy's folks, and he hadn't been able to stop it. Now, all these years later, she was marrying Gabriel Beckett.

So obviously Gabriel and Jodi had managed to work through their shared painful pasts. He guessed they'd found their "normal."

"It's not safe for us to be out here," Theo explained. "We need to get in my truck so we can talk."

She didn't budge, but she did follow his gaze when he looked around again. "You heard about the threatening letter," Ivy said.

No, he hadn't, but it got his attention, and Theo shook his head. "What letter?"

Ivy huffed, and she finally lowered her gun. "The latest one had a warning that my brothers, my sister and I would all be murdered on the anniversary of our parents' deaths."

Which was only two months away.

Ivy's tone practically dismissed the threat her family had gotten. But Theo wasn't dismissing anything. "You get a lot of letters like that?"

"Enough. Emails, too, and the occasional phone call from blocked numbers. If you didn't know about that, then why are you here?" she asked without hesitating. "And why did you say it wasn't safe for us to be out here?"

"Because it's not." He took a deep breath. "You know I'm a special agent in the DEA?"

Her mouth tightened, and she nodded. "Gabriel says you're what law enforcement calls a joe."

That was the slang term for it all right. An agent who

went into deep cover, sometimes years at a time. Just as Theo had done. In fact, he was less than a month out of a three-year assignment where he'd infiltrated a militia group to track the sale of drugs.

"Yes," he verified, "and I have access to criminal informants who give me intel from time to time. According to one of those informants, there's a killer coming here to the ranch tonight."

Her eyes widened. Then narrowed just as fast. She looked ready to bolt, of course, but he saw her quickly rein that in. "How reliable is this so-called intel?"

Good question. "Reliable enough for me to come to a place where I know I'm not welcome."

She stayed quiet a moment. "You could have just called," Ivy pointed out, confirming his notion about his not being welcome.

He shook his head. "According to the informant, the killer managed to bug both the sheriff's office and Gabriel's house."

Theo saw another punch of concern on her face, maybe some skepticism, too, and she had another look around as Theo did. "This killer is connected to my parents' murders?"

"The informant says the killer is." Theo paused. "But the informant also said this is the same guy who murdered your folks."

Ivy groaned. Mumbled some profanity under her breath. "We know who killed them. Your father, Travis Canton. And he's sitting in jail right now because there was more than enough evidence to prove he'd done it."

No, there was more than enough evidence to *convict* him. That was splitting hairs, but since his father couldn't remember if he'd murdered the Becketts, Theo still had his doubts.

"Travis hated my parents," Ivy reminded him as if he'd said those doubts aloud. "He threatened them just hours before the murders. And when the deputies found him by the creek, he had my father's blood on his shirt."

All of that was true. What she could have added was that Travis was an alcoholic who'd experienced blackouts, both that night and others. He could have killed the Becketts in a drunken haze and not even remembered.

Or someone could have set him up.

Someone waiting to finish the job by killing the Becketts' children.

"Your father was the sheriff at the time of his murder," he continued. What he was about to say would be old news to her, but he wanted to remind her that everything might not be black-and-white here. "Your mother was a former cop. They had plenty of enemies because of the arrests they made over the years. One of those enemies could be coming after you tonight, and that's why you don't need to be standing out here."

There was a bit more worry in her eyes this time when she glanced around. But she still didn't budge.

Now it was Theo's turn to mumble some profanity. "Look, I know Gabriel, Jameson and your sister, Lauren, won't want me inside—"

"Lauren's not here and won't be coming. She left town around the same time you did and hasn't been back."

Theo couldn't fault her for that. Lauren was the youngest, had been barely eighteen when she'd been made an orphan. Like Theo, she had no doubt wanted a fresh start.

"I'm sorry," he said, because it sounded as if Ivy

was hurt that Lauren wasn't there. It was a hurt he understood. "Hell, maybe my own sister won't want me here, either. But can we at least sit in my truck while I convince you that this threat could be real?"

"And how will you do that?" she asked. Yeah, he'd been right about that skepticism.

"I've got a recording from the criminal informant. He knew some things about the night of the murders. Things that weren't revealed to the press. He says the killer told him those things."

Her attention slashed toward the house. "Gabriel will need to hear this." And now there was some urgency in her voice.

Yes, he would. Jameson, too. And Jodi. "But not inside. Remember, there could be listening devices. If the killer knows we're onto him, it could send him back underground where he could prepare for another attack. And next time, we might not get a heads-up from a CI."

He could see the debate going on inside her, and with each passing second, Theo's unease escalated. It really wasn't a smart idea for them to be outside.

"Your brothers don't trust me," he added. "I get that."

Man, did he. Because for a short period of time after the Becketts were murdered, Theo had been a suspect.

His father wasn't the only one who'd had bad blood with Ivy's parents.

Just hours before their murder, Theo had had a run-in with Ivy's father, Sherman, and Sherman had told him in no uncertain terms that he was to stop seeing Ivy, that she didn't need a bad boy in her life. Theo had been furious, even though Sherman had been right—Ivy had deserved something better.

"Yes," Ivy whispered as if she knew exactly what

he was thinking. "But let's not allow old water and old bridges to play into this. Gabriel needs to hear this recording and decide if it's something we should be worried about."

Yes, and her brother *would* be worried once he heard what the CI had to say.

Ivy motioned for him to follow her. Not to his truck but rather to the back of the house. She hurried, thank God, which meant it had finally sunk in that she was in danger. But since she was clearly taking him inside, Theo had to speak up.

"Remember the part about a possible bug. When we're inside, whisper." That might not be enough if the listening device was sensitive and had a wide range, but at this point he just wanted her out of the line of possible fire.

She led him onto the porch and through the back door, but Ivy stopped in a mudroom, where there were raincoats on wall pegs and cowboy boots stashed beside a wooden bench. A reminder that this was indeed a working ranch. Gabriel wasn't just a sheriff, but also raised cattle and horses. There were cans of paint and what appeared to be scaffolding, as well.

"There was a fire last month," Ivy said, following his gaze. "An attack. That's why I want to make sure another one doesn't happen."

He wanted the same thing, especially since Theo had read about that attack. His sister had been the target, and even though the guy was now dead, he'd clearly left his mark.

"I'll have Gabriel come back here." Ivy put the rifle on the top shelf of the storage closet, took out her phone from her jeans pocket and sent off a text.

Theo had another look around, shut the back door and then glanced out the single window that was in the small room. Ivy reached for the light switch to turn it on, but he stopped her. Of course, that meant touching her, and he got another sucker punch of the old heat.

A third sucker punch when their gazes met.

She didn't say anything, but Theo thought maybe she had felt it, too. He also thought maybe she was fighting to push it away as hard as he was. Yes, she was a widow, but after everything they'd gone through, she probably didn't want to have another round with him any more than he did with her.

"It's not a good idea to be this close to a window," Theo insisted. And yes, he whispered. "We should at least get down."

She clamped her teeth over her bottom lip for a couple of seconds. A gesture he'd seen her do so many times. Nerves. But she finally ducked down so that her head wouldn't be anywhere near the glass. Theo ducked, too, but he stayed high enough so he could continue to glance out and make sure the killer wasn't sneaking up on them.

The moments crawled by, and with each one of them Theo became well aware of the close contact between them. It was hard to fight the attraction and the old memories when they were this close. And when he caught her scent.

Hell.

For just a split second, the image of her naked body flashed into his head.

Thankfully, the image didn't stay. It vanished when he heard the voice and the sound of footsteps. It was yet another voice he recognized. Gabriel's.

Theo braced himself for whatever Gabriel might dole out. He could just order Theo out of there, but Gabriel barely spared him a glance when he stepped into the doorway. That's because he was on his phone, and he took his sister by the arm and moved her out of the mudroom and into the adjacent kitchen.

Once Gabriel had done that, he finished his call, slipped his phone back into his jeans pocket and finally looked at Theo. This time, it was more than a glance.

"What the hell did you do? Who did you bring with you?" Gabriel demanded. But he didn't give Theo a chance to answer. "One of the ranch hands just called. He spotted an armed man crawling over the back fence, and the man's making his way to the house right now."

Chapter 2

Ivy's heart slammed against her chest. She had already been feeling so many emotions, including dread and fear, but this was a different kind of fear.

There's a killer coming here to the ranch tonight.

She hadn't exactly dismissed Theo's warning, but Ivy had prayed he was wrong. Apparently not, though. Because she doubted an armed intruder had good intentions. And according to Gabriel, he was on his way to the house. Ivy would have bolted toward the front stairs if Gabriel hadn't taken hold of her arm again.

"I've already told the others to lock up and get down," her brother said. "They're fine." He slapped off the kitchen lights and tipped his head to the back door where Theo and she had entered. "Lock that," he added to Theo. Theo did, and Gabriel used his phone to arm the security system.

"There could be listening devices planted in the house and at your office." Theo hurried into the kitchen with them. "Who else is here?" Theo asked at the same moment that Gabriel threw out a question of his own.

"What do you have to do with the armed guy?"

Judging from the glare Gabriel aimed at Theo, her brother felt his question had priority over Theo's. Theo must have felt the same way, because he started talking.

"I don't know who he is, but I have a recording of a CI who says that a killer is on the way to the ranch. I didn't call because supposedly this killer had managed to plant bugs in the house and the sheriff's office, and I didn't want to tip him off that we were onto him. But obviously we're past the point of being worried about tipping him off."

"Yeah." A muscle flickered in Gabriel's jaw. "How long had Theo been here before you texted me?" he asked her.

"Just a few seconds." That was possibly true. Ivy honestly had no idea how long it'd been. Time had sort of frozen when she'd come face-to-face with the man she'd never expected to see again.

Gabriel stared at her as if he might challenge that, but then he growled out, "Follow me."

Ivy was certain that put some renewed panic in her eyes, certain that her brother saw it as well, but Gabriel kept moving, anyway. "We'll go into my office."

Not upstairs. Though that's where Ivy wanted to go. "Nathan," she said.

"He's in the guest room with Jameson and Jodi," Gabriel quickly answered. "They moved him into the bathroom and will make sure he's all right."

That steadied Ivy a little. Jameson was a lawman,

and Jodi had been trained as a private security specialist. Still, Ivy didn't want a gunman anywhere near the house or anyone in her family.

"Nathan?" Theo asked.

"Ivy's son," Gabriel said before she could answer. "If this gunman makes it to the house, he'll be seriously outnumbered. But it might not even come to that, because I have three armed ranch hands headed out to stop him."

Gabriel must have made those arrangements shortly before he'd come to the mudroom. Good. Ivy wanted every precaution taken. Correction: she *needed* it, because she had to keep Nathan safe.

"You have a son?" Theo asked, his voice practically a whisper now.

"Yes." She didn't give any other details. No time. Because Gabriel spoke again.

"I want to know everything about the recording," Gabriel insisted, glancing at Theo again. "I want to hear what this CI has to say."

Theo nodded and followed Gabriel into his office, which was just off the family room on the bottom floor. There were plenty of windows here, but Gabriel had already shut the blinds and drapes. He also didn't turn on the lights. No doubt because it would alert anyone close enough to the house that there was someone in that particular room.

However, her brother did go to one of the windows that faced the back of the house, and he opened the blinds just enough so he could keep watch. Theo did the same to the window across from Gabriel. That one would give him a view of the side of the house. While the inside of the house was practically dark, there were security lights on the grounds, so maybe they'd be able to see this monster coming.

"Is there an extra gun in here?" Ivy asked.

"Bottom right drawer," Gabriel quickly provided. It was locked, but he rattled off the combination, and she took out a Glock he had stashed there. She wasn't an expert marksman, not by any stretch of the imagination, but she would use it to defend her son if necessary.

"The CI is someone who regularly gives me intel," Theo started. "I'll write down his name for you later. In case the place really is bugged, I don't want to compromise his identity. The other person you'll hear on the recording is a federal agent. He's the one who sent me this, and the voices have been altered—again so that no one will be compromised."

While still keeping a grip on his gun, Theo took out his phone and hit the play button. He held it up so that Gabriel would be able to hear it, and it didn't take long before the man's voice began to pour through the room.

"I heard some stuff," the man said. "Stuff about them Becketts. I figured I oughta tell you because that family's been through enough."

Yes, they had been. The murder of their parents. Also the near murder of Gabriel's bride-to-be, Jodi. It had changed their lives forever.

It was still changing them.

"There's a killer coming after them," the man went on. "I don't know the fella's name, but I heard him talking at the Silver Moon Bar over on St. Mary's Street. He said he'd been hired—and these are his words, not mine—*to put some more Becketts in the ground*. He said he was going to the Blue River Ranch tonight to finish off as many of them as he could."

A chill slid through Ivy, head to toe, and she felt her stomach clench into a tight knot. "God, will this never end?" she said under her breath.

Ivy clearly hadn't said that softly enough, because it caused both Theo and her brother to look back at her. Theo hit Pause. He stared at her as if he might need to intervene in some way. Definitely not something she wanted. Nor did she want to give in to the fear. So she went to the window next to Theo in order to help him keep watch.

Theo continued to look at her while he volleyed glances out the window, but he finally hit the play button again.

"Describe the man who said that." It was a second person on the recording. Theo's fellow agent, no doubt. "And did he say who hired him?"

"Didn't mention a word about that," the CI answered. "Of course, it wouldn't have been too smart if he had. And I couldn't exactly ask him without maybe gettin' my own self killed. But he was tall, bulky. Built like one of those navy SEALs or something."

Theo looked at Gabriel then, and her brother nodded. "That matches the description of the man the ranch hand saw."

"How do you know this hired gun is for real?" the agent asked the CI.

"'Cause he knew things, that's why. Things about Sheriff Sherman Beckett and his wife, Millie, who got killed ten years ago. It was all over the news, but this fella told me there was something the news didn't mention. Something that the cops kept out of the papers. He said the killer took Sherman Beckett's watch. Pulled it right off his dead wrist. And that he took Millie's necklace. It was a heart-shaped locket and had pictures of her kids in it."

It was true. All true. Those items had indeed been missing, though they hadn't been found on the killer, Theo's father, Travis. Ivy had always assumed that Travis had dropped them or hidden them somewhere, but how would this man have known that?

That didn't help the knot in her stomach, and Ivy had to fight to hang on to what little composure she had left. She had prayed this was all some kind of misunderstanding, that the CI had been wrong, but apparently no such luck. There really was a killer headed to the house who had plans to finish them all off.

"Did this hired gun say anything else?" the agent pressed. "Anything that would help us figure out who's paying him to do this?"

"Nope, but I figure it's gotta be Travis Canton. Yeah, I know he's in jail, but something like this could get him out from behind bars."

Theo didn't say anything, but even in the near darkness, she saw his jaw tighten. "I've already checked with the prison," Theo volunteered, "and other than his lawyer, my father hasn't had any visitors in the past week. Plus, he doesn't have the funds to hire a hit man."

So maybe this was the work of some kind of psycho groupie. There'd been so much interest in the murders, partly because Jodi had also been attacked and left for dead in a shallow grave. And all that interest had attracted some very sick people.

"I know you gotta tell this to the Becketts," the CI went on a moment later, "but you oughta be careful when you do it. The fella at the bar said he'd put bugs in the sheriff's place and his house. So if you say anything to them, sure as hell don't mention my name. I don't want that SOB comin' after me."

"That's the end of the conversation," Theo told them. "But you can see why I had to come."

Yes, she could. Since the CI had been right about the hired killer, maybe he was right about that bug, too. It sickened her to think that someone had been spying on them, listening to their every word. Someone who now wanted to kill them.

Her brother must have realized that, too, because he cursed and fired off a text. Several seconds later, his phone buzzed. He set it aside and put it on speaker, no doubt to keep his hands free for his gun.

"Sorry, Gabriel," the caller immediately said. It was Aiken Colley, one of Gabriel's ranch hands. "But we lost sight of the guy."

That was not what Ivy wanted to hear, and she made a frantic search of every part of the grounds that she could see. No signs of a gunman. No signs of anyone.

Gabriel cursed. "Where was he when you last saw him?"

"By the south barn."

That wasn't that far from the house. Worse, there were other outbuildings and fences between the house and that particular barn, and this man could use those to conceal himself so he could get closer.

"I never had a clean shot of him," Aiken went on. "The guy was running, and every few seconds, he would duck behind cover. Jake and Teddy are out here with me, and I've alerted the other hands."

Jake and Teddy were two other hands, and while none of the hands were in law enforcement, they all knew how to handle guns. But apparently this hired killer knew how to dodge those guns.

"If possible, I want this guy alive," Theo said.

Gabriel didn't disagree with that. Probably because a dead man couldn't give them answers, but at the moment Ivy cared only about keeping this monster away from Nathan and everyone else in the house.

"Kill him only if necessary. And be careful," Gabriel warned the ranch hand.

"We will. We'll keep looking for him until we find him," Aiken added before he ended the call.

Ivy got back to keeping watch. Not that she hadn't been doing that, but she adjusted her position just enough so that she could try to take in more of the yard and the pastures. Still no sign of him, but she could almost feel him closing in on them.

Who the heck was putting this monster up to this?

The CI had said it was Travis, and perhaps it was. Maybe he'd somehow gotten the money. But there was also another possibility. One that had been a thorn in her family's side since Travis had first been arrested.

"Could your uncle August be behind this?" Ivy asked Theo. "Because August has been adamant that Travis is innocent."

August was Travis's half brother. A hothead. In the past ten years, he'd never turned to violence to free his brother, but August could be getting desperate since Travis had exhausted all his appeals.

"I haven't spoken to August since I left Blue River," Theo answered. "I tried to call him, but he didn't answer. If he had anything to do with this, I'll deal with him."

Judging from Theo's tone, that would not be pleasant. Not a surprise. There was no love lost between Jodi and their uncle, and it appeared to be the same for Theo. Of course, that was probably because August was not an easy man to like, and he was always saying that Travis's "ungrateful kids" weren't doing enough to help their father.

Theo's phone buzzed. "It's the agent who recorded the conversation with the CI," Theo relayed to them, but he didn't mention the guy by name. However, as Gabriel had done, he put the call on speaker. "The gunman's here," Theo told the agent right off. "Not in the house, but it appears this is where he's headed."

The agent didn't jump to answer. It seemed as if he took a moment to process that. "You want me out there?"

"Not yet. This goon could fire shots at you as you drive up. Plus, I don't want to send him running."

Part of Ivy wanted him to run. To get as far away from Nathan as possible. But Theo was right. If the guy ran, he could possibly just regroup and come back for a second attempt.

"Did you find any bugs in the sheriff's office?" Theo asked.

"Not yet, but the deputies are looking. One of them spoke to Gabriel a little while ago. He stepped outside to do that."

"Cameron," Gabriel provided. "He called the moment the agent showed up at the office."

Of course he had. He wouldn't have kept Gabriel in the dark about something this big. That meant Gabriel had been plenty busy in the short time since all of this mess had started with Theo's arrival.

"The deputy wants to know if you need backup," the agent continued.

"Not yet," Gabriel answered before Theo could say anything. "But keep watch, because there might be more than one hired gun. Whoever's behind this could have sent someone there."

Oh, mercy. She hadn't even considered that. But if someone had indeed wanted to put the Becketts "in the grave," then the person might have gone looking for Gabriel at work.

"I just got a call," the agent continued. "The CI is dead."

Other than hearing she had a son, Theo hadn't seemed surprised by much of what had happened. But he was clearly surprised now. And riled. "How the hell did that happen?"

"We're not sure yet. We had a tail on him, just in case he tried to follow the hired gun or something, but the tail stayed a safe distance back. He saw someone dressed all in black gun the guy down."

Ivy doubted that was a coincidence, and that meant… Oh, God.

"Was this all a setup?" she asked. Neither Gabriel nor Theo jumped to deny that, and that only caused her heart to pound even harder. "You think the hired gun wanted Theo to come here?" she added.

Again, they didn't deny it. "If so, it worked," Gabriel mumbled, and he tacked on some profanity.

Yes, it had. But what did it mean? It didn't take Ivy long to come up with something that she didn't want to consider.

All the "survivors" of the murders were now under the same roof. Gabriel, Jameson, Jodi, Theo and her.

Along with their sister, Lauren, all five of them had been either in the house where her parents were murdered or on the grounds. Which meant they had all been possible witnesses to the crime.

Possible, but they actually hadn't been.

Ivy had been in her upstairs bedroom with her headphones on. And crying. Because of the blowup that Theo had just had with her folks. The music had been so loud that she hadn't heard her mother and father being murdered in the room just below her. Some people had told her that it was a blessing she hadn't heard because if she had, she would have gone downstairs and possibly been killed, too. But Ivy wished she had heard. Because she might have been able to save them.

Jodi hadn't heard the murders going on, either. She'd been outside, coming back from Gabriel's house, which was a short distance away. She'd been attacked that night. Not by the killer, though. But rather by her ex-boyfriend who'd been in a rage over their breakup. Since he was now dead, he was no longer a possible witness.

Jameson and Gabriel had been at their own houses, but they were close enough to the main ranch house that they could have seen something. They hadn't. But maybe the killer hadn't known or believed that.

"What could your father or August possibly hope to gain by eliminating witnesses?" Ivy came out and asked.

"They wouldn't," Theo answered.

She looked at Gabriel to see if he would argue that. He didn't. "If they wanted to clear Travis's name," Gabriel explained, "they could be desperate enough to arrange a murder. But Theo and Jodi wouldn't be the targets."

Because Travis still seemingly loved his children. Of course, that didn't exclude Travis's brother. August wasn't fond of Jodi or Theo. "This could all be something August put together."

"If August had come up with this plan to make my father look innocent," Theo went on, "he would have hired someone to stab his victim."

The way her parents had been killed.

Ivy was about to say that could be the hired thug's plan. But then she heard a sound that stopped her cold.

"Get down!" someone shouted. Aiken.

But there was no time to do that. Because a bullet came crashing through the window where Ivy was standing.

Chapter 3

Hell. Theo hadn't even seen the shot coming.

But he sure as heck heard it. Felt it, too, when the glass flew through the room and a piece of it sliced across his cheek. It stung, but he ignored it and scrambled toward Ivy so he could pull her to the floor. She had already started in that direction, but Theo helped her along by hooking his arm around her and dragging her about five feet away from the window.

Good thing, because another bullet tore through what was left of the glass.

"Stay down," Theo warned her, and he put her behind a huge leather chair so he could hurry back to the window. He didn't get directly in front of it but instead kept to the side.

This was exactly what Theo had been trying to stop. Ivy and her family had been through enough, but apparently that moron outside didn't feel the same. He was adding to their misery, and in doing so, he was putting an innocent child in danger. Theo didn't know how old Nathan was, but it was possible he was a baby.

"Do you see him?" Gabriel asked. He came to the window next to Theo and peered out through the edge of the blinds.

Theo looked over the grounds as best he could, but there were too many places their attacker could use for cover. A barn, several vehicles, shrubs and trees. However, it became a little easier to narrow down a hiding place when the next shot blasted through the air. Like the other two, this one slammed into the wall near the door, and it allowed Theo to pinpoint the man's location.

"He's on the right side of the barn," Theo relayed to Gabriel. "I can't see him, but I can see a rifle barrel."

Gabriel didn't waste any time. He tossed Ivy his phone. "Text Aiken and tell him to stay back from the barn." And like Theo, Gabriel took aim in that direction.

Theo didn't look back at Ivy, but he could hear the clicks on the phone as she wrote. However, they were soon drowned out by another shot. This time, it went through the window near Gabriel.

That must have been the final straw for Ivy's brother because he cursed, took aim at the barn and fired. Theo did the same, all the while watching to see if their attacker would show his face. He didn't. And he didn't seem put off by being shot at, because he continued to fire, as well. However, something was off because Theo could no longer see the rifle.

"I think he's trying to make a getaway," Theo mumbled. "I'll go after him." He didn't allow Gabriel or Ivy a say in that. Keeping low, Theo hurried toward the door.

"Disarm the security system so I can go out front but reset it as soon as I'm outside."

Theo had only been in Gabriel's house a time or two even though the man had lived there for going on thirteen years. Gabriel hadn't exactly been a fan of Theo's when he'd been dating Ivy, but Theo had dropped by a couple of times to pick her up there. That's why Theo knew the general layout, and he ran up the hall and through the family room to get to the front door.

Gabriel must have turned off the system because the alarm didn't go off when Theo eased open the door. However, he did hear a sound he didn't especially want to hear.

Footsteps behind him.

It was Gabriel. "You'll need help," Gabriel growled.

"You should stay with Ivy," Theo growled right back.

"She's the one who insisted I go with you." Gabriel didn't seem especially pleased about that.

This was part of that "old water, old bridge" thing between Theo and the Becketts. Still, Gabriel was a lawman, and he knew it was a stupid time to discuss this or anything else, especially all that old baggage. Gabriel rearmed the security system, this time using the keypad on the wall, and he shut the door. He then tipped his head to the left side of the house.

"I'll go that way," Gabriel said, "and make my way to the back. As soon as I get to the porch, I'll fire at the barn, but I'll keep my shots low to try to avoid a kill shot. You do the same from this side of the house. Ivy's texting the hands to let them know we're out here so they won't hit us by mistake."

Good. Gabriel had been thorough. Now, if everything played out as planned, they could catch this snake and get him to talk. If August or his father was involved, then there'd be hell to pay. Not just from Theo but from the Becketts.

Theo made his way to the side of the porch and peered around the edge. He was careful, but the gunman must have been looking for him because he sent a shot right at Theo. It smashed into the wood siding, tearing a hole in it.

That caused Theo to curse again, and he hoped like the devil that none of those shots made it through the wall where Ivy was or upstairs to the others. If the shots went in the direction of her son, Theo was almost certain that Ivy would go running up there, and in doing so she might get herself killed.

Theo waited, giving Gabriel a couple of seconds to get into place, and even though those seconds seemed to crawl by, he knew Gabriel was hurrying. And the next sound Theo heard was a shot coming from the direction where Gabriel had said he would be. Their attacker would obviously soon know that Gabriel was back there.

Theo leaned out, aiming low, and he fired two rounds. Almost immediately, he ducked back behind cover. Good thing, too, because the gunman fired off two rounds of his own at Theo. But Theo could also hear the man cursing. Maybe because he'd been hit. Perhaps because he realized that coming here alone had been a stupid mistake.

That last thought had no sooner crossed his mind when Theo felt that bad feeling crawl up his spine. It was a feeling that had saved his butt a few times, so he didn't ignore it. He pivoted, looking around him.

And spotted the second man near Theo's own truck. He was dressed all in black, armed with multiple weapons on an equipment belt. He had one weapon in his hand, as well. That's the one he aimed at Theo.

Theo fired first.

He double tapped the trigger, the shots slamming directly into the man's chest, and the guy dropped to the ground. Maybe dead or dying, but it was equally possible that he was wearing a Kevlar vest and had simply had the breath knocked out of him. If so, he could still be dangerous.

"There's a second gunman," Theo called out to Gabriel. "And there might be others."

Of course, Gabriel didn't need him to add that last part, but it was also, hopefully, a reminder for everyone inside to stay down. Especially Ivy. She was on the bottom floor and could easily be hit by bullets meant for Gabriel and him.

The guy by the barn fired another couple of shots, one of them in Theo's direction. At least one went toward Gabriel's office, though. Maybe the guy had thermal equipment or something because he seemed to know that there was still someone in that particular room. When the goon sent another shot at the office, Theo knew he couldn't wait.

He leaned out and fired.

Not low this time.

Theo sent some rounds in the area of the shooter's chest. And finally the shots stopped. Just like that, it was quiet again. Theo didn't hear any moaning or sounds of pain. Definitely didn't hear anyone trying to run away.

It was a risk. Anything he did at this point could be, but Theo left the porch and ran toward his truck, where the second gunman was still on the ground. He kept his gun ready, kept watch around him, too, but as he approached the man, he didn't see any movement.

But he did see blood.

It was on the ground around the guy, which meant he hadn't been wearing Kevlar after all. Theo touched his fingers to the man's neck.

Dead.

He didn't curse, though that's what he wanted to do. Maybe the other one was still alive.

Using shrubs for cover, Theo started making his way to the barn. "I'm back here," he called out to Gabriel.

But calling out to him wasn't necessary because Theo soon spotted the sheriff at the back of the house. Gabriel was closer to the barn now, heading toward the first gunman. And he wasn't alone. There was another man with Gabriel. One of the hands no doubt.

"Are the hired killers dead?" Ivy asked, and that's when Theo realized she was at one of the blasted-out windows.

"Get down!" Theo ordered her.

He hurried past Ivy but not before he got a glimpse of her face. She was too pale and had a death grip on the gun she'd taken from her brother's desk, but she appeared to be unharmed. Physically, anyway. This had to be triggering flashbacks of her parents' murders. Also triggering new fears of the danger to her son and family.

Gabriel and the hand got to the gunman ahead of Theo, and Theo braced himself for Gabriel to say the guy was dead. He didn't.

"Ivy, call an ambulance," Gabriel shouted. "Tell the medics to hurry."

Theo soon figured out why the hurry part was necessary. Just like the guy in the front yard, this one had gunshots to the chest, and he was bleeding out fast. Theo kicked away the guy's weapon just as Gabriel got right in the man's face.

"Who hired you?" Gabriel demanded, sounding very much like the lawman that he was.

The guy shook his head, and he opened his mouth as if to answer. But he didn't. His eyelids drifted down, and his head flopped back, prompting Gabriel to check for a pulse.

"He's still alive," Gabriel said, glancing at Theo. "Go back in and check on Ivy and the others. Ivy still has my phone so tell her to disarm the security system. Also let Jameson know what's going on."

Theo didn't like leaving Gabriel out there with just the hand, but he soon saw two other men making their way toward them. Not gunmen. These were dressed like ranch hands.

"I heard Gabriel," Ivy volunteered. Which meant she was still too close to the blasted window. "I turned off the alarm."

Good, because the sooner Theo got in the house, the sooner he could chew her out for taking a risk like standing too close to the window. But he didn't get a chance to even start the chewing out. By the time he was through the door and into the foyer, Ivy was already headed up the stairs. Theo shut the door and followed her.

She stopped at the top of the stairs, looked at him, and he saw that her bottom lip was trembling. Actually, she was trembling all over.

"There really could be others?" she asked. Her voice was as shaky as the rest of her.

"Maybe." And he hated that he even had to say that to her because it certainly didn't help with her frayed

nerves. "We just don't know who or what we're dealing with right now."

She nodded. But didn't budge. "I need a second to
calm down. I don't want Nathan to see me like this."

Theo understood that. As a single mom, she probably
wanted to be strong for her kid. But she took more than
a second, and the trembling seemed to be getting worse.
He figured it was a mistake, but since Theo didn't know
what the heck else to do, he put his arm around her.

Ivy automatically stiffened. Maybe because the last
time she'd been in his arms, they'd still been lovers.
But there was no trace of that attraction now, and Theo
heard her try to choke back a sob.

She pulled away from him, hiking up her chin. Or
rather, trying. She wasn't doing a very good job of it
until one of the doors opened and Jameson stuck out
his head.

"Are you okay?" Jameson asked, his attention going
straight to his sister.

She gave another nod. "Gabriel's with one of the
gunmen, the one who's still alive. The other guy's dead.
Theo had to shoot him."

Jameson's attention went to Theo then, and he
stepped back when Jodi came out of the room and into
the hall. She didn't hurry to Theo. She didn't curse him,
either. Considering that he hadn't contacted her in a
while, he deserved the cursing.

Ivy didn't linger in the hall, though. She pushed past
all of them and hurried into the room, no doubt to see
her son.

"You came because of these gunmen?" Jodi asked him.

"Yeah," Theo verified. "I tried to stop this."

Jodi made a sound of understanding, and this time

she went to him. Just as he'd done to Ivy, Jodi hugged him. For a couple of seconds, anyway. But then she eased back and punched him in the arm.

Hard.

"That's for not calling me." She punched him again. "That's for letting me think you might be dead or dying somewhere."

The emotion surprised him. So did the tears that sprang to his sister's eyes. Jodi wasn't the crying sort. Or at least she hadn't been the last time he'd seen her. But she hadn't been engaged to Gabriel Beckett then. Obviously, his sister had taken her life in a new direction.

"I love you," Jodi added. "And you're bleeding." She used the sleeve of her shirt to wipe his cheek.

Theo hadn't forgotten about the glass cutting him, but he also hadn't figured it was serious since he wasn't hurting.

"Who's with Gabriel?" Jodi asked.

"Three ranch hands."

Jodi glanced back at Jameson, and that seemed to be the only cue the Ranger needed to get moving. Maybe Jodi wanted her soon-to-be husband to have as much backup as possible.

"Wait here with them," Jameson said to Theo as he headed down the stairs. "And don't let them go outside until I say so."

Theo doubted Ivy would want to venture out of the house as long as that gunman was out there, but since his sister was already nibbling on her bottom lip and looking around, she might try to disobey Jameson's orders. Just in case that's what she had on her mind, Theo took Jodi by the arm.

"Is there a bathroom in here so you can get me a

cloth for this cut on my cheek?" he asked. Not that he particularly wanted to do that, but it would give Jodi something to do.

"Yes, this way."

Theo followed her into the bedroom and then to the attached bathroom. It wasn't that big, but it still took Theo a moment to spot Ivy because she was in the corner next to a claw-foot tub. She had a boy clutched in her arms.

Definitely not a baby.

This kid was older, school-age, and he was looking up at Ivy as if to comfort her rather than vice versa.

Jodi froze, practically in midstep. Ivy froze, too, but the boy turned and faced Theo. And Theo felt as if he'd just been punched in the gut. Because he knew that face. Or rather he knew the features, because he saw them every time he looked in the mirror.

Hell.

Ivy must have seen his reaction then, because she shook her head. Not a denial, exactly, since there was no way she could deny what Theo had just realized.

He was looking at his own son.

Chapter 4

Ivy could have sworn her heart stopped beating for a few seconds. Theo knew. God, he knew.

From the moment she'd seen Theo by the side of the house, Ivy had feared this might come. In fact, at first that's why she had thought Theo was there, that he'd found out about Nathan. It would have been safer if that's why he'd been there. But it wasn't going to be easy to deal with the storm that was brewing behind Theo's narrowed eyes.

"Who is that?" Nathan asked, his attention suddenly fixed on Theo. "He's not one of the bad men, is he?"

On the surface those were easy questions, but neither Ivy, Jodi nor Theo jumped to provide him with answers. Ivy wasn't even sure she could speak yet, and she doubted Theo could, either, because his jaw was clenched so tight.

"Uh, this is my brother, Theo." Jodi finally spoke up. "And no, he's not a bad guy. He's sort of a cop like your uncle Gabriel and uncle Jameson."

Because Ivy still had her arms wrapped around Nathan, she felt his muscles relax a little. It would probably be a while before he completely relaxed. Even when he did, this had changed everything for him. Her little boy had heard those gunshots, had felt the terror that went along with him.

There'd be nightmares.

Ones similar to hers, ones she'd been having for a decade. And Ivy silently cursed the gunmen for that. Silently thanked Theo, too, for warning them, or those two thugs might have made it all the way into the house. Then her son might have to deal with more than fear, tight muscles and nightmares. They could all be dead.

A thought that sickened her to the core.

At the moment, though, Theo probably wouldn't want her thanks. For anything. In fact, his shock had morphed into a glare that he was now aiming at her.

"How old are you?" Theo asked. His glare softened significantly when he looked at Nathan.

"Nine," her son answered, meaning Theo could narrow down the date he'd been conceived.

Theo clearly wasn't surprised by her son's answer. Not after seeing Nathan's face. In fact, Theo might even be able to remember the exact date of Nathan's conception. Because it was the same night of the big blowup between her parents and him. A blowup that'd happened because her mom had found Nathan and her in bed together.

All of those feelings came back, too.

Ivy pushed them aside, that mix of pleasure and

grief, and she got to her feet. It was obvious there were some things she needed to say to Theo. Obvious, too, that he had some questions for her, and she didn't want him asking those in front of Nathan. Eventually, her son would have to know the truth, but now wasn't the time. He wasn't ready for it. Heck, *she* wasn't ready for it.

"I'll stay with Nathan," Jodi volunteered. "He'll be okay."

Even though Ivy hadn't said anything to her, Jodi and she were on the same page about what needed to be done. But Ivy didn't want her explanation to Theo to come at the expense of her son's safety.

Theo didn't say anything, either. He just followed Ivy out of the ensuite bathroom and into the bedroom, and he pulled the bathroom door shut behind them. She didn't go far, just a few feet away. Hopefully close enough so she could still get to Nathan if there was another attack but far enough away from Theo so that they weren't in each other's personal space. Even though it did seem a little late for that since they'd once been lovers.

He stood there staring, and she could see he was trying to work out what to say to her. Hopefully, he wasn't going to yell at her, since she didn't want Nathan to overhear something like that. At least at the moment Theo wasn't yelling. In fact, he wasn't saying anything. Theo put his hands on his hips, shook his head and turned that glare on her again.

"Why?" he finally asked, and he did keep his voice at a whisper. An angry one that dripped with emotion.

Since that simple word could encompass a lot of territory, Ivy went with a simple explanation. "I couldn't find you to tell you I was pregnant."

Ivy watched him process that, and she knew it wasn't

something he could dispute. Theo had vanished shortly after the attacks. Jodi had been in the hospital, still recovering from her horrific injuries, and she certainly hadn't known how to get in touch with her brother.

"I left because you told me to leave," Theo reminded her.

She couldn't dispute that, either. Ivy had indeed ordered him out of her house and her life after the argument with her parents. In part, she'd done that for Theo's own safety. Because she'd been afraid her father was going to beat him up or have him arrested for something. No way would Theo believe that now, though. And even if he did, it would only make him madder than he already was. He wouldn't have wanted her fighting those kind of battles for him.

"Does Nathan know the truth?" Theo snapped.

Ivy shook her head, and she prayed Theo didn't rush out and tell him.

"How about your late husband?" Theo again. "Did he know?"

"Yes. His name was Chad Vogel, and Nathan was eleven months old when I married him. But Jameson, Lauren and Gabriel didn't know I was pregnant or that I had a child. Neither did Jodi. At least they didn't know until I came back to Blue River two days ago."

Now Theo cursed. "One of them should have called me. And don't say they couldn't find me, because Jameson's a Texas Ranger. He could have tracked me down if you'd asked him to do that."

"Yes," she repeated. "And FYI, Jodi said I should tell you after she finally met Nathan day before yesterday. I just thought it was best if I waited until after the wedding to do that."

Judging from his still-tight expression, Theo didn't agree. And maybe he was right. Maybe she should have searched harder for him, especially after her husband passed away.

Theo glared at her a few more seconds before he finally glanced away and cursed some more. "Is Nathan healthy? Is he okay?"

It seemed petty for her to hesitate even a second to give him that info. But she knew that with each new bit, Theo would only want to know more and more. Then he would want Nathan to know who'd really fathered him.

Theo. And not Chad.

Of course, Nathan didn't have a lot of memories of Chad anyway, since he'd died after losing his battle with cancer when Nathan had been only five.

"I'm sorry," she said. It didn't seem nearly enough, but there wasn't much else she could say or do at this point.

There was a sound outside the window, a car engine, and Theo hurried to look while motioning for her to stay put. Just like that, her heart revved up again. Not that it'd gone back to normal, and that might not happen for a long time.

"It's just the ambulance," Theo told her. He stayed at the window with his gun drawn.

She was glad that it'd arrived. Now maybe the medics could save the gunman so they could find out what the heck was going on. And soon. It was probably too much to ask to find the person responsible for this attack and get him behind bars so that Gabriel and Jodi could get on with the wedding, but Ivy prayed that would happen. Her brother and Jodi deserved to have their special day.

"Did you love him?" Theo asked.

The sound of his voice cut through her thoughts, and it took Ivy a moment to realize that he probably wasn't talking about Nathan. Of course she loved him. But Theo knew that and was asking about Chad.

"Yes. I did."

In some ways that was a lie, but Ivy wasn't about to get into that now. Besides, what Theo probably wanted to know was how she could go so quickly from him to another man. Especially when she'd had Theo's child. But it was because of Nathan that she'd agreed to marry Chad. Once Theo got past the initial kick of anger, she'd maybe tell him more.

More that he wasn't going to want to hear.

"Does it look as if the gunman is still alive?" Ivy said. It was definitely time for a change of subject, because whatever was going on outside that window was critical to their situation. A situation that didn't necessarily have to include Theo.

He nodded. "The guy's moving, clutching his chest."

Probably because he was bleeding and in pain. She wasn't certain of the details of his injury, but Ivy had heard Gabriel's quick phone chat that he'd had with Jameson.

And now she moved on to the part about Theo not having to be in Nathan's or her life. "For the record, I don't expect anything from you," Ivy continued a moment later. "We were practically kids when I got pregnant, and the feelings you once had for me are obviously long gone."

Theo gave her a look that could have frozen the hottest levels of Hades. "I'm not leaving," he spat out. He stared at her as if he might repeat it, but then he shook his head. "I just need to stop whoever sent those thugs, and then I can deal with everything else."

That sounded like some kind of threat. And Ivy wasn't immune to it. She'd never had to share her son with anyone. Not even Chad, who had been a "father" in name only, had been able to spend much time in the parent roll because of his health problems. She didn't feel ready to share Nathan with Theo, either.

"Yeah, we were kids," Theo went on, "but we sure as hell aren't kids now." He paused again, those jaw muscles stirring like crazy. "You should have found a way to tell me."

Ivy huffed. "You can say that now," she argued. "But we were in a different mind-set back then. Remember?"

"Of course I remember. Your mom caught us in bed. Your dad blew a fuse when she told him, and he ordered me to stay away from you. That should have been the time you backed me up, but you didn't. You agreed with him and told me to get out of the house."

Ivy had indeed told Theo to leave, but she darn sure hadn't agreed with her father. Sherman Beckett could be a hard man sometimes, and he hadn't approved of Theo and his minor run-ins with the law. Ironically, her dad had thought Theo would get her pregnant and then run out on her. Strange how all of that had worked out. Strange, too, that Theo had become a lawman, the last thing her father or she would have expected him to become.

"Then you and your brothers actually considered me a suspect in your parents' murders," Theo added. Judging from his tone, that was still an extremely sore spot for him.

It was for her, too.

Because she hadn't stuck up for Theo. That had obviously been the straw that had broken the camel's back.

As soon as Theo's name had been cleared, he'd left Blue River.

Ivy was about to put an end to this conversation, or a temporary end at least, but she heard the footsteps in the hall. Both Theo and she pivoted in that direction, and she felt herself gear up for another fight. If a gunman had actually made it into the house, he wasn't getting to Nathan.

"It's me," Jameson called out.

The relief came, but it didn't completely wash away the adrenaline punch she'd gotten when she thought they could be near another attack. A moment later, the door opened, and her brother came in.

Jameson's attention went to her first, and he no doubt saw her tense body. Perhaps saw a whole lot more than that, though, when his gaze shifted to Theo. Then to the bathroom door where he knew Jodi—and Nathan—were waiting. It didn't take Jameson long to piece everything together, and he cursed under his breath.

"Just in case there's a bug in the house, I'll whisper," Jameson said. "How much trouble is this situation with Nathan going to cause the two of you?" he asked. He didn't specifically direct the question to either of them, and neither of them answered.

However, Theo did ask a question of his own, and it was indeed meant for Jameson because he was staring at her brother. "Did the gunman say anything about who sent him and why?" He, too, kept his voice at a whisper.

Ivy figured that he hadn't, but Jameson nodded. He took a deep breath, and that's when she knew this was not going to be good news.

"The gunman died right after the medics put him in the ambulance," Jameson said.

Now Ivy wanted to curse. She didn't. Over the years, motherhood had taught her to rein in the profanity, but still this was a situation that warranted some cursing.

"He didn't know who hired him," Jameson went on. "Or at least that's what he said. According to him, it was all done through a third party. A San Antonio thug everyone just called Mack. I've never heard of him, and I know most of the CIs and other informants in the area. And yeah, I've already made a call about him."

That didn't sound very promising, especially since it wasn't a name her brother knew, but Ivy got the sinking feeling that it wasn't his not knowing Mack that'd put that troubled look on his face.

"The gunman said something else," Jameson continued a moment later. "This Mack hired other men. At least three more." He turned to his sister then. "And, Ivy, they have orders to use whatever means necessary to kill *you*."

Chapter 5

"Ivy's the target?" Theo immediately asked Jameson. He figured it was a question that Ivy wanted answered, as well.

Jameson lifted his shoulder. "That's what the guy said." Like the rest of them, he continued to keep his voice at a whisper. "That doesn't mesh with what the CI told you, though, does it?"

Theo had to shake his head. "But maybe the person behind this changed his mind and decided to go after one of us at a time. He or she might think Ivy would be the easiest to pick off."

Ivy made a soft gasping sound, and Theo wished he hadn't voiced that aloud. Still, it was true. Since they didn't know the person's identity or motive, anything was possible.

"Are you okay?" Jameson asked his sister. He gave her arm a soft pat.

She shook her head as if pulling herself out of a trance. "Yes." Ivy fluttered her fingers toward the bathroom. "I just need to check on Nathan."

"Give yourself a couple of minutes," Jameson advised her. "You're as pale as paper right now, and Nathan will pick up on that."

The kid probably would. Then again, Nathan and Jodi both had to be on edge waiting for news.

"Are you okay?" Jameson repeated. Not directed at Ivy this time, but at Theo.

Theo lied with a nod. He was far from okay. His mind was whirling. Hell. He'd thought this would be a quick in-and-out trip back to the Beckett ranch, but there was no way that was possible now.

He had a son.

And if that wasn't enough to get him to stay, someone wanted Ivy dead. Of course, the gunman could have been lying when he'd said that Ivy was the target of would-be assassins, but the attack had been real. Bullets had actually been shot into the house, and even if she was the sole target, that didn't mean others couldn't have been caught in cross fire. Nathan and anyone else could have been killed.

"Look, I know you two have plenty to work out," Jameson went on, "but you need to leave it here for now. Gabriel wants to take everyone to the sheriff's office. The medics will need to take a look at that, too."

It took Theo a moment to realize Jameson meant the cut on Theo's cheek. "I don't want a medic," Theo insisted. "But someone should check on Jodi and Nathan."

It wasn't the first time he'd said his son's name aloud, but for some reason, it hit him like a punch to the gut.

Theo actually had to take a moment just to regather his breath.

"Yeah," Jameson mumbled. Whatever the heck that meant. "You both stay here, pull yourselves together, and I'll go in and talk to Nathan and Jodi. Be ready to leave as soon as Gabriel has the cruisers in place."

Jameson stepped into the bathroom, shutting the door and leaving Ivy and him alone. Since Theo didn't want to keep glaring at her, he turned his attention back to the window so he could watch for the cruisers.

"Why would Gabriel want us to go to the sheriff's office?" she asked, her voice shaky. "Wouldn't it be safer to stay here rather than risk going outside?"

"No. There could be other gunmen in the area. Plus, he probably wants to set up some security measures here." He glanced at her and saw that didn't do anything to ease the tension on her face. "Gabriel knows what he's doing."

Theo hoped that was true, anyway. There was no love lost between Gabriel and him, but Ivy's brother had been sheriff for nearly a decade now. Maybe that meant he knew how to handle an attempted murder investigation along with keeping Ivy and the others safe. Theo had no intentions, though, of just backing off and letting Gabriel run with this. Not when his son's safety was at stake.

"When I first saw Nathan, he asked who I was," Theo reminded her. "He thinks your late husband is his dad?"

She paused a long time, and it was so quiet that Theo could hear Jameson talking in the bathroom. He couldn't hear what the Ranger was saying. Which was a good thing. Because it meant Nathan wouldn't be able to hear what Theo and Ivy were talking about.

"No. Nathan knows the truth," Ivy finally answered. "Chad was a widower and a lot older than me. He had a college-age daughter, Lacey, when we got married. Lacey told Nathan when he was about six." Her mouth tightened enough to let him know that was a sore subject. "My stepdaughter and I don't get along that well," she added.

Theo made a mental note of the woman's name. Right now, he needed to look at all the angles to figure out who was behind this, and a riled stepdaughter could definitely have motive for putting this together.

Of course, so could Uncle August.

Theo would be contacting him very, very soon.

August had been a thorn in nearly everyone's side since his brother's arrest for the Beckett murders. For whatever reason, August had become Travis's champion of so-called justice even though Travis had never asked him to do that. In fact, from everything Theo had heard, his father had accepted his fate and was willing to spend the rest of his life behind bars.

His phone buzzed, and Theo answered it when he saw Wesley's name on the screen. "I heard about the shooting at the ranch," Wesley greeted. "I'm still in Blue River, so you want me to head out there?"

"No need. The danger seems to be contained. For now, anyway." Theo didn't mention they'd all soon be going to the sheriff's office since this wasn't a whispered phone conversation. If there truly was a bug in the house, he didn't want to tip off the gunmen's boss about them leaving, since that would mean they'd be out in the open, at least for a little while.

"The deputy here got an update from Gabriel," Wesley went on. "The gunmen didn't ID the person who hired them."

"No. But I've got a lead. I'll tell you about it when I see you."

"A lead?" Wesley practically snapped. "Who?"

"The house might be bugged," Theo reminded him. "The info I got might not amount to anything, but it's a start."

"Text me what you have," Wesley added a moment later.

Theo hadn't thought it possible, but Wesley seemed even more on edge than Theo did. "I will." Theo ended the call so he could do that, but the bathroom door opened before he could even get started on the text.

And Nathan came out.

Jameson was in front of him. Jodi, behind. Both still had their guns in hand. Nathan gave Theo a long look, and Theo wondered if the boy recognized their similar features. If so, he didn't say anything. He just hurried to his mom, and Ivy looped her arms around him, pulling him close to her.

"Gabriel wants us in the cruisers," Jameson mouthed to Ivy and him. "Don't take anything with you in case it's bugged."

It was a good precaution, and while Theo wasn't exactly eager to have Ivy or Nathan outside, he understood why they were in a hurry when they followed Jameson out of the room and to the stairs. There wasn't exactly a peaceful, safe feeling in the house right now.

Jodi paused long enough for their gazes to connect, and he saw the questions in her eyes. How was he handling this? It was too long of an answer and one that he couldn't give her with just a mere glance.

When they made it to the front of the house, Theo

spotted the two cruisers that were now parked by the porch steps. There was a deputy behind the wheel of one of them and another deputy next to him, but Gabriel was driving the cruiser in front. "Ride with me so we can talk," Gabriel insisted. He motioned for them to get in with him, and he threw open both the back door and the passenger's side.

"Hurry," Jameson reminded them. "Jodi and I will ride in front. Theo, Ivy and Nathan in the back seat."

Jameson didn't have to tell them twice to hurry. Jodi and he took off running, and Theo got Ivy and Nathan moving fast. Nathan ended up in the middle between Ivy and him, and the moment they were buckled up, Gabriel got them out of there. The deputies followed right behind them, no doubt as backup in case there was another attack.

"Is everyone okay?" Gabriel asked.

Gabriel brushed a kiss on Jodi's forehead, and when his sister looked at her soon-to-be husband, Theo could practically see the love in her eyes. Not really a surprise, though. He had always suspected that Jodi was in love with Gabriel, and despite their painful pasts, it appeared that Gabriel felt the same way about her.

Each of them, including Theo, answered or made some kind of sound to indicate they were okay.

"He's not all right," Nathan said, and he motioned toward Theo. "He's bleeding."

Theo didn't exactly thank him for pointing that out, because Nathan seemed to be alarmed by the blood. Theo hated to add to the boy's anxiety, but he also didn't want anyone to make a fuss about a small cut. At least he thought it was small. He hadn't really had a chance to look at it, but he did know that his cheek was stinging.

Jameson opened the glove compartment, located a small first-aid kit and passed it not to Theo but to Ivy. "Since Theo said he won't see a medic, you make sure he doesn't need stitches."

That request seemed to add to Ivy's anxiety level, but she opened the kit and took out some gauze and antiseptic cream. She reached over Nathan and blotted the gauze against Theo's cut. It wasn't a very manly reaction, but he grunted from the pain.

"When Mom's fixing up my cuts," Nathan said, "I just think about a computer game or my horse, Willow. You have a horse?" he asked Theo.

Theo shook his head, but nearly cursed when that caused Ivy to press harder on his cheek. He decided it was best to keep still. Best not to make direct eye contact with Nathan, either, since it was obvious the boy was curious about him. Soon, Theo would satisfy that curiosity by telling him the truth, that he was his father. But for now, Theo just let Ivy continue to torture him while he kept watch around them.

Other than the cruiser behind them, there were no other vehicles in sight. Theo wanted to keep it like that. If he'd been alone, however, he would have wanted this SOB to come after him. That way, he could stop him and put an end to this.

No one in the car talked about the attack, though Theo was certain they wanted to do that. Best to wait until Nathan was out of earshot. The boy had already witnessed enough without having the details spelled out for him.

Two men dead.

Countless shots fired.

And a threat still hanging over their heads because this snake might indeed go after Ivy.

Once Ivy was finished cleaning and bandaging the cut, Theo took out his phone and texted a fellow DEA agent in the San Antonio office so they could get started on locating this thug named Mack. He didn't include Wesley on this, but he would fill him in at the sheriff's office. As soon as Theo was certain there were no bugs in the place. It was bad enough that he had Jodi, Nathan and Ivy on the road, but he didn't want anyone else knowing they were on their way to Gabriel's office.

It wasn't that far from the ranch to town, and Gabriel didn't dawdle. He made it there in probably record time, and he pulled the cruiser to a stop at the back door so they could hurry inside. First through the break room and then into Gabriel's office. Even though it was a good twenty feet away from the squad room at the front of the building, Wesley must have heard them, because he came hurrying back.

Ivy automatically stopped, and she pulled Nathan behind her. Jodi rushed to Ivy's side to shield the boy, as well. Jameson and Gabriel reacted, too, by taking aim at the man.

"This is DEA agent Wesley Sanford," Theo explained. "He's the one who gave me the recording from the CI."

That caused Gabriel and Jameson to relax a bit, but Jodi and Ivy still stayed in a defensive posture. Maybe because Wesley didn't exactly have a welcoming expression. Probably because he'd been in law enforcement most of his adult life, first as a San Antonio cop and then as a DEA agent. The man was tall and lanky with a thin face, and he rarely smiled. He certainly wasn't smiling now.

"You said you had a lead," Wesley reminded him, "and that you'd text me."

"*Possible* lead," Theo corrected. He motioned toward Gabriel. "This is Sheriff Beckett and his brother, Ranger Jameson Beckett. Are you certain the building isn't bugged?" he added to Wesley.

"The deputies and I have gone through the place and didn't see anything."

"I'm having the Rangers bring in equipment to check every inch," Jameson volunteered. "They should be here any minute. Until then, anything we say should be in one of the interrogation rooms."

Good idea. There was minimal furniture, and a person wouldn't have had easy access to those rooms to plant a listening device. Normally, the other option would have been to discuss this outside, but there was nothing normal about this situation.

Nathan was a reminder of that.

"Why don't you stay with Nathan here in Gabriel's office?" Theo suggested to Ivy.

She instantly looked torn, and Theo knew why. Ivy wanted to hear anything about the investigation, but she didn't want their son to be part of it. Neither did Theo. Jodi must have picked up on their wanting to protect Nathan, because she slipped her arm around the boy's shoulders and led him deeper into Gabriel's office.

"I'll wait in here with Nathan," Jodi offered. "I can probably download a movie or book for him."

"Is everything gonna be okay?" Nathan asked, volleying glances at his mom, his uncles and Theo.

"Of course," Ivy jumped in to say. Jodi, Gabriel and Jameson answered similarly.

Nathan settled his attention on Theo. Maybe because he didn't respond to the boy's question. "Will it be okay?" Nathan pressed.

Theo wasn't sure why Nathan wanted to hear his assurance when they'd only met a short while earlier. Maybe Nathan felt the connection? But Theo knew that could be wishful thinking on his part. He certainly felt a connection to his son, and it didn't matter that he hadn't shared the same years with the boy that Ivy had.

"We're all going to work to put a stop to this," Theo finally told him.

Nathan nodded, apparently accepting that as gospel, and he went with Jodi when she led him to Gabriel's desk. Part of Theo wanted to stay so he could just talk to him and get to know him better, but as long as Ivy was in danger, so was Nathan.

Gabriel motioned for them to follow him to one of the interview rooms just up the hall, and once they were inside, Gabriel shut the door. Each of them re-holstered their weapons. Except for Ivy. No holster for her, so she tucked the gun in the back waistband of her jeans.

"One of the gunmen gave us a first name or possibly a nickname of the person who hired him," Theo told Wesley. "Mack, someone the gunman described as a thug from San Antonio. Ring any bells?"

Wesley repeated the name, and he nodded. "Maybe. There's a bar. A *seedy* bar," Wesley added. "It's owned by a guy whose last name is McKenzie. I can't remember his first name, but he used to work as a bouncer at the place before he bought it." He took out his phone, stepping slightly away from them. "I'll see what I can find."

"I need to check on my own contacts," Jameson said, taking out his phone, as well. "I also need to keep tabs on anything the ME might find on our dead guys. Anything the CSIs might find, too."

Yes, because those gunmen had gotten to the ranch somehow, and that meant they'd maybe left a vehicle in the area. A vehicle that could contain possible clues as to who had hired them and why.

"I'll get to work on ID'ing the guys," Gabriel said. "Once we have that, then we might be able to find a money trail."

Again, it was a good idea, and Gabriel moved as if he might step to the other side of the room to start on that, but he stopped and looked at his sister. Then at Theo. "I don't want any yelling," Gabriel warned Theo.

That didn't sit right with Theo. Of course, nothing much would at this point unless they found the clown who'd orchestrated all of this. But Gabriel wasn't talking about the danger. He was talking about Nathan.

"You don't think I have a right to yell?" Theo asked him.

Gabriel's eyes narrowed for just a moment. "Maybe. But it won't happen here. Anything you and my sister have to hash out can wait."

With that "advice" doled out, Gabriel moved away from them and made a call. Of course, that left Ivy and Theo standing there, staring at each other. Theo knew he had his own calls to make. And he wanted to check on this situation with Ivy's stepdaughter to make sure she didn't hate Ivy enough to do something like that.

And Theo did pull his phone from his pocket, but Ivy spoke before he could make a call.

"Don't tell Nathan that you're his father," she said. "Let me do it, please."

Theo thought about that for a few moments. "What will you say to him?"

"The truth. More or less," she added. "I don't want to get into specifics. I'll just tell him that it didn't work out between us."

He gave that more thought, too. "I don't want him to think I knew about him and then left. I'm not the bad guy in all of this."

Something flashed through her eyes. Not anger. But hurt. Theo wished he'd phrased that better, but it was the truth. There was only one person who knew Ivy was carrying Theo's child, and that was Ivy herself.

Ivy nodded, finally. "I'll tell him I screwed up," she said, dodging his gaze. But she didn't do the dodging before he saw something else in her eyes.

Tears.

Hell. It was too bad Gabriel hadn't added "no crying" along with the "no yelling." Theo wasn't an ice man—not every day, anyway—and those tears cut away at him. They also brought memories back to the surface. Ivy had been crying the night she'd ended things with him. He hadn't wanted to hold her and comfort her then. Too much anger had been bubbling up inside him. But for some stupid reason he wanted to try to comfort her now.

He resisted.

In part because it truly would be stupid to have her back in his arms and also because her brothers were watching her. Jameson and Gabriel were both on their phones, but they had their attention nailed to their kid sister.

Gabriel finished his call first and came back to them, and judging from his expression he looked ready to blast Theo for making Ivy cry. But Ivy gave a little shake of her head, a gesture for her brother to back off. Gabriel did—eventually.

"They got an immediate match on one of the gunmen's prints," Gabriel explained several long moments later. "Ted Mintor. He has a long record, and they're looking for a match on the second one."

Good. A name could lead them to possible bank records. From what Theo could hear of Jameson's conversation, he was already working on that.

"I'm having the hands beef up security at the ranch," Gabriel went on. He was looking at his sister now. "I'm debating whether to go back there or move Nathan, Jodi and you to a safe house."

"Jodi won't go," Theo quickly said.

Gabriel didn't argue with that. Probably because he knew Jodi well. Jodi was a well-trained security specialist and would consider it an insult if she was tucked away while others were in danger. But maybe Theo could put a different spin on this to get her to go.

"What if Jodi realizes she'd be protecting Ivy and Nathan if she went?" Theo asked.

Gabriel nodded. "That could work. It'd also work if you went with them. That way, I wouldn't have to tie up a deputy."

Theo felt as if Gabriel had just turned the tables on him. He did want to be with Ivy and Nathan. He wanted to protect them. But it would be hard to find the person behind this if he was shut away in a safe house.

Before Theo could respond to Gabriel, Wesley finished his call and joined them. Theo could tell from the agent's expression that he'd learned something.

Something that Theo might not like.

"I just had a tech do a computer search on our person of interest," Wesley explained. "Birch McKenzie. Like I said, he owns a bar in San Antonio, and it's not exactly a five-star place. When I was a beat cop, we were always getting calls to go out to the place. Anyway, SAPD's bringing in McKenzie now for questioning, but the tech found an interesting connection. To you," he added, looking at Theo.

Theo shook his head and was certain he'd never heard the man's name before today. "You think I know McKenzie?"

"No. But your uncle August does." Wesley paused, his mouth tightening. "August lent McKenzie the money to buy the bar."

Gabriel mumbled some profanity under his breath and took out his phone again. "I'll get August in here right away for questioning. And he'd better have the right answers."

Chapter 6

Ivy tried to put on a brave face for her son's sake, but she felt none of that braveness inside her. She was terrified, not for herself but for Nathan. He was much too young to be caught up in the middle of this.

"How much longer do we have to be here?" Nathan asked her. Considering they'd been at Gabriel's office for well over an hour, she was surprised he hadn't asked that sooner. Maybe, though, that was because he'd been interested in the movie Jodi had downloaded for him.

"We'll be able to leave soon," Ivy told him, and hoped it wasn't a lie. Actually, she wasn't certain how long it would take Gabriel to set up a safe house.

One where Nathan, Jodi and she would apparently be going. With Theo. That caused her stomach to tighten even more than it already was. Because there was little chance that Theo would keep the truth from Nathan much longer.

"But what about Aunt Jodi and Uncle Gabriel's wedding?" Nathan pressed. He yawned. No surprise there, since it was a little past his nine o'clock bedtime. Plus, it'd been the day from Hades what with the attack.

"We might have to delay that a day or two," Jodi answered. She was in the corner of Gabriel's office, working on a laptop. Theo was in the other corner, doing the same. All of them waiting for the deputy to bring in August.

Nathan made a sound of disappointment. In his case it was probably because he'd been expecting cake and party food. But Ivy figured what he felt was a drop in the bucket compared to what Jodi and Gabriel did. They'd waited a long time for this wedding, and now it might have to be delayed indefinitely.

Jodi stood, stretching, and she set the laptop aside. "I'm getting a bottle of water. Anyone else want one?"

Theo, Nathan and Ivy shook their heads. Gabriel had already brought in burgers from the café just up the street, and the only one who'd touched any of it was Nathan. Nothing seemed to dampen his appetite.

Jodi stepped out, closing the door behind her. A precaution no doubt, so that Nathan wouldn't be able to hear anything that was being said in the squad room where Gabriel, Jameson, Wesley and two deputies were working.

"It's like there are a bunch of secrets going on," Nathan said, snagging both Ivy's and Theo's attention. Nathan looked at both of them, probably waiting for them to verify that.

They didn't.

Mumbling something she didn't catch, her son got up from the desk and went to the small bed that Ivy had made for him on the floor. Basically, it was a couple of blankets and a pillow that she'd gotten from the break room. It wouldn't be long before Nathan was sacked out—which was a good thing, considering the loud voice she heard out in the squad room.

Not August Canton.

But it was a familiar voice.

"Lacey," Ivy provided when Theo looked at her.

Ivy got up, and with Theo in front of her, they stepped into the hall. Yes, it was her stepdaughter all right, though it was hard for Ivy to think of Lacey as any kind of daughter since they were practically the same age.

"You did this," Lacey snapped the moment her attention landed on Ivy.

Ivy first checked on Nathan. He was indeed going to sleep, so once Jodi was back in the office with him, Ivy pulled the door shut so this wouldn't disturb him. The trick, though, would be to keep Lacey's voice in the normal range. She looked ready to start yelling.

Gabriel stepped in front of Lacey, but she just tried to go around him. "I want to have a little chat with Mommie Dearest. Because of her, the cops want to talk to me."

"And *I* want to talk to you," Theo snarled right back, and there was no shred of friendliness in his tone.

Lacey peered around Gabriel, and the moment she actually looked at Theo, her eyes widened a little. She didn't smile exactly, but it was close.

"Theo Canton," Lacey provided.

Because Theo's arm was against Ivy's, she felt him tense a little. "How do you know me?"

"I've made it my business to know you and anyone else associated with my dad's wife. Your name and picture were in the papers. You were a suspect in the murders of Ivy's parents." The slight smile stayed on her face.

And Ivy knew why. Even though she'd never told Lacey about Nathan's father, Lacey could no doubt see the resemblance. Of course, the papers that'd covered the murders had gone into the fact that Theo and Ivy had broken up that night and that was his possible motive for murder. It wouldn't be a stretch for Lacey to do the math and realize that Nathan had been born nine months later.

"So," Lacey said, dragging that out a few syllables. Her attention stayed fixed to Theo. "What'd you want to see me about?"

He went closer. "Someone tried to kill us. What do you know about that?"

Despite Theo's harsh tone, Lacey hardly reacted. Instead, she turned to Ivy. "You put him up to this. You want him to suspect me of something I didn't do so you can get me out of the way. Well, it won't work. I'm not stopping the fight to get what's rightfully mine."

Ivy groaned softly. "Chad left everything to Nathan and me in his will," she explained to Theo.

"Because you brainwashed him," Lacey insisted. "I've filed a lawsuit to rescind his will and give me what's rightfully mine."

"Your father didn't want you to have that money," Ivy reminded her. This was old news to Lacey, but Ivy repeated it, anyway. "He thought you already had too much from your mother's trust fund and that you needed to learn some responsibility."

Lacey cursed. "You don't know me, and you don't

have a right to say anything like that to me. He was my dad."

"And he was my husband," Ivy pointed out just as quickly.

"Are you here for your interrogation?" Gabriel asked when Lacey opened her mouth, no doubt to return verbal fire.

Lacey gave him a withering look. "By you? I think not. You're Ivy's brother. And not you, either," she added to Theo. "I won't have Ivy's ex-boyfriend trying to pin something on me."

"What about me?" Wesley asked, standing. "I'm not related to Ivy or Theo. And the sooner you answer questions, the sooner we can clear your name. Or maybe you'd rather I take you into custody now and drive you back to my San Antonio office."

Maybe in that moment it occurred to Lacey that it hadn't been a good idea to come storming into a sheriff's office with wild accusations against the sheriff's sister. She was almost certainly weighing her options, and considering her expression, she didn't like any of them.

"I'm not talking to anyone unless my lawyer is here," Lacey concluded.

"Then you'd best be calling him or her right now," Gabriel said, and he added a glare to it.

Lacey glared back. Cursed. But she took out her phone to make the call to her attorney.

"Get her into the other interview room," Gabriel told Wesley and Jameson. "She can wait for her lawyer there."

When Gabriel looked out the window, Ivy followed his gaze and realized why there'd been some urgency in her brother's order. That's because August had just gotten out of his car and was making a beeline for the sheriff's office.

Round two was about to hit.

Wesley and Jameson had barely enough time to get Lacey out of there before August came waltzing in. Ivy braced herself for August to unleash some anger on Theo. After all, August had always said that Jodi and Theo hadn't done nearly enough to help clear their father's name. But unlike Lacey, there was no anger on August's face or in his body language.

"Ivy," August greeted. "Welcome home. It's been a long time."

Yes, it had been. Ten years. She would never be able to make her brothers understand why she'd cut them out of her life. Sometimes, she didn't understand it, either.

August was the same as he had been ten years ago, and he still didn't look as if he ran his brother's ranch. He dressed more like a rich businessman, emphasis on the rich. And he was. In fact, he probably had as much money or more than Ivy's family thanks to August's wealthy mother, who'd died shortly after marrying Travis's father and giving birth to August. Travis, on the other hand, had been a cowboy. One with a drinking problem. And despite the fact that August and Travis had been as different as night and day, that hadn't stopped August from spearheading the fight to clear Travis's name.

August turned to Theo next, and while Ivy wasn't sure how the man would react, she certainly hadn't expected him to go to Theo and hug him. Clearly, Theo hadn't expected it, either, because she saw him go stiff.

"Good to have you home, Theo," August said.

Ivy was instantly suspicious. August had always been somewhat of a hothead, and from everything Ivy had heard from Jodi, August had plenty of resentment for Theo.

"Will you be seeing your dad?" August asked when he stepped back from that hug.

"No," Theo said without hesitation.

Now there was that flash of anger in August's eyes that she'd been expecting. He aimed some of that anger at her. "Then why are you here?" August didn't wait for him to answer. "Oh, I get it. You came for Jodi's wedding. That figures. Instead of her saying 'I do,' you two should be helping me. Did you know your dad has been stuck in prison all this time?"

Ivy knew that, of course, but it caused her breath to go thin just thinking about it. She wanted Travis to pay for her parents' murders, but nothing they did now, including Travis spending the rest of his life behind bars, would bring them back.

"I know," Theo answered. "But he was convicted of murder."

More anger went through August's eyes. "On circumstantial evidence. Heck, he doesn't remember anything about that night, and that's why it was so easy for the Becketts to pin this on him."

Since there were three Becketts in the room, August obviously didn't mind letting them know he thought they had railroaded his brother. They hadn't. She started to remind him that when Travis had been found that night, he'd had her father's blood on him. But August knew that, too, and he probably thought they'd planted it there.

Or else maybe August had been the one to do the planting.

"There was another attack at the ranch," Ivy said.

August nodded. "Yeah, whenever somebody goes after you or your kin, your brothers start hauling me in for questioning. They have this warped notion that if I kill one of them, or you, then it'll get Travis out of jail. It won't. The only thing that'll do that is for the truth to come out."

Both Jameson and Gabriel huffed as if this were old news. It gave her a glimpse of what they'd been having to deal with for the past decade.

"So, is that why you told me to come?" August went on. "Because you want to pin this latest attack on me?"

"Yes," Theo readily admitted. "Did you have anything to do with it?"

August tossed him a glare before he gave one to Gabriel, Jameson and her. "No. Of course not." He turned to Theo to finish that. "Your father loves both your sister and you. Why, I don't know, since you rarely go to see him. But if I were going to do something to help him, it wouldn't be by harming one of you."

Gabriel stepped closer to August. "Then explain your connection to the man who hired the two gunmen who came after us."

No glare this time. August's eyes widened. "What the hell are you talking about?"

"Birch McKenzie," Gabriel said.

Ivy carefully watched August's reaction. First, there was more surprise, and then he cursed. "Birch didn't hire those men. Someone's setting him up, and by doing so, they're setting me up, too." He cursed again, snapped back to Theo. "I wouldn't have done this."

August was so adamant about it that Ivy almost believed him. Almost. But then she remembered that his loyalty wasn't to anyone but his brother. Why, she didn't know. Since Travis was a lot older than August, maybe he saw Travis as more of a father than a half brother. Of course, there was another reason, too.

August had had motive to kill her parents.

Like Theo and Travis, August had also had a recent run-in with Ivy's father. August hated him, and there'd been a long feud between them over land rights. Maybe August had killed them, and if so, his guilty conscience could be causing him to do everything humanly possible to free his brother from jail.

That wasn't a new theory, either. Both of her brothers had been investigating it, especially now that the threatening letters and emails had started. Someone was sending those, and it wasn't Travis since he didn't have computer access in his maximum-security cell. Also, his mail was being monitored.

While August stood there still mumbling profanity, the door to Gabriel's office opened. Both Ivy and Theo instantly looked over their shoulders to see Jodi pulling Nathan back into the room.

"Sorry," Jodi said to them. "He woke up and got to the door ahead of me."

"Mom?" Nathan rubbed his eyes and yawned. "When can we leave?"

"Soon," Ivy assured him, and Jodi took him back into the office and shut the door.

But not before August had gotten a glimpse of her son.

Just as Theo and everyone else had done, August saw the resemblance, and he smiled. He moved as if he might go to Nathan, but both Theo and she stepped in front of him.

"So, I guess things weren't as over between you two

as you thought," August said. "Are you two back together?"

"No," Theo and she said in unison. It was Theo who continued. "I came back because I got a warning about an attack at the Beckett Ranch. Ivy could be the target." He leaned in closer. "But if she's the target, then her son is in danger, too."

"Your son," August corrected.

Theo didn't confirm that. Didn't deny it, either. "If Travis really doesn't want Jodi and me hurt, then how do you think he would feel about someone harming that little boy?"

Travis's grandson. Theo didn't spell that out, but August clearly understood what Theo was saying. And his eyes narrowed again.

"What will it take to convince Jodi and you that I'm not behind the attacks?" August asked.

"Proof," Theo said. "Proof of who's doing this. And if it's not you, then I'll owe you an apology. For now, though, you have some questions to answer."

"Questions that I'll be asking in the interview room," Gabriel stated, and he motioned for August to follow him.

Thank goodness Jodi had shut the door so that August couldn't get another glimpse of Nathan. It wasn't pettiness on her part. Ivy just didn't want her son to be exposed to his great-uncle until she was certain August was indeed innocent.

Theo looked at her. The kind of look that asked if she was okay. She wasn't. Her nerves were right there at the surface, and Theo must have seen that, because he muttered some profanity under his breath.

"Why don't we go ahead and take Ivy, Nathan and

Jodi to the safe house," Jameson suggested. As they'd done in the house, he kept his voice at a whisper.

"It's ready?" Ivy asked.

Jameson nodded. "Just don't expect too much. I didn't have a lot of time to put it together."

Ivy was about to say she didn't care about that, but then it hit her. "What if Nathan gets hurt because of me?" she asked. "The gunman said I was the target."

"And he could have been lying," Theo pointed out just as quickly. He huffed. "I'd rather Nathan and you not be under the same roof as our suspects."

He had a point. Of course, the real culprit could be out there, waiting for them to leave so he or she could attack again. Maybe it was someone who wasn't even on their radar. Her parents' murders had drawn a lot of press, and it was entirely possible this was a sicko who'd glommed on to them. A sicko who was not only sending threatening emails and letters, but a person who could also hire thugs to kill them.

"I'll pull the cruiser up to the back door," Jameson offered. "Once I have all of you settled, then I can come back here and help Gabriel with the interrogations."

Jameson headed off to do that, but before he made it into the hall, his phone buzzed. "SAPD," her brother said, looking at the screen.

He took the call but didn't put it on speaker. Since this could be an update on the case, Ivy decided to wait to go in and tell Jodi and Nathan about plans to leave for the safe house. She couldn't hear Jameson's conversation, but whatever the caller had said to him, it caused Jameson's forehead to bunch up.

"What?" Jameson snapped a moment later. He paused, listening. "You're sure?"

Ivy glanced at Theo to see if he knew what was going on, but he only shook his head.

"Birch McKenzie's dead," Jameson said when he finally ended the call. "Murdered. A gunshot wound to the head."

Ivy hadn't known the man, of course, but he'd been the link between the gunmen and the person who'd hired them. A link, too, to August.

"Who killed him?" Theo asked.

"SAPD doesn't know. They went out to question him about his possible involvement in this, and they found him dead. The cops also found his phone, and they glanced through his recent calls. The last call he made was to one of our suspects."

"August," Ivy muttered.

But Jameson shook his head. "No, McKenzie called Lacey."

Chapter 7

As little sleep as Theo had managed to get, he figured Ivy had gotten even less. After they'd arrived at the safe house, she'd quickly taken Nathan to the room they would share, but since Theo's room was right next to theirs, he'd heard someone moving around in there most of the night. He figured that someone was Ivy.

He showered and made his way into the kitchen to get some coffee started, but got confirmation that Ivy hadn't slept when he saw her at the kitchen table already sipping a cup. Her eyes confirmed his theory, too. She looked exhausted.

And beautiful.

Yeah, Ivy was probably one of the few women on the planet who could have managed that. Despite her rumpled hair and tired eyes, she still looked amazing.

He felt that old ripple of attraction. Always did whenever he was around her. But he told that attraction to take a hike. It would only distract him at a time when he needed no other distractions. And besides, he still hadn't cooled off from her not telling him about Nathan.

"Are Jodi and Nathan still sleeping?" he asked.

She nodded. "But I figure they'll be up soon. Anything new on the case?" she added. "I heard you talking on the phone a couple of times."

He had, but Theo felt he'd gotten nowhere. "Gabriel questioned Lacey, and she denied knowing McKenzie. Lacey said he called her to set her up."

Ivy groaned, and Theo silently groaned with her. With his coffee in hand, he went to the window to look out. The safe house was on an old ranch, only about thirty miles from Blue River, and it was out in the middle of nowhere. Which was a good thing. The pastures were flat, and he had a clear view of the road. That meant it'd be hard for someone to sneak up on them. Added to that, Jameson had put out a motion detector on the road to alert them if anyone drove up.

"Lacey lawyered up," Theo went on. "So did August. And Gabriel doesn't have enough to hold either of them. That means we're at a stalemate unless SAPD or the CSIs find something to link the attack or McKenzie's murder to someone."

Someone in this case being August or Lacey.

And that brought Theo back to something he'd been wanting to ask Ivy. "Just how much does Lacey hate you?"

She looked at him for a moment before she answered. "A lot. Why?"

He lifted his shoulder. "Lacey said she made it a point to get to know anyone connected to you. It's a

long shot, but she could have discovered the link between August and McKenzie."

He was talking softly enough not to wake Jodi and
Nathan, and Ivy got up from the table to go closer to
him, probably so she'd be able to hear him better.

"But if she wanted to set up August to take the blame
for this," Ivy said, "then why would she have allowed
McKenzie to call her?"

"Maybe she didn't allow it. He could have just
screwed up. Or it could be he got spooked when he realized someone was trying to kill him and he tried to
get in touch with her. Either way, McKenzie would have
been a loose end."

That was true even if Lacey or August wasn't behind
this. McKenzie had a link to two dead gunmen, and the
mastermind pulling their strings wouldn't have wanted
to keep McKenzie around.

"August's motive is to clear Travis's name," Ivy whispered. "But Lacey won't inherit her father's money if
she kills me." She made a soft gasp and touched her fingers to her mouth. "She'd have to get rid of Nathan, too."

That wiped away the fatigue in Ivy's eyes, and the
fear quickly came. Theo had had a similar reaction earlier when he'd thought of how this might all play out.

"God, she can't hurt him," Ivy said on a rise of
breath. Tears sprang to her eyes.

Hell. He didn't handle these tears any better than he
had the ones the night before at the sheriff's office. This
time, though, Theo put his arm around her.

Ivy melted against him.

That definitely wasn't good because she felt soft—
and right—in his arms. The years vanished, and for
a few seconds, she was his lover again. Thankfully,

it didn't go past the thought stage because Ivy pulled away from him.

"Sorry," she said, her voice low. He wasn't sure if she was apologizing for the tears or the reaction they'd just had to each other. And Theo decided it was best if he didn't have the answer to that.

"I'm not going to let anything happen to Nathan," Theo promised her, and somehow that was a promise he'd keep.

She stayed at the window with him, and her gaze connected with his again. "Is there something you aren't telling me?" she asked. "You're not thinking of telling Nathan the truth, are you?"

That was two unrelated questions. "Nathan will eventually need to know," he reminded her.

She kept staring at him. "But?"

"It can wait a little while longer."

He was pretty sure the breath she blew out was one of relief. "Then what's wrong?"

"It's maybe nothing." And that's why Theo hated to even say it aloud. Still, it was bothering him. "It's about Lacey and Wesley. By any chance, did she ever mention him?"

"No." Ivy had the reaction that Theo expected. Confusion and surprise. "Why?"

"Wesley didn't even ask who Lacey was when she came into the sheriff's office. At that point, we weren't expecting her."

"Yes," she agreed after several moments. "But you don't think Wesley could be behind the attack?"

Theo certainly didn't want to believe it, but he just couldn't shake this feeling. "I've worked with Wesley a long time. In fact, we were teamed up on our last case where a fellow DEA agent was murdered."

She shook her head. "You believe the attack last night could somehow be connected to that?"

Theo scrubbed his hand over his face. "If it is, I can't see it."

That didn't mean he would stop looking, though. He would also be more careful about the info he got from Wesley. After all, it was Wesley's intel about the impending attack that had sent Theo running to the ranch.

"I called a DEA friend this morning," Theo explained. "His name is Matt Krueger, and he's someone I know I can trust. I asked him to look for any connections between Lacey and Wesley. Between Wesley and any of this," he added.

"But why would Wesley want to go after you?" she pressed. "Why would he want to go after you like this?" Ivy amended. "By including our families?"

"This is just a guess, but the attack last night could be the ultimate smoke screen, a way of making sure no suspicion fell on Wesley."

Still, that didn't answer one big question.

Why?

Was it somehow connected to the botched investigation and death of the DEA agent? Theo had spent hours going over every transcript and all the surveillance footage he could get his hands on, and even though he couldn't see anything wrong, he felt it. Deep in his gut. Something about all of it wasn't right.

"Are you thinking that Wesley could be dirty?" she asked.

He had to shrug. "That whole undercover operation had hitches right from the start," Theo explained. He couldn't give her some details because they were classified, but he could tell her the big picture. "There was a militia group dealing arms and drugs, and some of those came from a cache of weapons that'd been seized in a federal raid. The agent who was killed was at the heart of both the bust to seize those weapons and the undercover operation of the militia group."

And now that the agent was dead, there was no way he could answer the questions that were eating away at Theo.

"God," she said. "If Wesley had anything to do with this…"

"Wesley doesn't know the location of the safe house," Theo told her when he realized all of this had put the alarm back in her eyes. "Only Jameson, Gabriel and the four of us know. And just in case something else goes wrong, if someone did manage to follow us, Jameson is working on setting up a second safe house. A backup."

The sound of footsteps stopped him from saying anything else, and Theo automatically slid his hand over his gun in his holster. But it wasn't a threat. It was Nathan.

"Aunt Jodi's taking a shower," he greeted. "Is there any cereal and milk? I'm hungry."

Ivy went to the counter, where there were bags of groceries and supplies, and she rummaged through them. "No cereal, but there are some granola bars."

Nathan didn't seem disappointed with that, and he opened the fridge to take out the carton of milk. Since he couldn't reach the cabinet and because Ivy was opening the box of granola bars, Theo got a glass for him and set it on the table. Nathan poured himself a glass, all the while keeping his attention on Theo.

"I'm not dumb, you know," Nathan said. "I heard

Aunt Jodi and Uncle Gabriel on the phone. She was whispering, but I heard her." He had a big drink of the milk. "You're my dad, aren't you?"

Even though Theo could feel the question coming, it was still a shock to hear it. A shock for Ivy, too, because she stood there, her hand frozen while she reached out to give Nathan the granola bar.

"Yeah, I am," Theo answered. He braced himself in case Ivy was going to blast him for revealing that, but she merely put the bar on the table and sank down in the chair next to Nathan.

Nathan nodded. "We look alike. Aunt Jodi said."

His sister was a regular font of information, but Theo couldn't fault her for that. Nathan was her nephew, and with Ivy keeping that a secret, it meant she'd kept Nathan a secret from all of them.

"We do look alike," Theo agreed, and he turned to Ivy to see if she had anything to add to that.

"Are you mad that I didn't tell you?" she asked Nathan.

While he shook his head, he bit off a chunk of the bar. "I knew Dad wasn't my real dad. Lacey told me, remember?"

"I remember." Ivy's jaw was suddenly a little tight.

Theo waited for Nathan to ask more—such as why Theo hadn't seen him in all this time—but he continued to eat his breakfast as if this were an ordinary day.

"Are those bad men going to find us?" Nathan finally said.

Theo wished they'd stayed on the subject of fatherhood, but he hadn't expected Nathan just to forget the attack. "No. That's why we're in this house. If we have to stay here long, I'll have one of your uncles bring out some cereal for you."

"Thanks." He finished off the last bite of the granola bar and looked up at Theo. "Will you and my mom be together? You know, like some moms and dads?"

Theo was certain he had the same deer-in-the-headlights look as Ivy, but Ivy didn't seem to have trouble finding her voice. "No. But you will get to see Theo if that's what you want."

"Sure." Nathan stood and cleaned up after himself. "Can I go play a game on the computer now?"

Ivy nodded, and she seemed to release the breath she'd been holding when Nathan took off. However, he quickly stopped and whirled back around. "I think Aunt Jodi's a little sad. Because this was supposed to be the day she got married to Uncle Gabriel."

"I'll talk to her," Theo assured him. That was apparently all the answer he needed, because Nathan hurried to the bedroom.

Theo waited to see if Ivy would start to cry again, but she blew out another long breath and sat next to him. "I thought Nathan would take it harder than that."

Theo made a sound of agreement. And since she'd brought it up—and wasn't crying—he pushed the conversation a little. "When this is over, I want to see a whole lot more of Nathan. I want to get to know him."

She stared at him. "But what about your job? You're rarely around."

"True, but that could change. I've been a joe for a long time, and the DEA would probably like to see me behind a desk for a while."

"You'd want to do that?" She made it sound as if he'd be jumping off a cliff.

Nothing so drastic, but it would be a total lifestyle change for him. One that Theo hadn't thought he'd ever want to make. Then again, he'd never thought he would have a son, either.

"I'm not walking away from Nathan," he warned her. "He'll get to know me as his father, the way he should have from the start."

He hadn't meant for that to sound so harsh, but it was hard to rein in the emotions when it came to the boy. Ivy held all the emotional cards here. She had the history and connection with their son. He was going to have to build it from the ground up.

"Gabriel, Jodi and Jameson will want to spend time with him, too," Theo went on. "After all, Nathan is their only nephew." And he waited for her to dismiss that or accept it.

One way or another, Ivy was going to have to accept it.

He didn't have to wait long. She gave another of those weary sighs. "I didn't plan to keep Nathan from my brothers or Jodi. Or from you. It all got mixed up into one giant mental mess. The murders. Our breakup. Jodi nearly dying. Gabriel and Jameson weren't in a good place mentally, and they had their hands full with the investigation. When I suspected I might be pregnant, I decided to leave." She paused. "They honestly didn't know about Nathan. I made sure they didn't know."

Because Gabriel and Jameson would have gone after her and tried to bring her home. He got that.

"And you didn't stay around, either," she reminded him.

No, he hadn't. "I had to get away, too." He'd had his own mental mess to deal with. "I kept thinking I should have been there to protect Jodi. I shouldn't have let that monster nearly knife her to death. That got mixed up with me being a suspect. Then my father's arrest."

Ivy stayed quiet a moment. "Do you think Travis is innocent?"

He couldn't give her a simple answer. Because there wasn't one. "I thought he was. Then Jodi and the rest of you started getting those threatening letters and emails. I'm a lawman, so I had to look at it from the angle that maybe the real killer was doing this so he could taunt you."

"Or it could be August trying to create doubt for his brother," she quickly pointed out.

Yes, that was more than possible. Still, he doubted his father would have gone along with a plan if it'd actually endangered either the Beckett children or Jodi and him. That meant there was still the possibility of a real killer out there or someone with a sick obsession about all of this.

Theo's phone buzzed, and he saw DEA agent Matt Krueger's name on the screen. He answered the call while he went to the window to have a look outside.

"Please tell me you found something about that militia raid I was asking about," Theo greeted.

Matt hesitated a moment. "Yes, that. I did go over everything, and I see what you mean about maybe the pieces not fitting. I'm thinking someone could have tipped off the militia about agents having infiltrated them."

That's what Theo had considered as well, but it still twisted at him to think that a fellow agent could have done that. "Is there any proof?"

"Maybe. I just went through the surveillance footage

we have, and Wesley made a call about thirty minutes before the attack. Since he was using a prepaid cell, there's no way to trace it. Any idea who he called?"

"None." In fact, that was the point in the assignment, when he, Wesley and the agent who'd died— Ross Callahan—should have been keeping watch for an arms shipment that was about to come in.

"I think it's time for me to ask Wesley about this," Theo added. "I'll give him a call—"

"You haven't heard?" Matt interrupted.

"Heard what?" Theo asked.

"I just got the news a couple of minutes ago. Gabriel apparently took Wesley into custody. Don't know the details yet, but the sheriff found some kind of evidence to link Wesley to those dead gunmen."

Everything inside Theo went still. "What kind of evidence?"

"I'm not sure. Gabriel's holding that close to the vest. But Wesley claims that you set him up, that you're the one responsible for those gunmen who attacked last night."

Theo cursed. "And why the hell would I have done something like that?"

Matt hesitated again. "Wesley said you did it to get Ivy out of the way so you could get custody of your son."

Chapter 8

Theo was still cursing under his breath after they got in the cruiser, and even though Ivy hadn't timed it, it'd been well over an hour since his intense phone conversation with Matt Krueger.

During that time, Wesley had accused Theo of attempted murder.

And that's why Theo had immediately started making plans to go to the sheriff's office in Blue River. He did that by arranging for Jameson to come out and stay with Nathan while the deputy, Cameron Doran, drove with Theo as backup into town. Theo and Cameron had been friends since childhood, and Theo trusted him. But Ivy made sure she was in on those plans, too, even though Theo had insisted it wasn't the right thing to do.

Heck, she wasn't sure it was the right thing, either, but she did want to be there when Gabriel interrogated

Wesley. And Lacey, as well. Gabriel had had to reschedule her interview so that her lawyer would be there with her.

"If Wesley's the one behind this," Theo said to her, "then you're not the target. That means there's no reason for you to be there."

Theo had already voiced several variations of that argument to get her to stay at the safe house, and it might be true. The investigation had certainly taken a strange turn, what with Wesley's accusations. Too bad that it might take them a long time to sort it out.

Time they didn't have.

Nathan was okay for now at the safe house with Jodi and Jameson, but Ivy hated the thought of him being shut away. Hated more that her little boy was in danger. Maybe they would get some answers, and soon, and put an end to that.

Theo continued to mumble profanity while he read a text. He did that while volleying glances all around them. So did Cameron while he drove them toward town. Thankfully, it was a rural road with no other traffic, so it should be easy to spot someone trying to follow them. Unfortunately, there were plenty of old ranch trails and even some thick woods between the safe house and Blue River. That's the reason Theo had wanted Cameron to make this drive with him.

"SAPD can't find a money trail for McKenzie and either of the dead gunmen," Theo relayed to her once he'd finished reading the text.

It was frustrating but something she'd expected. None of their known suspects would have left that kind of evidence behind.

"What about the phone call McKenzie made to Lacey?" she asked.

Theo shook his head. "SAPD can't even be sure McKenzie made that call. There were no prints on the phone. It'd been wiped clean."

Ivy huffed. "That means someone could have killed McKenzie and then used his phone to set up Lacey."

"Yep. And Lacey could have done it that way to throw suspicion off herself. That way, if her name did show up on any of McKenzie's other outgoing calls, then she could say she was being framed."

"And she might be," Ivy admitted. "If someone wants us dead, Lacey would be the perfect patsy since she has motive. Well, motive to go after Nathan and me, anyway. But the person behind this could plan to make it look as if the real target was caught in the middle." She paused. "Of course, we don't know who the 'real target' is."

Theo made a sound of agreement. "About how much money does Lacey think she lost out on with the inheritance?" he asked.

"Four million," she answered after a pause.

That got the reaction she expected. Shock. Yes, she'd married a rich, older man. Practically a cliché. But what was missing from that cliché was that Chad had loved her and had taken very good care of Nathan and her.

"Four million is a lot of motive for murder," Theo pointed out. "You said something about your late husband wanting Lacey to learn to be more responsible. I take it they clashed?"

"A lot. Lacey hated me right from the start and thought I was trying to replace her mother. She died of cancer when Lacey was just a little girl. I think she would have resented any woman her dad married, but it didn't help that she and I are so close in age. She probably would have called me a gold digger, but I had my own money."

Not as much as Chad, but it was close.

"Anyway, Chad divided his estate between Nathan and me," Ivy added. "He left Lacey only a small amount that'll remain in a trust until she's forty."

Theo shifted his position a little until their gazes connected. "Chad loved Nathan."

"He did, in his own way. More like an uncle's love than a father's." Chad had loved her, too, but Ivy figured she didn't need to spell that out. She especially didn't need to spell out that she'd never loved the man who had made her his wife.

"Good," he said under his breath just as his phone dinged again with another text message. The texts had been coming in at a steady rate since the earlier call from the DEA agent.

"Wesley brought my boss in on this," Theo read. "He's also demanding that Gabriel take me into custody."

She was betting her brother wasn't going to do that. Well, unless Wesley came up with some kind of evidence that would force Gabriel's hand.

Theo groaned softly. "I didn't do what Wesley said I did."

"I know," Ivy readily agreed. Theo turned toward her, fast, as if he hadn't expected her to dismiss the charges so easily. "You're not the sort to break the law," she added. "Well, not since you were sixteen."

The corner of his mouth lifted into a smile. One that lasted only a couple of seconds. But it was nice to see it even for that short time. It brought back memories of other smiles, of happier times.

That seemed a lifetime ago.

"My run-ins with the law were petty," he said. "And stupid."

"Yes. I remember the time you and your friends took my dad's tractor apart and reassembled it in the hayloft. Must have taken you hours."

"All night," Theo admitted. "Your dad had warned me not to touch you when I took you out so I wanted to give him a little payback."

Well, it had certainly struck a nerve with her dad, that's for sure. But then her father had never liked Theo. Sherman had thought right from the start that Ivy could do a whole lot better than the likes of Theo Canton.

She hadn't.

In some ways, no man had ever lived up to him. And that wasn't an especially comforting thought. Things between Theo and her were tense. Maybe not as much as they had been just twenty-four hours earlier, but they were a long way from getting over their pasts.

Something they would have to do for Nathan's sake.

"Has anyone gotten in touch with your sister?" Cameron asked Ivy. "Because Lauren could be in danger, too."

Ivy nodded. "Jameson called her. She didn't answer her phone, but then she usually lets any calls from family go to voice mail."

She met Cameron's eyes in the rearview mirror and saw the flicker of emotion. It was gone in a flash and probably something he hadn't wanted her to see. But Ivy could guess what this was about. Cameron had once been in love with her kid sister, and the murders had torn them apart. Just as it'd done to Theo and her. Now, Lauren had built her life far away from Blue River. Far away from family and friends.

"Lauren is taking precautions in case this guy goes after her?" Theo pressed.

"She texted Jameson back and told him she'd be careful. She has a son now, so I'm sure she will do anything to protect him."

Theo glanced at Cameron, and even though neither man said anything, everyone knew that Lauren was still a raw nerve for Cameron. It probably hadn't helped that she'd gotten married and become a mom. A single mom, though, since her husband had died a little over a year ago. Or so Ivy had heard. Lauren hadn't exactly stayed in touch with her, either.

"So many lives got messed up that night the Becketts died," Cameron mumbled. "Lauren blamed me for a lot of that."

She had. And the blame was partially warranted. Cameron had been a rookie deputy at the time, along with being friends with Theo's family. Just a couple of hours before the murders, Cameron had run into Travis drunk outside the town's bar. He'd taken Travis's keys, but he hadn't arrested him for public intoxication. If Cameron had, then Travis would have been locked up, and he couldn't have committed two murders. She doubted Cameron would ever forgive himself for that.

And neither would Lauren.

"What the hell?" Cameron said, getting Ivy's attention. Theo's, too.

She followed the deputy's gaze to the road ahead and spotted a blond-haired woman. Ivy didn't recognize her, but she was on the gravel shoulder, her hands in the air as if she were surrendering.

"You know her?" Theo immediately asked Cameron.

"No. She's not local. I have no idea why she's in the road, but I don't think she's carrying a gun."

Ivy agreed, and since the woman was wearing a body-clinging cotton dress, it would have been hard for her to conceal a weapon. Not impossible, though, and that's probably why Theo motioned for Ivy to get down on the seat. She did, but not before trying to get a better glimpse of whatever the heck was going on.

"You see anyone else?" Theo again, and the question was directed at Cameron.

"No," the deputy repeated, and he slowed the cruiser to a crawl. "Keep the windows up," he instructed—probably because they were bullet-resistant. "She doesn't have on any shoes, and her feet are bleeding. It's possible she got stranded by the river or something."

It was the possibility of that "or something" that troubled Ivy, and when Cameron brought the cruiser to a stop, Ivy could see the woman. She still had her hands in the air. And looked dazed. Her hair was a tangled mess, and while Ivy didn't have a view of her feet, there was also blood and what appeared to be a bruise on the right side of her face. What she didn't do was rush forward.

Strange.

After all, they were in a Blue River Sheriff's Department cruiser that was clearly marked, and both Cameron and Theo were wearing their badges.

Cameron called for an ambulance for backup. He did that because he probably wanted a cop to go with her to the hospital. Then he lowered his window just a fraction.

"Are you all right?" he asked her, sounding very much like the lawman that he was.

She shook her head. "I think I was kidnapped."

Yes, definitely strange. A person should know for certain if they were kidnapped or not, but maybe someone had drugged her. Whoever had done that perhaps caused that injury to her face.

"What's your name?" Cameron pressed. "And who kidnapped you?"

Another shake of her head, and a hoarse sob tore from her mouth. "I'm not supposed to be here."

Cameron huffed. "Then where are you supposed to be, and who brought you here?"

Several moments crawled by, and while Theo was watching her, he continued to glance around. Ivy wanted to help him do that, but she knew it would only make him more on edge if she did.

"I'm sorry," the woman said.

"For what?" Cameron snapped.

But she didn't get a chance to answer. That's because a shot cracked through the air and the bullet slammed right into the woman's chest.

Theo didn't see the shooter, but he certainly heard the bullet. And he had no trouble seeing the damage it did.

The blonde made a sharp sound of pain, clutched her chest and dropped to the ground. Theo didn't think she was dead, but she soon would be. The blood was already spreading across the front of her dress.

"We have gunfire," Cameron said to whoever he had called. Probably Gabriel, who would in turn have to hold off on sending in an ambulance.

"Can you pull her into the cruiser?" Ivy asked, as she sat up to get a better look at their surroundings.

Theo was already debating doing just that. It would be a risk, but at this point anything they did would be. The woman had clearly been drugged and was probably part of a trap to get them to stop. It'd worked, but if she was truly innocent in all of this, she could die.

He didn't have long to dwell on his decision, though, because there was another sound. A second shot, and this one didn't go into the woman.

It blasted into the window just above Ivy's head. The glass held though it did crack, but it wouldn't hold for long if the shooter kept firing into it.

And that's exactly what he did.

"You see the gunman?" Cameron asked.

"No. But he must be in those trees across the road." The woods were thick there, and even though the morning sun was bright, the light wasn't making it through the dense branches and underbrush.

Who the hell was doing this?

Theo didn't know, but at the moment their best bet for telling them that was lying on the ground, bleeding out.

"Can you open the window on the front passenger's side just enough to return fire?" Theo said to Cameron.

Cameron glanced back at him, and he didn't look any more certain of this than Theo felt. "You're going to get the woman in the cruiser?"

Theo hoped he didn't regret this, but he nodded. "Get down on the floor," he instructed Ivy. That would not only get her a few inches farther from the window, it would free up the seat so he could drag the woman inside.

"Please be careful," Ivy said, the fear and emotion

thick in her voice. It was in her expression, too, and Theo would have liked the time to assure her this was the right thing to do, but there was nothing he could say that would take the worry off her face.

Hell, he was worried, too.

Not for himself and Cameron. But for Ivy. If she was indeed the target, then all of this could be designed to get to her.

Several more shots came at them, each tearing through the window next to Ivy. Obviously, the gunmen were focusing on her. Or else the thug wanted them to think she was the focus. Theo wasn't going to take any of this at face value.

Cameron kept the engine running, but he moved to the passenger's window, lowered it just enough to stick out the barrel of his gun and looked at Theo to give him the go-ahead.

Theo nodded.

And Cameron fired.

The moment the deputy did that, Theo threw open his door, and he glanced over his shoulder to make sure Ivy was still down. She was. But she was watching him and mumbling something. A prayer, from the sound of it.

Theo moved as fast as he could and hoped he didn't do any more damage to the injured woman when he latched onto her arm and started dragging her to the cruiser. The shots didn't stop. In fact, the gunman picked up the pace, and this time he fired at Theo. The bullets slammed into the ground, kicking up the gravel that was on the shoulder.

The woman cried out in pain, and that's when Theo realized she'd been hit again. This time in the shoulder.

Theo hadn't needed any more incentive to move as fast as he could, but that did it.

And he got some help.

Unwanted help.

Ivy scrambled over the floor of the cruiser, and the moment Theo was back at the door, she reached out and helped him drag the woman inside. By doing that, she put herself in even greater danger. Later, Theo would tell her what a stupid thing that was to do, but then he saw the bullets slam into the ground where he'd just been. If Ivy hadn't helped, he could be dead.

"Get us out of here," Theo said to Cameron as soon as he had the woman on the seat.

Cameron was already moving to do that, and as soon as he was back behind the wheel, he hit the accelerator.

The cruiser sped away as the bullets continued to rip through the window.

Chapter 9

Ivy tried to force herself to focus. There was a lot going on at the Blue River sheriff's office, but she couldn't grasp it all. That probably had to do with the spent adrenaline that had left her exhausted.

Too bad the exhaustion hadn't stopped the sound of the gunshots from echoing in her head. Or stopped the fear that was still racing through her. Mercy, she wanted that gone most of all, because at the moment most of those fears were for her son.

The gunman who'd fired those shots had gotten away. And it wasn't as if no one had looked for him. Gabriel had sent out two deputies almost immediately, but by the time they'd arrived, there'd been no sign of him. That meant the man was out there, probably waiting to attack. Or worse, waiting to follow them to the safe house where Nathan was with Jameson and Jodi.

"How did the gunman even know we'd be on that stretch of the road?" she asked. It wasn't the first time she'd wanted to know that, and Ivy didn't direct the question at anyone in particular.

Theo, however, put away his phone after making his latest call and went to her. He skimmed his hand down her arm, probably a gesture to try to comfort her, but Ivy figured nothing much was going to soothe her right now.

"There are only two roads leading into Blue River," Theo reminded her. "There could have been a gunman on both."

Yes. And that meant there could have been another woman or hostage to force them into stopping. Or coerced. If so, Ivy hoped they found the person, and the thugs hadn't done to him or her what they'd done to the woman they'd encountered. She couldn't imagine that someone had volunteered to be shot as part of the plan to lure her out into the open.

"Jameson is on full alert," Theo went on. "If anyone tries to get near the safe house, he'll let us know."

She didn't doubt that. Didn't doubt that her brother and Jodi would be vigilant. But this monster could still get to them.

"I just want to rush back to Nathan," she said. Ivy cursed the tears that she was having to blink back. Tears weren't going to help this, and they only put more stress on Theo because it was obvious he was concerned about her. Ivy quickly waved that off. "But I don't want to lead the guy straight to Nathan, either."

Theo nodded to let her know they were on the same page about that. Actually, they were on the same page about several things, and it wasn't all related to the in-

vestigation. The attraction that kept rearing its head and
the fact that they would do anything to protect their son.

"Any updates on the woman who was shot?" Ivy
asked. Maybe if she talked about the investigation, she
could get her mind off Nathan. "Or Wesley?"

Even though the agent was still in the building, he
was in an interview room with Gabriel and Theo's boss.
Gabriel hadn't wanted Theo to be part of that, maybe
because he now had Theo on his suspect list. Even if
he hadn't been a suspect, though, it could still compromise things since Wesley and he were fellow agents.

"There's nothing on Wesley," Theo answered, "but
whatever he's telling Gabriel is a lie. I didn't have anything to do with this."

"I know," she assured him, and it wasn't lip ser-
vice. Theo wouldn't do anything to harm Nathan and
her. And no, that wasn't the attraction talking. Now,
though, she might have to convince Gabriel of Theo's
innocence—something she hadn't tried to do ten years
ago. That was a mistake she didn't intend to make again.

"As for the woman, I just talked to a doctor at the
hospital, and she's still alive," Theo went on. "That's
the good news. But she'd been heavily drugged, and
one of the gunshot wounds is serious. She's in surgery."

Ivy already knew the woman hadn't said anything
in the cruiser on the drive to the hospital because she
was unconscious through the entire trip. She also hadn't
moved at all when the medics had taken her away on
a gurney. Of course, Theo, Cameron and Ivy hadn't
waited around to talk to the doctor. It was too dangerous. Instead, Theo had rushed them to the sheriff's office, where they'd been for the past hour.

"The woman didn't have an ID on her," Theo went

on, "so we're not positive who she is. But she matches the description of a woman, Belinda Travers, who went missing the night before. From McKenzie's club."

That got Ivy's attention. "She knew McKenzie?"

He lifted his shoulder. "It's possible she just went into the bar, one of the hired guns saw her and decided to use her as bait."

So she could be innocent in all of this. It sickened Ivy to think of how many people had been hurt—or could be hurt—and they didn't know why or by who.

"They did a bug sweep of the sheriff's office and the rest of the building while we were at the safe house," Theo said a moment later. "And they found one."

She could have sworn her heart skipped a couple of beats, and the panic came. It was so strong that she nearly bolted for the door so she could go after Nathan. Theo took hold of her arm and anchored her in place.

"It was by the dispatch desk," he explained, "and it's been removed."

The dispatch desk was also Reception. That meant anyone who'd come into the building could have put it there. Heck, it could have been there for weeks or longer.

"Remember, we whispered whenever we talked about the safe house," Theo reminded her.

Yes, they had. Maybe that had been enough to keep those thugs away from her son.

"Come on." Theo still had hold of her, and he got her moving toward the hall. "We can go to the break room and maybe you can get some rest."

Rest was out, but her legs suddenly felt too wobbly to stand. Maybe she could at least sit down and wait for news about when they could return to the safe house. However, they only made it a few steps down the hall when the interview room door opened, and Gabriel stepped out. Judging from her brother's expression, things hadn't gone well. She got further confirmation of that when Wesley and the other man came out.

Dwight Emory.

Even though Ivy hadn't met the man, she knew this was Theo and Wesley's boss. He didn't look especially pleased, either, but then, one of his agents—Wesley—was accusing a fellow agent—Theo—of a crime.

"Well?" Theo prompted when no one said anything.

"We're sorting it out," Emory answered.

"We're not close to sorting it out," Wesley snarled. He nailed a glare to Theo. "How could you do this to me? We've been partners for years. Friends," he amended. "At least I thought we were, and then you start asking questions. You're treating me like a criminal."

Theo huffed, and his hands went on his hips. "Seems to me you're the one who said I wanted Ivy out of the way so I could get Nathan."

"Don't you?" Wesley challenged.

"No." And Theo moved closer to her, sliding his arm around her waist. He probably did that because she wasn't looking so steady, but it was also a signal to Wesley and Emory that the old baggage between them wasn't as toxic as it had once been.

Ivy wasn't sure when that'd happened exactly. Maybe around the time Theo had been trying to save her life.

Theo volleyed glances between Emory and Gabriel. "What kind of proof did Wesley produce to make an accusation like that against me?"

"A CI told me," Wesley volunteered.

Ivy wasn't sure who gave Wesley the flattest look,

but Gabriel, Theo and even Emory weren't jumping to embrace the so-called evidence.

"We're trying to find the CI now," Emory finally said. "If he confirms Wesley's claim, then we'll still have to consider the source." Emory looked at her then. "As you can imagine, CIs aren't always truthful, and this could be a situation of someone wanting to get back at Theo."

"Yeah, Wesley could be doing that," Theo insisted. "Because he might want to get suspicion off himself."

Wesley howled out a protest, but Gabriel made a sound of agreement. "I got the security footage of McKenzie's bar. It's grainy and there are only a few good camera angles—"

"I didn't go there to pay off anybody," Wesley interrupted.

Ivy glanced at Theo to see if he knew what any of this was about, but he only shook his head. "What happened on that footage?" Theo asked Gabriel.

Her brother took a deep breath first. "When Wesley entered the bar, he took out an envelope from his jacket pocket. And, yeah, he was wearing a jacket despite the fact that it was ninety degrees outside. It gets grainy when Wesley goes to a booth in the corner, but it appears he gives the envelope to a known thug by the name of Nixon Vaughn."

Oh, mercy. That wasn't good, and Ivy immediately wondered if this Vaughn was a hired gun. Maybe the very one who'd attacked them today and shot that woman.

"He's not on payroll for the DEA or any other agency," Emory added.

Theo's jaw was very tight when he turned to Wesley. "Did you pay off Vaughn?"

Wesley's jaw wasn't exactly relaxed, either. "Yes. Because you told me to."

A burst of air left Theo's mouth. "No, I didn't. And what makes you think I did?"

"I got a text from you." Wesley muttered some profanity under his breath. "You said to give Vaughn five hundred bucks, and that you'd pay me back. You said Vaughn had info about the threatening letters the Becketts had been getting. So I gave Vaughn the money, but he said he didn't know anything about the Becketts."

"The text came from a burner cell," Emory provided.

"Theo uses burners all the time," Wesley snapped.

As the daughter and sister of cops, Ivy knew what a burner was. It was a prepaid phone that couldn't be traced. Theo probably did use them for his job, but in this case someone had used it to set him up.

To maybe set up Wesley, too.

But why would someone have done that?

Maybe the person hoped to get both Theo and Wesley thrown off the case. If so, it wasn't working. Theo wasn't going to let this go whether he was officially on the investigation or not, and she doubted Wesley would just walk away, either.

"Obviously, I need to look into this further," Emory said. "But at this point, Wesley is going back to his office, and, Theo, the sheriff and I decided you should continue with protective custody for Ivy and her son."

Emory hesitated before "her son," as if he weren't sure whether to include Theo in that parent label or not.

Theo thanked his boss, though it wasn't a very enthusiastic one, and he shot Wesley a glare before he started with her toward the break room. Both Emory and Wesley walked away, but Gabriel stayed put.

"Your dad's lawyer called first thing this morning," Gabriel said, stopping Theo in his tracks. "August visited Travis and told him about Nathan. Travis asked if he could see him."

"No," Theo answered without giving even a moment's thought. Then he shook his head, cursed. "Even if it were safe to take Nathan out, I don't want him visiting a prison."

Both Gabriel and Ivy added a sound of agreement, though they were in tricky territory here. Nathan was Travis's only grandchild, but since Travis was also a convicted killer of her own parents, then Ivy didn't want to give Travis the chance to say anything to the boy that could possibly upset him. Nathan had already been through enough, and she had told him only a few sketchy details about her folks' deaths. She certainly hadn't told him that his grandfather was a convicted murderer.

"The lawyer said he could set up a Skype call with all of you and Travis," Gabriel added. "I told him if you were interested in that, you'd let him know. I didn't tell him that hell might freeze over before that happened."

Theo smiled, muttered a thanks. He turned to get her moving but then stopped again. "What about Jodi's and your wedding? You were supposed to be getting married today."

"Yeah." Gabriel sounded and looked disappointed. "It's still on hold. Jodi and I are okay with that."

They no doubt were okay, but Ivy hated that their plans had been derailed because of some sick monster who wanted at least some of them dead. Of course, all the danger seemed to point to Theo, Nathan and her. At least Jodi didn't seem to be in the path of a killer. After she had already survived not one but two attacks, Ivy didn't want her soon-to-be sister-in-law to go through anything else like that.

Theo led her to the break room, such that it was. It had a microwave, small fridge and a beat-up leather sofa. Theo had her sit, got her a bottle of water from the fridge and then took out his phone. At first she thought he was going to make another of those calls to get updates on the investigation, but when he put it on speaker, she heard Jameson's voice.

"How's Nathan?" Theo immediately asked.

"Fine. Jodi and he are watching a movie. Are Ivy and you okay?"

Since Jameson knew about the attack, he was aware that they hadn't been injured. Not physically, anyway. "I think Ivy will be a lot better if she can talk to Nathan." And Theo handed her the phone.

Other than the initial call to the safe house after they'd arrived at the sheriff's office, Ivy hadn't considered talking to Nathan. She hadn't wanted him to hear the fear in her voice, but the moment her son came onto the line, that fear vanished.

"Uncle Jameson taught me to play poker," Nathan proudly announced.

"Kiddie poker," Jameson corrected.

Ivy figured it was the real deal since her brother favored that particular game, and she honestly didn't mind. Nathan sounded excited as if this were some kind a treat, and that was better than the alternative. Plus, he was getting to spend time with his uncle, something that Nathan hadn't ever had a chance to do.

"Aunt Jodi can't cook at all," Nathan went on. "She burned the toast and cut her finger when she was trying to make a sandwich. But Uncle Jameson can make grilled cheese and popcorn."

"Hey, I'm giving him some fruit, too," Jameson called out.

"Yeah, fruit and chocolate milk," Nathan concurred.

Again, her son sounded happy. "I miss you," Ivy told him. "But maybe it won't be long before Theo…your dad and I can come back."

"Okay. Can you bring some pizza?"

Ivy had to smile. "I'll try." Even after all the food that was just mentioned, she wasn't surprised that Nathan had pizza on the mind. It was his favorite. "See you soon, sweetheart."

Even though she was so glad she'd been able to speak to Nathan, the moment she ended the call, Ivy felt the loss. She had spent so little time away from him that even this short while felt like an eternity.

"I've missed so much," Theo said.

She looked at him, saw the loss on his face, too, but it was far worse than hers. After all, she'd had Nathan all these years that he hadn't. It hadn't been a decision to keep Nathan from Theo. At first, it'd been because of the rift between them and then because she couldn't find him. But after seeing Theo's raw expression, Ivy wished she'd done more.

Theo had indeed missed a lot.

She stood and went to him, and though it wasn't a smart thing to do, she pulled him into her arms. At least that's what she started to do, but Theo did some pulling of his own. Maybe it was the emotion of the moment or the fact that they'd just escaped death. Either way, it was as if he snapped. He dragged her to him.

And he kissed her.

It had been ten years since Theo's mouth had been on hers, but the memories—and the feelings—came flooding back. Ivy hadn't especially needed a kiss to remind her why Theo and she had been together in the first place, but the heat was just as hot as it had been back when they were teenagers.

He'd been the first boy to kiss her, and she had lost her virginity to him. And yes, there was still enough attraction there that she remembered exactly why that had happened. Theo had had her hormonal number then, and he still had it now.

She heard herself make a sound of pleasure, something she often did whenever she was around Theo, and the sound only increased when he deepened the kiss. He added some nice body pressure, too, with his chest moving right against her breasts. It didn't take long for her body to recall just how good the pleasure could be. It also didn't take long for Ivy to find herself wanting more.

Theo was obviously on that "more" page as well because he turned her, moving her so that her back was against the wall. He made the adjustment with her, still touching her with his body. Especially one part of him. In the maneuvering, his thigh ended up between her legs, and the pressure started to build there.

She broke the kiss so she could breathe, and when she pulled back a few inches, Ivy was staring right into his eyes. Those eyes had always had her number, too, and it didn't seem to matter that ten years had passed, because her body was on fire. Still, she forced herself to remember they were in the break room where anyone could come walking in at any second. No way would Gabriel approve of such a thing, and she shouldn't approve of it, either, since they had so many more important things they should be doing.

She repeated that last part to herself. It didn't help. Every inch of her was still zinging from the kiss.

"I should say I'm sorry for that." Theo's voice was husky and deep, and it did nothing to cool her off. It also did nothing to make her want an apology from him or even regret that it'd happened.

But she should regret it.

There were still a lot of unsettled things between Theo and her. Added to that, someone was trying to kill them. The last thing she should have been doing was kissing him. Or wanting to kiss him again.

Which she did.

Ivy might have done just that, too, but the break room door opened, and Gabriel came in. Theo and she immediately stepped apart. She was certain they looked guilty, and equally certain that her brother was aware of what'd happened between them. And yes, Gabriel scowled in a way that only a big brother could manage when he believed his kid sister was making a mistake.

The same mistake she'd made a decade ago.

"I would offer to give you a moment," Gabriel grumbled, sarcasm in his voice, "but this is important."

That got her heart pumping. "Is Nathan okay?"

"This isn't about Nathan. A courier just arrived with some very interesting things that you should take a look at." He turned, headed back toward his office and said the rest from over his shoulder. "Cameron is calling Lacey now to get her in here. She's in town, staying at the inn, so it shouldn't take her long to get here. Once you see this, you'll know why I might have to arrest her."

Chapter 10

Theo forced his attention on Gabriel and what he'd just told them. It should have been an easy thing to do, what with the investigation and the danger, but he first had to shake off the effects of that kiss.

What the hell had he been thinking?

He had no idea, but Theo knew for a fact which of his body parts had encouraged him to do that, and it was the very part of him that could make stupid choices just like that one. Later, he would owe Ivy that apology he'd skirted around, but it would have to wait for now. Clearly, Gabriel had something important to show them.

"The courier is still here," Gabriel said to them as they walked into his office. "I've put him in an interview room so I can find out more about who had him deliver this. The envelope just has the name John Smith, no address, and the courier only had a vague description of the guy."

It was probably vague because the person hadn't wanted to draw attention to himself. Or could have even been wearing a disguise. If the person who'd attacked them was behind this, he or she probably wouldn't have done something so stupid as approaching the courier themselves. They would have hired someone to do that. Someone who couldn't be traced back to them.

Theo figured Gabriel was going to clarify all of this very soon, but for now he had one big question. "What does Lacey have to do with this?"

"Maybe everything." Gabriel tipped his head to his desk where Theo saw not only a manila envelope, but the item that was lying next to it. It was in a clear plastic evidence bag.

A silver watch.

Hell. What was going on here? The watch face was ordinary, but the band had small copper insets. Theo had only seen one other watch like that.

It had belonged to Ivy and Gabriel's father.

Ivy gasped, pressed her fingers against her mouth and took a step back. She shook her head. "Is that…Dad's?"

"According to this, it is," Gabriel said. He seemed to be struggling with seeing the watch, too. Of course, it didn't help that Sherman had been wearing it at the time of his murder.

And that the killer had taken the watch—probably as some kind of sick trophy.

The watch hadn't been found on Theo's father, though. For that matter, neither had the knife that'd murdered Sherman and his wife.

"It's a lab report," Gabriel said. He didn't touch the paper next to the envelope, but he pointed to it. "Someone claims to have had prints and trace run on the watch." He paused, his forehead bunching up. "There's a small amount of blood. A DNA match to Dad."

Ivy didn't gasp again, but she made a soft, strangling sound, groped around for the chair that was behind her and sank down onto it. "Where's it been this whole time?"

Gabriel shook his head. "The lab report doesn't mention that. Of course, my theory was that Travis had hidden it somewhere. Or ditched it like he did the knife. And maybe he did."

Someone had found the knife, though, hidden it away and then tried to use it to kill Jodi. That'd happened only a month earlier. But the person who'd done that was dead and couldn't have been the one to send the watch.

"I'll have it tested, of course," Gabriel continued a moment later. "Not just for blood but also to verify the partial prints that this report says were on the watch band."

"Prints?" Ivy repeated. "Whose?"

Theo figured it was Travis's prints. Since Sherman's blood had been found on Travis's shirt, it wouldn't be much of a stretch for the prints to belong to his father, as well.

Apparently they didn't, though.

"They're Lacey's," Gabriel said.

Oh, man. That explained why Gabriel had wanted Ivy's stepdaughter brought in, but that was about all it explained.

"Lacey was twenty when our parents were killed," Ivy pointed out. "And she didn't know them. She didn't even live close to Blue River when the murders happened."

"That's exactly why I want to talk to her," Gabriel continued. "If those are really her prints, then she must have touched the watch at some point—either at the time of the murder or afterward."

"*Afterward* could mean someone is setting her up," Theo pointed out. But then there was a problem with that. "Who had the watch to be able to do something like that, and why set up Lacey this way? If someone wanted to tie her to the attacks, there would have been an easier way to do that by just creating a fake money trail."

Obviously, neither Gabriel nor Ivy had answers for that, and if it was a setup, Lacey might not know it, either. But it could mean she'd come in contact with someone who'd been present at the murders. *Could.*

Theo hoped Ivy didn't take this the wrong way, but he had to ask. "Is it possible that your late husband knew your parents?"

She shook her head. But then she paused. "I honestly never asked him. All of that was still so raw and painful when I met Chad, and he seemed to sense that I didn't want to talk about it."

Theo looked at Gabriel, who was already taking out his phone. "I'll see if Chad's name came up at any point during the investigation or the check of the old police records."

That brought Ivy to her feet. "You can't think Chad killed them." She didn't seem to have any doubts about that. "Because he was a gentle man. He definitely wasn't a killer."

Theo took her hand and had her sit again. "I believe you, but it's possible he had some connection to my father. He might have known him, might have sympathized with the feud that was going on between the Becketts and the Cantons. Yeah, it's a long shot," he quickly added, "but we're working with nothing but long shots here."

And that meant Theo might have to talk to Travis after all. Not to have him meet Nathan. Not a chance. But rather to start ruling out any association he could have possibly had with Chad.

"How'd you meet Chad?" Gabriel asked the moment he ended his call.

She narrowed her eyes a little at her brother. Obviously, she wasn't pleased that her late husband was coming into question. Probably because it was too hard to wrap her mind around the fact that she might have been living with the man who'd had some part in her parents' death. And maybe he didn't. Again, this was a long shot.

"I met him at a livestock auction near Houston," Ivy finally answered. "I'd just bought a small place and wanted to buy a horse. Chad sat next to me, and when Nathan started fussing, he started making funny faces at him and got him to stop."

For reasons Theo didn't want to explore, hearing that caused him to scowl. He figured what he was feeling was some old-fashioned jealousy, but hell, it was hard to hear of any man having that kind of interaction with his son when he hadn't had the chance to even see the baby.

Hard to hear about Ivy being with another man, too.

That kiss was responsible for him feeling that. And in this case, the jealousy didn't make a lick of sense. He'd been with other women since Ivy, but then, he hadn't married any of them. In fact, he hadn't even gotten past the casual sex stage. Theo had always blamed that on his job, but after that kiss with Ivy, he knew that his feelings for her were still there, and they had probably been playing into it even after all these years.

Ivy pushed her hair from her face, looked away. "After we met at the auction, Chad asked me out for coffee, and eventually I went…four months later."

So Ivy hadn't exactly jumped at the chance to be with another man. Not that Theo believed she had. Nathan had been nearly a year old when she'd married Chad, and that meant by then Theo had been out of her life for almost two years. She'd moved on. But she'd moved on with a man who could have some connection to the Beckett murders.

"If Chad had known my parents or had anything to do with that watch, why would he have asked me out?" Ivy questioned. "Why would he have married me? Because I can promise you that he never asked a question about my parents, and he certainly never tried to hurt me. So you're wasting your time trying to link Chad to Lacey's prints on that watch."

"You're wasting your time to link me to it, too," Lacey said.

The woman came into the doorway. Cameron was right behind her, and judging from the deputy's frustrated expression, he'd been trying to hold her back.

Lacey aimed glares at all of them, including Cameron, and her glare was still in place when her attention landed on the watch. "That's why you brought me in here?" she asked Gabriel.

Gabriel gave her a glare of his own. "Your prints are on it. Why?"

Theo carefully watched her expression, and if she was the least bit concerned about the accusations against her, she didn't show it. Instead, she shrugged. "About a week or so ago, I was at the mall, and when I came out, that watch was lying on the hood of my car. I picked it up. I figured someone walking by had found it, thought it was mine and left it for me."

Theo didn't glare, but he was certain he looked skeptical. Because he was. "How'd the watch get from you to here?" he demanded.

"How should I know? I tossed it on the ground, got in my car and left. I didn't want to leave it on the hood because I thought it might hit my windshield and chip the glass."

"And you didn't think it was suspicious that someone would put a watch on your car?" Ivy asked. There was skepticism in her voice, too.

Lacey hadn't seemed to object too much to Theo's question, but she clearly didn't like Ivy's. "No, because like I said, I thought someone believed it was mine. Obviously, it's not my style, and it belongs to a man. I don't even have a current boyfriend."

If Lacey was telling the truth, then someone indeed had set her up. But Theo wasn't convinced that it'd been the truth that had come out of Lacey's mouth.

"Did you see anyone near your vehicle before you spotted the watch?" Gabriel pressed.

"No. Now, what's this about? Why is that watch so blasted important?"

"It belonged to my father," Ivy answered after everyone paused. "It went missing the night of his murder."

Now Lacey had a reaction. Her eyes widened, and she shook her head. "Oh, no. You're not going to try to pin that on me. It's bad enough that I'm stuck in this cowpoke town because the sheriff here thinks I might be behind the attacks to kill the likes of you. I won't have you accusing me of your parents' murders."

"How about your father?" Theo asked, ignoring the

insults Lacey had peppered into her comments. "Could Chad have killed them?" He knew that wasn't going to earn him a kind look from Ivy. It didn't.

Lacey howled out a protest, but she didn't limit it to just Theo. She snapped toward Ivy, too. "You're behind this, aren't you? You think if you can get me out of the way, then I can't get what's rightfully mine."

Ivy blew out a long breath and stood, facing Lacey head-on. "I'm not behind this. If I'd found my father's watch, I would have given it to the cops because it might have some kind of evidence on it. I darn sure wouldn't have put it on your car, knowing that you could toss it."

That didn't seem to soothe Lacey any. The veins in her neck were practically bulging, and her nostrils were flared. "Please. You'd do anything to stop me from getting my father's money."

"Not anything," Ivy argued. "But there is something I can do to make sure my son is safe, and I did it. I had a lawyer redo my will. Since I'm trustee of Nathan's inheritance, I can make decisions about that, too. So if anything happens to Nathan and me, all of your father's money will go to charity."

The color drained from Lacey's face, and she looked at Theo for confirmation of that. He had no idea if it was true or not, but he nodded. "This way, you have no motive to come after our son."

"I never tried to kill him!" she shouted. Then she snapped back to Ivy. "You have no right to a single penny of my dad's money."

"Neither do you." Ivy huffed again, and Theo could see she was having to wrestle with her own temper. "Look, I would give you the money but your father asked me not to do that. It was his dying wish, something he told me many times over, and I'm going to do what he wanted."

Good call, because at this point just giving Lacey the money might not put an end to the danger. It seemed to Theo that Lacey wanted Ivy and Nathan completely out of the picture.

"My father loved me," the woman stated through clenched teeth.

"And he knew you," Ivy agreed. "He didn't think you were responsible enough to handle another large sum of money. Plus, he knew you wouldn't share it with me."

"Because it wasn't your money to have! You brainwashed my father. You got him to fall for you because he'd always wanted a son. Well, your brat kid isn't his son and never will be."

"No, because he's my son." Theo probably shouldn't have blurted that out, but Ivy wasn't the only one having to put a choke hold on her temper. He started to address the brat comment but decided against it. He'd already said too much.

"Like I care whose kid he is," Lacey grumbled. "This isn't over," she added to Ivy, and she turned as if to leave.

"No, it's not," Gabriel agreed. "And you're not going anywhere just yet." He ignored her protest and went into the hall, motioning for Cameron to join them. "I need you to continue this interview with Miss Vogel, and if she refuses, lock her up. Based on what I have here, we won't have any trouble getting a court order."

Lacey fired glances at all of them. "You'll be sorry for this," she spat out, and she slung off Cameron's grip when he took hold of her arm.

However, Lacey didn't head out the front door, something Theo had thought she might try to do. She followed Cameron to his desk.

Gabriel stepped back in his office and shut the door. "You think she's lying?" he asked Theo and Ivy.

"I don't know," Theo admitted when Ivy shook her head. "But I don't trust her."

Both Gabriel and Ivy made sounds of agreement to that.

"Who could have left that watch for her?" Ivy asked, but she didn't wait for them to answer. "August, maybe? I know he wasn't at our old house the night of the murders, but maybe Travis gave it to him?"

No, August hadn't been at either the Beckett or the Canton house. Instead, he'd been with a woman one town over, and she'd provided him with an alibi for the time of the murders. That didn't mean, though, that August hadn't run into Travis later, since Theo's father hadn't been found until the following morning. Those were a lot of hours when a transfer like that could have taken place, and there was no way August would have volunteered that Travis had had the watch because it would have added another nail to his conviction for the murders.

"If Travis gave him the watch, August wouldn't have turned it over to Gabriel," Theo pointed out. But Theo had some trouble finishing that theory. "Why wouldn't August have planted the watch on someone who's a more plausible suspect, someone we would actually believe could have killed your parents if my father hadn't done it? Or he could have just tossed it in the river, where it probably would have never been found."

Obviously, Theo wasn't the only one having trouble coming up with a reason for August to do this.

"Now, Wesley—yes," Theo went on. "I can see an

angle for him on this. If he'd somehow managed to get the watch, then he could have used it to frame Lacey so it would take suspicion off him."

"How would Wesley have gotten the watch, though?" Ivy asked.

Theo had the answer for this one. "Wesley was around during the murder investigation. In fact, he was a San Antonio cop then, and a group of them came out to help comb the area when everyone was looking for Travis. He could have found the watch then."

That didn't explain, though, why a cop would have kept something like that, but maybe Wesley had been dirty even back then. If so, he'd certainly kept his dirty deeds hidden away.

"There's a third theory, though," Theo continued a moment later. One that he hated to even consider. "Someone could be playing a cat-and-mouse game with us. Maybe a person my father has somehow managed to hire." He paused, not really wanting to consider this one as well, but they needed to look at all of the possibilities. However, it was Gabriel who finished that train of thought for him.

"Or your father could be innocent, and the real killer is out there," Gabriel said.

None of them believed that. Or at least they didn't want to believe it. Because if it was true, it would turn this investigation—and their lives—upside down. Again. It also meant Theo had no way of protecting Ivy from a nameless, faceless monster who could have already butchered at least two people and had plenty of others in his or her sight.

Maybe even their son.

If this was truly someone wanting to spill Beckett

blood, then Nathan could be a target. Of course, a killer could also use the boy to draw out Ivy and Theo. And it could work, since both of them would lay down their lives for the boy.

Theo hadn't intended to do it, but he slid his hand over Ivy's shoulder. Gabriel noticed, too. But then he was also the one who'd walked in on Ivy and him shortly after that kiss. Judging from Gabriel's expression, he was about to dole out some big brother advice. Maybe even a big brother warning. However, his phone rang before he could do that.

Theo kept his hand in place, and Ivy looked up at him. Their gazes connected for just a second before Gabriel interrupted them.

"It's the doctor who performed surgery on the injured woman." Gabriel put the call on speaker.

Theo braced himself for the doc to say the woman was dead. That would be tragic not only because she might be truly innocent in all of this, but also because they would lose their chance to question her.

"She's awake," the doctor announced. "And she says her name is Belinda Travers."

So she was the woman who'd gone missing from McKenzie's place. "Did she say anything else?" Theo asked at the same moment Gabriel said, "How soon can I talk to her?"

"Give it another hour," the doctor answered. "By then, she should be a little more alert. And as for the other question—yes, she told me something else. She said someone kidnapped her from a bar. She doesn't know the person who did that, but the reason she was there was to meet August Canton."

Chapter 11

Ivy wanted nothing more than to go back to the safe house so she could see Nathan. But there was no way her brother could spare the manpower right now. No way that Theo would let Ivy and him drive back there alone, either. Not after the other attack on the road and with the possibility of hired thugs still being in the area.

So she paced the hall in front of Gabriel's office. Waited. And worried.

Gabriel had already questioned the courier and hadn't uncovered anything new, but her brother was definitely hoping to learn something from the watch, which he'd already sent for processing. Also to learn something from August. Once the man came in, that is. August had some answering to do over Belinda's accusations that she'd been at McKenzie's bar to meet him.

At least Lacey and Wesley wouldn't be around. Or

rather they shouldn't be. It was unnerving enough having August return, and Ivy didn't especially want to be under the same roof with all three of their suspects.

The worries kept coming, too. Because the greatest danger might not be with August, Lacey or Wesley. Gabriel had mentioned the possibility of Travis being innocent, and if by some serious long shot he actually was, then God knew who'd killed her parents. But whoever it was could want her and the rest of her family dead.

Not exactly a reassuring thought.

That could explain why she and other members of her family had been getting those threatening letters over the years. There'd been details in some of those letters—such as her mother's necklace being taken—and the police had purposely kept those out of the reports. It'd been a way of putting a lid on false confessions. So the person who'd written those threats had either managed to hack into those reports, or else he'd been there that night to take the necklace while he'd murdered her mother.

Ivy had to close her eyes a moment to shut out the images. She'd been the one to discover her parents and had actually stepped in her mother's blood when she ran to the bodies. There'd been nothing she could do, and she didn't even remember making the frantic call to Gabriel. Good thing she had, too, because when he'd run to their parents', he'd discovered Jodi on the path. She was within minutes of bleeding out, and he'd managed to save her.

Something Ivy hadn't been able to do for her folks.

There were times, like now, when she reminded herself that the horror that'd gone on that night could have been even worse. Jodi could be dead, too. Maybe even Gabriel as well, since Jodi's attacker was probably nearby when her brother had found her. Remembering that soothed Ivy a little. But not enough to make the ache fade in her heart.

Theo finished the call he'd just made to the crime lab, glanced at her and frowned. "You can't dwell on it," he said.

It was as if he'd looked right into her mind—something he'd always had a knack for doing—but she didn't care much for it now. In some ways it made it worse that he knew how much she was still hurting. In some ways, though, it made it better. This wasn't a case of misery loving company, it was just that Theo understood how much she'd lost that night. Because he'd lost so much himself.

"How do you forget?" she asked. "How do you push it all aside?"

He stared at her, shook his head. "You don't." On a heavy sigh, he went to Gabriel's fridge, grabbed a bottle of water and brought it to her. "There's no permanent fix for grief. It keeps coming back."

Yes, it did. Like now. It was washing over her.

"Sometimes, it helps if I think about the good stuff," he added. He pushed her hair from her face, his fingers lingering on her cheek. "How close Jodi and I once were. The times I was with you. I just force myself to remember that there were more good times than bad."

Good advice. Too bad she couldn't take it. It was impossible to push away the fear. Or so she thought. But then she looked at Theo, their gazes connecting, and just like that, things were a little better.

And worse.

Because even now with all the bad memories flooding her mind, she noticed him. That rumpled hair. That mouth. Mercy, he had a way of getting right past the fear and into places inside her where he shouldn't be. Like her heart. Of course, her heart wasn't the only problem at the moment. Theo also knew how to stir up things in her body.

Yes, there'd been plenty of good times, and most of those moments had centered on him.

"I would ask you to go to the break room…" he said, arching his eyebrow as if that were a question rather than an attempt at a joke.

Despite everything going on, Ivy had to fight back a smile. "Probably not a good idea."

Theo kept his eyes on her as if waiting for something more. Conversation, maybe? An assurance that she was okay?

Another kiss?

If it was the kiss, then Ivy imagined it would be the kiss that people gave each other when they were used to kissing. When that kiss would suddenly make all the bad things go away. Something that it couldn't do. But it could cause the old heat to slide right through her. In fact, just the thought of kissing him did that to her. It also helped that Theo was so close to her that she caught his scent.

More of that heat came.

"I've seen that look before." He brushed his fingers over the center of her forehead, which was bunched up.

Now she waited, because she wasn't sure where he was going with this. Maybe he had noticed the need in her expression. Or perhaps he was picking up on all the other things—the worry, the fatigue and, yes, the fear.

He didn't take his fingers from her face. Instead,

Theo slipped them lower, to her cheek, and his touch—warm and soothing—lingered a moment there. Even though he didn't say anything, they had an entire conversation. About this mutual attraction that was messing with their minds. About what had torn them apart in the past. Even what might bring them back together in the future.

Nathan.

Theo must have realized this wasn't going to be something they could hash out now. Nor should they be doing this. Not with the danger still out there. And that's probably why he stepped back. Not far enough, though. Of course, several rooms over might not have been far enough to get her body to cool down.

"I'm sorry," he said, the frown returning.

Those two words certainly started the cooling-down process. "For what?"

"For not being able to keep you safe."

That's where she thought this was leading, and she didn't like it one bit. "I could be the reason you're in danger," she reminded him. Ivy was about to repeat his apology to him, but then she stopped when an idea went through her head. "Has anyone checked to see if my father was maybe investigating Wesley?"

She expected Theo to look surprised at the abrupt change in conversation, but he merely nodded. "I did last night. All your father's cases aren't digitized, but Gabriel did a summary of each of them and put the info in a master file and shared it with me."

Now Ivy was the one who was surprised, and she felt her eyes widen. She hadn't known about the master file or the sharing part, and Gabriel must have been able to get over the rocky past with Theo for him to give him that info.

"And?" she asked.

"Your father didn't specifically mention Wesley's name, but he was working on a case that involved SAPD. Sherman had busted some guys for drugs, and he found some guns on them that had been confiscated in a raid in San Antonio. The weapons had been reported as destroyed, but clearly they weren't."

Ivy took a moment to think that through. "So a San Antonio cop sold or gave them the gun?"

Theo lifted his shoulder. "Or it could have been a paperwork error. It happens," he added. "I'll keep digging, but so far I haven't found anything that connects Wesley to the chain of custody of those guns."

And without that, it would be almost impossible to tie Wesley to it—and to her father's murder.

Ivy shook her head. "Maybe I'm overthinking this. Your father was convicted of the murders, and he has never denied doing it." Of course, that was mainly because Travis had been drunk and couldn't remember. "Anyway, maybe Wesley isn't dirty at all. Maybe that drug bust my father made is just muddying already muddy waters."

Theo certainly didn't argue with that. Which meant they were back to Lacey and August. And speaking of August, Ivy heard the man's voice in the squad room. A very unhappy voice. It wasn't a shock that he was riled about being brought back in again for questioning.

"There'd better be a damn good reason you dragged me back here," August shouted. And yes, it was a shout. "Because I'm sick and tired of being accused of things I didn't do."

Gabriel had been at one of the deputies' desks, but he got to his feet and motioned for August to follow him. Her brother didn't shout, but he was scowling.

Both Theo and she stepped to the side so that Gabriel could lead August into his office. The watch, envelope and report were no longer there. They'd been couriered to the crime lab.

"First things first," Gabriel said to August. "Tell me about Belinda Travers."

"Who?" August made a face. "Never heard of her."

"Well, she's heard of you. She says you were supposed to meet her in a bar in San Antonio, but then someone kidnapped her."

"What?" August howled. "She's lying."

Gabriel and Theo exchanged glances, both of them clearly not happy with that denial. Maybe when the woman was able to talk to them, she could prove that August was the liar.

Gabriel dragged in a long breath and turned his computer monitor in August's direction. "Tell me about this," Gabriel ordered him. It was a picture of her father's watch.

Before August's attention actually landed on the screen, he'd already opened his mouth. No doubt to shout something again about how innocent he was. But he not only closed his mouth, he also moved in closer for a better look.

"Where did you get that?" August demanded.

"I asked you a question first," Gabriel fired back. He didn't add more, maybe because he wanted to see where August would go with this.

It didn't take long for August to respond. He cursed. It wasn't exactly angry cursing, though. His shoulders dropped, and while he shook his head, August sank down on the edge of Gabriel's desk.

"Hell," August mumbled. That definitely wasn't a denial, and neither was his body language. "I need to know where you got the watch," August said, and this time it wasn't a demand. Even though he didn't add a *please*, it was there, unspoken.

"I figured it'd come from you," Gabriel answered.

Since August was a hothead, his normal response would have been to verbally blast Gabriel for suggesting that. He didn't. Mercy, did that mean it'd actually come from August? If so, how had he gotten it, and why had he used it to try to set up Lacey?

"Start talking," Theo ordered him. He stepped closer to his uncle, violating his personal space, and August spared him a glance before his gaze darted away.

"I found the watch shortly after Travis's trial," August explained after a long pause. "It was in the barn at Travis's ranch." He looked up at Theo. "You know that corner where your daddy used to store sacks of feed? Well, there were some loose boards on the wall," he said when Theo nodded. "I looked behind them and saw the watch."

Theo tilted his head, his mouth tightening. Gabriel had a similar expression—one of skepticism.

"SAPD went through that barn," Theo reminded him. "So did Gabriel and Jameson."

August nodded. "So did I, and I didn't see it. Someone had tucked it up behind the boards. I think the only reason I found it was that some of the nails had given way and caused the board to come loose."

Ivy supposed it was possible that Travis had taken the watch and then hidden it there. Well, it was believable if you discounted the fact that Travis had been drunk the night of the murders. Apparently, he'd been so drunk that he'd passed out shortly thereafter.

"How do you think my dad's watch got there?" Ivy came out and asked.

"I have no idea." Now August shifted his attention to her. "But this still doesn't make my brother guilty. The killer could have easily planted it there hours and even days after the crime. Like I said, I didn't find it until after the trial, and that was months later."

"You found it and yet you didn't turn it over to Gabriel?" Theo's mouth was in a flat line now.

"I couldn't see the point of it," August answered without hesitation. "Travis had just gotten a life sentence. I didn't think it would do much good if folks knew a dead man's watch had been found in his alleged killer's barn."

"It wasn't alleged," Gabriel said. "He was convicted. And you should have given the watch to me instead of trying to use it as some kind of ploy to set up Lacey Vogel."

"What?" August jumped to his feet, and she saw that flash of temper that'd been missing the last couple of minutes. "Is that what she said I did? Because I sure as hell didn't."

Theo and Gabriel exchanged more glances. Confused ones. Ivy was right there with them.

"Someone put the watch on Lacey's vehicle," Theo explained. "She tossed the watch aside, and that person then took it and sent it to a lab. It has both Sherman Beckett's blood and Lacey's prints. Not your prints, though. Why is that if you're the one who found it?"

August's gaze slashed between the two lawmen, and

his eyes widened before he cursed again. "My prints weren't on it because I used a paper towel to pick it up. I then wrapped it in that towel and put it in Travis's house. In plain view on the coffee table in the living room. I figured if Jodi and Theo came back, they'd see it and turn it in."

Theo huffed. "Why the hell would you do that?"

Ivy wanted to know the same thing. To the best of her knowledge, Theo and Jodi had never gone back to the house. Like her own parents' house, Travis's place had been empty. Abandoned.

"I didn't want the watch at my house," August said as if that explained everything. "I just figured it'd be better if I left it at Travis's."

"Better because it would seem as if someone had put it there to taunt the police," Theo snapped. "You did that to try to make my father look innocent. Or at least that's why you did if you're telling us the truth."

"I am," August insisted.

Maybe he was, but if so, he didn't deny Theo's accusation about leaving the watch to make Travis appear innocent.

"Someone must have taken the watch from Travis's house," August went on. "But why would that person then want to set up Ivy's stepdaughter?"

Ivy didn't know, but she had a theory. "Lacey hates me and would do anything to get back at me. It wouldn't surprise me if she had had someone go through both my parents' and Travis's places. Maybe so she could find something she could use against me. Something to help her win a lawsuit to get her hands on her dad's money."

All three men were staring at her now. Maybe waiting for her to come up with more, but Ivy didn't have more. She didn't have a clue how Lacey would hope to connect the watch to her.

But Theo apparently did.

Still, there was something about all of this that didn't make sense. Ivy gave that some more thought but had to shake her head. "That seems like a lot of trouble to go through just to cast some doubt on my name."

Theo lifted his shoulder. "Maybe it's all she could find and figured she'd use it. By having her own prints on it, too, she might think it takes suspicion off her. It doesn't." Theo shifted his gaze to August. "Nor you. Gabriel could file charges against you for withholding evidence."

August's mouth practically dropped open, and he snapped to Gabriel. "By the time I found the watch, the investigation and the trial were over."

"Doesn't matter," Gabriel answered. "Anything connected to the case should have been given to me."

"What the hell would you have to gain by bringing charges against me?" August's temper was not only back, but it had also risen a couple of notches.

"Justice," Gabriel answered without hesitation. "Plus, if you'd given me the watch, we'd wouldn't be in this situation now of wondering who's trying to use it and why."

August would have no doubt responded to that with a fury-laced tirade, but Theo's phone rang, the sound knifing through the room. The moment Theo glanced at the screen, Ivy knew from his suddenly tight expression that there was a problem.

"It's Jameson," Theo told her, and he answered the call.

Ivy moved even closer to Theo so she could hear

what her brother was saying, but it was a very short conversation. One that ended with Theo cursing and taking hold of her arm.

"We need to leave now," Theo said. "Jameson said there's an armed intruder on the grounds of the safe house."

Chapter 12

Theo had been on plenty of assignments where he'd faced down killers, but that suddenly felt like a drop in the bucket compared to what he was facing now.

His son could be in grave danger.

That in itself was bad enough, but in the back of his mind he also had to wonder if this was a trap to draw Ivy and him out for yet another attack. Hell, even that wasn't worse than an intruder going after Nathan.

"Just stay calm," Jodi said from the other end of the line.

She was whispering, something she'd done since she had taken over the call from Jameson. His sister was in the bathroom with Nathan while Jameson was at the front of the house to make sure the intruder they'd seen didn't get inside. She was keeping her voice low so that anyone outside the house wouldn't be able to hear her and pinpoint her location.

"Any idea where the intruder is now?" Gabriel asked from the front seat of the cruiser. He was driving— something he'd insisted on doing—not just so they'd have more backup but also because he'd been concerned that Theo and Ivy were too upset to be speeding down the rural road.

Gabriel was right. Theo was upset. But Ivy was to the point of being panicked. That was no doubt why Jodi kept reminding them to stay calm.

"Jameson just said he spotted the guy again," Jodi relayed. "He's in the ditch near the front of the road."

That probably meant the guy had tripped the motion sensor and that's how Jameson had known he was there in the first place. Maybe now that Jameson knew his location, he could just shoot him or keep him pinned down until they got there. Theo would have liked to have the guy alive, but he didn't want that to happen at the expense of Nathan, Jodi and Jameson.

"The ditch doesn't lead to the house," Jodi added. "Even if the man crawls toward us, the nearest he can get is about twenty yards."

That was still close. Too close. The goon could fire into the house, and the shots could make it through the walls and into the bathroom. Of course, if the gunman lifted his head to fire, Jameson should be able to take him out.

Provided the goon didn't shoot Jameson first, that is. But since that made Theo's own panic soar, he reminded himself that Jameson was a capable lawman. A lawman who was protecting his nephew and his brother's fiancée.

"How did this person find the safe house?" Ivy asked. Her voice was hoarse, no doubt because her throat was tight. Her knuckles were turning white from the grip she had on the seat. "Did he follow us the first time we went there?"

Not likely. Theo was almost certain they hadn't been followed, and it would have been fairly easy to spot someone doing that on this road.

"The listening device," Theo guessed. "Even though we whispered when we were inside, someone still could have heard us. Plus, all three of our suspects were in the sheriff's office and could have overheard something."

Ivy whispered the profanity that Theo was thinking. They'd known about those possible bugs, but they'd gotten so caught up in the danger and investigation that they might not have been as careful as they could have been. Not just with the bug, either. Because it was also possible that someone had sneaked into the parking lot of the sheriff's building and planted tracking devices on the cruisers.

"Is Jameson sure there's just one intruder?" Ivy asked several moments later.

"He thinks just the one," Jodi answered.

His sister could be saying that to calm Ivy's nerves. But Theo figured the only thing that would calm her was for Ivy to see Nathan and make sure all was well. That might not happen for a while. For one thing, they were still a good ten minutes out. For another, the thug might start shooting at them the moment they got there. If he wasn't alone, then Gabriel could be driving right into a trap. That's the reason Theo took out his backup weapon and handed it to Ivy.

"It's just a precaution," he said when her eyes widened.

"Keep watch around us," Gabriel reminded them, and then added to Ivy, "That's a precaution, too."

A huge one. Because this stretch of road had plenty

of trees. Ditches, too. More thugs could be lying in wait for them.

Those last few miles seemed to take an eternity, though Theo was certain Gabriel was going as fast as he could safely go. When Gabriel finally reached the turn to the house, he slowed and glanced around.

"Jodi, I'm going to hang up and text Jameson," Gabriel told her. "I've got a visual on the house and the ditch, but I can't see the gunman." Gabriel did text his brother, and it only took a few seconds for Jameson to reply.

The guy is near the mailbox, Jameson responded, and Gabriel read the text to them.

"Get down on the seat," Theo instructed Ivy, and he lowered his window just a fraction. "If you drive up closer, I'll see if I can get this idiot to surrender," he added to Gabriel.

Gabriel did begin to inch the cruiser closer just as his phone buzzed with a call. "It's not Jameson," he said. "It's the hospital, but I'll call them back." Instead, he kept his attention on the ditch.

"Stand so we can see you," Theo called out to the man. "And put your hands in the air."

Theo figured there was no way that would work, and it didn't. Almost immediately, the man got to his feet. But he definitely did not put his hands in the air. Nor did he surrender. Instead he turned, aiming his gun at the cruiser, and he fired. The shot slammed into the front windshield. Just like the other attack, the glass held, but Theo couldn't risk this idiot firing shots that stood any chance whatsoever of hitting any of them.

"Stay down," Theo reminded Ivy, and he lowered

the window even more. When the goon lifted himself to shoot at them again, Theo fired first.

His bullet hit the man squarely in the chest.

The goon fell backward, his weapon thudding to the ground next to him. Gabriel didn't waste any time driving the cruiser closer to him. Jameson came out the front of the house as well, but he stayed back on the porch. Probably because there could be other gunmen in the area.

Gabriel stopped the cruiser right next to the wounded man, and Theo opened his door wide enough to snatch up the thug's weapon. Of course, he could be carrying a backup, but at the moment he wasn't reaching for anything. He was clutching his chest.

And he was bleeding out.

Gabriel called for an ambulance, but Theo doubted it would get there in time. That meant anything they could get from the guy, he had to try to get it now.

"Who are you?" Theo demanded.

The guy shook his head. "My name won't mean anything to you."

"Try." Theo kept his gun pointed right at him.

"Morris Carlyn." He groaned in pain, pressing his hands even harder over his wound.

The name didn't mean anything to Theo, but it soon would. Gabriel fired off a text, no doubt to get a background on this guy. Once they had that, they might be able to link him to one of their suspects.

"Who sent you, Morris?" Theo asked.

Another headshake. "There's no threat you can make that'll be worse than what'll happen if I talk."

"Wanna bet?" Theo took aim at the guy's leg. "I can start putting bullets in you. It won't kill you any faster, but it'll make your last minutes on this earth very, very painful."

It was a bluff, of course. He couldn't shoot an unarmed, dying man, but mercy, that's what he wanted to do if it would help them put a stop to the danger.

The guy looked at him, their gazes connecting. "My family could be hurt. That's why I can't tell you. That's why I agreed to do this."

All right. So someone had maybe blackmailed or coerced him. Theo glanced at Gabriel to see if he was already on that. He was. Gabriel sent another text that probably included cops going to this guy's house to check on anyone who might be there.

"How did you find this place?" Theo continued.

"I was just told to come here and kidnap the woman, Ivy Beckett. I was supposed to take her alive."

Hell. That was hard to hear. Obviously hard for Ivy to hear, too, because she gasped.

If the guy was telling the truth, and that was still a big *if*, it didn't rule out any of their suspects. Wesley or Lacey would want Ivy alive so they could use her as a bargaining chip to get whatever it was they wanted. In Lacey's case so she could get the money. For Wesley, it could have been so he could maybe force Theo into a rescue situation so he could kill him. Because there was no way Theo wouldn't go after Ivy if this idiot had indeed managed to kidnap her.

It was ironic, though, that Wesley would be doing that because he thought Theo knew something about that botched militia raid. Other than a gut feeling, Theo had nothing, and you couldn't use gut feelings to make an arrest.

"Protect my family," the guy said, and his eyelids

fluttered down. Dead, probably. But Theo wasn't about to get out and check on him.

Apparently, Gabriel wasn't, either, because he sped toward the house, and he pulled the cruiser to a stop directly in front of the porch. Ivy immediately bolted out, running past Jameson and going inside.

"Any sign of other gunmen?" Gabriel asked his brother as they rushed in behind Ivy.

"No. But the sensors are still working because they went off when you got here." Jameson armed the security system and then tipped his head to the ditch. "Is the guy dead?"

"Probably," Gabriel answered, and he went to the window to keep watch while he made a call. No doubt to follow up on the thug's family.

"Go ahead. Check on Nathan," Jameson told him when Theo kept looking in the direction of the hall bathroom. "Once we've regrouped and gotten more backup out here, we'll have to leave, though."

No way would Theo disagree with that. He wanted backup and plenty of it, but he also wanted Ivy and his son out of there. The location had been compromised, and that meant there could be another attack. Or another attempt to kidnap Ivy. Either way, they were all at risk.

The moment Theo stepped into the bathroom, Jodi hurried out, saying that she wanted to check on Gabriel. Theo stood there a moment and watched his sister go to the man she obviously loved. He saw the fear now, on her face and in her body language. The relief, too, that Gabriel was all right.

Theo felt that same relief when he looked at Nathan. Well, what he could see of him, anyway. Ivy had him wrapped in her arms, and even though she wasn't crying, she was blinking hard. No doubt to try to stave off the tears.

"Did you do something to the bad man?" Nathan asked him. He maneuvered himself back just enough so that he could make eye contact with Theo.

Theo nodded and hoped that would be enough of an explanation. He really didn't want to have to tell Nathan that he'd just killed someone.

"Does this mean we have to leave?" Nathan added.

"Yes," Ivy and Theo answered in unison.

Nathan didn't seem upset about that, but he did volley some glances at both Ivy and him. "Will you two get together?" he asked.

It was a repeat of the same question the boy had hit them with earlier. It was understandable for him to want to know. After all, whatever Ivy and he did would affect Nathan's future.

"I mean, since Mr. Chad is dead and you're my parents and all," Nathan added. "I just figured you'd get together."

Considering that Theo's mind was still whirling from the attack, it was hard to switch gears in the conversation. Especially when the switch was this big. Theo looked at Ivy to see if she had an idea of how to answer that.

She didn't.

The blank stare that she gave Theo let him know that.

"We'll talk about that soon," Theo settled for saying. "For now, why don't we go ahead and start gathering up your things so we'll be ready to leave when the other deputies get here?"

Nathan got moving right away, and Ivy and Theo followed him to the bedroom not only to stand watch but to make sure he didn't go near the window. The blinds were down, curtains drawn, but there was no sense taking the risk.

"I can't go to the new safe house with him," Ivy said. Her voice was a hoarse whisper, and he saw that her hand was trembling when she touched her fingers to her mouth. "If someone is truly after me, I can't put him in danger like that."

Theo was already thinking along those same lines, but he doubted that Gabriel had two safe houses ready to go. That would take time.

Ivy turned to him, took hold of Theo's sleeve and pulled him out into the hall. "Just hear me out before you say no," she started.

And Theo groaned. Because he figured he wasn't going to like what would follow that comment.

"I think Jodi and Jameson should take Nathan to the backup safe house. Right away," Ivy added. "The deputies who are coming can follow them as backup. That'll get Nathan out of here in case there are other gunmen."

He couldn't object to any of that, but Theo could practically see where this was going. "You're not going to make yourself bait," he insisted.

"Not bait." She glanced in at Nathan, then pulled Theo even farther away from the room before she repeated those two words. "But we can't let things continue like this. If whoever's behind this can't get to me, they might decide to go after Nathan."

Just the thought of it twisted his gut. So did the fact that Theo couldn't deny that. If this person became even more desperate, then things might escalate fast.

"You're still not making yourself bait," he warned her.

"Controlled bait," Ivy corrected, and she kept on

talking despite Theo's protest. "While Nathan is safe with Jodi and Jameson—and you—Gabriel, Cameron and I can go back to Gabriel's place. We can use the ranch hands for extra protection. Maybe even set up some sensors like the ones that are here."

Theo was shaking his head before she even finished, but she took hold of his chin to stop him. "We can make things as safe as we can possibly make them," Ivy added.

That wasn't much of an argument, but then, no place was going to be completely safe. And yes, the ranch hands along with some motion detectors would beef up security. Maybe not enough, though.

"If we can sell Gabriel on this—and I'm not even sure I want to do that," Theo said, "then I wouldn't go with Nathan and the others. I'll be with you since the attack is most likely to happen at the ranch." Just saying that didn't help with the knot that was tightening even more in his stomach. "But first we need to find out if we can find the snake responsible for this before we have to do something this dangerous."

Ivy made a sound of agreement. "You mean talk to Belinda Travers. Gabriel got that call from the hospital, and it's probably about her. Maybe she's talking."

"Wait here with Nathan," Theo instructed, "and I'll find out."

Theo went back to the living room, where he found Jodi, Jameson and Gabriel all standing watch at the window. "Is Nathan okay?" Gabriel immediately asked him.

Theo nodded. "Ivy wants to send him to a separate safe house."

Even though Theo didn't explain Ivy's "controlled bait" idea, Gabriel obviously filled in the blanks because his mouth tightened. What he didn't do was dismiss it.

And that caused Theo to curse. "Belinda's not talking?"

Gabriel gave a heavy sigh. "She's dead."

Hell. Well, there went the notion of questioning her, but it was more than that. From the looks of things, Belinda had been innocent in all of this, and someone had murdered her. That someone wanted to do the same to Ivy, too.

"Please tell me someone didn't sneak into the hospital and finish her off," Theo said.

"No. She developed a blood clot. The doc told me that sometimes things like that happen."

Yeah. Bad things happened all the time. Theo had to make sure now that the bad things didn't continue with Nathan and Ivy.

"I think it's too late for the guy in the ditch, but just in case, the ambulance is on the way," Gabriel continued while he volleyed glances between Theo and the window. "The deputies will be here soon, too."

"What about the guy's family?" Theo wanted to know. "Any idea if they're really in danger?"

"I called SAPD as soon as we were all back in the house," Jameson volunteered. "They're on the way to check on them."

Theo hoped they were all right, but after what had happened to Belinda, it was possible the man's family was also in danger.

"Is there another safe house?" Theo's question got all of their attention. Ivy's as well, since she was now in the hall with Nathan behind her.

"One that's ready now," Gabriel answered. "It'll take me a while to set up another one."

"Wait in your room for just a few more minutes," Ivy told Nathan.

Judging from his pinched expression, that was the last thing Nathan wanted to do. The kid was no dummy, and he must have known that something big was about to happen. Still, he went into his room, and Ivy came closer to them. That's when Theo saw that she was blinking back tears again.

"Look, I don't want to be away from my son. Nor do I want to die." Ivy's voice was shaking, and one of those tears made it down her cheek. She quickly wiped it away.

Theo went to her and slid his arm around her waist. He doubted it would help. Nothing much would at this point.

"We have to put an end to this—*now*," Ivy insisted. "That means using me to draw out this monster."

Since Theo had already voiced his opinion on this, he stayed quiet and waited for Gabriel to tell her no way in hell was he going to put his sister in danger like that. But Gabriel didn't get a chance to say anything because Jameson's phone buzzed.

"It's SAPD," Jameson said. He answered the call but didn't put it on speaker. Several moments later, he cursed. "The gunman's house has been ransacked, and his wife and two kids are missing." Jameson paused, his attention going to Ivy. "Someone left a note on the guy's door."

"A note about me?" Ivy asked. Theo felt the muscles in her body tense.

Jameson nodded. "The note said, and I'm quoting, 'Tell Theo that Ivy will be next. She dies tonight.'"

Chapter 13

The note had chilled Ivy to the bone. It still did even several hours later. But it had been the final straw needed to convince Theo and her brothers that the only way to end this was to draw out the killer.

Not just for their sakes but for the gunman's family, too.

Ivy now knew that Morris Carlyn's family had indeed been kidnapped, and the cops didn't think it was a staged crime scene, either. The person who'd hired Morris had likely taken them to get him to cooperate. If he'd lived, that is. He hadn't, and Ivy prayed that meant the family would be released soon. While she was praying, she added several for Nathan and the rest of them.

She dies tonight.

If that was true, then she only had five or six hours before this monster tried to come after her. Five or six hours to get everything in place so that at least Nathan would be safe.

"It's time to go," Gabriel said as he disarmed the security system.

That was Ivy's cue to give Nathan one last hug and kiss before he went off with Jameson, Cameron and Jodi. Ivy trusted all three of them to keep her boy safe, but even though she seemed to be the target, there were no guarantees the culprit might not try to use Nathan the way he or she had used Morris's family.

"It'll be okay?" Nathan asked, but it took Ivy a moment to realize he'd aimed that question at Theo. "You'll take care of my mom?"

Theo certainly wasn't the ice man–lawman right now. His eyebrows were drawn together, and muscles in his shoulders looked stiff. "I will."

Nathan seemed to accept that because he nodded, went to Theo and hugged him. Everyone in the room looked surprised. Especially Theo. He hesitated just a moment before his arms went around Nathan to return the hug.

Ivy had been near tears all day, and seeing that put some fresh ones in her eyes. Over the years she hadn't allowed herself to consider how Theo would be with Nathan, but she could see how much he loved their son.

Theo brushed a kiss on top of Nathan's head, and the boy pulled back, meeting his gaze. "Will you teach me to ride a bull? Because Aunt Jodi said you used to ride them and that you were good at it."

Theo shot his sister a "thanks for nothing" glance. "Maybe when you're a little older," he answered.

Again, Nathan seemed to accept that because he smiled, gave Theo another hug and then hurried to the door next to Gabriel. "I know," Nathan said to him. "We gotta run fast when we get outside."

Since every one of them had mentioned that in some way or another, Ivy was glad it had sunk in. She went to the door, too, and from the side window, she saw that Cameron had pulled an unmarked police car next to the porch. Earlier, he'd gotten Nathan's things and put them in the trunk, and he'd already opened the back passenger's door.

Jodi and Jameson didn't waste any time getting Nathan outside and into the vehicle. Cameron immediately sped away. A second car with two reserve deputies followed them for backup.

"The new safe house is about ten miles from here," Gabriel said, "but it'll be a while before they get there."

Yes, because Cameron would have to drive around to make sure they weren't being followed. Gabriel had already explained that to her along with the assurance that all the vehicles had been checked and double-checked for bugs and tracking devices. Gabriel and the others had made it as safe as they possibly could, considering that Nathan would essentially be out in the open.

"Now it's our turn," Gabriel instructed.

Another of the deputies, Edwin Clary, pulled a cruiser in front of the house. This one was definitely marked with Blue River Sheriff emblazoned on the side, as was the one behind them that Deputy Jace Morrelli was driving. Along with Gabriel and Theo, that meant there'd be four lawmen driving her back to the ranch.

As Nathan and the others had done, they hurried to get into the cruiser, and Edwin drove them away. Ivy ended up in the middle of the back seat between Gabriel and Theo, and she automatically sank lower since she figured one of them would soon tell her to do that.

However, she kept her head just high enough to help them keep watch.

"We're going straight to the ranch," Gabriel continued, "even if someone follows us."

Ivy had figured that's how things would be, but it still sent a chill through her to hear it aloud.

"What's the plan once we're there?" Edwin asked. The deputy made eye contact in the mirror with Gabriel as he turned onto the road that would take them back to the ranch.

"The hands know we're coming, and they're all armed. Not out in the pastures, though. They've been setting up some sensors and cameras they got from the office to set up motion detectors and surveillance spots on the paths that lead to the house. Once they're finished, I want them out of sight."

It was smart to set up the equipment. Because the road was highly visible from Gabriel's house, but there were two paths that someone could use to get to them. In fact, the man who'd attacked Jodi ten years ago had used one of them. Maybe Travis had as well the night he'd murdered her parents. Those paths were lined with bushes and trees—the perfect place for a person to hide.

"Whoever comes after you," Gabriel continued, "we need to take him or her alive. That's the only way we're going to be able to figure out who's behind this."

Yes, especially considering that Belinda and Morris were dead and Morris's family was missing.

"That's why I want the hands and all of us tucked away. I don't want whoever's coming to see too many guns and turn back."

In other words, Gabriel was going to make it look like it would be an easy attack. Of course, the person behind this likely knew that it wouldn't be and would probably bring lots of firepower.

Ivy looked up at Theo the moment he looked down at her, and she saw something in his eyes that she was certain was in her own. A parent's worry. This was still a fairly new feeling for Theo, and she wished she could tell him that it would go away. It didn't. Even when there wasn't this kind of danger looming over them, she always worried about Nathan.

"Don't worry," Theo said. "I won't teach him how to ride a bull. Not anytime soon, anyway." The corner of his mouth lifted for just a moment.

Ivy was glad at his attempted humor. Glad, too, that it eased her racing heart just a little. She wanted to tell him she was glad he was there, but because he was there, with her, he was also at risk of being killed.

"How does Nathan do in school?" Theo asked. He glanced away from her to keep watch.

It seemed like such a, well, normal conversation. Definitely not the gloom and doom they'd been discussing since his return to Blue River.

"He gets As and Bs," she answered. "He struggles some with math, but he's way ahead in reading. In sports, too. He loves playing baseball."

Ivy realized she, too, was smiling a little, and she understood that's why Theo had talked about Nathan in the first place. That was probably the only thing that could help with the nerves. For a few seconds, anyway. And then Ivy felt the blasted tears threaten again.

On a heavy sigh, Theo slid his arm around her. She had on her seat belt, but Theo didn't, and he eased across the seat toward her. As he'd done with Nathan, he brushed a kiss on the top of her head.

"Thank you," she whispered. She automatically slid into the crook of his arm.

"Don't thank me yet," he whispered back, and she got the feeling they were talking about more than just the danger yet to come.

She looked up at him and got confirmation of that. The heat was still there. Simmering. And the kisses in Gabriel's office hadn't done a thing to cool it down. However, what did help was when Gabriel's phone buzzed, because that quickly got her attention. Theo's, too, since he moved back across the seat.

"It's nothing to do with Nathan," Gabriel said right off. "It's one of the hands. They have everything in place, and they're moving to their hidden positions now."

Good. Because they weren't far from the ranch now. Only a couple of minutes out.

"When we get there," Gabriel went on, looking at her, "I'll have Edwin pull up in front of the porch, and Theo, you and I will go inside. Edwin will leave and drive back toward town, but he'll actually pull off on a trail not far from here so he can make a quick response if necessary."

Ivy hoped it would be quick enough.

"I want you and Theo to go upstairs to the guest bathroom," Gabriel continued. "The hands have put a laptop there so you can watch the security cameras."

It took Ivy a moment to process that, and she didn't like where this was going. "If an attack happens, it'll likely be on the ground level of the house—where you'll be."

Gabriel nodded. "And I'll know they're coming before they even get here. I don't want to make this easy for whoever's after you by giving someone the opportunity to just start firing shots into the place. There's also another cruiser parked out of sight in the barn, and if things get bad, I want Theo to get you there and drive the two of you off the ranch. Don't worry, the hands and I will get out, too."

That caused every muscle in Ivy's body to tense. She didn't want her brother or anyone else right in the line of fire, but that might happen no matter where they were on the grounds. The trick would be to spot a possible attacker and capture him before he could even pull the trigger.

"The hands have made sure someone's not already on the grounds?" Theo asked.

"As much as humanly possible. They've been looking around since I called them a couple of hours ago."

But the hands could have missed a gunman who was hiding. The ranch was huge, and there were a lot of places for someone to stay out of sight of the hands.

"Hell," Gabriel grumbled.

Theo cursed, too, and Ivy lifted her head even higher to see what had caused their reactions. She soon saw the cause. There was a car parked just off the road where they were to take the final turn to the ranch.

And Wesley was there, leaning against the car as if waiting for them.

It wasn't an ideal spot for an ambush since there were no trees nearby, but that didn't mean Wesley didn't have something up his sleeve.

"What the heck does he want?" Theo added under his breath. His gun was already drawn, but he turned it in Wesley's direction.

"Should I stop?" Edwin asked.

The muscles in Theo's face tightened. "Yeah. Stop right here."

They were still a good twenty yards from Wesley, and Theo took out his phone. Since Ivy was sitting right next to him, she saw when he pressed Wesley's number, and when the man answered.

"I'm not going to shoot you," Wesley snarled. "You can come closer."

"This is close enough," Theo snarled right back, and he put the call on speaker. "Why are you here?"

She had no idea how long Wesley had been there, and since he was a good half mile from the ranch, the hands probably had no idea he was there. Still, for someone who'd come out this way to see them, he didn't jump to answer Theo's question.

However, Wesley did mutter some profanity that she could still hear from the other end of the phone line. "I came to apologize. I was wrong to accuse you of anything criminal."

"You were wrong, but you didn't have to come out here to tell me that. How'd you even know I'd be here?"

Wesley lifted his shoulder. "I went by the sheriff's office, but no one would tell me where you were. I wanted to talk to you face-to-face, and figured sooner or later Ivy would want to come home. And that you'd be the one to bring her."

To most people that probably wouldn't have sounded like a threat, but it did coming from this man. Of course, that probably had something to do with the fact that he was still a suspect.

"I didn't have anything to do with what went wrong with that raid," Wesley went on. "It's important you know that."

"Why?" Theo didn't ease up on the intensity in his voice. Nor his expression, either.

Wesley cursed again, and looked away. "I don't want anybody watching my every move. I don't want people to think I'm a dirty agent."

"Too late. They already think that." Theo paused a heartbeat while he kept watch around them. Edwin and Gabriel did the same. "Let me guess—Dwight Emory has started some kind of internal affairs investigation on you?"

Bingo. Even though Wesley didn't confirm that, Ivy could see enough of his face to know that it was not only true but that Wesley was riled about it. He certainly wasn't looking apologetic now.

"I won't let this ruin my career," Wesley spat out. "Or my life," he corrected. "Just know that I expect you to stop it. You need to tell Emory I did nothing wrong."

Ivy figured there was little or no chance of that happening, which made her wonder why Wesley had really come. Was it to find out if they were at the ranch? If so, he now knew they were, and if he was the person after them, they might not have to wait long for this to all come to a head.

"Drive," Theo instructed Edwin. "We've wasted enough time here." And with that, he hit the end call button but not before Ivy heard Wesley curse some more. The man continued to curse, too, when Edwin sped past him.

Ivy braced herself in case Wesley took out his gun and fired at them. But he didn't. She watched as he got back in his car, and he drove away—in the opposite direction of the ranch. Of course, that didn't mean he wouldn't just double back.

"What the hell was that all about?" Gabriel grumbled.

Theo shook his head. "I figure Emory put him on suspension, pending an internal affairs investigation."

An investigation that could be connected to the attacks against them if Wesley was indeed trying to silence Theo. Maybe Emory could find something against Wesley before things went from bad to worse.

Edwin took the turn to the ranch and drove through the cattle gate. She didn't see any hands, cameras or sensors, but Ivy figured they were all there. Another thing that wasn't in sight was the wedding decorations that had been on the fences. Someone had taken down the blue bows, a reminder that Gabriel's and Jodi's lives had been thrown into chaos, as well. They should be on their honeymoon by now, and here Gabriel was, preparing to face down a killer.

A ranch hand stood in the opened doorway of Gabriel's house, and the moment Edwin stopped the cruiser, Gabriel, Theo and she rushed inside. Gabriel set the security system.

"It won't be dark for a while," Gabriel reminded them, "but I don't want you two out of the bathroom. If you need something, call me, and I'll bring it to you," he added. "Oh, and you can use the laptops to monitor the security cameras. The motion detectors shouldn't pick up slight movement like a small animal or such, but if you hear a beep, it means we've got someone where they shouldn't be."

Someone who would almost certainly be there to kill them.

Theo and she didn't waste even a second. They went upstairs to the guest bath suite, and they locked the door just in case someone managed to break in.

"Don't turn on the lights." Theo put his hand over

hers when she automatically reached for the switch. Both his touch and the warning caused her to look at him. The warning because it was a reminder that they could still be targets here. The touch, well, because even something that simple could cause a swirl of heat to go through her body.

Of course, the timing sucked for that, so Ivy stepped away. It wasn't a tiny space, not with the private toilet area, bathtub and massive walk-in closet all in separate rooms. But she suspected it wasn't the large space that had caused her brother to want them there. It was the natural stone walls in the shower. Like the cruisers, it would be bullet-resistant.

Ivy had been using this bathroom and adjacent bedroom during her stay at the ranch, but someone had added a few things. There was bottled water, a gun with extra ammo, some snacks and a laptop—which Theo went to right away. He sank down on the floor with the computer and booted it up.

"Stay away from the window," Theo added.

She did, though it was impossible to see in or out of it since it was made of glass blocks. Still, it wouldn't stop bullets like the stone.

Ivy watched the laptop, and it didn't take long for the images from the security cameras to appear on the screen. Six total. And while the cameras covered the ranch grounds, that still didn't mean someone couldn't snake their way through the trees and shrubs, staying out of sight of both the cameras and the hands. Though if that happened, maybe the motion sensors would detect them.

"I used to sneak to your old house this way," Theo said. He tapped the screen to the right of her parents' house. No one lived there now, but once there'd been a trail of sorts that led from the road and then coiled around to the back of the place where Ivy met him at the back door and let him in.

"Sneaked him in" was closer to the truth. Her parents had never been keen on her seeing Theo, so to avoid the arguments with them, it was just easier to let them believe she wasn't seeing him.

"I remember. My bedroom was on that side of the house, and sometimes I'd sit in the window and watch for you when you were coming over."

Actually, she'd done that even when he hadn't said he would be over. Theo had pretty much dominated her thoughts in those days.

In some ways, he still did.

Like now, for instance.

His attention was on the laptop, but in profile she could still see enough of his face to bring back the old memories. Of their first kiss. The first time they'd made love. Ivy had been a virgin—Theo hadn't been—but it had felt incredibly special. Like something that'd never happened between two people before.

She silently cursed just how naive she'd been in those days. Because many couples probably felt that way. Couples who had managed to stay together and not be ripped apart by something as tragic as murder.

Theo went to another screen, this one on the trail that led from the old house to Gabriel's. Something caught her eye, and it must have caught Theo's as well because he zoomed in on a spot on the ground. She sank down on the floor next to him, their backs against the vanity while he made the necessary keystrokes to get the right angle.

Ivy hadn't realized she'd been holding her breath until she got a closer look and then relaxed. "It's one of the blue bows that'd been on the fences. A wedding decoration," she added. "It must have blown off and landed there."

Theo made a sound of agreement but zoomed in even more. Maybe to make sure the bow wasn't covering something like a weapon. But it wasn't. They were able to determine that when the wind blew it again and it skittered against one of the shrubs.

"Blue, Jodi's favorite color," Theo remarked. "She used to plan her wedding to Gabriel when she was just a kid. She had a notebook with pictures she'd cut out of magazines."

Ivy nodded. "I remember. I also remember Gabriel always saying he was too old for her."

"At the time, he was. Five years is a big gap when she was just thirteen, and he was already legally an adult."

Yes. But that hadn't stopped Jodi from making those plans or her feelings for Gabriel. Now, here all this time later, she would finally get to marry the man she'd dreamed about, the man she loved.

"I used to plan our wedding," Ivy mumbled. Oh, mercy. She hadn't meant to say that aloud, so she quickly added, "You know, when I was a kid."

Actually, she'd been a teenager and was still planning it right up to the time of the big blowup and murders.

Theo turned to her, and she got a much better look at his face now that it wasn't just his profile. And she felt that old punch of heat. Definitely not a good time for it, so she looked away.

Theo didn't, though.

From the corner of her eye she could see he was still

watching her. Probably because he was stunned by what she'd just said. As a teenage boy, he certainly wouldn't have been into wedding planning and such.

"Did you ever hate me for leaving?" he asked.

Now she was the one who was stunned. "No." It probably would have been a good time for her to at least pause and pretend to think about that. A good time, too, for there not to be so much heat in her voice. It was probably in her eyes, too. They'd been skirting this attraction since they'd come back to Blue River, but the skirting stopped suddenly.

Theo slid his hand around the back of her neck, pulled her to him and kissed her.

This kiss had *mistake* written all over it. And worse, Theo had known he was going to kiss Ivy from the moment she sat on the floor next to him. He also had known it would be good.

It was.

But that still didn't mean they should be doing this. For one thing, it was the quickest way for him to lose focus. Of course, Theo's body had a comeback for that—at the moment, there was no danger, and if that changed, the sensors would alert them to it. Still, this wasn't the right time or the right place. Too bad the thing that overrode that solid argument was that while everything else about it was wrong, Ivy was the right woman.

She always had been, and even though it'd been ten years since they'd been together, it was as if all those years vanished. All the old baggage, too. A good kiss could do that.

Along with making him stupid.

Theo should just end the kiss, move away from her

and go back to watching the computer screen. But he didn't. Not only did he keep things at the stupid level by continuing the making out, he upped the ante by deepening the kiss and pulling Ivy even closer to him.

Ivy didn't exactly shy away from this, either. In fact, she was the one who moved the laptop to the counter so that there was nothing in between them. No reason for them not to position themselves so that his chest ended up against her breasts.

Theo kept kissing her, too. Kept moving her until she was practically in his lap. All in all, it was a good place for her to be if they were going to have sex, but he was pretty sure that shouldn't happen. Of course, he felt the same way about the kiss, but that hadn't stopped him.

Ivy finally stopped, though. She took her mouth from his, eased back and met him eye to eye. He figured she was about to apologize or say something else before she moved back to the floor.

She didn't.

"Don't overthink this," she said.

Since that's exactly what he was doing, Theo hesitated and stared at her. Along with the old baggage vanishing, so did the years. Suddenly, he was nineteen again and wanting Ivy more than his next breath. He hadn't had much willpower, but that ate up the rest of it.

Theo pulled her back to him and kissed her.

This time there was definitely no overthinking. Hell, no thinking at all. He just kept kissing her until the fire was burning so hot inside him that he knew sex was going to happen even if it shouldn't.

Thankfully, Ivy was on the same page. Without breaking the kiss, she lowered her hands to his shirt and started to unbutton it. It was not a graceful effort.

For one thing, Theo was trying to get her clothes off, too, and their hands kept bumping against each other. Still, he was finally successful at pulling off her top. He flung it to the side, and in the same motion, he turned Ivy and laid her back on the floor.

Because they'd been teenage lovers, they'd rarely had the luxury of a bed for sex. And Theo hated that they didn't have it now. Ivy darn sure deserved better than this, but there was no way he could risk taking her into the bedroom.

"Don't overthink this," she repeated.

She went after his shirt again, succeeded in getting it off him, and then she went after his jeans' zipper. Since things were moving fast, Theo got in some foreplay before the heat built to a point that they'd be beyond that. He took the kiss from her mouth to her neck. Then to her breasts. That brought back some sweet memories, and they got even sweeter when he unhooked her bra, bared her breasts and kissed her the way he wanted.

Ivy made a sound of pleasure and pulled him on top of her. Not a bad place to be, but he wasn't done yet. Theo went lower, dropping some kisses on her stomach while he unzipped her jeans and shimmied them off her.

Her panties went next.

And Theo probably would have kept kissing her for a few more seconds, but Ivy had a different notion about that. She latched onto him, hauling him back up to her so that she could kiss his mouth. And unzip him.

Theo didn't have much of a mind left. Not with his body burning to ash. But he did remember to take the condom from his wallet before Ivy got him out of his jeans. He also remembered how to put it on. No easy feat with Ivy still kissing him and trying to pull him into her.

The moment he had on the condom, he stopped resisting her attempts, and he slipped into her. Hell. He got another slam of memories. Of the first time they'd been together like this, and that slam only fired up his body even more. Definitely not something he needed, because this was already going to end much too fast. The pleasure was always too fast with Ivy, and like those other times, Theo tried to hold on to it.

She lifted her hips, bringing him even deeper into her, and Theo had no choice. There was no holding back, no more trying to draw this out to savor the pleasure. So he took control of the pace. As much as he could, anyway. He kept moving inside her. Kept holding her. Kept kissing her.

Until it was impossible to hold out any longer.

Especially when Ivy came in a flash. She made that sound of pleasure again. Gathered him in her arms. And she gave Theo no choice. He let Ivy take him right along with her.

Chapter 14

Ivy dressed while she waited for Theo to come out of the private bathroom area. She figured he wouldn't be in there long, which meant she needed to try to compose herself before she had to face him.

The sex had been amazing, and while that pleasure was still causing her body to hum, she doubted that Theo would be humming. No. He was probably already regretting this.

He would see it as a lapse in judgment, something that had caused him temporarily to lose focus. Heck, he might even regret it because it was too much, too soon between them. Either way, she didn't want to look as if she expected something more than sex between them.

Don't overthink this, she'd told him.

Well, it was advice she needed to take, as well. What was done was done, and she'd just have to deal with the consequences later. In hindsight, though, Theo and she should have worked out a few things before having sex.

Ivy pushed all of that aside, put on her clothes and sat back on the floor with the laptop. There were still no signs of an intruder. Both a blessing and a curse. Part of her wanted this to come to a quick end so she could see Nathan. Another part of her wished there was a different way. One that didn't involve her brother and the hands in possible harm's way.

Theo's phone was still on the floor, and when it buzzed, she started to tell him he had a call. But then she saw Jameson's name on the screen and hit the answer button.

"Is Nathan okay?" she immediately asked.

Jameson hesitated a moment, maybe because he'd been expecting Theo to answer, and Theo must have heard the buzzing sound because he raced back into the main part of the bathroom. He was dressed for the most part but was still zipping up his jeans.

"He's fine," Jameson answered, and with a huge breath of relief leaving her mouth, she put the call on speaker and handed the phone to Theo. "We're all fine. Jodi and he are eating right now so I stepped into the bedroom to call you. I just got an update on Morris's family. I've already told Gabriel, but he said I should call you because he's basically got you and Theo locked in the bathroom…together," her brother added.

Even though Ivy couldn't see Jameson's face, he'd probably lifted an eyebrow over that. He knew that Theo and she couldn't keep their hands off each other. And they hadn't. But no way was she going to get into that.

"Did the cops find Morris's family?" Theo prompted when Jameson didn't continue.

"Yeah. They were in a motel just off the interstate. A maid found them. They were tied up, gagged and blindfolded but otherwise physically fine."

Ivy was betting that wasn't true of their mental state. Unless they were faking this, that is. "Who do they say took them?" Ivy asked.

"They don't know. The wife said that she and her daughter got back from shopping, and someone was in the house. The person used a stun gun on them. The guy carried them to a car and drove around with them for hours. In fact, he drove so long that he had to stop for gas."

"Certainly the thug made or got a call or two during that time," Theo pointed out.

"He made one call at the beginning of the drive and told the person that he had the 'goods,'" Jameson answered. "Neither the wife nor the daughter could hear anything the caller said, but their kidnapper assured whoever it was that he would keep driving until he got further orders."

All of this had no doubt happened while Morris was on his way to the safe house to attack them.

"The kidnapper received a call right before he dropped them off at the motel," Jameson added. "By then, they must have known Morris had failed and there was no reason to hold his family."

Yes, and the kidnapper's boss could have already started lining up the next thug he or she could use to storm the ranch. Thank God the person had seen no value in killing Morris's family. Of course, there was another thing to consider. If Morris had voluntarily been in on this, then his family could have faked the kidnapping and release. They might not know the truth about that unless they caught the man or woman who was responsible.

"The guy who stun-gunned Morris's family wasn't wearing a mask?" Theo asked her brother.

"No. The wife was able to give a description of the man, but it's a pretty vague one. Not sure we'll actually get much from it."

Even if they did, the guy was probably long gone by now.

"I'll get in touch with you if anything else comes up," Jameson assured them, and he paused again. "I guess you two have plenty to talk over once we're out of this mess. Let me know if I can help with that." And he ended the call before Theo or she could even respond.

Theo put his phone in his pocket, and even though his attention went back to the laptop, Ivy knew he was thinking about what her brother had just said. She certainly was. But she didn't have time to dwell on it because there was a soft knock at the door.

"It's me," Gabriel said.

Since he could have critical information, Ivy hurried to let him in. Theo stood, too, but he volleyed his attention between Gabriel and the laptop. Gabriel's eyes did some volleying as well—between Theo and her.

"Is everything…okay?" Gabriel asked her.

She nodded and hoped it didn't look as if Theo and she had just had sex. But judging from her brother's huff, it did look that way.

"The last time Theo and you tangled, you left town for ten years," Gabriel reminded her. "I'd rather that not happen again. In fact, when this danger is over and done, I want you to consider moving back here. It'd be a good place to raise Nathan."

It would be. Though she'd been comfortable enough at her own ranch, it had never quite felt like home.

"You wouldn't have to move in here," Gabriel added. He must have taken her silence to mean that she needed more convincing. "We could build you a place or you could have the old house."

"Definitely no to the old house. Too many bad memories there."

If she came back for good, Ivy would want a fresh start. Something that didn't add to the weight on her shoulders. Of course, that led her to the next thought that was on her mind.

Where did Theo fit in with this fresh start?

He'd said something about a desk job in San Antonio, but Ivy wasn't sure if he was certain of that or not. It was one thing to love his son and want to spend time with him, but it was another thing to completely alter his life.

"Is something wrong?" Theo asked, his attention on Gabriel now.

Because she'd been so caught up in the conversation, Ivy only then realized that Gabriel probably hadn't come up there to talk about their future. That sent her pulse racing, and it raced even more when Gabriel didn't jump to answer.

"Look at the camera that shows the old house," Gabriel instructed Theo. "You'll have to zoom in."

Ivy practically ran back to the laptop so she could see what was going on, but after frantically searching the screen, she had to shake her head. She didn't see anyone moving around or lurking in the shadows. But she did see an open window on the second floor.

"I'm pretty sure that window was closed last time I checked, and I didn't notice it until a few minutes ago."

It was open, not fully, though, only by a couple of inches. Since there were no lights on in the old house, it was just a gaping dark space. However, Ivy could see the reason for his concern—that window was lined up directly with Gabriel's house.

"The hands searched the place when we were on the way here," her brother continued, "but someone could have been hiding."

Yes, there was a huge attic along with enough rooms and closets that the hands could have missed someone. Someone like a gunman.

"Have you seen any kind of movement in the window?" Theo asked without taking his attention off the screen.

"No. And I considered having a deputy and a couple of hands go down there to check it out, but I decided against it. Too risky at this point."

Definitely, because the deputy and hands would be out in the open and could be gunned down.

"Just keep a close watch on it," Gabriel told them. "I'll focus on the other cameras."

Good idea, because whoever had opened the window could have meant to do that as a distraction. Maybe to lure them out. Or maybe just to take their attention off another hiding place.

Gabriel started to leave, and Ivy followed so she could relock the door. But Theo said a single word of profanity that stopped them both. With Gabriel right behind her, Ivy went back so she could see for herself what had caused Theo's reaction.

And her heart went to her knees.

Because of what was now in the open window of the old house.

The barrel of a rifle.

From the moment they'd come back to the ranch, Theo had known an attack was possible. Likely, even. But it still gave him an adrenaline spike to see that weapon now pointed at Gabriel's house.

"Get in the shower now," Theo told Ivy.

Gabriel rushed out of the bathroom, no doubt so he could get to one of the windows downstairs so he'd be in position to return fire if it came down to that. Theo locked the door behind him and carried the laptop into the shower with Ivy and him, but not before Ivy grabbed a gun.

Her breathing was already way too fast, and Theo considered trying to do something to help her level it. But if he pulled her into his arms now, it would definitely be a distraction, and he needed to keep his attention on the rifle.

It was already dark, but there was enough of a moon to see the light glint off the barrel. Enough to see, too, when the barrel shifted just a little, and Theo spotted the scope on it. The shooter was taking aim at something, and he hoped it wasn't a ranch hand or deputy who wasn't hidden well enough.

"A shot from there would be able to make it here," she said.

It wasn't a question. She knew it could. But he hated to hear the slight tremble in her voice. Both of them wanted this showdown, but there was plenty of worry and fear, too.

Theo watched as the barrel shifted again, and he

steeled himself for what he figured would come next. He didn't have to wait long.

The gunman fired.

Three shots, one right behind the other. Theo couldn't tell exactly where they'd landed, but they'd definitely hit Gabriel's house.

The shooter turned the barrel again, and the goon fired more shots. Not at the house this time. It didn't take Theo long to figure out what had been the gunman's new target.

One of the security cameras.

He'd shot out the one in Gabriel's backyard. That portion of the laptop screen went blank.

"The security system is still on," Theo reminded Ivy when she made a slight gasp. "If anyone tries to get into the house, the alarm will sound."

Plus, there were five other cameras and motion detectors. Theo figured, though, that the shooter would try to take out most of them.

And he did.

The next round of gunfire destroyed the camera on the side of the house, the one that had allowed them to see the rifleman.

"He's setting up an attack," Ivy said, her voice a little shaky, but she kept a steady grip on the gun she was holding.

Theo hoped like the devil that she wouldn't have to use the weapon. While he was hoping, he added that maybe the ranch hands would spot this snake before he could get anywhere near Ivy.

They lost a third camera with the next shots. This one near the front porch, and it meant they now had a huge blind spot in the area that divided the two houses. Since that was also where the shooter was, Theo doubted that was a coincidence, and it meant the gunman would probably try to make his way to Gabriel's.

The silence came, and in many ways it was worse than the shots. As long as the guy was firing, Theo had known his location. Now he had no idea where the shooter was. However, he kept watch on the three other cameras since someone could be coming from that direction, too.

There was some movement on the screen from the camera on the other side of the house. Not an attacker. It was Al Talley, one of the ranch hands. He was at the back of a shed, and since Theo hadn't spotted him earlier, it meant Al had probably been in the shed itself. Maybe the gunfire had drawn him out.

Hell, or Al could have heard the sound of someone approaching.

Theo was about to text Gabriel to see if he knew what was going on, but the next shot stopped him cold. Because this one didn't go downstairs. It slammed into the window just a few feet from the shower. The bullet tore through the chunk of glass and sent it flying across the room.

"The shooter knows we're in here," Ivy whispered. Her grip tightened on the gun. She made a strangled sound of fear that came from deep within her chest.

Yeah, he did. That probably meant he was using some kind of thermal scanning equipment that could pinpoint them. The next shot proved it, too, because it tore through another chunk in the window, and the gunman kept firing, kept chipping away at it until the entire floor was littered with the sharp glass.

"Why didn't the breaking window trigger the security alarm?" she asked.

"Probably because this one wasn't wired into the system." It couldn't be lifted, which meant it wouldn't normally be a point of entry for someone trying to get in. It still wasn't, not with those jagged shards of glass sticking out all over.

"We'll just stay put," Theo said when the shots moved from the window to the wall. The wall adjacent to the shower. "The bullets can't get through the stones."

He hoped.

But the shots sure as heck could cause debris to fly through the air. It seemed as if the guy was trying to rip his way through the wall.

Theo's phone dinged, and he saw Gabriel's text message pop up on the screen. Are you both okay?

Fine, for now, Theo texted back.

He caught on to Ivy and lowered her until they were lying on the shower floor. It was larger than average size, but there still wasn't a lot of room with both of them in it. They were practically wrapped around each other.

I have a deputy and one of the hands moving in on the shooter, Gabriel added in his text a moment later. I think we can get this snake.

Theo was about to answer, but then he heard a strange sound. Definitely not an ordinary bullet this time. It was something else. Something that was about to make their situation a whole lot more dangerous than it already was.

A small metal canister.

It dropped onto the floor and started spewing tear gas.

Theo tucked the laptop under his arm, yanked Ivy to her feet and they started running. But it was already too late. The tear gas was burning their eyes and causing them to cough. Slowing them down, too. Not good. Because the gunman started firing bullets again, and this time Ivy and he were right in the path.

He crouched as low as he could, making sure Ivy did the same, and Theo somehow made his way to the door. The moment he had it unlocked and opened, he scrambled out in the hall, shutting the door behind them so it would hopefully contain some of the tear gas. Not all of it, though. It was already starting to seep right out at them.

Ivy was coughing so hard that she couldn't catch her breath, and he was certain her eyes felt as if they were on fire. His did, too, but Theo kept moving. Not downstairs, though. He took her to the hall bathroom. It had a tile floor but didn't have the stone protection of the other room. Plus, it had a massive window over the vanity.

It wouldn't take a gunman long at all to shoot through that.

But the last time Theo had checked, the ranch hand, Al, had been on that side of the house. Maybe he'd be able to put a stop to anyone who tried to put bullets or more tear gas into the room.

"Text Gabriel and make sure he's okay," Theo said, handing Ivy his phone. "I'll look on the laptop and see if we have any security cameras left."

They did. Three that were on the opposite side of the house from the shooter. Nothing much seemed to be happening there, but Theo heard more gunfire. This time, though, it came not from just one weapon but two. The gunman and someone else outside the house. Maybe a hand who had finally gotten in position to take out the shooter. Or at least stop him from sending more tear gas their way.

"Gabriel didn't answer," Ivy relayed to him. There was a new round of fear in her voice.

Theo was about to reassure her that Gabriel was probably just keeping watch and that nothing bad had happened to him. But he heard something that made Theo realize that might not be true.

The security alarm went off, the sound immediately blaring. And that wasn't the only sound. He also heard Gabriel's voice.

"Someone's in the house," Gabriel shouted.

Chapter 15

Ivy hadn't thought her heart could beat any faster, but she'd been wrong about that. Just hearing what her brother said caused every part of her to start racing.

Her first instinct was to run downstairs and help Gabriel, but Theo kept his hand on her arm, no doubt to stop her from doing just that. Because it would have been a dangerous thing to do. She could get shot from friendly fire or cause such a distraction that it could get Gabriel killed. Still, it was almost impossible to just sit there and wait when the adrenaline was urging her to fight.

The security alarm went silent. Probably something Gabriel had done so he could hear what was going on. It was entirely possible that her brother had no idea where the intruder was in the house. Neither did she, but she took the laptop from Theo to try to have a look. There weren't any cameras inside the house, but maybe she could spot how the snake got inside.

Theo let go of her and opened the bathroom door a fraction so he could look out. He aimed his gun in the direction of the stairs, but if the intruder made it to that point, it meant he or she had gotten past Gabriel and the others. Rather than think about what that could mean, Ivy forced herself to focus on the computer screen.

And what she didn't see told her loads.

"No open windows or doors on the side, front or back of the house where we still have cameras," she relayed to him in a whisper.

That meant he'd come from the area between the two houses. Since the gunman was no longer shooting tear gas or bullets at them, it was entirely possible that he was in the process of trying to join his intruder comrade for a joint attack.

But how had the intruder gotten past the hands?

If it was just the one in the house, then it would make more sense. One person would have an easier time slipping into the house, especially on the side where they no longer had surveillance.

Ivy tried to pick through the darkness and see if there was anybody else out there. Al was no longer by the shed, and it took her a moment to find him. He was next to some shrubs that were only about ten yards from the back porch. He turned suddenly, taking aim at something on the blind spot side of the house, and he fired. Maybe he'd managed to take out anyone who was trying to sneak in.

Theo glanced back at the screen and muttered some profanity. At first she thought he'd done that because Al had likely killed someone who could have given them answers about all of this.

But no.

Ivy soon smelled more tear gas. And it didn't seem as if this was coming from the guest bath where they'd been but rather from the direction of the stairs.

"We'll have to get out," he told her.

No way could she argue with that, because Ivy was already starting to cough. It wouldn't be long before they would be so overtaken by the gas that they wouldn't be able to escape.

She wanted to ask him if that meant Gabriel had gotten out, but she soon saw that he had. On the computer screen, she saw Gabriel running from the front porch to the side of the shed where Al had been earlier.

Even though her brother was firing glances all around him, he was also doing something on his phone. A moment later Theo's own phone dinged, and she saw Gabriel's text.

There's a collapsible fire escape ladder on the shelf in my bedroom. Use it to get out the window.

She showed Theo the screen, and he immediately got her to her feet. He took his phone from her and shoved it back into his pocket.

Since he didn't know the location of Gabriel's room, Ivy pointed to the end of the hall. There was a window on the "safe" side of the house where Gabriel was, and they could get out that way.

First, though, they had to make it down a very long hall.

Theo positioned her ahead of him no doubt so he could try to shield her from any attacker who made it up the stairs. If someone was indeed on their way to try to kill them, then he or she had to be wearing a mask since there was now a tear gas mist blanketing not only the stairs but the hall, as well.

Ivy coughed the entire way to Gabriel's room, but with each step also came the fear. At any point someone could come up those stairs and start shooting. If that happened, Theo would be right in the line of fire.

She thought of Nathan and prayed nothing like this was going on at the new safe house. Maybe, just maybe, they could put an end to this tonight. Of course, that meant catching one of their attackers, and right now, that didn't seem probable.

The moment Ivy reached Gabriel's bedroom, she hurried inside. Theo rushed in behind her, closed the door and locked it. Ivy didn't waste even a second. While Theo stood guard, she went to the closet, but since she didn't know exactly where the portable metal ladder was, she had to waste precious time looking for it. She finally found it, folded up like an accordion, and ran to the window with it. Theo helped her with it.

Or at least that's what he started to do.

Before the shot blasted through the bedroom door.

The sound was deafening, and it felt as if it had blasted into her. Despite her shaking hands, Ivy forced herself to stay as steady as possible. Panicking now wouldn't do them any good. Instead, she hooked the ladder frame over the windowsill and let the chain rungs drop.

She spotted Gabriel and hoped he would be able to stop anyone from shooting them while they escaped, but even if he couldn't, Theo and she couldn't stay put. Especially not when another shot came at them. This one smacked into the wall right next to her.

"Go now!" Theo ordered her. "Leave the laptop so

your hands will be free in case you have to shoot." And he returned fire.

Even though there was no way Theo could see the shooter, he obviously had a general idea of where the guy was because of the angle of the shots coming through the door.

Ivy scrambled out the window, and moving as fast as she could, she backed down the steps. Above her, Theo stayed put, volleying glances between the door, her and the yard. When she was halfway down, Theo followed her, and Ivy knew this was probably the best time for their attacker to go to the window and shoot at them.

If that happened, she prayed Gabriel would be able to stop him.

There were more shots from inside the house, and then they stopped. Did that mean the shooter was hurrying outside after them? Maybe. Ivy hadn't needed any other motivation to speed up their escape, but that reminder did it. When she got to the ground, she helped Theo and then turned so they could run to the shed.

But the sound of Theo's shout stopped her. "Gabriel, look out!"

Ivy saw it then. Something she definitely didn't want to see. A ski-masked gunman was behind Gabriel and was taking aim at him.

Theo immediately pulled Ivy to the ground, though there wasn't much cover here by the side of the house. The only thing was a line of shrubs, but since bullets could easily go through those, he knew they couldn't stay there for long. Right now, though, there was a more immediate problem.

Gabriel.

Ivy's brother had to dive to the ground, too. In his case it was on the side of the shed facing them. And it was barely in time. Because the masked gunman fired a shot at him, and if Gabriel had stayed put, he would have taken that bullet.

Theo levered himself up and fired the gun, sending the man scrambling out of the line of fire. He didn't want to keep firing in the guy's direction, though, because he didn't know if there was a ranch hand out there.

"There's Al," Ivy whispered. Of course, she was trembling. Terrified, too. And Theo was scared for her.

Theo followed the direction of where she'd tipped her head, and he saw Al halfway between the shed and the barn. The very barn where there was a cruiser. Somehow, Theo needed to get Ivy there since it would be the safest place for her right now. Gabriel and he were obviously on the same page about that, and the text Theo got from him proved it.

I'll keep this thug occupied while you take Ivy to the barn, Gabriel said. It was a group message, and he'd included Al and several of the other hands and deputies.

Good. That way, all the people on their side knew where Ivy and he would be so they were less likely to get hit by friendly fire. Of course, it was the unfriendly fire that they had to worry about.

Gabriel and Al did, too.

Both Al and Gabriel adjusted their positions and got their weapons ready to fire. Theo didn't move yet. He waited for Gabriel to go to the other end of the shed, and he started firing in the direction of where they'd seen the gunman disappear. Al joined him in the shots, and that was Theo's signal to get Ivy out of there.

Theo pulled her to her feet, and while keeping low,

they started running. It wasn't that far to the barn, but he knew that each step could be their last. In hindsight, this had been too dangerous of a plan. However, there was no turning back now.

They ran to the end of the house, and Theo paused only long enough to glance around the back to make sure someone wasn't lurking there. If someone was, maybe Al would be able to take them out. Just in case, though, Theo angled his gun as best he could, and then he caught on to Ivy's arm with his left hand. They made it to the barn door, and he pushed it open.

"Stay behind me," he warned Ivy.

Despite the gunfire that was going on in the yard, Theo still took a moment to look around the barn. The overhead light was off, but there was a light on in the tack room, and it gave him some decent visibility. He didn't see a gunman inside, but then, there were plenty of places to hide.

Including the cruiser.

It was impossible to watch every corner of the barn, so Theo turned Ivy so they were back-to-back. Not ideal, since she could end up facing a would-be killer head-on, but at this point nothing was ideal.

"Shoot at anything that moves," Theo told her, because there shouldn't be any hands or deputies in the barn.

Without taking his attention off their surroundings, he reached out and slid the barn door shut. Having the place closed off didn't help with the visibility because it shut out what little moonlight there was, but Theo didn't want to risk one of those stray shots coming in the opening.

"See anyone?" she asked.

He didn't. But that didn't mean someone wasn't there. "No," he answered. "Let's move closer to the cruiser."

Outside, the gunfire stopped, but that didn't give Theo any peace of mind. He hoped it didn't mean Gabriel or Al hadn't been shot. But it could also mean the gunmen were running away. While part of him would have liked that, he didn't especially want to give them a chance to regroup and come at them again.

"I don't see anyone in the cruiser," Ivy said. Theo hadn't thought it possible, but her voice was trembling even more than it had before.

He, too, looked on the seat of the cruiser. No one. Well, unless someone was hiding on the floor. Someone could be on the other side of the vehicle, as well. That didn't help with the bad feeling that was snaking its way down his spine.

"When I open the cruiser door, get in," he instructed. "And slide across the seat so I can drive."

She moved to his side and gave a nod that was as shaky as the rest of her. She also still had a hard grip on her gun. A gun he wanted her to use if there was anyone lurking in the cruiser that they'd missed.

Theo shifted his body a little, and the moment he opened the door, Ivy scooted across the seat. She also locked the door on that side and then looked on the floor of the back seat.

"No one," she told him.

Theo was right behind her, and he locked up as well when he was behind the wheel. Thankfully, the keys were in the ignition, but he didn't start the engine. Not yet, anyway. He didn't want to risk the carbon monoxide building up while he was trying to contact Gabriel.

Plus, the sound of the engine might cover up someone trying to sneak up on them.

"Keep watch," Theo reminded her, though he was certain it wasn't a reminder she needed. Still, he wanted to be sure because texting Gabriel would divide his attention for a couple of seconds.

We're in the cruiser, he texted Ivy's brother. And Theo waited for a response.

A response didn't come, though, and after a couple of minutes crawled by, he had to consider that Gabriel might not be in a position to respond. He figured that Ivy realized that as well because her breathing kicked up a notch.

The silence came and everything suddenly seemed so still. As if waiting for something to happen. And something happened all right.

More gunshots came.

All of them slamming into the sides of the barn. Both of them. Theo didn't know exactly where the shooters were, but it felt as if they were closing in on them. He couldn't wait any longer for Gabriel's response. He needed to get Ivy out of there in case these thugs had something more than bullets to launch at them. They could have explosives.

"Hold on," he warned her.

The moment that Theo started the engine, he hit the accelerator, and the cruiser crashed through the barn doors. But almost immediately he had to slam on the brakes. Because there in front of them were two gunmen.

And they had taken a hostage.

Chapter 16

Because she wasn't wearing a seat belt, Ivy jolted forward when Theo brought the cruiser to a quick stop only a few yards in front of the back porch. And she didn't have to figure out why he'd done that.

There were two gunmen on the porch, their backs to the house.

They were both wearing ski masks, and they had their weapons pointed at Al's head. Al was standing in front of the two men, their human shield. They'd no doubt taken up that stance so that Theo or someone else couldn't shoot them.

Ivy's breath froze. Not her thoughts, though. The thoughts and fears came at her with a vengeance. These men were killers. Or that was their plan, anyway, and now the pair had them exactly where they wanted.

She pressed her left hand to her heart to try to steady it. Also tried to rein in her too-fast breathing. If she panicked now, it certainly wouldn't help them. No. She needed to keep a clear head and try to figure out how they could all get out of this alive.

But how?

They couldn't shoot at the men, and if they sped off, then they'd kill Al. At least Theo and she were in a bullet-resistant car, but that wouldn't help anyone else out there—especially Al. Ivy didn't know the hand that well, but he was out here because he'd been trying to protect her. That reminder twisted away at her, and once again she had to remind herself to stay calm.

"Step out of the cruiser," one of the gunmen shouted.

"Stay put," Theo told her, and he didn't hesitate, either. However, he did lower his window a fraction so he could yell back an answer to the men. "Put down your weapons. There's no way you can get out of this alive."

If Theo's threat bothered them in the least, they didn't react to it. They certainly didn't put down their guns. Ivy had to wonder if these men had been in similar situations as Morris. Had their loved ones been taken as well to get them to do this or were they merely hired guns?

Either way, this situation could be deadly.

"Get out of the cruiser," the thug repeated. "If not, we start puttin' bullets in your friend here."

"Hell," Theo said under his breath, and he glanced around, probably looking for Gabriel or the other hands.

Ivy looked for them, too, and she spotted Gabriel still near the shed. He was at the wrong angle to have a shot to stop this, and if he stepped out from cover, one of the gunmen could easily shoot him.

Maybe someone could come through the front of the house to get to the men. But then she had to mentally shake her head. The house was probably still filled with tear gas.

"Who hired you?" Theo called out to the men. "Because whatever he or she is paying you, it's not enough for you to lose your lives. That's exactly what will happen, too, if you don't stop this now."

Even though she couldn't see their faces, Ivy thought the one who'd been doing all the talking laughed. "Just get out of the cruiser. I don't think you want your woman to watch as we shoot this guy."

No, Ivy didn't want to watch that, but she figured the moment Theo and she stepped out, these thugs would gun them down. She didn't want to see that, either, but they didn't have a lot of options here.

"Who exactly is it you're after?" Theo asked. "Me or Ivy?"

The two didn't jump to answer but did have a short whispered conversation. "Ivy. If she wants to save you or anybody else, then all she has to do is open the door and come to us."

"You're not going out there," Theo told her right off. "They won't want any of us alive because we're witnesses."

Because her mind was whirling with fear, she hadn't actually realized that. But it was true. Heck, the thugs probably had orders to kill them all.

But why?

That was the million-dollar question. And they still didn't have the answer. Because any of their suspects could have hired or coerced these men into doing this. It was even possible that their boss was nearby, waiting to make sure his or her orders had been carried out.

"I have men all around here," Gabriel called out.

Her brother had moved his position just a little but was still thankfully behind cover. Or at least he was unless someone came from the back pasture. Hopefully, though, there were still hands out there to make sure that didn't happen.

"So do we," the thug answered back. "And time's up." He lowered his gun to Al's arm. "Either she gets out of the cruiser, or I fire the first shot. Just how much blood do you think he can lose before he dies?"

It was impossible for her not to think of Belinda Travers. She'd been shot and certainly hadn't survived. The same could happen to Al.

"I can't just sit here and watch him die," Ivy said.

Theo cursed again, glanced around as if trying to figure out what to do. "Get lower on the seat," he instructed. The moment she did that, he added to the men, "Give us just a few seconds. Ivy was hurt when we ran into the barn, and I'm trying to stop the bleeding. She's not in any shape to stand right now."

Ivy doubted the men would buy the lie, but it seemed to give them a little time because the thugs had another whispered conversation.

"They're wearing masks," Theo said, but it sounded as if he was talking to himself more than her. "The man who attacked Morris's family didn't wear one."

She considered that for a moment. "You think these are men you know?"

"Maybe." Theo shook his head. "Or maybe they're just cocky enough to think they can kill us all and escape." He turned back to the window. "Ivy needs an ambulance," he shouted to the men.

Theo then took out his phone, and while keeping watch of the situation on the porch, he also sent a text to someone. Probably Gabriel. Because a few seconds later, Ivy saw her brother glance down at his phone screen.

"Put on your seat belt," Theo told her.

Ivy was certain her eyes widened. "Why? What are you going to do?"

"Play a game of chicken to get these guys to scatter so that Gabriel can pick them off. But I want you belted in and as far down on the seat as you can go in case something goes wrong."

And there was plenty that could go wrong.

She managed a nod and did as he said. Ivy also kept her gun ready just in case this situation went from bad to worse.

"Hold on," Theo said the moment they were in place, and he hit the accelerator.

The cruiser lurched forward, but Ivy couldn't see what was going on. However, she could hear it. The men cursed.

And then a shot blasted into the windshield.

Theo had already braced himself for the shot that came right at them. The ones that followed, too. He gave the steering wheel a sharp turn so that his side of the cruiser bashed into the back porch railing. The impact certainly jarred Ivy and him. Seemed to jar the house, too.

But it didn't stop the gunmen.

Four more bullets came crashing into the cruiser's engine and his window, cracking and webbing the glass to the point that it was nearly impossible for him to see.

He could hear, though.

And what he heard was Gabriel returning fire. Good.

It was just as Theo had instructed him to do with that text he'd sent him.

Judging from the angle of the returned fire, Gabriel did indeed have the right angle or at least enough of one to get those gunmen. Maybe that meant Al had scrambled out of the way so they could put a quick end to this.

Since the side of the cruiser was now directly in front of the porch, Theo tried to peer through what was left of the glass. It took him a few seconds, but he saw the gunmen. Both were now in the back doorway of the house and didn't seem to be reacting to the tear gas. Maybe they had some kind of filtering equipment beneath those ski masks.

Both of the gunmen were leaning out from cover to continue firing. The one on the left was shooting into the cruiser. The one on the right was aiming in Gabriel's direction. No doubt to try to pin him down.

There was no sign of Al.

It was possible the thugs had dragged him into the house, and because the lights were off, Theo couldn't see anything in there, much less try to figure out if the man was alive. Later, he would need to do that, but for now he had a much more immediate problem.

There was another round of shots, these going into the engine, and it didn't take long for it to start spewing steam. They'd obviously shot out the radiator, which would make it impossible for Theo to use it for an escape. They certainly wouldn't get far enough away from those gunmen to do any good. Still, he'd known that right from the start. That meant they had to make their stand here and hope Gabriel and the hand could do enough to capture the shooters.

Now that they'd disabled the engine, the shooter

shifted back to his window. The bullets tore a big enough hole in the glass that the shots started coming into the interior of the cruiser. He was betting these guys had a lot of ammo, and as long as the one kept Gabriel out of the picture, it meant the other one could continue blasting until he shot Ivy and him.

Another chunk of the glass came flying right at him, and Theo had no choice but to duck down. He didn't stay there, though. He came up off the seat, and he used one of the holes in the window to take aim so he could fire. He double tapped the trigger and sent the thugs ducking back inside.

It didn't last.

After only a few seconds, the thugs started shooting again. This time the glass fell right onto Ivy. She quickly lifted her hand, putting it over the back of her head, but Theo knew that wouldn't be enough to keep her protected.

The shots continued, coming at them nonstop, but there was other gunfire, too. It was coming from the pasture behind the barn. Probably one or more of the hands. Hopefully, that meant they knew that Al was out of the way so that he wouldn't be hit.

"Stay put," Theo told Ivy.

As expected, she lifted her head just enough to make eye contact with him, and he saw her shake her head. "You're not going out there."

It darn sure wasn't something he wanted to do. Not with bullets seemingly coming from every direction, but he couldn't just sit there and let Ivy be hit. Something that could happen any moment now that the shots were coming into the vehicle.

"I'll use the door for cover," he told her.

She still shook her head and reached for him. Theo wanted to take the time to reassure her, but maybe that wasn't even possible, anyway. He put his hand on the door handle.

And then heard the sound crack through the air.

Not another bullet. It was a tear gas canister, and it smacked onto the ground just a few feet from the cruiser.

Hell.

Theo ditched his idea to open the door and instead try to start the engine to get them out of there. No such luck, though. The gunmen had seen to that. This had likely been their intention all along, and Theo had no choice but to move Ivy.

"We'll go out your side," he told her. "Open the door and get out but stay low. Wait for me, and then we'll run to the shed where Gabriel is."

It wasn't an especially good plan, but he didn't have a lot of options here. Especially not with the tear gas starting to ooze its way into the cruiser. His only hope was that the tear gas would hide his and Ivy's escape. Then he had to hope they didn't collapse along the way. It wouldn't be a long run, but it would feel like a marathon with that gas burning their eyes and lungs.

Coughing again, Ivy threw open the door, and she practically tumbled out, landing in a crouching position on the ground. Theo kept low since the bullets were still coming, and he crawled toward her.

"Watch out!" Gabriel shouted.

Despite the gunfire, Theo heard him loud and clear, but he had no idea why Gabriel had yelled out that warning. Not until he saw the movement.

Someone was walking out of that cloud of tear gas.

That someone had a gun, and he latched onto Ivy, knocking away her gun. In the same motion, he took aim.

And the man fired.

The shot was so close to Ivy that the sound blasted through her head. She braced herself to feel the pain from being hit. But nothing.

Well, nothing other than the pain in her ears from the noise.

From what she could tell, the shot had gone into the ground right next to her. Maybe he'd just missed. Or else it could have been some kind of warning shot. If so, it had certainly gotten her attention.

Despite the man's having hold of her and that fired shot, she was alive, and she needed to do something to keep it that way. Ivy turned, ready to push her attacker away before he could fire again, but she was already too late. He hooked his arm around her and put the gun to her head. Worse, he was in position so neither Theo nor her brother might have a clean shot to take out this guy.

She tried to elbow the man in his gut, but he only tightened his grip on her until he had her in a choke hold. It was already hard enough to breathe because of the tear gas, and that certainly didn't help.

The man, however, probably had no trouble breathing. That's because he was wearing a gas mask. Ivy caught a glimpse of it when she managed to glance back at him.

"Let her go," Theo growled. That's when Ivy realized he had taken up cover behind the back of the cruiser.

Of course, the man didn't release her, and he didn't respond to Theo's demand. He just started dragging her onto the porch. Only a few steps, and he would have her inside where there were at least two other gunmen waiting.

She forced herself to stay as calm as she could. Which probably wasn't very calm. But she needed to think. Needed to do something to make sure no one got killed before she even tried to diffuse this.

"If this is about my husband's money," she said. "We can work this out."

Again, no response. So if Lacey was indeed behind this, then she'd convinced the men not to bargain with her. Maybe by kidnapping their families. Maybe because Lacey had just paid them too well.

The man just kept dragging her, and the moment they reached the doorway, he pulled her inside. Ivy had been right about the gunmen being there. One was on each side of the door. A door they didn't close. They stayed there, no doubt ready to shoot anyone who came after her.

At least the tear gas inside had thinned out enough for her to breathe. But the bad news was that the goon still had her in a choke hold.

"I gave birth to Travis's only grandchild," she tried again. She needed to hit some kind of nerve so she knew who she was dealing with. "He wouldn't like it if anything bad happened to me."

The man still didn't say anything. That didn't mean August wasn't behind this, though. In fact, it didn't rule out anyone.

"Everything's in place," one of the thugs said to her captor.

She didn't recognize the voice, but it made her wonder if Theo would. Ivy peered out through the door but could no longer see him. Could no longer see Gabriel, either, but maybe either he or one of the hands was making his way to the front of the house where the man was taking her.

The lights were all off in the house, but Ivy looked around for anything she could try to grab so she could club the guy. The only thing she could spot was a vase on a table in the family room, but when she reached for it, the man snapped her back so hard that Ivy nearly blacked out from the pain and loss of breath. She couldn't try that again, not while he had her in a choke hold, anyway, or he might kill her. Still, she didn't intend to go with him without a fight.

But where was he taking her?

Better yet, how did he plan on getting her off the ranch?

She soon had the answer to her last question. There was a third masked thug by the front door, and he opened it. When the man dragged her onto the front porch, she saw the black SUV parked by the steps. Maybe this was the vehicle the shooter in the old house had used. It could have been driven up the path between the two houses. Given the limited visibility from the gas fog and the darkness, it would have been hard to see. Still, she couldn't imagine one of the hands not spotting it. Did that mean these thugs had killed them?

It sickened Ivy to think that could have happened, but with all the gunfire going on, it was impossible to know.

There was a new round of shots. This time at the back of the house where she'd last seen Al and those two hired thugs. Gabriel was in that general area, too, and she prayed that none of them had been hit.

In one last-ditch effort to save herself, Ivy dropped

down her weight, trying to throw the man off balance, but he just hooked his other arm around her waist and kept going. Straight for that SUV.

"Wesley?" someone called out.

Theo.

Ivy couldn't see him, but judging from the sound of his voice, he was on the side of the house toward the front of the SUV.

As the man had done the other times Theo or she had spoken to him, he didn't say a word, but she felt his arm tense just enough to let her know that Theo had been right. This was Wesley or else someone working for him.

But why would Wesley want her?

"Ivy has nothing to do with this," Theo continued. "This is between you and me."

Again, her captor's arm tensed, but he still didn't talk.

"You don't want me to hear your voice," Theo added. "But I recognized one of your hired guns. He's a criminal informant. I know because I've used him myself. My guess is you got him to do this for cheap or else you threatened him with arrest. Either way, it doesn't matter. This ends here."

The gunmen at the front door came onto the porch, took aim at Theo and fired. Ivy's heart went to her throat, and her breath stalled in her chest until she realized Theo had dropped back in the nick of time. He hadn't been hit.

However, he could be.

In fact, this could end badly for all of them. That's why she had to try to bargain with this man.

"I'll go with you," she told him, "but you need to leave Theo and everyone else here alone."

Wesley or whoever this was certainly didn't jump to agree to that. The man started backing her down the front porch steps, and it would be only a matter of a few seconds before he had her in that SUV. Heaven knew then where he'd take her. Or what he'd do to her. Plus, that would leave the hired guns in place to keep attacking Gabriel, Theo and the hands.

Theo came out from cover again, and he fired at the gunman who wasn't holding Ivy. The bullet hit the thug and despite the fact that he was wearing a Kevlar vest, he dropped onto the porch. That's when Ivy saw the blood and realized Theo's shot had gone into his neck. If he wasn't dead already, he soon would be.

Her captor mumbled some profanity under his breath and started moving her even faster. It was a mistake. Because it gave Ivy the chance to trip on the last step. She paid for it with pain when he bashed her upside her head with his gun, but that only got him out of position to shoot Theo.

Theo, however, was in position.

Now that Theo had a clean shot, he didn't hesitate; he fired three shots. All three bullets slammed into the guy's chest. He was also wearing Kevlar, but the bullets must have knocked the wind out of him because he fell, his head smacking onto the side of the SUV.

The driver's-side door flew open, and the gunman inside took aim at Theo. However, he barely had brought up his hand when someone fired. Not the gunman or Theo. It was Gabriel. He was now in the doorway of the house, and he'd taken out the thug with a shot to the head.

While Theo ran toward her, Ivy kicked the gun out of the fallen man's hand, and it landed a few feet away.

Once Theo reached her, he maneuvered her next to the porch railing, where she'd have a little cover in case there was another attack, and he went to the man. The guy was wheezing and clutching his chest, but Theo ripped off the gas mask.

It was Wesley all right.

He cursed Theo and then smiled, his head dropping back onto the ground.

"You just signed their death warrants," Wesley said.

Theo was no doubt about to ask Wesley what he meant by that, but then she heard something she didn't want to hear.

An explosion.

She whipped toward the sound of the blast. Her parents' old house. And it was now in flames.

Chapter 17

Theo cursed. He hadn't exactly relaxed, but he had thought the worst of the danger was over. Maybe not, though. His instincts were to go running to the old house, to make sure no one was inside, but that could be a trap. Something that Wesley had set up in case he failed here.

Which he had.

The agent was moaning in pain, but he still had that stupid smirk on his face. A smirk that could be there because he'd put someone in that house. Someone who was now dying because of the fire. The flames were quickly eating their way through the place, and even if they could get the fire department out right away, it might still be too late to save it.

"Three of the ranch hands are on the way down there," Gabriel said after reading a text. "And Edwin's just up the road. He'll be arriving at the old house in just a couple of minutes."

Maybe that would be enough, because it was also possible that Wesley had stashed the rest of his hired guns near there. Hired guns who would kill anyone who came their way.

Theo checked the SUV to make sure no one else was inside. It was empty. Theo also picked up Wesley's gun and shoved it in the back waistband of his jeans.

"Where are the gunmen who were at the back of the house?" Theo asked Gabriel.

"Dead," Gabriel answered while he tossed Theo a pair of plastic cuffs that he took from his pocket. "Al's back there, and he's keeping watch to make sure no one else sneaks up on us. The hands in the pastures are reporting that they're not seeing any other gunmen. Not live ones, anyway. They had to shoot a couple of them. Jace has rounded up a couple of them, too."

Theo released the breath he hadn't even noticed he was holding. Of course, there could still be a straggler out there, but maybe that person would just surrender now that his boss had been captured.

From the end of the trail, Theo saw the cruiser lights as the vehicle pulled to a stop near the burning house. Edwin, no doubt. At least now the hands had law enforcement help.

Gabriel made a call to someone else, but Theo didn't wait to hear who he was talking to. He first cuffed Wesley, and since it was still too dangerous for Ivy to be outside in the open where a sniper could pick her off, he put her on the passenger's seat of the SUV.

"Stay down," Theo warned her.

She gave a shaky nod and caught on to his arm when he started to move away. That's when he spotted the marks on her throat. Bruises and scrapes from Wesley putting her in that choke hold. It sickened him to think of just how close she'd come to dying.

And all because of him.

"I'm so sorry," Theo said.

Ivy shook her head, took hold of the front of his shirt and pulled him to her. She kissed him. It didn't last long. Just enough to soothe some of the raw nerves inside him. Still, he wanted to beat Wesley senseless for doing this.

Standing guard in front of Ivy, Theo turned so he could face Wesley. "Who's in the old house?"

"Just tying up some loose ends." The smirk finally faded, and he glared up at Theo. "You might as well go ahead and kill me. You know what they do to former agents in prison?"

Yeah, he did, but since this piece of slime had tried to kill Ivy, Theo didn't care what happened to the man.

"Who are the loose ends?" Theo pressed.

Wesley groaned in pain. Probably because he had cracked ribs. Or maybe the realization of what he'd done was finally hitting him. "One loose end," he amended. "Someone who helped me fund this little operation. Don't worry. I sent proof of the money trail to the sheriff's office so you'll know who paid for all these hired guns."

Hell. That could maybe be August or Lacey. Theo was hoping, though, that it was just a bluff and the only person dead in that house was the guy who'd fired those rounds of tear gas.

"It wasn't supposed to work this way," Wesley mumbled.

"No. If things had gone according to your plan, you

would have kidnapped Ivy and used her to get me to do whatever you wanted me to do."

That could involve anything from destroying evidence to murder. Because Wesley knew that Theo would do anything to get Ivy back.

But there was another angle to this.

If Lacey had been the one to "fund" all of this, then maybe Ivy had been as much of a target as Theo. This attack could have been designed to kill them both.

"The fire department, an ambulance and two more backup cruisers are on the way," Gabriel relayed after yet another call. "I'll stay here with Ivy and you until we're sure it's safe."

Good. But judging from Gabriel's tone and the way his gaze kept darting to the burning house, that's where he wanted to be. So did Theo, but it was too big of a risk to leave Ivy alone. Once backup arrived, Theo could get her out of there. Maybe they'd have more answers by then. Answers that Wesley could give them.

"I had no proof you did anything wrong in that botched raid," Theo told the man.

"Didn't matter. You suspected I had something to do with it, and you wouldn't have let go of it."

Theo shook his head. "I didn't suspect it until the attacks started."

Wesley made a sound as if he didn't believe that. And maybe he was right. In the back of Theo's mind, he'd always felt something was wrong. He wouldn't have let go of it, either, and eventually he would have started digging. That digging would have led him to Wesley.

"Did you think you could kill and silence everyone who could figure out you were dirty?" Ivy asked Wesley.

Wesley turned his head to the side, spared her a glance before making a weary sigh. "Yes. You don't understand. I can't go to jail." He groaned. "I'll die there."

"You didn't mind killing innocent people to save yourself. That makes you a coward," Theo told him. "And Belinda's kidnapping and murder is going to put you on death row."

Gabriel's phone buzzed, and he answered it right away but again didn't put it on speaker. Nor did he say anything. For several slow, crawling moments, Gabriel just listened to whatever the caller was telling him.

"The ambulance should be here any minute," Gabriel finally said, and he ended the call. He looked at Theo. "It's Lacey."

"She came here with Wesley?" Ivy asked her brother.

"Was forced here, according to what she said. She's alive, but Wesley had stun-gunned her and left her in the house with a firebomb that was on a timer before he and the thug came over here. She wasn't burned but took in a lot of smoke before the hands pulled her out."

Now it was Ivy's turn to curse. "Lacey is the one who funded Wesley."

Gabriel nodded. "Wesley apparently went to her with the plan, but she's saying she didn't have anything to do with any deaths. When Wesley tied her up, though, he told her he was going to pin all of this on her by making it look as if she'd died while launching an attack."

Yeah, and it might have worked, too. If they hadn't gotten lucky.

"I had no idea she'd go this far," Ivy said. She tried, and failed, to choke back a hoarse sob. "Nathan could have been hurt, or worse." Another sob. "We all could have been."

Theo kept watch, but he pulled Ivy into his arms for a short hug. It didn't help. Nothing would at this point. That's why he kissed her.

"I love you," he whispered. "And we're going to get through this."

She blinked, clearly surprised by his L-word bombshell. He'd never told her that, and she probably thought it was the adrenaline talking. It wasn't. He'd always loved Ivy. But now hadn't been the time to tell her.

And she certainly wasn't telling him she felt the same.

Definitely the wrong time, because Ivy had enough whirling through her head without adding that.

Theo got a good distraction—he heard the sirens. Lots of them. And he knew it wouldn't be long before he could finally get Ivy out of there. He took out his phone and handed it to her.

"Call Jameson," he instructed. "See if you can talk to Nathan."

The moment the cruiser pulled into the driveway, Gabriel came down the porch steps. "Arrest him," Gabriel told the two deputies who got out of the cruiser, and he tipped his head to Wesley.

Gabriel must have already instructed the ambulance where to go because it sped past them and went to his parents' house. The fire truck was right behind it. The two cruisers, however, came to Gabriel's. Both stopped, and a pair of deputies got out of the first vehicle and a third one exited the cruiser behind them.

Ivy kept watch of everything going on, but she continued her conversation on the phone. Obviously, she'd reached Jameson and could assure him that everything was okay. Well, as okay as it could be considering just how close she'd come to dying.

"Wesley said he sent something to the sheriff's office," Theo told one of the deputies who approached him. Her name was Susan Bowie, someone he'd known since he was a kid.

Susan nodded. "A courier delivered some papers about thirty minutes ago."

Right about the time the attack had started—though it certainly felt as if the gunfire had lasted a lot longer than that. "The papers implicated Lacey Vogel?"

Another nod. "They're records to show withdrawals from an offshore account in Ms. Vogel's name. There were other bank accounts to show where the money went."

Theo was betting they could match the deposits to the dead gunmen scattered over the ranch. Lacey had been an idiot to use a bank to pay for all of this, or else she'd been so hell-bent on revenge that she didn't take precautions. Of course, Wesley wouldn't have helped with those precautions, either, since he'd probably intended to set Lacey up right from the beginning. Lacey had helped him by making herself a prime suspect.

Gabriel stayed right by Wesley until Susan and a male deputy hauled the man into the cruiser. Theo watched, too, and even Ivy got one last look at Wesley before the deputy shut the door. At least Wesley wasn't smirking or smiling now. It had probably set in that he would never be in a position to hurt them again.

Nor Lacey, for that matter.

The ambulance would take her to the hospital, but after that, she'd be arrested. Not only had Wesley ratted out Lacey as funding this attack, Lacey herself had admitted to paying for the thugs used in the attacks.

"Susan, you and Mick go ahead and take Wesley to jail," Gabriel told the deputy. "Read him his rights. Do everything by the book." After Susan nodded, he turned to the third deputy. "I want you to stay here and help Edwin wrap things up. I need to use your cruiser to take my sister somewhere."

Gabriel didn't say where that somewhere was, but Theo figured it was the safe house. There was nothing that would get that look of terror off Ivy's face faster than seeing her son.

Their son, Theo mentally corrected.

He figured it would help settle him down, as well.

Theo hurried when he helped Ivy from the SUV and into the cruiser, and she ended her call with Jameson, probably so she could hear an update from Gabriel and him. As they'd done on their other trips, Theo got in the back seat with her, and as soon as Gabriel was behind the wheel, he took off.

"Please tell me we're going to the safe house," Ivy said.

"We are," Gabriel answered. "I'll drop you two off there and come back here and deal with the investigation."

That wouldn't be a fast or easy thing to do. Heaven knew how many dead bodies there were, and there was a huge crime scene to process. If there were any gunmen left alive, they would also have to be arrested and interrogated. Gabriel would be putting in a lot of long hours and all because of a dirty agent and a greedy stepdaughter.

"Wesley sent bank documents to the sheriff's office," Theo told Ivy and Gabriel, too, in case he hadn't heard what Susan had said earlier. "It should be what you need to bring murder charges against Lacey."

"Murder?" Ivy repeated on a rise of breath.

"Yeah. Because of Belinda, the CI and McKenzie. Since Lacey paid for the attacks, both Wesley and she will be charged."

Ivy stayed quiet a moment, probably letting that sink in. Then fresh tears sprang to her eyes. "It's over." Her voice was mostly breath and filled with relief. So, the tears weren't from sadness this time.

"It's over," Theo assured her.

Gabriel took the turn from the ranch, and once he got onto the main road, he sped up. "The safe house isn't far. Ten minutes or so. That should give you two a little time to…talk or something."

Theo met Gabriel's gaze in the rearview mirror, and even though Gabriel didn't come out and say it, he seemed to be telling Theo to go for it. But what Gabriel didn't know was that Theo already had. He'd told Ivy he loved her, and she hadn't said a word about her feelings for him.

Maybe their pasts were just too painful for her to put behind her. Hell, maybe she didn't even want him in her and Nathan's lives. Well, tough. He was going to be there. At least in Nathan's, anyway.

"I'm taking that desk job in San Antonio," Theo said. Unlike Ivy's voice, there was no relief in his. But there was some anger. "I could try to put in for a transfer to Houston or wherever you end up—"

She slid her hand around the back of his neck, pulled him to her and kissed him. Hard. That was probably the fastest way to get him to shut up.

"I love you," she said when she broke for air.

Ivy went back for another kiss. Apparently, that was another way to get him to hush, because it stunned him to silence. Strange considering how much he wanted to say to her. But at the moment, he just mentally repeated those words.

And savored them.

Until she'd said it, Theo hadn't realized just how much he'd wanted to hear them. Not just now. But for years. Because that's how long he'd been in love with Ivy.

"I want to stay at the ranch," she continued, her breath as ragged as his was. A good kiss could do that. "Maybe build a house." She paused. "With Nathan and you."

That felt like a punch. A good one. Because it caused a warmth to go through him from head to toe.

"You'd sure as hell better ask her to marry you," Gabriel grumbled. "After all, you did get her pregnant ten years ago. She's crazy in love with you, and Nathan needs a dad. Heck, Ivy needs *you*."

Theo hadn't been certain that Gabriel was listening, but obviously he was. And he was right. That wasn't just Ivy's big brother talking. This was right between Ivy and him, and the past was the past.

"Well?" Theo said, turning to her. "Will you marry me?"

Just in case she had any notion of saying no, Theo kissed her. He made sure it was long and deep. Made sure he poured his heart into it, too. Which wasn't hard to do. Because Ivy already had his heart.

"Yes," she managed to get out before the kissing continued.

Later, they could celebrate. And he could get her

an engagement ring. Later, there'd be time for a lot of things—like living the rest of their lives together. But for now, it had to wait, because Gabriel took the turn to the safe house.

The moment they pulled into the driveway, the door opened, and Theo saw something that made this complete.

Nathan.

His boy was there, right between Jameson and Jodi. And Nathan was grinning from ear to ear.

"Mom," he called out to Ivy.

Ivy scrambled out of the car, and before she made it to Nathan, Theo saw more tears in her eyes. This time he knew for certain they were happy ones. She pulled Nathan into her arms, kissed him and kept on kissing him until the boy was laughing.

"Dad," Nathan said when Ivy finally let go of him. He went to Theo and hugged him.

Theo had to blink back some happy tears himself. Not very manly to cry, but he suddenly realized he had everything he'd ever wanted right here. He gathered both Ivy and Nathan in his arms and held on tight.

* * * * *

Jen Delaney loved Bent, Wyoming, the town she'd been born in, grown up in. She was a respected member of the community, in part because she ran the only store that sold groceries and other essentials within a twenty-mile radius of town.

From her position crouched on the linoleum while she stocked shelves, she looked around the small store she'd taken over at the ripe age of eighteen. For the past ten years it had been her baby, with its narrow aisles and hodgepodge of necessities.

She'd always known she'd spend the entirety of her life happily ensconced in Bent and her store, no matter what happened around her.

The reappearance of Ty Carson didn't change that knowledge so much as make it...annoying. No, annoying would have been just his being in town again. The fact their families had somehow intermingled in the last year was...a catastrophe.

Her sister, Laurel, marrying Ty's cousin Grady had been a shock, very close to a betrayal, though it was hard to hold it against Laurel when Grady was so head over heels for her it was comical. They both glowed with love and happiness and impending parenthood.

Jen tried not to hate them for it.

She could forgive Cam, her eldest brother, for his serious relationship with Hilly. Hilly was biologically a Carson, but she'd only just found that out. Besides, Hilly wasn't like other Carsons. She was so sweet and earnest.

But Dylan and Vanessa… Her business-minded, sophisticated older brother *impregnating* and marrying snarky bad girl Vanessa Carson… *That* was a nightmare.

And none of it was fair. Jen was now, out of nowhere, surrounded by Carsons and Delaneys intermingling—which went against everything Bent had ever stood for. Carsons and Delaneys hated each other. They didn't fall in love and get married and have *babies*.

And still, she could have handled all that in a certain amount of stride if it weren't for *Ty* Carson. Everywhere she turned he seemed to be right there, his stoic gaze always locked on *her*, reminding her of a past she'd spent a lot of time trying to bury and forget.

When she'd been seventeen and the stupidest girl alive, she would have done anything for Ty Carson. Risked the Delaney-Carson curse that, even with all these Carson-Delaney marriages, Bent still had their heart set on. She would have risked her father's wrath over daring to connect herself with a *Carson*. She would have given up anything and everything for Ty.

Instead he'd made promises to love her forever, then disappeared to join the army—which she'd found out only a good month after the fact. He hadn't just broken her heart—he'd crushed it to bits.

But Ty was a blip of her past she'd been able to forget about, mostly, for the past ten years. She'd accepted his choices and moved on with her life. For a decade she had grown into the adult who didn't care at all about Ty Carson.

Then Ty had come home for good, and all she'd convinced herself of faded away.

She was half convinced he'd returned simply to make her miserable.

"You look angry. Must be thinking about me."

Don't miss
Wyoming Cowboy Ranger *by Nicole Helm,*
available June 2019 wherever
Harlequin® Intrigue books and ebooks are sold.

www.Harlequin.com

HIEXP0519

Need an adrenaline rush from nail-biting tales
(and irresistible males)?

Check out **Harlequin Intrigue®**,
Harlequin® Romantic Suspense and
Love Inspired® Suspense books!

New books available every month!

CONNECT WITH US AT:

Facebook.com/groups/HarlequinConnection

 Facebook.com/HarlequinBooks

 Twitter.com/HarlequinBooks

 Instagram.com/HarlequinBooks

 Pinterest.com/HarlequinBooks

ReaderService.com

**ROMANCE WHEN
YOU NEED IT**

SGENRE2018R

SPECIAL EXCERPT FROM

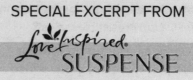
Love Inspired.
SUSPENSE

*When a guide-dog trainer becomes a target of a
dangerous crime ring, a K-9 cop and his loyal
partner will work together to keep her safe.*

Read on for a sneak preview of
Blind Trust *by Laura Scott,*
the next exciting installment in the
True Blue K-9 Unit *miniseries, available*
June 2019 from Love Inspired Suspense.

Eva Kendall slowed her pace as she approached the
training facility where she worked training guide dogs.

Using her key, she entered the training center, thinking
about the male chocolate Lab named Cocoa that she would
work with this morning. Cocoa was a ten-week-old puppy
born to Stella, a gift from the Czech Republic to the NYC
K-9 Command Unit located in Queens. Most of Stella's
pups were being trained as police dogs, but not Cocoa.
In less than a month after basic puppy training, Cocoa
would be able to go home with Eva to be fostered during
his initial first-year training to become a full-fledged guide
dog. Once that year passed, guide dogs like Cocoa would
return to the center to train with their new owners.

A few steps into the building, Eva frowned at the loud
thumps interspersed between a cacophony of barking. The
raucous noise from the various canines contained a level
of panic and fear rather than excitement.

LISEXP0519

Concerned, she moved quickly through the dimly lit training center to the back hallway, where the kennels were located. Normally she was the first one in every morning, but maybe one of the other trainers had gotten an early start.

Rounding the corner, she paused in the doorway when she saw a tall, heavyset stranger scooping Cocoa out of his kennel. Panic squeezed her chest. "Hey! What are you doing?"

The ferocious barking increased in volume, echoing off the walls and ceiling. The stranger must have heard her. He turned to look at her, then roughly tucked Cocoa under his arm like a football.

"No! Stop!" Panicked, Eva charged toward the man, desperately wishing she had a weapon of some sort.

"Get out of my way," he said in a guttural voice.

"No. Put that puppy down right now!" Eva stopped and stood her ground.

"Last chance," he taunted, coming closer.

Don't miss
Blind Trust *by Laura Scott,*
available June 2019 wherever
Love Inspired® Suspense books and ebooks are sold.

www.LoveInspired.com